STARZEL

The First Priority

Mark Bertrand PhD

Not A Real Publisher LLC

Not A Real Publisher LLC

Publisher: Not A Real Publisher

ISBN Print: 979-8-9889234-2-8
ISBN Ebook: 979-8-9889234-3-5

About The Author

Mark Bertrand is an acclaimed author known for his compelling works of science fiction and metaphysical exploration, including "Starzel," "Love Reincarnate," and "A Conscious Thing."

With a background in aerospace, neuroscience, and mathematics, Mark brings a unique blend of scientific knowledge and philosophical insight to his writing. His deep understanding of Buddhist principles and Zen teachings infuses his storytelling with a thought-provoking and introspective quality.

As a seasoned traveler and seeker of knowledge, Mark draws inspiration from diverse cultures and experiences, enriching his narratives with a global perspective. When he's not crafting captivating stories, Mark can be found enjoying the serene landscapes of southern Spain, reflecting on life's mysteries.

With his unconventional thinking and ability to challenge conventional norms, Mark's writing captivates readers, offering a fresh and immersive reading experience. He maintains open lines of communication with his readers and critics, fostering a strong commitment to his craft and staying at the forefront of his field.

Engage in his literary journey by visiting his website or social media platforms and discover a world of boundless imagination and philosophical exploration in Mark Bertrand's evocative works.

Acknowledgments

Cover Art Provided by: Andrly Cover title, North America Post 15th Aryan War.Story Edit Provided through Beta Reading Provided by: Allison Beta Reading Provided by: Nsikak Edet Illustration, Banyan by: Olesla Illustration. Eulər by: Brian Flores SEO & Advertising Provided by: Mariam Zahra

Publisher: Not A Real Publisher LLC

First Edition: September 2023

Visit the author, Mark Bertrand on his website:

Please be sure to give five-star reviews. Thank you for your continued support of independent authors.

Contact: info@notarealpublisher.com

Not A Real Publisher LLC

Contents

Chapter One

Planet Forty-Four

When it comes right down to it, there are just two sides to everything. Ludicrous, I say. Should I accept the simple duality of everything? There are just two things I have to say about two choices. First, who cares? Second, so what? What I found as far as this, when there seems to be a choice between one thing or another, that's a red flag, the siren, the lightning flash, the warning. When this happens I know the choice isn't obvious and I have to choose neither of the two. Instead, this is when intelligence opens the heart to listen and discover truth.

Still, and silly as it might seem, I often catch myself comparing my life between being here on Planet Forty-Four, home of the Syganoid, a highly advanced humanoid race, to what I have learned about life on Planet Earth. In theory, Planet Earth sounds pretty sweet, but just being a generic human on Planet Earth? That's not for me. No way!

Here's a good example of why not. On Planet Earth, the water, air, and ground are all part of how human life evolved. It's the only natural environment for sustaining human life. Meanwhile, on Planet Forty-Four, we live inside massive domed habitats that are floating on a fully poisonous gas planet. One tiny crack in the dome and this planet's natural environment will end, killing every person here. Fortunately, our superior technology and enhanced minds make it possible for us to survive. You could even say we prosper.

A gentle breeze is always present inside the dome and the atmosphere is rich with every element needed to produce water, soil, and nutrients for growing plants and producing building materials for everything we need. The smell and sound are neutral as it is our way to experience life as The Source intended it. No conflicts with too hot, too cold, too rainy, too bright, etcetera. Every day is perfect in temperature and feels comfortable on the skin. Smells are clean and refreshed and every sensation provides a longing to experience the beauty of our advanced civilization.

Life here gets even better when you compare it to how people live on Planet Earth. So, when I hear someone saying they wished to visit or go on vacation to Planet Earth, I shake my head in disagreement. Why would anyone want to go someplace where everything wants to destroy you? Natural air, they say. Filled with diseases, viruses, and pollution that destroy DNA and spawn cancerous cells in your organs, I say. And the water? Water is even worse than the air for destroying the body's natural existence. Everything on Planet Earth competes to exist at the expense of everything else. Plants consume soil and water, rob the sunlight and convert all that stolen energy into growing their physical structure. Small fish are eaten by larger fish, who are eaten by still larger fish is exemplified throughout. All of it is a necessary effort to survive on Planet Earth. Every facet of energy exists because it can be devoured, in one way or another, by some other source of energy.

Then there are the people. What they don't consume they destroy in their quest for pleasure. They take pleasure in everything. Everything they consume destroys the very planet they need for survival. Do you know the difference between being dumb and being stupid?

Dumb is when you do something wrong but you didn't know any better and stupid is knowing better but doing it anyway. People on Planet Earth, yeah, they're stupid.

This brings up the major difference between a highly enhanced, very capable, and super intelligent Syganoid like me, and a generic human. Humans occupy their life by doing. They are always doing something. Even when they sleep they're busy, busy, busy. They designed sophisticated words for it such as efficient, productive, and meaningful. A Syganoid is all about being. We don't have to do anything to exist or be happy, we don't need to buy things, make things, or try to live better lives than everyone else. We are happy and alive. Be real, be content, and be here.

As I contemplate the contrasting realities of our existence, the immense gulf between the advanced Syganoid civilization and the seemingly primitive life on Planet Earth becomes abundantly clear. The marvels of our technology, the splendor of our environment, and the profound sense of contentment we experience form the foundation of our superiority, evoking a profound mix of curiosity and pride within me.

How do I know all this about Planet Earth, you ask? My mother is a biological scientist who works with a team of scientists on Planet Earth. Most of the time, she's there and her team develops biomechanical enhancements that give Syganoids more enhanced lives. We already enjoy sixteen senses. Compare that to generic humans living their entire lives with just five senses. Anyway, my mom tells me a lot about living on Planet Earth and she brings me recent data files from various places around the planet.

My father and I love her and she loves us back. He is a genius, my dad. His mind has added more to the evolution of space and the expansion than any of us can fathom. We share a home and have so much in common. My eyes, like all Syganoids, are the unmistakable ylnmn blue, and my thin but wavey blonde hair is just like his. Most people say that I have my mom's nose and smile. Anyway, love is another example of the differences between humanoids and humans.

Here, we love being alive. Love is the core of existence and we love the well-being of all that is. But on Planet Earth, people made love a thing to do rather than a thing to be. They fall in love, whatever that means. They announce their love of things and for things. Ridiculous things like food, shoes, transportation, buildings, sports teams, towns, and schools. They select one person to --give-- their love to and then the doing of love gets even more busy. They get an engagement ring, have an engagement party, set a wedding date, and spend more money on wedding preparations and gifts than most of them earn in half a lifetime. Do the wedding, do the honeymoon, do the make a baby, do the baby, and a few years later, when there's nothing else to do, they do the divorce. Return to fall in love at step one, and start it all over again.

For them, love is just a word they attach hundreds of actions to the word and it becomes an aggregate that causes both anxiety and limited moments of joy. In comparison to my humanoids and how we love, it is very different. But rather than tell you, I think you'll enjoy it more if I show you. Come on, follow me. I'll take you to where it all gets started and then I'll share my typical day with you. We'll visit my friends, and I'll take you to where I work. Later will catch up with my father for a hearty meal and a chat. Let me warn you right now, he'll talk your leg off.

***

Before we catch up with my friends who have been telling me for several weeks now that I need to go to the doctor for a check-up. "You're acting peculiar," they say, "you need a physical or something, and blah blah blah." Be like me and just ignore them. First, though, let's head over to that building. The five-story all glass with the silver light beams chasing from bottom to top illuminating the corners. It's our medical center. Is Quantum Jumping new to you? With intention, we can sense our way to be wherever we want to be. We call it quantum jumps, which is the fourteenth sense. It doesn't work from Dome to Dome though. It only functions intradome. Duh, right? Let's go.

Through these doors here. The chief of surgery is on the other side and says, "Hey, Eulǝr. Where's it all happening, man?" That's my name, by the way. I'm Eulǝr. My father named me after his favorite mathematician, Leonhard Euler. The upside down ǝ in my name, is an emphasis for the Euler Number represented in mathematical formulas by an e. The Euler Number is used in defining almost everything including the discovery of the code to the Universe. Anyway, that's fairly boring stuff. Righteous and powerful, but wicked boring.

"Who are you talking to?" the chief of surgery asks me. We are standing inside her spacious operating room. The walls are opaque with a pearlesque tint and the ceiling above is luminous with brilliant color-enhancing light that gives everything in the room a high-definition appearance. There are four, Bio Organoid Operating Machines (BOOM) positioned in each corner of the room with a sliding table to insert and extract a patient down the center of the tall rectangular-shaped machine. The outside of the BOOM is an organized group of conduits, hoses, and tubes with little room to spare that are all connected through the walls and ceiling. Midway of the long side on the front is an operations control center with multiple monitors and several keypads, toggles, and metered dials.

"Don't be rude, man. That's not chibusa. An apology would be nice." After a long pause between us, her blank expression tells me she isn't going to apologize. "Are you performing any procedures today?" I ask.

She looks at me with a quizzical expression, "I'm not sure who owes whom an apology Eulər. Otherwise, yes. I have two seven-year-old patients today. Do you want to watch the operation? I'll be using the new O. I. techniques your mother and team developed." She throws her arms around me. "I'm so sorry for your loss. Your mother was always wonderful and provided enhanced quality of life for every Syganoid for more than three hundred years. She treated me with respect and friendship."

"Thank you for your kindness and yes, can we observe the procedures?" I ask.

Her quizzical expression returns as she catches her speech and decides on another thought. Her eyes express concern, "Did you take mine and your father's advice from our lunch last week? Have you made an appointment with your doctor for a checkup?"

"Like I told you guys, there is nothing wrong with me. I feel fine and my systems are not reporting any issues."

"You didn't answer my question, Eulər. Did you make the appointment?"

"Pardon me," says the porter as he comes into the operating room with the patient on a gurney. The patient is unconscious and anesthetized. He's a seven-year-old which is the age our civilization agrees is the correct age for a human to transform. After today, following the operation, the young man will be a humanoid, a highly advanced Syganoid, and a new member of our kuudere.

We help the porter lift the child onto the litter and then watch as he is conveyed into the BOOM. "I'll need authorization," the porter says as he holds the reader to the surgeon. She takes the small cylinder holds it to her right eye and then after it flashes to her left eye. Taking the reader back from her he says, "Thank you." We wait for him to exit the room.

"These are exciting times in medical history," she says, almost giddy. "We've come a long way with organoid intelligence. Thanks to your mother and her team back on Planet Earth. God bless her." She cups the side of my face with her soft, cold, hand. Stroking my cheek with her thumb as she mentions Mom, her sympathy is shown with an exaggerated facial expression.

"Come over here." She stops touching my face and takes me by the hand. Leading me to the center of the operating machine. We stand, looking at the high-definition monitor and the surrounding metered displays. Each of the smaller displays is scrolling data for specific outputs of vital signs, injections, harmonics, resonances, and dozens of other pieces of information that I'm unfamiliar with. "You can watch the entire process with me, while I perform the implants for enhancements. We'll make this person one of our kuudere. Very exciting times!"

Before it starts, I stand in this advanced operating room, the hum of the medical equipment, the smells of a sterile medical environment, and the soft beeping of monitors. I'm witnessing the transformative procedures and hearing the surgeon's excitement, while a profound sense of awe and the weight of my heritage washes over me, blending pride with an overwhelming sense of expectation.

Through the monitor, I can see the first three Neurolinks being lifted from their containers. "Every device is keyed and serialized to one body." She says as she points to a display noting the serialized codes being registered. The devices are then dipped into a Petri dish and swished around in what looks like a thick gravy before being lifted back out of the dish.

"What is that?" I ask, pointing at the Petri dish.

"That my young Eulər, is your mother's new solution of organoid intelligence. The microscopic-sized biobrains attach to the circuitry of the Neurolink and bond to the device. Like some miracle of magic, she found a way to get the individual brain cells to become embedded into the circuitry, not just attached to it, but they evolve to become one super-intelligent machine. Imagine tens of thousands of micro brains operating at computer speeds without the need for an interface or for operating systems. Wait, look there." She points to the monitor. "Here's your father's mathematics at work."

With curious intensity, I watch, as the infused and saturated Neurolinks are positioned and then laid on top of the young boy's shaved head. A second or maybe two later the Neurolinks disappear. I struggle to believe what I saw as the devices seemed to melt into the boy's head as they submerged and disappeared.

"Did I see what seemed to be the head absorb the devices?" I ask.

"It's so amazing. Isn't it?" she boasts. "Here. Let me adjust the view so we can see what's going on inside his skull now." She moves a few switches and then the monitor displays the inside of the boy's head. "Through the harmonic resonance, the organoids synchronize with the host's body and brain. They already know where to go inside the brain and where to connect to the autonomic and peripheral nervous system, the pineal plexus and the pituitary plexus, etcetera. See there." She points at one of the neurloinks as it begins to reappear and attach itself to the brain.

"That's the HUD monitoring system. Right now it is attaching itself to the eyes' visual cortex. The other two will join themselves to the pineal and thymus. These give us an awareness of the energy of the universe and how we can use the power that creates worlds and the power that makes life. From these first three Neurolinks, we have thousands of times more intelligence, energy, and strength. Our sixteen senses bring us into harmony with all of space and we control time and energy at the foundation of reality. We are the ultimate creators.

"Without a single incision or invasive procedure is the real miracle. Your father perfected the harmonics and your mother perfected the biomechanics. Your family's heritage will always be known as the beginning of our existence and the beginning of the kuudere of Planet Forty-Four."

While the words she says make me proud, they also overwhelm me. The accomplishments of my parents are too much for me to live up to. I often feel like I live in the thick, dense shadows of their lives.

The monitor returns to the surface view of the boy's body and the operation machine is placing four neurolinks along his spine and two spiral-shaped devices are placed on the meaty part of each buttock.

"Attached to our spinal columns are more autonomic and anatomic nervous system organoid-rich devices. These give us superhuman strength and intelligence as it increases our neurological operating speeds. We can think fast, move fast, and make perfect decisions based on universal knowledge. Truth. Universal knowledge is truth," she says. "Those memory storage devices connect us to the individual experiences of our separate life as well as provide communication with other kuudere.

"Completion of the entire operation takes another fifty minutes. The machine monitors and adjusts the implants and runs a series of calibrations. Then, when everything is in balance, I'll have the porter return the boy to the recovery room. It's an amazing, painless, and invasion-free process to become humanoid. We live in amazing times, Eulər."

***

Science has always been a key component of my family heritage. As far back as my family tree goes, all the way back to our first family who lived in Glenwood Springs Colorado, on Planet Earth, they were all scientists. That's another long and boring topic and there are more important things to do and talk about for now.

"This has been an exciting treat for me. Thank you for letting me see how my mom's work continues to make Syganoid life for all the kuudere better. And thank you for your kind words. I miss her so much. But, hey. I need to go. My friends are expecting me at the center and I have to be at work in a few hours."

"Wait," she says as I start to walk away. "Have you had any more vivid dreams? My hunch tells me you had something recent that shook you in its vividness and realness. Am I right?"

Hesitant and still unsure how she seems to know when I have these amazing and realistic memory-shaking dreams, I take a breath. "Yes," I tell her. "Last night. I saw a few dozen monks, robed in saffron colors wandering through a thick forest.

"The Source spoke to me but . . . I think these dream states are often the vessel of knowledge as The Source communicates with the part of me that is pure energy."

"Very true," she says. "Some kuudere call it the soul, and most, and more precise in their naming of it, call it the True Self or, Self. Go on then. Tell me about the dream."

As I recount the dream and its ethereal elements, an indescribable longing welled up within me, like that old bittersweet melody that tugs at the strings of the heart, invoking a profound yearning for understanding and connection. I feel odd.

"A sage in the form of a large stone gate adorned with jewels and hinged with bands of gold tells me a parable.

"Your son's son will complete the pathway to paradise. It will be through his emotional commitment to love that the gateway will be found and from there all humans who so chose to do so can evolve. Until then, life will be one and the same with suffering. You must replace the data and put it back into the sacred files but more so, you must understand and experience The First Priority. You must define the characteristics of true love and then The First Priority will be known throughout the universe. It began this way. Listen. Learn." The Gate says.

>>// Long, long ago when Ibrahim was growing up he spent as much time at the nearby monastery as he could. That is, when his parents didn't need help on the farm to feed the goats and wrestle eggs away from the rowdy gaggle of geese. Otherwise, every free minute he had he would run the three and a half kilometers from his home to the monastery. The Abbot observed young Ibrahim and could sense, though he was still in his youth, that Ibrahim had a mind that was ripe for human liberation. The Abbot instructed the elders of the abbey and the monks of the monastery to allow Ibrahim full access to the teachings and to teach him the way of monastic life. Ibrahim drank in every lesson as a man in the desert drinks water. He performed every chore as a student does, and he learned how to free his mind from thoughts and how to tame the wild thinking monkey mind.

When Ibrahim reached the age of maturity his parents held a celebration and kept the custom of civilized peoples. They invited everyone from the community to join them in a celebration. Ibrahim was well-liked and admired in the community because he was always willing to lend his help and join in public conversations. If someone was ill, he would help tend to their crops and livestock until they recovered. When someone was sad he would walk with them and hold their hand and embrace them as they worked through their sadness. When someone was preparing a celebration he would help set up the tables and decorations for the festivities and he would always help to clean up when the celebration was finished. Everyone knew him and had respect for him.

As the people of the community began to arrive for his coming-of-age celebration he stood at the gateway to the family farm and greeted them one by one. A strong gust of wind brought a surprising harsh scattering of dirt and plant debris. But a few heartbeats later it was gone and the gentle breeze returned. When he looked in the direction of the gust he couldn't help but notice a family never before seen coming up the street toward his home. When they came to the gateway of his family's farm he greeted them with the same respect and admiration he was accustomed to showing everyone. Just then his mother and father joined him at the gateway.

"Ibrahim this is Yahya and his wife Mariyam from the mining city of Baloc," his father said. "Our families have known one another's for many centuries."

Ibrahim's mother placed her hand on Ibrahim's left shoulder and with her other hand she motioned towards a young woman, one of the guests' children, Ibrahim assumed. But then his mother said, "My son, this young girl here will be your wife. Her name is Lizet and she will live with our family from today and you will be married to her in one year from today."

Ibrahim was very happy and somehow, meeting Lizet he felt excited for the future. He stood there looking at the strangers and after a few moments collected his wits. Finally, he stepped forward and offered the crook of his arm to Lizet. "Here, take my arm, and please allow me to show you around your new home," Ibrahim said. She cautiously reached out her hand to take his arm. The two of them turned to walk the path which led through the gateway and towards the farm.

Until this day there was never before in history a love at first sight. It started on that very day and at that very moment. Ibrahim and Lizet became more enamored with each minute they spent together. Their zest for life and affinity for each other was contagious and anyone and everyone who was around them for even a moment couldn't help but feel good inside.

Together they helped families near and far. When someone was sick or injured Ibrahim and Lizet would take care of the crops, and livestock or run their store until they were healed. When someone was sad and depressed they would walk with them and would hold their hand and embrace them as they recovered. Ibrahim and Lizet would travel to other cities throughout the provinces visiting and helping everyone in need. Their popularity grew. They had a combined wealth between their families that provided them with all the comforts life can offer. They had fame and popularity, and even the mayors, governors, and elected officials frequently counseled them in matters of great importance.

When one day it was time for the Abbot to begin preparations for the seasonal ceremony he asked the monks to send for Ibrahim. The monks told the Abbot about Ibrahim becoming promised to marry a woman of high position and that he had not been seen at the monastery for many months. The Abbot was not deterred by the news. He repeated his request of the monks, bowed to them, and departed. //<<

***

Making my way to the door, I see the chief of surgery is glued to the operating machine monitor and recording devices. I doubt she heard a word I said.

"Obvious to me, this dream," I say, though she isn't listening, I feel I want to hear myself say it, and express my poetic appreciation for capturing what I sense in this oft-recurring dream. "In this idyllic setting, as the golden sun bathed the lush forest, a soft breeze whispered through the leaves, carrying with it a symphony of scents--the earthy aroma of moss and foliage mingling with the delicate fragrance of wildflowers. The air was alive with the chatter of guests, their laughter like sparkling notes of joy. As Ibrahim extended his arm to Lizet, their hands met in a tentative touch, setting in motion a journey of intertwined destinies. At that moment, the world seemed to hold its breath, anticipation, and trepidation entwined in the hearts of those witnessing this love's enchanting beginning."

As I push the doors open with my back, I continue to look at her and when she doesn't turn toward me, I wave goodbye to her back and leave.

As I walk through the hallway and before transporting to the recreation center to meet up with friends, I recall a memory of my mother telling me about her medical team's work. . .

"genuine biological computing that harnesses brain organoids using scientific and bioengineering advances in an ethically responsible manner. Standardized, 3D, myelinated brain organoids can now be produced with high cell density and enriched levels of glial cells and gene expression critical for learning. Integrated microfluidic perfusion systems can support scalable and durable culturing and spatiotemporal chemical signaling. Novel 3D microelectrode arrays permit high-resolution spatiotemporal electrophysiological signaling and recording to explore the capacity of brain organoids to recapitulate the molecular

mechanisms of learning and memory formation and, ultimately, their computational potential. "Biological computing (or biocomputing) could be faster, more efficient, and more powerful than silicon-based computing and AI, and only require a fraction of the energy. Oh Eulər, I'm sorry baby. I'm boring you to death with all of my excitement."

Never in all my life would she ever bore me with her words. And her excitement? That enthusiasm of hers made it okay with me that she was gone for long periods of time while working with her team. But she and Dad both treat me as if I don't understand their maths and sciences. They think I'm uninterested in any and all of it. I've never understood why they talk and dumb it down for me. Anyway, I guess it doesn't matter. Let's go see some friends of mine.

Most of the time everyone is hanging around right here. While I scan the large auditorium turning clockwise looking for my friends the open floor plan, the pyramid-shaped, glass-enclosed building is full. Kuudere are seated everywhere in small clusters and everyone is in the lotus position. Their hands poised with thumb and forefinger touching, open palm placed upward on either knee, eyes closed, head slightly tilted forward and down. Their faces are emotionless, and they glow with a light almost unnoticed at first but it provides an ora of various shades of the rainbow.

A sudden tap on my shoulder and as I turn to see who, they moved too fast for me. Another tap on the opposite shoulder and again I look but they moved in anticipation of my reaction. "Okay, okay, very funny," I say.

"How are you today, my lovely and wonderful Eulər? Still playing with your imaginary friends while ignoring the rest of us?"

This is Casper, and he is the most powerful Syganoid I know. I've seen him move objects with his mind and I've caught him levitating in a deep trance state while he glowed with a brilliant white ora.

"Where is everyone?" I ask.

He motions for me to follow and after twenty or more paces we find where my friends are sitting and playing. This is what we love about being here on Planet Forty-Four. In every domed city you'll find most of the kuudere spend their none work time in the auditorium playing.

"Will you join me at our field today, Eulər?" Casper asks. "Or are you still inept?"

"If I can," I say. "This week has been challenging for me to say the least."

Something has been causing me to be distracted this week, and I don't know, I just can't get my true self to emerge in the fields on the other side. Taking the lotus position I acknowledge my core energy centers. From the first energy center, the inferior mesenteric plexus, I call my attention to be aware of the energy of space around it, then upward I take my concentration, one by one, through the seven energy centers. Then, when I'm no longer anyone, and no longer someplace, I remove the veils from the sense of sight, smell, hearing, taste, and touch. The energy of the universe replaces the senses and in those places emptiness takes hold. Join me. Give it a try, just stop labeling the stuff you see, hear, smell, etcetera. You don't simply stop seeing, it's more like there is no sight. So think of it as not doing and instead as nothing done or not done. The senses aren't stopped, on hold, paused, but they never existed.

Once the practice of aligning the energy centers is mastered, the present moment, or the reality of being manifests. For me, it starts as a vacuum or hollowing sensation as if my consciousness is pulled into a void. This part of the practice is difficult because it's very easy for the mind to want to identify and label the sensation. If that happens, then I have to start all over again. Then there's the outer existence and realms of vast energy flows. It's hard to put words to this because

I'm describing things that are real using words that are used to define illusionary existence. It is one of the few times that saying you had to be there to understand it, is true. Come on and be with me. Stop doing and start being.

You see? This is how we play. Don't do the meditation, don't do the practice, don't just sit there, do nothing. If you want to have a good experience with knowing the difference between being and doing, don't think about it.

****

About a month ago my energy centers stopped aligning and I haven't been able to get out of my body. Meanwhile my friends are there waiting for me, well not waiting. It's more like they miss my energy. Our entire population of kuudere spends countless hours in the fields out beyond the illusions of sensual existence. We absorb the suffering from the sensual illusion of life and replace it with love. We fill the universe with loving energy and when we fill the universe the illusion and suffering life will disappear into the energy of love we create. The closer we get to ending suffering, the more difficult it is for the sensual existence, and in our sensual existence we see life getting worse. It seems as if evil and disrespect, dishonesty, and ignorance are becoming more powerful. But that's part of the illusionary existence, called Mara, straining to stay in control as we replace it.

Look over there. That's my friend Gatlia. We have decided to have a child together. Here she comes. Gatlia waves, and comes over closer to sit beside me. She has an egg-shaped head and face with a wide forehead and narrow chin. Her eyes are often gunmetal grey but can appear to be the typical ylmnm blue in the right light. Her lips are thin and her eyes are narrow slanting up on the outside with soft brow and smooth cheeks. Today her hair is twisted into a coil and pinned over the crown of her head with two long, bright green pins. Most of the time she lets her long straight black hair fall down her back and tucked behind her ears to stay off her face. Like most of the kuudere, she's thin, healthy looking, and well-proportioned.

"Have you been to the medical clinic to find out what is wrong with you?" she asks.

Several of my friends nearby open their eyes when they hear her ask me. They nod. acknowledging me, and then close their eyes slipping back out of the body.

"No, I know you haven't," she says. "Why are you so stubborn? So, listen. I decided our son's name will be Magallan."

"A son now, is it?" I say. "Last week a girl, the week before a boy. Here we are today and a boy again."

"Stop being rude," she grins.

"After all of the weeks of not being in the fields with all of you I guess I'm lucky you still want to breed with me."

Tilting her head to the left she says, "It's just your family's DNA I'm hoping to capture for our son's inheritance, and since you are their only child. What choice have I? Stop playing with me and come be with the kuudere in the fields." She closes her eyes and slips out of the body.

There is no sense in wasting my time here. I know my energy centers aren't going to align right now. Let's go to my office and you can see where I work. Though, it is the most boring and mundane job on Planet Forty-Four. I'll warn you now and if you would rather not, we can go instead to catch up with my father. Perhaps we can have an early dinner.

Do you remember how to get to my office? All it requires inside the domed city is the intention to be somewhere. You see, there is always the opportunity on Planet Forty-Four to practice being rather than doing. Come on and try it with me. Let go of doing what you're doing and manifest the intention for being at my work.

That was awesome, well done. Here we are. I suppose this is an odd place to work when you look around and all you see is floor-to-ceiling cloud storage racks. Remember when my mother would bring me news from her travel? She always met me here when she returned from her work. Of course you wouldn't remember that. How could you?

Look a little closer and you'll see that none of these storage devices have external power connections and you won't even find battery packs for power. The smell of sandalwood incense is a bonus, and I still don't know where that comes from, but I enjoy it. Listen close. Can you hear that gentle but steady hum? It sounds like the universe. The vibration from all the energy is in motion everywhere, all at once. It resonates with the sound -- om!

Inside this one location is all of the universe code. The laws and rules that govern and expand at the speed of light. The heart of all that ever is, so to speak, and all that ever was. Everything that happened before you got here was the preparation for you being here, and everything from this point on is the result of you being here. This place, where I work, is the operational center of all the universal energy, the center of the power that creates galaxies and worlds. Cool eh?

Except that it is boring and mundane. This bench here, against the wall, is where it begins. I suppose it could be worse. The bench seat could be unupholstered and less comfortable, but even with the plush cushion and the diamond-patterned blue-on-blue tapestry, the work is uneventful.

After sitting on the bench the vibrational sound in the room increases in decibels and the illumination of the room fades until I'm in total darkness. The senses become aware of the vastness of space and my body and heart-mind are in harmony with the energy of space. Now all I do is wait and stay alert. If anything were to ever go wrong with the laws of space, the energy of the universe, I would be alerted. So they tell me. It's never happened in fourteen billion years so nobody knows for sure. But this is my job. I am the keeper of the code of the universe.

As the vibrations of the universe resonated through the darkness, I can't help but feel a gnawing emptiness within, longing for something more than this monotonous existence as the keeper of the code.

Meticulous and without fault, maybe redundant to an extreme, and as you can see for yourself this job sucks. Shall I tell you a secret? Sometimes I open up the code history and look back at the time. Sort of testing the archives and historical records. Once I changed a data fact. Nothing major of course, just a little piece of data. What can I say? Bored out of my comfort zone I suppose. But it's harmless. Changes to the past could be dangerous, but I'm a high-functioning superior humanoid and a high-ranking Syganoid. If I wasn't then I wouldn't have this critical job.

***

Imagine if I did something minor on a nondescript planet in a tiny galaxy far out in the not-so-dense part of the universe. The consequence of altering the code's historical data in such a meaningless and remote location would be -- inconsequential. Then it came to me in thought. I know the perfect place to tinker and add some recreation to my work. You guessed it. Humans on Planet Earth.

It started with a simple experiment. All I did was move a flower from one side of a brook to the other side. Lateral and unchanged during a time before apes stood upright. Simply moved the plant across the brook. Another time I moved the walnut on a tree branch. Same branch, same tree, but I moved it just about an inch closer to the trunk. This sort of recreation was harmless because when my work day is done, and the cloud storage room manifests, I can see nothing in our existence is any different today from yesterday. Harmless and entertaining. The Universe is dynamic and capable of sustaining such small changes as these.

Think about it. How much harm can I do on a planet where barely evolved talking apes are at the top of the hierarchy? Did you know these people created a verbal language so that they could share information and learn from each other? Remarkable for simple creatures, but then they spent the next fifty thousand years inventing accents, slang, and a variety of characters and different dialects so that they couldn't understand one another. They always strive to separate themselves.

One time I introduced the ways of centering their internal energy centers through meditation to one of the more promising ancient cultures. Over the next ten thousand years they invented a hundred different gods to worship and praise. Every human god they invented was devoted to love and peace yet, somehow, the people invented war, killing machines, and hate all in the name of their gods. What harm could a little recreation with an otherwise gouge your eyes out from boredom job do here?

Best of all, I can do some good for a suffering individual and make a difference in a few ordinary lives. For example, I found historical code where this child was clumsy and had difficulty with a speech impediment. So I altered the code. Only just a bit to make this boy named Genghis Khan right-handed rather than left-handed. A change like that could have a major impact and a ripple of difference in our current lives. So I watched when I got back to now, present time and . . . since nothing has changed in our current time. No impact.

As I recall and contemplated the potential repercussions of my tinkering with historical events, a sense of both exhilaration and apprehension dance in my mind, a delicate balance between the thrill of exploration and the weight of responsibility is exciting.

Check this one out. It made me feel pretty good about myself and our kuudere and how we can provide so much benefit to humans. Okay, so there was this husband and wife who were madly in love, desperate for children and to raise a family together. Except the husband comes from a long line of men who have performance anxiety. He's as sterile and impudent as a blackhole. So, I went back into the code and changed his DNA a bit so that Alois and Klara Hitler could have children. That man went on to produce nine children. Cured from the physical ailment.

Something like that would seem dangerous, but again, once the workday was over I couldn't see that there was any difference in our lives. Imagine though if something significant changed such as the evolution of life. If that was paused or accelerated for even one-hundredth of a second over twenty million years later, life would be nothing like we know it.

If anything ever did change, you know, something went wrong from something I've altered, all I would do is go back into the code and make it right. I know, I know. Syganoid wisdom tells us that being has no consequence. Doing has continuous, harmful, and duel consequences. But it's fine, trust me.

Serendipity . . .time for dinner with Dad. We are supposed to meet at the lower dome at his favorite place. The starlight down there is much dimmer than here in the second city. You'll see once we get down there. The stacked domed cities stretch from the near outer atmosphere down towards the center. Each city mines a different layer of gas on Planet Forty-Four and the deepest city is fifteen thousand miles down. The light from Galp, our main sequence star, is faint, but the engineers figured out how to imitate natural light so as long as the kuudere stay inside the city we won't have to worry about losing spacial awareness.

Up to now, as you've been with me in three locations, we travel inside the dome using our thoughts. When an individual intends to move to a different location, their thoughts interact with the underlying quantum field that permeates the city. This interaction creates a quantum entanglement between the individual's consciousness and the target location. Through this entanglement, the individual's physical body is transported across space, appearing instantaneously at the intended destination.

This quantum travel within the domed city offers a multitude of advantages. First and foremost, it eliminates the need for physical vehicles and infrastructure, reducing pollution and congestion within the city. It also allows for an unprecedented level of convenience and efficiency, as travel times are nonexistent. Whether one wishes to be at work, visit and be with friends, or explore various parts of the city, it's simply a matter of conscious intention of being.

To ensure the safety and accuracy of this quantum travel system, the domed city employs advanced quantum computers and sophisticated algorithms. These systems continuously monitor and optimize the quantum entanglement processes, ensuring that individuals arrive at their intended destinations reliably and without any unintended consequences.

However, mastering this form of travel requires individuals to undergo training and develop a heightened awareness of their thoughts and intentions. The city provides specialized education programs to help its residents understand and control their conscious interactions with the quantum field.

Intention won't work this time though. We cannot transport in a quantum leap since Dad is meeting me in a different dome. We'll have to travel the traditional way. Let's catch a shuttle cab to the tubes.

Chapter Two

Planet Te

"They're confined to individual experiences limited by life with just five senses," Mother says. "It's rare, but not impossible for them to experience the shared consciousness. But the large majority of people on Planet Earth believe the world is physical. They think it is all about matter, things, and doing. Their mind won't believe what their eyes can't perceive. In our world, with our sixteen senses enhanced by artificial and organoid intelligence, we know consciousness and nonduality instinctively."

Those words from the last conversation I had with my mother, three weeks ago, are a prominent, recurring memory today. For the first time since her death I am alone and as I remember her words I can almost hear her. "If you ever visit human-occupied planets, Eulər, you'll kill people." Her last words to me just before she died. "Not on purpose and not because of anything you do, but it will happen all around you. Be careful, and never let anyone discover who and what you are. If they do, they will execute you."

These are important memories for me because today I have decided to go to planet Earth. I'll attempt to explain my decision in full detail in a journal.

Log entry one, day one. Everything that happens within my sixth sense of awareness in the present moment is the definition of magic. While awareness of the space where everything happens is consciousness. Make no mistake by my simple definition because it may not be obvious that it includes all things that happened in the past combined with the awareness of the things that are happening now, and knowing that things will happen in the future. An aggregate definition of consciousness. Then given these are truths of magic and consciousness, I can only present to those in the distant future who will look back on our lives today my deepest regret and apology for the way these things are.

Mistakes were made and everything has consequences. I am writing this with great hope that at long last perhaps this lengthy exposure can magically correct the momentum. Perhaps the conscious energy fields can obtain the harmonic balance. Sitting here in my office, the guardian of humanity files for the Universe gone missing. All I can do is try to recover them.

From the beginning, we intended to provide humanity with a better life. Improved health, reduced suffering, or less stress as most people don't call it suffering, they call it stress. But it is suffering and suffering is exacerbated by media, consumerism, advertising, politics, and all-in-all every day life is necessarily stressful. But to right the wrongs and repair the damage done, then I must go back to where it all started. Though the missing information wasn't known to be missing and as best I can determine it has been slowly disappearing for sixty years. It's as if humanity is being erased from the archives of time. How I did not see it until today matters not.

When I discovered there was information missing from a file called "The First Priority" it was too late. The damage was done. We were exiled from Planet Earth and had to flee to a planet where no one could find us. Here on our planet The First Priority is our way, and still there is suffering. How was it possible that information would be missing from something so critical to human existence? But even more shocking to me than discovering code is missing was discovering that it had been erased, destroyed, and the evidence was hidden.

Upon investigating the discovery I could only find a trace of magnetic residence that seemed out of place. For decades no one ever noticed the sector of data that had been deleted from the original storage device. At first, it appeared to be a bad sector on the drive. But as I investigated it further the sector had been written over in all zeros. A binary technique to hide code and make the sector rewritable to the operating system. However, this device is sacred and nothing was ever added to the drive. So nothing was ever written over the erased data. There is, I estimate, between eight and twelve thousand Bits of missing code and the missing Bits are the beginning of The First Priority.

After several weeks of trying every technique to recover the erased data, it was unrecoverable. So, I turned instead to learning everything I could about the origins of The First Priority and the person who wrote the document. There isn't very much information about the man. His name was Banyan and he was born in a small town somewhere in Colorado late in the year 2005. In 2007 he became an orphan when his parents went missing after a fishing trip on Lake Ontario. From the age of two until he was forty-nine there are no records about his life. No schools, no address of residence, no adoption or orphanage. The only historical information is of his writing the document and his death three years later.

Then, there is the mystery of the writing itself and the creation of The First Priority. The now legendary tale of Banyan and his writing of the original document on the hard drive also tells how he handwrote two hundred and twenty-five copies of the document. Some of his copies were distributed throughout planet Earth. The legend also tells us that he was in Culver City, California when he wrote the original copy.

So the only thing I can think to do now is to make this right for humanity by logging my efforts. Everything from the moment I discovered the missing code to the day it is recovered, or I die, must be tracked and recorded. There is a high probability that I will fail in my efforts to recover the missing code but at the very least, I will leave the record for someone else to follow through. If, on the other hand, I should succeed then I will have great wealth and benefit merits beyond imagination. Before I can move forward with this journey of discovery, I'll need to complete today's physical examination scheduled with the medical center. However, this physical will not be easy to head off, and I can't cancel the appointment.

***

Apologies if I'm being repetitive from our previous conversations, but it bears repeating. Planet forty-four, as the Syganoid government calls our planet of five stacked and interconnected domed cities, is a gaseous planet. Toxic gasses are abundant in the atmosphere of our world and the predominant color of our sky is ylnmn which is a vibrant shade of blue that occurs when the compound manganese oxide, like our planet's outer atmosphere, contains vast quantities and is heated at two-thousand degrees Fahrenheit. Mostly though, far below the upper atmosphere, our planet contains helium which is critical for our fusion energy needs and the production of our bio-mechanical organoid implants. That's why I'm here at the medical center in the capital dome at level two. My harmonics have been causing my HUD display to malfunction, and the government has a mandatory upgrade.

"This is a rare disorder you've described," said Froptil. He's a neuroscience specialist who decided to work at the medical clinic so he could better experiment with frontal lobe implants. "Preliminary scans of your Neurolinks indicate an unbalanced energy center in the fourth mind. Do you know what that means? The fourth mind is the thymus, heart center, and critical to cognitive abilities. The heart is the first organ to develop in a fetus and has a deep neuro connection to the body and the mind. Have you been under any unusual stress? I'm guessing the loss of your mother has caused harsh emotions. Am I correct?"

"There have been some dark moments and my thoughts have frequently been sad. It's nothing unusual given the circumstances and I'll move on with time," I say as we make eye contact.

In that moment of eye contact I'm reminded how in this doctor's office of the medical center, a unique and intriguing sight awaits the patient. The doctor, amidst the compact and congested space, has a distinguishing feature that captures immediate attention – one brown eye and one eye that is completely white. The contrast between the warm, natural hue of one eye and the striking whiteness of the other creates an otherworldly and enigmatic presence.

The doctor's gaze, with one eye grounded in familiar tones and the other seemingly carrying the essence of the unknown, exuded a sense of both depth and mystery. It is as if his eyes are windows into different realms, hinting at a profound connection to the secrets of Planet Forty-Four.

"Stop trying to tell me my diagnosis, Eulər," his scorn jolts me from my daydreaming. "Just answer the questions and drop the psychological jargon."

Froptil sighed, adjusting his spectacles as he looked at me. "Apologies if I came across as presumptuous. It's just that understanding your emotional state can provide valuable insights into your condition. However, let's focus on the medical aspect for now."

He tapped a few commands into his interface, bringing up a holographic representation of my brain. The display highlighted the fourth mind, depicting a swirling energy center that seemed off-balance. Froptil continued, "The unbalanced energy center in your thymus, heart center, and fourth mind is likely the root cause of your harmonics malfunctioning.

"Bio-mechanical organoid implants are commonplace, organoid intelligence plays a crucial role in enhancing HUD (Heads-Up Display) communications and optimizing the functioning of the fourth energy center, the thymus and heart center.

"Organoid intelligence refers to the integration of artificial intelligence algorithms with bio-mechanical organoids, specialized implants designed to interact with and augment humanoid physiology." He points to the triangular section highlighted in the holograph. "These organoids, constructed from advanced nanomaterials and bioengineered components, possess a level of intelligence and adaptability that allows them to interface seamlessly with the humanoid body.

"Importantly in your case, in the context of HUD communications, the organoid intelligence within the implants serves as a bridge between the user's thoughts and the visual display projected onto the HUD. By analyzing the user's neural signals and interpreting their intentions, the organoids translate the desired information into a visual overlay that appears directly in the user's field of view. Your condition, and until you receive these upgrades, your HUD communications are highly suspect.

"So it's something at work that is stressing you and combined with depression from the loss of your mother. Still, it seems to me there's something else that's causing the issue. It's not mechanical, it's organoid.

"Have you been practicing some new type of meditation or mysticism?"

"Tell me more. I haven't heard about new meditation practices," I say.

"There aren't any new practices. You've misunderstood my question."

"Oh. Well then, no I haven't been doing any new methods or tactics," I say.

Lucky he hasn't put me on the mind scanner or he'd see I'm lying.

"Then I'll get you over to the transport and we'll get your Neurolink update done tomorrow. There's a good chance the upgrade will make the HUD issues go away."

"Please not today, Doctor. I can't take a week or two off right now. The issues at work can't wait."

He's tapping away on the medical center's central computer tablet. I can't see what he's typing though I'm straining to look over his shoulder without being too obvious. If he insists on sending me for the operation today, it will be impossible to refuse. The government mandate will impose penalties and I'll get a police escort.

"I'll postpone your upgrade operation for one hundred days. Not a single day more. But, if the problems get worse or you discover any more malfunctions, it's for your safety to get this upgrade as soon as possible."

Without another word, before he could change his mind, I left the medical center. The door to his office seals closed behind me with the whisper of vacuum. Outside his office, the air smells less sterile and more vibrant with ions and electrolytes.

As I pause here in the waiting room of the medical center, the air from outside carries a faint metallic tang, a hint of the technological advancements that permeate every aspect of our Syganoid world. The sterile touch of the holographic door interface on my skin sent a shiver of anticipation down my spine, a mix of excitement and trepidation. Turning to look over my shoulder as I step out of the center, I glance out of the window, catching a glimpse of the swirling ylnmn hue in the sky, a constant reminder of the toxic gasses that surround us. The weather outside, a perpetually clouded and turbulent atmosphere, mirrored the conflicting emotions brewing within me. It is as if the universe itself is directing my thoughts through some kind of mystery story brewing a world of possibilities and dangers, where my own ingenuity and the restrictions of the government clash, creating a charged and uncertain emotion deep in the pit of my stomach.

With a sharp shake of my head, I snap out of the daydream and consider the doctor's words and advice. His diagnosis is correct and I should have thought of it myself. There is a new mysticism I've been refining. Something I had been working on. It's a method of generating a wormhole between Class M planets by matching the electromagnetic harmonic resonance of the planet with my location's resonance. Casper and his students have perfected a method, but it is unsustainable. I have been modeling a different algorithm that uses Lorentzian geometric pathways. But there has been capacity over usage, and the old system's strain is the culprit.

Of course, the new system the government is forcing everyone to migrate to will be a problem for this new practice. Everyone will be accountable for the unsanctioned and unlicensed use of biomechanics. They have passed a new law requiring all forms of algorithms and mind-altering meditation practices to be sanctioned by the central government before being used by individuals or groups.

***

The plan is not complicated. I'll open a wormhole from my home office directly to the coordinates my mother provided me. She had a close friend and work colleague on Planet Te, where the vortex opens up on the other end. I'll explain to her why I need to get to Planet Earth and arrange for her payment for the transport. After that, well, I'll have to get to California and find Banyan. As I said, not a complicated plan but that only means there is little chance of my success. Because as you well know, I've got just one hundred days to get it done.

Once the harmonic resonance syncs the vortex opens and I get through to the other side in an instant. It's a quantum field which means there is no time-space through the vortex. But my HUD isn't able to switch instantly between the satellite relays and that's causing my bio-mechanics to give me migraine headaches and dizziness.

"That is precisely the same entrance your mother used when she would drop in," she laughs enthusiastically while helping me to my feet. "You must be Eulər. I recognize your mother in your brilliant yln-mn eyes and naturally curly blonde-colored hair. My name is Rupirah and I'm thrilled to meet you." Her smile and laugh are contagious. She greets me with her hands pressed together and the tips of her thumbs touching her breastbone. Just like my mother used to do when she would greet people.

"Thank you," I say.

"God I miss your mom," she continues, not giving me a chance to say hello. "Trista was my best friend of best friends. You know what

I mean? Do you still talk to your imaginary friend? She was always worried about that most of all, your mother."

Before I can say a word, she continued without taking a breath. "She always knew how to make me feel good about being me. Such a shame she took her life away from our present reality. I mean our place of perception. You know? Of course, you do. She told me she raised you and your brother with the knowledge and wisdom of The First Priority. It is such a pleasure to finally meet you, Eulər.

"Listen to me dominating the conversation and babbling along like an old woman at an old folk's social dinner. You will require some assistance from me or you wouldn't be here. No one would just drop in on an old woman like me if he didn't need something. I know that and it's okay and perfectly alright. So tell me how can I help?"

She motions for me to take a chair at a pearl white with deep blues and green marbling stone-topped table. The oblong-shaped table had six comfortable chairs with thick padded arms, backs, and seats covered in green wool fabric. The color of the fabric matched the tabletop. I took the chair at the nearest head of the table.

"I had a feeling you would sit there. If you're not in too big of a hurry, I'll make tea." She disappears through the doorway at the opposite end of the table.

As I pour out my thoughts and desires for getting to Planet Earth and once there to find Banyan's writings, my eyes wander around the cluttered apartment. The space is cramped, with piles of paper, books, and various other Earthly objects strewn haphazardly throughout. It was a chaotic environment, reflecting a mind consumed by the pursuit of history, artifacts, knowledge, and understanding.

Rupirah listened attentively, her eyes filled with a mix of empathy and wisdom as she poked her head through the doorway from time to time. When she returned to the table, She nodded slowly, under-standing the weight of my quest.

"The First Priority... Ah, Trista held that knowledge close to her heart," she said, her voice tinged with a touch of nostalgia. "She knew the importance of preserving the ancient wisdom that had been passed down through generations."

With a gentle yet firm motion, Rupirah cleared a path through the cluttered apartment, leading me to a small nook near the single window. She brushed aside some boxes and papers, revealing a worn-out leather armchair. "Sit, Eulər. Find comfort amidst the chaos," she suggested, her voice warm and reassuring, but somehow odd.

I settled into the worn-out armchair as Rupirah shuffled around the cluttered apartment, her movements slow and uncertain. She picked up random objects, examining them with a childlike curiosity before setting them back down in a different place.

"Sit there, dear," she mumbled, pointing vaguely in the direction of the armchair. Her eyes seemed distant, lost in memories that flickered and faded like fragments of a dream.

As I watched Rupirah amidst the clutter and confusion, a deep sense of empathy welled up within me. Rare for me to experience a non-humanoid, kuudere. No, she's not a kuudere, she's a person. Even though she's just human, I understood the weight of her fading memories and the bittersweet nature of our encounter, where fragments of connection fought against the constant motion of time.

From my seat, I spoke softly, trying to catch her attention. "Rupirah, it's me, Eulər. Trista's son."

Rupirah turned toward me, her eyes momentarily focused. A flicker of recognition crossed her face, and a faint smile formed on her lips. "Trista... yes, I remember her. Such a bright soul."

My heart skipped a beat, hoping that she would share something meaningful about my mother. But the moment quickly passed as Rupirah's expression shifted once again, her gaze drifting away.

"No, no, you're mistaken," she muttered, her voice filled with confusion. "I don't know who you are. Trista... she's gone."

Hope deflated, but I remain patient. I know that trying to force coherence from Rupirah's scattered thoughts would be futile. Instead, I decide to ask a simple question, hoping for a fragment of insight.

"Rupirah, if you could offer any guidance, any words of wisdom, what would they be?"

Her brow furrowed as if searching for words buried deep within the recesses of her mind. After a brief pause, Rupirah's eyes regained a momentary clarity, and she spoke softly, her voice filled with sincerity.

"Embrace the unknown, dear Eulər. The answers may elude us, slipping through our fingers like grains of sand, but within that uncertainty lies the beauty of discovery. Cherish the moments of clarity, for they are like stars in the night sky, used wisely they can guide you through the darkness."

***

"The tea is from the planet Oban and it's called Padmottara. It tastes of bitter tree bark if it seeps too long," Rupirah says as she reappears after being absent for fifteen minutes. "It just makes me laugh every time I make it. You know, because the people on Oban believe they are living in a different world system called Padmottara. Isn't that as funny as a squirrel with its cheeks full of nuts?"

"It is odd. That world system doesn't exist in our three-dimensional Newtonian Universe. If I recall it correctly, the Padmottara World

System only exists in the Quantum field," I reply shocked by her clarity and focus.

The sound of her laughter causes me to wonder more about her mental stability. It was one of those quirky moments when you suspect the other person in the room isn't safe to be around.

"You are all like, a matter of fact and scientific. Just like your mother told me once, not too very long ago."

She pours the tea from the ancient metal pot. The steam rises from the blue-colored glass cups. The color of the cups and saucers match the marbling of the tabletop. I join her back at the table for tea.

"Come on then. Out with it. How can I help the handsome and rugged, Eulər on his epic journey? Is it a journey and a quest you are on, yes?"

"There's something I need to find in California on Blue Origin."

"You mean Planet Earth. Nobody calls it Blue Origin except you, Syganoids. And if you are going there, you can't let anyone find out you are a humanoid or they will execute you. Humanoids are not welcome on Planet Earth and have been outlawed since the year 2046. They call it The Musk Law. Named after the father of humanoids. The day the world accepted the law they executed him at a public execution and his eleven humanoid children too.

"Yes. I can help you with the quest, but I want something from you before I do."

"There isn't much I can provide for you. But you're on point with thinking that I am on a journey. So, if I can do something for you, ask. Please," I say.

"When the world governments back on Planet Earth discovered you humanoids, it shocked the planet's population. The media frenzy hyped the Neurolink implants and bio-mechanical implants to the point where everyone believed you all were evil and bent on destroying humanity. They went to war against bio-mechanics and there was no safe place for humanoids to escape execution. They killed humanoids on sight. In military terms, they adopted a policy of extreme prejudice. Basically, they didn't care how many civilians were in the line of fire as long as they executed a humanoid in the process of blowing up a building, sinking a ship, or destroying a town or an airport. It was horrible.

"The development of space travel using nuclear energy rockets and fusion power was hidden during the early twentyfirst century by Elon Musk and his secret companies. He hid his advancements behind the disguise of a company he called, SpaceX. People were amazed at his self-recovering rocket systems and the advancements he was making on the colonization of Mars and the moon. But nobody knew he was using that technology as a subterfuge for his advanced society of super-intelligent humanoids, conscious machines, and the colonization of planets outside of the local solar system.

"The chaos on Earth spurred the great civil war in the United States, which separated the country into eight new and autonomous countries. Parts of Mexico and Canada took over or joined the new countries voluntarily. It was a time of the great reset of civilization and governments that went around the world. No country was left unscathed and even now, the planet is still unsafe from terror and power struggles.

"California, where you want me to arrange your travels, is now part of the country called Starzel. Yes, I can get you there, but you will find it difficult to survive unless you can fit in. Before I tell you more, you must tell me how the implants and bio-mechanics give your humanoid body super strength and super intelligence."

While she tells me the story I sip at my tea and observe her arms and hands. She's demonstrative and displays emotions with her movements and voice inflections. Her loud voice and occasional bursts of laughter are out of context. The gravity of the wars on Planet Earth and the policy of extermination are grave. Somehow she has separated her emotions from the ugliness of the horrors and describes it more from a perspective of childlike mistakes. Putting it all aside I try to answer her question.

"How do I describe the difference? It's sort of hard to put words to it since I was only seven years old when I had my first implants. I don't remember what it was like to not be a Syganoid."

"There must have been some education process," she huffs. "They didn't just check you out of the hospital and then send you on your way."

"My parents taught me how to use my mind. I mean, when I went home they guided me and showed me the practice. Always reminding me of The First Priority and the way."

"Share it with me," she says. "What do you recall from those first lessons? Not The First Priority, we are very much familiar with that Glorious Light Doctrine as we call it here. Just tell me how your parents guided you. And then I will tell you how to survive in Starzel.

***

"Right. Okay," I say. "Uhm . . . well there are eight energy centers within the human body. Seven of them operate at the subconscious level and are part of the autonomic nervous center. Each of them has a separate mind and a specific effect on the epigenetic rhythm in the three-dimensional genome."

"Alright, genius," she stops me. "Let's just back up way far to over here on the other side of Musk's engineering intelligence where I'm sitting. You have to break it down into some simple words. Think about explaining this to your little sister who has just started the fourth year of school."

"Sorry. Let me see," I start again. "Well, let's imagine you went for a walk on a warm, quiet, day in your favorite place. The effect of exterior surroundings affects your feelings and mood. The sounds too have an effect that makes you feel content, maybe even happy. That is epigenetics, the environment affects your DNA, cellular chemistry."

"Okay. Got it." Her arms swirl around as if she's gathering in all of the information and then she pushes her hands onto her head as if she's stuffed it all into her brain.

"Inside your body are these things called glands and these glands make chemicals that get released into your blood. The chemicals do all sorts of things. They help you digest the food you eat, and they help you fight off viruses and infections and many thousands of other things. And basically, the glands cause your health and emotions to maintain your life."

Then I wait to see if Rupirah is keeping up with the science. She rolls her eyes in a clockwise rotation a few times and then switches them to roll counterclockwise. When she stops rolling her eyes she smiles and gives me a quick nod.

"There are seven glands inside the body that work independently of one another. We say they have a mind of their own because they essentially do, but these minds are not part of our consciousness. I mean, we can't hear or know their thoughts in the same way as our thinking mind which is the seventh gland. We call it the hypothalamus and the pituitary gland and it lives almost at the center of your brain. Just a little forward of center. That's where our conscious thoughts and experiences are known.

"The first gland is located at the bottom of your crotch. It's called the sex gland and the next one up is in the lower abdomen called the pancreas gland and the third is below the stomach called the adrenal gland. These first three are making chemicals and keeping your body healthy. Their minds want to procreate, digest food, and fight off disease. But we can't hear those minds because they operate on the subconscious level. Like when you dream. It's not part of the awareness of your awakened conscious thoughts.

"The next gland up is the thymus and this is where life gets interesting. This gland is responsible for the heart and lungs. It circulates oxygen and blood throughout the body to give all your cells the energy they need to maintain and rebuild themselves. It's the first energy center that becomes aware of the outside world. The first three centers are focused solely on the body, but the thymus discovers the nutrition from the food we eat and the air we breathe comes from outside the self. But it too operates at the subconscious level and we don't hear it.

"Anyway, with the Neurolink implant in our thinking mind, the hypothalamus operates at a much faster level and the frequency becomes variable. That is to say, we can tune into the subconscious and the conscious all at once. We can use the subconscious minds with our consciousness to make our bodies and our mental abilities much improved. Some say we operate with five to six hundred times basic human capability."

"Slow down there Zippity Skippity," Rupirah again stops me. "You skipped way ahead in the lessons. What about the other two subconscious glands and the sixth one? You thought you could get away without telling me everything I asked for and that I would send you off to California without paying me in full. Didn't you? You think I'm stupid. Don't you?"

She stands up and leans across the table twisting her head slowly from one direction to another to look at me from the sides of her eyes. As if she sees me with some unusual focused point of view. Then she laughs hysterically with a few short loud bursts while she fills my cup with more tea from the kettle.

"It has nothing to do with my perception of your intelligence or lack of it," I say.

"Stop sweating the jive, Eulər. You'll get the crack of your ass chapped if you keep that up. Just give me the four-one-one on the whole picture."

Her eyes are exaggerated and wide open and her toothy grin gives me more concerns for her mental stability.

"Before I share more details of the Syganoid practice of coherent messaging, I think it's your turn. Tell me what I need to know to survive in Starzel."

"Trust is an important part of collaboration. Okay, I'll share a little though I don't think you have told me one iota of what I asked you for." Her eyes never looked up from the cup of tea she holds with both hands. In careful and deliberate slow motion she sets the cup back on the saucer, places her hands on her legs, and then closes her eyes while she speaks.

"Though I have never been to Starzel, you aren't the first person I sent there. The last was your mother. What I tell you now is what she told me when she returned. This would have been about six months ago so something there might have changed. Starzel is a feminist republic. It is a rule of law society where the law doesn't just defend women's rights, it ensures their livelihood."

After a short pause, her eyes open, she stands and takes a few hesitant steps away from the table. "Where did I put that ring your mother wanted me to give you? It was a white gold herringbone design and I can't recall where I put it." She rifles through the drawers of the credenza then she rushes across the room to another cabinet that fills the wall from floor to ceiling with shelves and drawers. I hear her mumbling and clicking her tongue against the back of her teeth as she can't find it in each vase, bowl, and drawer she checks. Then she swings the small ladder attached to the ceiling rail into the center of the cabinet. She climbs up a few steps and continues her search.

"Wait a sec!" she shouts with her loudest voice yet. "It's in the safe under my bed! I just knew I would remember." She laughs in several short hysterical bursts as she disappears from the room through the opening just behind where I'm sitting.

The sound of her laughter, intermingled with mumbled words and tongue clicks, adds to the strange and slightly comical atmosphere. I can't help but feel exasperated yet entertained by this unpredictable exchange.

***

After several minutes of waiting, I wonder if she will remember I'm here. I walk to the small window and take in the view outside. Planet Te is always covered in clouds but it never rains. The planet has limited water and they mine a nearby asteroid belt for ice. Several other worlds in this planet-rich part of the galaxy also mine the asteroids so they can sell or trade ice for the diamond battery products Te produces. The planet is mountainous and the land is covered in lush vegetation that absorbs the water from the humid air, rich in oxygen and breathable nitrogen.

"Are you still here?" she yells out from somewhere in the distant part of her home. Before I can answer she emerges from behind the door on my right.

"Golly man, I'm so sorry," she says. "There are times when I find myself wandering around looking for something not remembering why or what I'm looking for. Then, all of a sudden, like just now, I was sitting on the dry loo when I remembered that you were here." She shakes her head. "Well anyway, the incinerator on my dry toilet hasn't been working properly and I have to get the system checked soon . . . if you catch my drift." She laughs half-hearted.

"Did you find the ring?" I ask.

"Of course, I found the ring. Don't be so smug." She makes a tongue clap and rolls her eyes. "Your mother gave this to me," she says, displaying a silver-colored ring with a deep herringbone pattern. "It's supposed to store her journal from the last visit she made to Starzel. I'm not a humanoid so I cannot access the stored information. Anyway, it's yours now." She quickly snatches it with her tight-fisted grip. "But only after you finish telling me about the eight energy centers. There's more to these glands than what you've shared yet. But I like what you are telling me in these simple basics. So that when you define the eighth center I can comprehend -- the way.

"Come on back over here to the table. Finish the lecture and then I'll give you the ring and you can be on your way to Planet Earth."

We walk to the table and take our seats. She fast steps ahead of me and quickly sits in the chair where I had been. "Why don't you sit over there this time?" with a mischievous snicker, she then points to the chair where she had been.

"Further above the heart, that is the thymus gland, there is the thyroid. This gland is at the center of the throat and it too is aware of the outer world." I sit in the chair as I continue. "The mind of the thyroid takes its cues from the taste buds, the smells from the olfactory, sounds from the ears, and interprets them to produce chemicals, protect our body, and also to communicate with those around us. Don't drink that, look over there, don't eat that, call out the warning, and so on and so forth.

"The sixth energy center, or gland as it is called, is located at the base of the brain. Just above the area where the tongue and throat join. The pineal gland. It is aware of the outer world through the eyes, and it also listens through the skin and hair follicles that pick up electromagnetic energy from outside and inside the body. The chemicals it produces are in millions of varieties to generate strength, run, climb, or react to dangers. Not just to avoid predators, fires, and the like but also nutritional dangers. For example, if you have a potassium shortage in the blood, it triggers a craving for bananas or broccoli. If you need vitamin E, you'll want fisheye stew or cashews. The creativity of the pineal gland is a marvel of miracles."

"That is the genius gland isn't it?" she shouts excitedly and dances in her seat. "The one that makes some people able to figure out how to make flour from wheat, and to make butter and cheese from milk. It's the thingamaglobin that gives a person super strength to lift heavy objects off of a trapped person and unimaginable athletic ability. You know, it's not like there was some divine cookbook just handed down from the gods like the Quran with everything humankind would ever need for eternity or something. Somebody had a supernatural inspiration every now and again throughout history to all of a sudden figure out stuff like iodine and penicillin. Who can know what we will come up with next?"

"Well, sort of. I guess, Rupirah. Though not entirely on its own." I pause to again let her focus. "The consciousness at the center of the mind...Remember, the hypothalamus? It is the seventh energy center.

That is what plays a larger role in developing products and improving life through inventions."

She settles back in her chair with a look of disappointment waning toward irritable skepticism. She quietly hums and moans. "Mmmh-mm"

"The eighth center is above us, about a foot and a half over the top of the head. Let me think. I've never had to put words to describe this energy and how the Neurolink brings this all together."

She reaches across the corner of the table with her left hand to take hold of my wrist and with her right hand, she gently pats the back of my hand. "It's okay sweetheart. Take your time and explain it to old Rupirah. I'll wait patiently while you figure yourself out."

"Thank you. I think. Well, the Neurolink works to make our consciousness aware of the other six energy centers and makes it so we can communicate with and get all seven centers working together in a coherent, unified body. Once all seven energy centers are, well, centered I become more aware of and can communicate with the eighth energy center.

"There are two ways we experience reality. The internal awareness we call I or me, and the external awareness we call you or they . . . or them. Everything that's not I and me. So, this eighth energy center now connects our consciousness and generates an electromagnetic field that surrounds the body connecting us to the outer realization."

Still holding on to my wrist, she gives the back of my hand a few quick rubs and then stops to say. "You should have just said, I don't know in the first place, and saved us both a lot of time. You just wasted half my day telling me a bunch of hoohah -- nothing."

"Nothing!" I exclaim infuriated. "The power and intellect that comes from aligning the energy centers is not anything to you. You said it yourself how a humanoid is several times smarter and far stronger than ordinary humans."

"That's not what we agreed to," she says. "I said I would give you your mother's ring in exchange for you telling me how it all works. All you gave me was a bunch of epigenetic science on glands and the autonomic nervous system. If I had wanted to know more about epigenetics, I could have asked Alexa."

"Of course, but I told you that Neurolink provides a Syganoid with the cognitive ability to communicate with each gland's mind. We can pull the mind out of the body and join it with the conscious mind."

"Woopty doo! So what? I can pat my head and rub my tummy at the same time. Here, watch."

As she performs the stunt she crosses her eyes and sticks her tongue out at me. Then she flips me the bird with both hands and nearly hits me in the face as she stretches her arms out exaggerating and waving her middle fingers in my face to ensure I didn't miss the symbolic gesture. Then as quick as she first begins, she switches hands and rubs her belly, and pats her head again.

"Now you try," she says as she grabs Mother's ring off the table and holds it in her grip. "You won't be taking this ring. You cheated me."

"Listen. That's my ring and you know my mother told you to give it to me."

"No, you listen. I arranged for the transport to take you to Burbank, in Starzel. Take the elevator up to the forty-fourth floor and tell the clerk Rupirah sent you. He'll take care of everything."

"There's more to it than aligning the energy centers. The real key to gaining super intelligence and superhuman strength comes when I change the perspective," I say.

"What do you mean, perspective?" She asks.

"So, you want to know how to get the universe to work for you, and how to cause the source to favor your will? I can tell you how it works, I can tell you how to make your visions become a reality and how to heal your body by making it free from pain and sickness, and give you superpowers," I say almost pleading.

"Come on then and do it. Tell me how," she smirks. Adding a tongue clap.

Holding my right hand open, coaxing her to give me the ring, "Stop praying to fix everything that you think is broken. People spend their days sheltered in their imposter feelings. Thinking they are unworthy and that they don't have enough food, never enough money, are always tired or never happy. And then they pray for help to make this and that better and they pray for help with all their problems. All that prayer and feelings do is exaggerate the focus and make the problems worse. It communicates nothing to The Source. When you need money, The Source cues up all the money you need. When you need better health, The Source cues up all the healing. When you need help, The Source prepares all the answers and solutions. But when you ask for help to solve the issues, all you're doing is blocking The Source from delivering everything it has readied for you.

"Change the perspective of feeling like you are unworthy and need help. Be like this instead of asking to have the issue fixed. -- If I am a miracle of the Universe, if I'm this amazing being who experiences consciousness and I'm filled with Source energy, then prove it. Show me I'm special. -- That's the correct perspective. Then don't wait for the problems to go away before feeling better. Adopt the emotion of joy and gratitude because The Source has already given you everything you need."

She walks to the wall of shelves and cupboards and opens a cupboard door. Then she turns to look at me and points towards the front door.

"Get out of my home!" She screams.

Her other hand, still in a tight fist, holds my Mother's ring.

"The ring is mine. If you won't give it to me willingly I'll find another way to take it off you."

Pushing my chair back from the table I stand and walk around the table towards her.

"Leave me alone! Don't touch me!" She wails. Her grip on reality fades once again.

"Take it easy. I'm not going to touch you. I mean you no harm."

She screams and turns to run out of the room, but as she turns her head collides at the temple with the corner point of the cupboard door. Before I could catch her, she collapses in a heap.

"Holy goddamn hell!"

Dropping to my knees I roll her onto her back.

"Rupirah!"

She doesn't respond. I check for a pulse on the side of her neck. There's nothing there. Lifting her arm I check her wrist. No pulse there. Then I push my ear to her chest. I hear no breathing and no heartbeat.

"You can't be dead! No way. This can't be happening."

As grief and guilt intertwined within me, I realized the weight of the truth in my mother's words. A memory of her voice,

You possess a power unlike any other, but with it comes great responsibility. If you go to Planet Earth, people will die because of you. Your very presence there will be destruction and chaos.

My superior humanoid powers, untamed and unpredictable, had inadvertently led to tragedy. I had become the harbinger of doom she had foreseen, bringing about destruction and death. But amidst the anguish, a new determination flickered within me. I couldn't undo the past, but I could shape the future. I had the power to harness my abilities, to control and channel them for the greater good. Rupirah's death would not be in vain--I would use this tragedy as a catalyst for learning.

Rising from the floor, I gazed at Rupirah's lifeless form and made a solemn vow. "I will not let your death be in vain, Rupirah. From this moment on, I will try to better control my failing systems and wield my powers responsibly. I will protect those around me and prevent further harm from destroying innocent human lives."

My eyes survey the room. Two cups of tea and a teapot. What did I touch? My fingerprints . . . I have to remove evidence of my having been here. The window. My head turns to look at the window where I stood waiting for her when she went to look for the ring.

"The ring."

As I look at her hand I see the ring in her palm. I take the ring and slide it over my finger. As I do, my HUD instantly recognizes the Syganoid device.

__new device found__

__attaching to new hardware__

__storage device ready__

__name this device:__

--Mother--

__storage device named MOTHER__

As I continue to push the ring over my finger it automatically resizes to fit my hand.

--open files, Mother--

__there are no files__

--scan Mother for content--

__the storage device MOTHER contains no data__

This makes no sense. Why would Mom give this ring to Rupirah and tell her it had information about Starzel? There's no time to investigate the mystery. Right now I need to get out of here. I won't change anything. When they find her dead, they won't suspect anything. It was an accident. If anyone ever asks, I'll just say she was in good health when I left.

***

Before closing the door I scan the room. From this day forward I'll wear my mother's ring and carry the memory of crazy Rupirah's death. The door latch catches the strike plate and the frame secures automatically. Then I pull the backpack to a comfortable position over my shoulders while I use my biometrics to scan the passageway locating the elevator.

A moment later the elevator door chimes louder than necessary. As the holographic door disappears, retracting into the wall to my left. A mechanical voice prompts, "What floor number, please."

"Forty-four."

Stepping forward into a dapper, transparent pod that uses holographic technology to create a virtual elevator experience. A loud chime again as the nonexistent holographic doors close. The sensation of movement is slight and there is no sound of the vacuum lifting the car up through the building. The pod projects stunning visuals and immersive sound effects as the walls depict a bustling futuristic cityscape, with sleek hovercraft zipping through towering skyscrapers that seem to stretch infinitely into the digital sky. Neon lights dance in vibrant hues, creating a mesmerizing tapestry of color that pulses in harmony with the elevator's movement. I counted thirty-one seconds and then the nonexistent holographic door retracts to the right and the piercing chime announces the arrival.

As I step out I'm instantly met with the sounds of several dozen people all speaking at once. They swarm and clammer around me speaking dialects I cannot interpret. Language translation implants embedded in my ears instantly translate only four languages at any one time. This encounter has dozens of languages and the otherwise seamless communication with people from different cultures and backgrounds is nothing less than garbled noises.

When my biomechanical voice recognition system begins to identify the different voices and attaches the language to their face recognition, the noises turn into coherent words.

Planet Te is not an easy life for many of the inhabitants. Those who do not secure a corporate assignment do not earn tokens. Without tokens, there is no sustenance on Te where even the air we breathe has a price-per-breath tax. It carries a rich taste that causes the mind to crave more of it. The few who can afford the minimum beggers fee, charged by the transport company, come here to beg and plead to go with the traveler. They offer every service, committing themselves to slavery, promising to be loyal and attentive to whatever demands the traveler may have. Desperation cannot adequately define what my ears hear and my eyes see.

As I struggle to make my way through grasping hands, and those who step into my path face me and express the sincerity of their promises. My senses are insulted by the pungent scent of unwashed bodies, and the sight of people willing to offer themselves into servitude for a chance at survival. Trudging forward, at long last I reach the clerk's station. A shimmering barrier was in place between us. It is not made of physical material, but rather an advanced electronic force field. The force field emits a soft, pulsating energy, creating a faint glow that outlines its shape.

On the other side of a transparent barrier sits a slender man. He's well-dressed and perfectly manicured. A stark contrast to the barely clothed and unclean beggars that clammer for attention around me. His small chamber is undecorated. The walls of his office appear to be covered with brushed stainless steel. The office is well-illuminated and there's an off-white credenza that stretches across the wall behind him. On top of the credenza stands a single, thick stick of incense that billows an uninterrupted line of smoke.

"Where to, traveler?" he asks.

"Starzel, please."

The sudden silence was a shock to my ears. For a brief moment, it felt as if the entire room expanded and everyone pulled as far away from me as the room permitted. A few people laughed and everyone moved away as they head back toward the elevator to wait on the next traveler to arrive.

"That's a country on Planet Earth. I must warn you it's not a safe country and Planet Earth is a very dangerous planet too. Everybody knows that and I'm sure a man like you isn't worried about dangerous places." A sincere smile and assuring nod of his head as his small thin eyes look in my direction but he looks through me rather than at me.

"How much money and tokens will you be taking with you?"

His assuming tone makes me feel uneasy. "It isn't any of your concern how many tokens I'll carry with me. The transport has been arranged for me by Rupirah. That's all you need to know."

"Well, you should have mentioned Rupirah from the start." He lifts his voice and head when he says her name as if sending a signal to the room outside his chamber. As I scan the room I see two barely clothed and obvious call girls whispering together, sharing occasional nods and glances in my direction.

"Here it is. I have the reservation to Starzel here. Indeed, Rupirah did arrange general boarding and standard transport for today. Are you sure about the standard transport, mister?" This time his eyes are looking at me.

Before I answer I watch the two women cross the room to approach a giant of a man. As they speak to him all three of them took a quick look in my direction. Then the giant leaves the room in a hurry and the two girls pretend to act casual. They go in separate directions and now and again look back at one another with a suspicious giggle.

"There's probably some mistake on the reservation." He says after waiting for my delayed reply. "Let me send a messenger down to Rupirah's home and check with her. I'm sure she didn't expect you to travel in standard class."

"That isn't necessary," I say while turning my whole body to face him. "She's not to be bothered. That is, I'm sure standard class is fine."

"There's no problem in checking with her. Her home is right here in the building. It won't take but a few minutes to check with her. Trust me, mister. You don't want to travel in standard. Not with that fancy backpack and all your fancy clothes and accessories. Someone would steal them before you were ten minutes into your cryogenic sleep.

"Yeah, you need a private suite for your safety. Have you been vaccinated? There are half a dozen viruses on Planet Earth that will keep you trapped there for months in quarantine. If they don't kill you first. The viruses I mean. Of course." He chuckles to himself and rocks in his chair as if entertaining himself with a private joke. "I'm not suggesting anyone would kill you in Starzel. Though at last count it was reported there are fourteen guns per person on average in that country. They're just insane about having guns and shooting each other. Aren't they?"

"I'm sure I don't know. I've never been to Planet Earth before," I say.

"Never been to Planet Earth and you're going to Starzel on the first trip?" His voice was raised and shrill. A few people behind me burst out with a brief hysterical laugh. "I can take care of everything. I'll get your vaccinations, upgrades, and insurance for the safest trip. Customer service is what I'm all about."

***

The door to his left slid open and a woman dressed in all black enters his ticket office. With a quick snap of his fingers, he mutes the room. I watch their pithy exchange and unemotional demeanors. Her short and shiny black hair is a stark contrast to her form-fitting matte black pantsuit. The jacket top with a wide neck and a single button well below her moderate breast and then the design opens again to reveal and accentuate her tiny round belly button. The trousers also enhance the second jacket opening with untied flaps that cause the eyes to double-take a glance and then stare at her ultra-white feature that appears like a recessed nipple. She's wearing no blouse, exposing a generous amount of her breastbone leading up to her thin throat and rubbery face. As she leaves his office my eyes follow her slender form. She will be a memory I will not easily forget and oddly, I sense a craving to see her again.

My mind wanders back in time and I recall a conversation with my mother.

"Are you happy, Mom?" I asked, my voice filled with genuine concern as I approached the kitchen table. The matte black pantsuit she wore, a departure from her usual attire, caught my attention, but it was the distant look in her eyes that worried me.

She turned her gaze towards me, her expression a mix of contemplation and sadness. There was a weight in her response as if she had been grappling with this question for some time. "Happiness is a complicated thing, my dear," she finally replied, her voice tinged with a hint of melancholy.

She motioned for me to take a seat beside her, and I obliged, silently urging her to continue. She took a deep breath, her eyes scanning the world beyond the window before settling back on me. "Life is a series of ups and downs, moments of joy and moments of struggle," she explained. "Sometimes, happiness may seem elusive, but it's important to find contentment in the small things and cherish the moments of joy that come our way."

Her words struck a chord within me. I realized that happiness was not a constant state but rather a fleeting emotion, influenced by circumstances and perspective. It was a lesson in appreciating the present and finding joy in the ordinary moments of life.

Leaning closer, I asked, "Are you content, then? Do you find moments of joy in your life?" Her eyes softened, and a gentle smile played on her lips. "Yes, my dear. Despite the challenges and uncertainties, there are moments of immense joy that make it all worthwhile. You, your brother and father, and the love we share are my greatest sources of happiness and contentment."

Her words reassured me, and at that moment, I understood that happiness was not a destination but a journey. It was about finding meaning and purpose amidst the complexities of life.

As the memory faded, I returned to the present, the image of my mother in the matte black pantsuit lingering in my mind. I clasped the ring tightly, drawing strength from the memory of her resilience and the lessons she had imparted.

"There you are mister, uh Eulər is it? Not to worry, my new assistant will be back in a few minutes and we will get this matter of first-class transport arrangement completed for you. While we wait. Let's talk about insurance."

"There's no need to bother Rupirah." I try to use a forceful tone hoping to will him to call the assistant off. He won't, I realize, but if she discovers Rupirah's dead body she'll notify galactic-security. That will delay my leaving for Planet Earth and put me at risk of being discovered. "I'm sorry but before I can continue, is there a service nearby? I need to pee."

Without another word, he raised his left hand above his head, snapped his fingers to mute the microphone and at the end of his finger's snap motion the pointing finger directed me to a wall over my right shoulder. Just above the entry scanner was the word, toilets. Adjusting my backpack I started for the elevator. Impatient and with my thoughts giving way to images of my persecution for the murder. A failed defense claiming she hit her head on the cupboard door and why I didn't report the accident. It must be murder. So then, when the lift is slow to respond to my request I jump into the stairwell and run down the four flights to the apartment.

The door to her apartment is open just a crack. I listen to my feelings and use my sixth sense to anticipate what's next. I know I closed the door when I left. My memory is certain. Careful as a mouse slipping past the house cat I enter the apartment and close the door behind me. The vacuum of the door seal breaks the silence. My eyes scan the clutter but nothing looks out of place. My ears detect nothing, only the steady hum from the oxygen-generator fan. I take four quiet and long steps forward and look to the floor on the left. Rupirah's body is still there, but she has been moved onto her side.

My head jolts forward and my body falls forward and onto the ground. The sudden blow to the back of my head triggers my HUD to open and my physical strength-enhancing spinal implants automatically engage.

Using the force of the strike to my advantage I somersault forward, turn, and spring to my feet facing the assailant. It is one of the prostitutes from the transport waiting room. She's holding a short, solid, copper-colored pipe in both hands. She raises the pipe like a samurai warrior ready to strike. Then her partner jumps onto my back and wraps her arms around my throat and head, putting me in a perfect sleeper hold.

Careful here. Don't use hyper-strength now or they will know I'm a humanoid.

But before I can figure out how to neutralize these two, the woman in black attacks the first prostitute. In a blur of fast motion that lasted less than a heartbeat, she pulled the copper-colored pipe from her hands, placed her arm around her neck, and locked the arm in place while at the same time tightening the pressure with her free hand. The prostitute, fearing for her life, rips her shirt open to expose her breasts to me and tries to speak but can only just mutter, "Help me."

The exposed breast action caught me by surprise and I near laughed as I realized how her training in prostitution has taught her to use her sex to manipulate the male ego and psyche. She hoped it would put me into protective mode and trigger the male fight to save the weaker sex aggression in me. Meanwhile, my right hand has managed to grip the right thigh of my assailant and I squeeze it with the force of a vice clamp. The intensity of pain surging through her brain caused her to release the sleeper hold.

As I throw her to the floor with her right arm twisted and held in a hammerlock position behind her back. I press my knee on top of her arm and hold her to the floor.

"Stop!" I shout at the woman in black.

She looks into my eyes and without a second thought or any hesitation she snaps the prostitute's neck with the sound of a walnut caught in the jaws of a nutcracker. Her limp body falls to the floor with a great thud. Then in another blur of motion, she smashes the copper-colored pipe into the head of the woman I have pinned on the floor under my knee. The prostitute's head splits open with the sound of a log being split under the force of a well-swung ax.

Springing to my feet like a man who just discovered he's been kneeling on a cobra snake, I watch in shock as the blood pours from the headwound.

"Why would you do that? I had it under control," I say.

"You looked like you had it under control," she smirked. "That little girl hit you so hard and you never heard it coming. And then her partner had you in a sleeper hold before you could blink an eye. Yeah, you had it under control alright."

***

The air in the room turned thick and suffocating, each breath tainted with a metallic tang of blood. The taste mixed with a feeling of panic lingered on my tongue, a bitter reminder of the violence that had erupted before my eyes. My skin prickled with a mix of shock and adrenaline, sending shivers down my spine like electric currents. The room, once filled with unemotional exchanges, now reeked of raw emotion. The sight of lifeless bodies and the crimson pool spreading on the floor only intensified the heart-pounding fear that surged through my veins. In this moment, the boundaries between friend and foe blurred, leaving me grappling with a strange sense of gratitude towards the woman in black who had intervened, forever altering the course of my journey.

"People being killed in rapid succession isn't something that I'm used to experiencing -- ever. I've never seen anyone killed before, and to make this whole thing worse, I was holding the woman down when you split her skull open! That makes me an accomplice to your murderous act."

"Relax cheery boy. You are not an accomplice to anything and it's not a murder. They already killed Rupirah," she points to the dead body lying on the floor behind several small tables that are stacked from floor to ceiling and a wheat-colored woven basket with a wooden framed top and bottom that lay on the floor underneath the bottom table. The basket is filled with white stick candles. Rupirah's open hand is visible and extends beyond the basket into view.

That's the hand I took my mother's ring from.

"They broke into Rupirah's apartment and killed her. No doubt they planned to rob her and got caught. I saw the door was open when I arrived and lucky for you I was hiding here by the door behind the very tall credenza.

"Death isn't anything to get yourself all worked up over. It's just an individual experience in an otherwise always-on consciousness. First, the individual experiences the awareness of birth, and finally, the self has the final experience that ends in death. I use awareness and consciousness interchangeably. Not everyone does, but I do. Anyway, birth and death have been going on for hundreds of millions of years. Feeding the conscious expression of itself."

Her description of the individual experience and the universal consciousness is precise but unusual. She speaks like my friend Casper, but I don't recognize her from our circle of friends. Still, I can't stop my egoic self from fantasizing about her exposed flesh and the form-fitting outfit. I imagine she uses sexual allure to throw people off of her intellect and her killer skills. She camouflages her true self and intentions.

"Cheeryboy!" She snaps her fingers in rapid succession and shouts. "Are you paying attention to what I'm saying or are you imagining what you want to do with me in your bed?"

"Of course I am. That is, no, of course not. Fuck it all! I mean yes, I'm listening to you. Now you listen to me. I need to get to Planet Earth on the next transport." I hasten the conversation to get back to the present emergency. "There's no way I can get caught up in whatever this thing is with all these dead bodies."

"Listen to me," she mocks me. "I'm your transportation contact, Eulər. Your friend Casper hired me as a Boundrian Creator to provide you with my protection services. As a freelancer, I don't usually work with the government, but Casper said you are on a project that is off the books." She chuckles, "I guess that makes you a freelancer too."

The conversation I had with my father as I was leaving our home on Planet Forty-Four comes to mind. "This is an unnecessary risk, Eulər. There is nothing so important that you should chance a visit to that war-torn planet. Planet Earth has a human history of murder and suffering barely above that found in the Hungry Ghost hell realm.'

His concern was evident in his tone and his furrowed brow. The flesh of his neck twitched when he was nervous and causes me so much distraction that in any ordinary conversation, with him I tune his words out and count the pacing of twitches per second. In this particular conver-

sation, he captured my full attention when he mentioned the Boundrian Creator. I wonder if he and Casper had made this plan.

"There's a select few Syganoids with the ability to open wormholes between Class M planets. Something to do with the harmonic frequency of the planets. I don't understand much more. But you cannot use wormholes or vortexes to travel from here to Planet Earth. It's a traceable echo imprint. But once you are there you can use a vortex to reach most cities and countries. I'm going to hire someone to go with you. For your safety, Eulər. Follow the advice of the Boundrian Creator."

My memory of the conversation stops when the woman in black speaks.

"Anyway. I'm going to take care of this murdering bunch of prostitutes and then I'll catch up to you on Planet Earth in a day or two. For now, you need to get out of here and back up to the transportation deck."

"What about the check-in clerk? He's expecting you to go back and report about your conversation with Rupirah."

She looks across the congested apartment toward Rupirah's body. "Well she's not saying much is she?" Her sarcasm is followed by a stern look my way. "I'm sure even a cheery boy like you can handle that check-in clerk." Then she motions with over-dramatic flailing arms directing me to get out of the apartment.

When I walk out and turn to close the door, out of the corner of my eye I catch the motion of somebody entering the lift. The chime fades as the sound of the doors seals. Back into the stairwell I climb the four flights to the forty-fourth floor.

With a firm but slow push, I open the door and enter the waiting room. The clerk is sitting in his office and I can see him through the large, electronic opening. He appears to stay busy as he switches from typing to glancing from one monitor to another, checking each of his six displays. I zig-zag my way through the crowded room and over to his window. He greets me with his exaggerated and very toothy welcoming smile.

***

When the elevator chimes, the beggars clammer on cue toward the doors. They swarm and shout their pleas to the strangers getting off the elevator. I turn my attention away from the scene and instead look through the electric window and at the clerk.

"Let's wrap up this oneway transportation. I want first class with the private room."

His fingers hammer away at the keyboard as his eyes dart from monitor to monitor. The look of a determined hunter and his body coiled in anticipation of finding treasure in the monitors.

"Yes sir. Whatever you need, I will make this transport work for you. I see that my assistant is still not entered the information we need from Rupirah. But . . ."

I interrupt and give him my stern demand. "I will take care of Rupirah myself. Just book the transport and give me the keycard. Right? Okay then."

His fast-paced efforts stall as his eyes lock on the scene behind me. His expression suggests momentary fear before he regained composure and put his eyes and fingers back to the task. I turned to look. The gathering of beggars has given way and they are retreating back to their places, leaning against the walls, sitting on the floor, and waiting for the next arrivals announced by the chime of the elevator. The giant of a man has returned. I recall he had been speaking with the two prostitutes who are now dead and lying in Rupirah's apartment.

The woman in black, my transport connection. I wonder how she will convince the criminal investigation that she was protecting herself. As the thoughts run through my head and I replay the way she snapped the first girl's neck and then caved in the head of the second without remorse, I see the giant of a man point at me.

His bald head and pear-shaped face are surrounded by a ring of thick, curled, reddish-blond hair. The ring of hair covers his chin and cheeks about an inch long and in a circle about an inch wide that carries up his sideburns, across the top of his head, and back down and around the other side. His facial features with a narrow but deep-lined forehead, a broad nose, and round deep-set eyes that are spread too far apart even for his size, and his sunken cheeks seem to cave in from the circle of hair. He's wearing a green onesie uniform reminiscent of the infamous Omar Sharif Guard who are rumored to have pirate ships throughout the Milky Way Galaxy. His arms are as big around as my head and each of his thighs is as large as my entire trunk.

He's too big to be allowed to roam around in public.

Without making eye contact with him and trying to act as if I hadn't seen him pointing at me, I turn back to the clerk who is staring at me, waiting for my attention before he speaks.

"I'll just need to collect the insurance and we do take most all NFT and of course Dogecoin is preferred."

"Insurance?"

"Oh absolutely sir. In all good consciousness, I couldn't let you travel without insurance. The Planet Earth is the final stop which means everyone on that transport ship will be woken and off the ship before you. You'll sleep right through and even in a private room . . . well with all that fancy equipment and backpack you have there. You might even consider doubling the coverage."

"Right. Well, whatever," He doesn't realize that I won't go into stasis sleep. I'm a Syganoid, and I can't stay in general transport sleep chambers or they would discover what I am. "So, charge the balance to my aunt Rupirah's NFT wallet that you have on record."

I can see the reflection of the giant of a man in the reflective window. He's taken a seat on the farthest wall from the boarding gate. He's watching me like a hawk stalking a rat. He probably knows I had something to do with the death of his two prostitute friends. He no doubt wants to get revenge for their deaths.

The air in the room is thick with palpable tension as if the very walls hold their breath in anticipation of an imminent clash. The sharp gazes of the beggars and the calculated movements of the giant of a man have me on edge, as I maintain an air of nonchalance.

"Here's your boarding certificate and the card for your private room. Enjoy your trip."

"The insurance certificate?" I ask.

"Oh goodness me. Why I would forget my head if it wasn't attached," his fingers click away at the keyboard as he speaks. "My wife is always on my case for forgetting things. There, that's got it." He slides the three cards through the narrow slot at the bottom of his window.

I take a few steps away from the clerk's station while tucking the cards into the zippered sleeve of my waist belt. The blaring chime of the elevator sounds, and the clamoring begins the performance as if the conductor of the orchestra has motioned for the first act. The performance ends quicker than it began as two robo-security units, Androps, glide out of the elevator.

The security units raise their detector beacons and scan the long narrow corridor of the waiting room. I start off toward the seating area opposite where the giant of a man sits. I move as slow as a drip of water making its way down an icicle on the last day of winter. When the Androps begin to move further into the room I take the first seat in front of me. I'm right between two men who look like business travelers. They barely notice me, like everyone else in the room, their attention is on watching the Androps.

Chapter Three

Transport to Earth

I'm certain at any moment one of the security forces will arrest and take me away. Before they do, I must continue to make this journal of every effort taken to recover the missing data. Whoever you are reading this and taking my place on this mission . . . I pray the recording of my every moment helps.

Three deaths that I have been involved with on my first day on Planet Te. I recovered my mother's ring and secured transport to Planet Earth. According to my documents, I will arrive in Burbank on June 4, 2188, and accommodations are made for me in Culver City. Both locations are located in the Great Starzel Republic. Culver City was reported to be the location where Banyan wrote his final novel. There I would search for clues and I hoped to discover copies of all his work. I'm sorry that I failed to complete the task and therefore I cannot replace the missing code for the Arya Sangata Dharma Paraya. I am certain to be taken into custody for these deaths.

The Androps stop and question the giant of a man. Meanwhile, the people in the waiting room go back to their regular conversations and activities. The waiting room hums with the mingling of many voices and dialects spoken.

Special log entry tag identification, #Androps. These robo-security units are imposing figures that command attention wherever they go. Standing at a height of approximately seven feet, they are designed with an eye-catching esthetic. Their bodies are composed of a combination of durable metallic alloys and reinforced synthetic materials, giving them a robust and formidable appearance.

The Androps' overall shape is android, with broad shoulders and a muscular build, emphasizing their strength and authority. Their limbs are agile and precise, allowing them to move with fluidity and grace. The surface of their metallic exterior gleams with a polished finish, reflecting the ambient lights in the room.

At the core of their design, the Androps have a head unit that houses their advanced sensor systems and facial recognition technology. Their faces are innovative and featureless, lacking traditional human characteristics. Instead, a series of glowing lines and symbols run across the surface serving as indicators of their current state or activity.

The most notable feature of the Androp is its detector beacons. Located on their forearms, these beacons emit a soft pulsating light that scans the environment for potential threats or anomalies. When raised, the beacons emit a faint humming sound, signifying their active scanning mode.

In terms of locomotion, the Androps glide rather than walk. They hover slightly above the ground, propelled by an advanced anti-gravity system, which adds to their otherworldly appearance. Their movements are smooth and calculated, making them seem both efficient and unstoppable.

While their physical presence alone is intimidating, it is their unwavering dedication to security and enforcement that truly defines the Androp. Programmed with advanced algorithms and protocols, they carry out their duties with unwavering precision, always ready to respond to any breach of regulations or suspicious activities. End of log entry tag #Androps.

The businessmen I'm sitting between eye me over from top to bottom as if surprised to find a body has materialized unnoticed. The man on my right speaks first, "Looks to me as the bots found their target suspect, eh. Hooya, stranger. I have to admit to not seeing you sit here. While I was busying me self watching them." He discreetly motions a hand toward the security units on the far side of the room.

Several dozen rows of seats down the center of the room with ten seats in a row evenly spaced from a few meters before the clerk's office all the way through to the elevator and stairway entry. On each side of the room, seats are facing toward the center but two meters between the seats make a natural passage. The elevator area is packed with beggars and they have taken up positions along the walls and the first six or seven rows. Close enough to swarm anyone coming off the elevator.

From the seats along the wall, the two business travelers and I can observe all of the activity of the beggars, the passengers, and the security units. I see the giant of a man looking at me except to occasionally look at the Androp while he responds to their demands. I can't hear what they are saying to one another. I decide the best strategy for me is to fit in with the businessmen.

"Sorry, I crowded in on the both of you. When I saw the security officers come in, well I suppose I just took the first seat. Sat down and watched."

"Ye have not crowded neither tawone of us. Nare ye mind. Tis good to have the company of a fellow traveler for a change. Usually tis me and me friend just thar on these trips." He nods his head to point toward the man on my right.

"Security Officers, he says," laughing with a high-pitched squeal. "Did cha hear him call dem robots officers?"

"Aye. Of course, I heard em. Him is sat right beside mine and I taint deaf." He bumps a shoulder into mine to catch my attention. "Dem machines taint no officers. Dey is a simple machine filled with circuits and scripted programs. No heart, no emotions, no compassion. Dem chines don't deserve any honorable title."

Then the man on my right says, "All in all tis this legal fight for who owns space. Nowadays we have the Galaxy Patrol, the Space Police, and Galactic Detectives all battling one another fur jurisdiction. None of dem is more dan simple mafia. Like all governments before um. Nuttin but maffia. Last year, for good example. Last year we was making our trip to Elonia Colony from Te in less dan two day each way. So den come the Galactic Detectives with dare new law dat nobody can travel faster den sub-light speed. Now it take three month and some transports are a year or more for dis same route. Taint nuttin but robbery for us businessmen."

"Dat dare taint de only robbery on transporting," says the man on my left as he leans forward from his seat to look around me to the man on my right. The chime sounds before he can expound on his thought. The beggars spring into action. Their words fill the room with a roar of indiscernible voices. Only the tones of their sorrow and desperation and needs can be perceived. When the visitor comes out of the elevator it is another Androp. This one is identified as Galaxy Patrol.

The room returns to a quiet murmur of voices and everyone again finds their place and settles. I see the units have closed in tighter and surround the giant of a man. Even with their proximity he still eyes me. His emotionless stare causes me to quake as I experience deep regret for the death of his prostitute friends. I imagine him taking me into his giant hands and snapping my neck the way the woman in black took the life of the prostitutes.

"Dat fandangled insurance dey sell ta travelers is the biggest robbery of all," the man on my left picks up the conversation right where it fell off.

"Oy yay!" nods the man on my right in agreement.

"Not one robbery in all the years of space travel on deez transport and still dey charge premium fee for insurance. Dat is crimnal, eh."

The third Androp is followed off the elevator by a plasma energy forcefield-controlled holding cell. A paddywagon as they are usually referred to. Being held inside the transparent cell is the woman in black.

***

The paddywagon is a mobile holding cell designed to hold criminal suspects as they are transported from the place of arrest to the formal jail holding cell. The platform of the paddywagon contains the necessary components and energy packs to power the mobile jail. It measures a little more than one meter wide and twice as long. The height and width are expandable, electrified, holograph bars, and are automatically sized as determined by the size of the arrested person.

Inside the holograph holding cell, the arrested person is held in place by a plasma force field with arms outstretched from either side, palms of the hands forward with fingers outstretched, and legs spread a bit wider than shoulders width.

The businessman on my left turns to me and says, "The purdy gal in dat jail is sure eyeballing you, mate. Supposin she might be to know ye?"

"Probably she is just hypnotized by my incredible good looks." I laugh as I turn my head from side to side looking at the two of them sharing a sheepish grin on my face. When they begin to laugh I laugh louder coaxing them to open up and fill the waiting room with the sound of laughter.

"Where are you men traveling?" I ask.

The louder of the two men says, "We are stopping at the Asteroid Gateway for a day of meetings and from there, we're going to the old city, Erebus Montes on Planet Mars."

"There have been a lot of rumors about the meeting rooms and the business complex at the Asteroid Gateway complex. I've even heard one traveler tell me it makes the Lunar Gateway look like a small family vacation center," I say prompting them for another round of laughs.

His business partner says, "It might be but I never been to dat Lunar Gateway. Actually, I've never been dat far into the inner planets at all. We represent a large group of investors who own several dozen asteroids inside duh belt. We're meeting wit a mining group called Astrobotic. Dey is a small affiliate company owned by Space X. Dat isn't important. What dey are mining is important. Dey be chasing after duh mineral, Ilmenite which is rich in oxygen as you probably know. And dey is even more interested in a few of our asteroids dat contain large amounts of spartic."

"Spartic?" I ask.

He makes a quick look toward the other guy who gives an assuring nod. "It's an enzyme-producing mineral. When it mixed with water, it make us magic water, Adam's Ale as some people call it."

The louder of the two adds, "Duh benefits of the electrolyzed water be endless and valuable. It requires no cleaners, no chlorine, or filtering, and provide dem what drink it an hallucination of powerful super intelligence. I've never tried it because I can't afford of it."

A loudspeaker with an overmodulated voice announces the arrival of the transportation ship in docking port five. Thirty-plus people stand and gather their luggage and begin to take their place in the queue outside of port number five. The small opaque windows along the wall provide a shadowy visual of the ship as it glides into the docking bay. A moment later the disembarking passengers come through the doorway from the bay into the waiting room.

An odd metallic, synthetic ion smell is vivid when the doors to the loading bay open. The passengers appear groggy as they scan their boarding cards with an audible bleep, and a turnstile flashes green allowing them to exit the docking bay.

Both of the traveling businessmen follow me into the queue as they continue to chuckle and remind each other of my last statement.

"You didn't tell us where you're going to, mate," he says.

"You never asked me, mate." I laugh a hardy laugh. And the two of them join me again in a loud and long round of laughter. "I'm heading to Planet Earth. Going into Burbank in The Great Starzel Republic."

"Dat's not a good place to visit. Dat planet is the definition of human suffering." His traveling partner asks, "How do you mean suffering? I think we all are suffering, but most people accept the struggle of life as what life is. You know what I mean?"

"I think I know what you mean. It all goes back to that first hour and a half when Adam and Eve were thrown out of the Garden of Eden. Do you know that story?" I ask.

"No, tell me," they say at the same time.

"We haven't got the time. We'll be boarding soon," I say.

"We got better dan a half hour. Dez very slow boarding transport. Tell us dis story. Come on with it."

"Imagine how he felt as he walks out of Eden, Adam. He's experiencing anger for the first time and he feels the strain on his body, working every muscle as if nothing will come easy anymore. Never again. He turns to Eve and said, 'We had everything and everything was so amazing and peaceful and fun. Now look at this I'm hot, my feet hurt, and I'm thirsty. I'm really really thirsty.' They keep walking through the land and Eve replies with a venomous edge to her voice. 'Oh, so now it's all about Adam and his complaints? Typical. No one ever thinks about how I feel. No one cares about the burden I carry,' she sneered.

"They walk through the tall grass of the prairie. Tripping in the shallows and slipping in the muddy patches. Adam twisted his ankle once and Eve was stung by a bee or a hornet. Nobody knows for certain which it was. Then they walked across the barren land of rocks and gravel mixed with soft earth and when Adam stubs his toe on a dead tree branch raised a few inches above the ground, he said, 'This is horrible. We have no idea where we are going, all we can do is struggle along this rugged land and feel the heat of the sun and I'm still very very thirsty.'

"Again, Eve interrupted, her voice seething with resentment.'Typical of Adam, always whining and complaining. What about me? What about my pain and suffering? No one cares how much I've lost. It's always about him!' she spat. Tears stream from her eyes and stain her dirty cheeks with trails of moisture.

"An hour and a half after they left Eden, Adam spots a stream. He takes Eve by the hand and leads her down a steep bank as they head down to the stream. They fell twice and skinned their knees once, and Eve sobbed without stopping except to take in a few struggling series of short stuttering inhales. Finally, they reached the stream and Adam knelt to quench his thirst.

"Eve scoffed, her voice dripping with scorn. 'Oh, how convenient. Adam gets his sweet and satisfying drink, and suddenly everything is alright with the world. What about me? What about my pain? Does anyone care?' she exclaimed bitterly.

"From that day forward until the day he died, he never experienced a drink as sweet and satisfying as that first one.

"Now that is how we live every day. It is the memory of what we lost that always makes us seek happiness outside of ourselves, but always judged and judging, we are never satisfied for more than a brief moment, now and again."

The loud one says, "So den, at dare story maken me wonder -- what is the purpose of life? I din not tink I ever would ask dat question, but yuh make me wonder sum."

Waiting for a moment before I answer him, as I watch the giant of a man step into the paddywagon. The plasma forcefield instantly expands to surround him and force him into the spread eagle pose. I respond to the question without second thinking my words for who I am speaking to, "Happiness. The purpose of life is to be happy. Not giddy or silly or filled with laughter, but an absolute serene happiness."

The Androps escort the paddywagon carrying the woman in black and the giant of a man over to the clerk still seated behind the electronic window. "Excuse me for a moment gentlemen, do you mind holding my place in line here?" As I start to walk toward the security units and the paddywagon the businessmen take hold of me.

"Ye don wanna be messin' wif dem, Eulər."

"It will be okay," I assure them as I pull free of their holds and continue toward the security units.

***

The giant of a man's eyes grow wide as I approach, but then I turn back to the two businessmen. Their arms and hands were still outstretched in midair. Fear in their eyes and hesitant questioning expressions over their faces.

"Before I got too far away, I was thinking, I didn't finish what I was telling you about the story. You see, all of us keep getting hung up on this pursuit of happiness and we keep finding the path to be like that slippery slope down to the creek. Slipping, sliding, skinning our knees, and twisting our ankles. When it comes to happiness, the illusions are outside of us. New relationships, new jobs, new wotsits and they all bring temporary happiness and then later they bring a lot of major disappointment. Because, and finally I get to the point," I share a smile and a snorkel laugh, "true happiness can only come from within. Search within yourself."

With that said, I turn and walk straight to the closest Androp. The designation -- Android Security Unit 1777 Type E is stenciled across the front and below the black glass panel that appears to be the face of the thing. "Can I ask where are these people being taken?"

"Move along, please. Reactionary questions and idealism are criminal behaviors. These two individuals are no business of yours," it replies.

"It is my business as a taxpayer the whole process of your service and your job itself is paid for by me. You were built because of my work and for my benefit. Of course, it's my business. Don't be daft."

The security unit flashed a red light into my eyes. A foul-smelling puff of air wafts. "You need to move on and go about your business now. You are being reactionary and speaking of reactionary idealism. You will be arrested and prosecuted. This is your last warning."

Sirens blast and drown out the otherwise dull roar of conversation and fill the waiting room causing everyone to cover their ears. The woman in black is trying to escape the plasma forcefield and has set off an alarm. Her attempt to get my attention and cause the Androp to move away from me works.

"Move these criminals into the transport ship. Let's get them into the status chamber as soon as possible," orders the Androp as it slides toward the cargo doors of the docking bay.

The clerk opens the doors marked Cargo Bay Two and the sirens from the paddywagon stop their penetrating, pulse waves. The green light bars illuminate above the doors and the paddywagon, led by two Androps disappears through the opening and is followed by the third. The cargo bay doors close the moment the last Androp is through.

"Attention passengers. Thank you for choosing to explore space on Relativity Starships. Our mission is to take you to the planets of your choice on a safe and comfortable cruise. The transportation starship will begin boarding in two minutes. Destinations to Planet New New Deli, Asteroid Two One Zero, Asteroid Gateway, Planet Mars, and the final destination ninety-three days from today will be Planet Earth."

The announcement comes over the overmodulated speaker and is ignored as almost everyone is busy complaining about the ridiculous and exaggerated loud siren from the paddywagon.

Right on schedule, the boarding doors open and the display illuminates above the door in bright green letters, Gate Five. "You must have your boarding card ready to scan as you enter the ship," the announcement squawks and chirps as the line begins to shuffle toward the ship.

The boarding doors, marked with the faded green letters "Gate Five," open with a creak and a shudder, revealing a dimly lit corridor that lacks the inviting ambiance one would expect. The lighting is patchy, with some areas too bright and others barely lit, casting disorienting shadows. The once high-tech and informative displays now flicker intermittently or display distorted images, their poor maintained, outdated technology struggling to function properly.

As passengers enter the ship, the decline in maintenance becomes even more evident. The corridors, instead of being meticulously clean and polished, are marred by scuffed and worn-out flooring. The walls, once adorned with elegant artwork, are faded and peeling, with only remnants of their former beauty remaining. Interactive information panels, once instructive and interesting, now glitch and portray outdated or wrong information.

The ship's interior no longer hums with the seamless operation of advanced systems. Instead, there are occasional buzzes, groans, and the sound of dripping water, indicating leaks and malfunctioning equipment. The transparent viewports, once offering breathtaking views, now show signs of fogging or accumulated debris, obstructing the once-clear vistas.

The paddywagon is already on the ship and the passengers single-file past the prisoners after they scan their boarding cards. The Androps check each passenger and wave them toward the Sleepy Joes which is the brand name for the torpor stasis chambers.

"Move along and get into your assigned Sleepy Joe stasis chambers. The chamber number is on your boarding card. Do not get in any chamber other than the one you are assigned," said the Androp. "The transport can not leave the dock until everyone is in their assigned stasis chamber."

"What about them?" I ask as I point toward the woman in black and the giant man.

"You're in private room number eight." The Androp points toward the open doors that line the bulkhead on the right side of general passenger Sleepy Joes.

Following the slow-moving line of passengers as we move further into the ship I can't help but take note of the Sleepy Joe stasis chambers. While they undoubtedly represent an advancement in long-duration space travel, some aspects hint at potential shortcomings in their design and maintenance.

The chambers' outward appearance retains a sleek and streamlined design, suggesting a level of sophistication. However, upon closer inspection, signs of wear and inadequate maintenance become apparent. Scratches mar the once flawless surface, and faded labels on control panels hint at years of use without proper attention.

Within the chamber, the integration of biometric sensors and monitoring devices reminds me of the advanced capabilities of their technology. However, I doubt these systems receive the necessary updates and calibrations to ensure accurate readings. But, despite the outward appearance the records indicate flawless performance from this fleet.

The cryogenic technology employed to induce torpor sleep is impressive. Yet, my lingering question remains: How often are these systems serviced and maintained to ensure consistent and reliable performance? The success of the torpor sleep process relies heavily on precise temperature control and regulated atmospheric conditions. Any human negligence in maintaining these critical factors could jeopardize the occupants.

Furthermore, the life support system, responsible for maintaining the occupant's physiological needs, raises my concerns about its proper functioning. Adequate supplies of breathable gases, the removal of waste gases, and control of humidity are crucial for the occupant's well-being during extended periods of stasis. All these systems and operations rely on human attention to detail In my experience and knowledge of history, humans are not something that has ever been reliable.

As I walk past the paddywagon the giant of a man watches me. His eyes never lift nor blink. My HUD unit opens and the field of view indicates a message has been received.

Is he a Syganoid? Is the incoming message from him?

I look over my left shoulder for just a moment to confirm he is still watching me. He is.

"Keep moving passenger Eulər," Androp Unit 1777 says.

With the blink of an eye, I accept the message.

__you have a message from MOTHER__

--allow communication--

→Help him, Eulər←

--the giant of a man?--

→you must help him←

My thumb rubs the ring on my finger as I think,

How is this possible? I checked the external storage device when I took it from Rupirah, it was empty. There is no operating system, no program, and no data. The device is empty. How can it communicate with me?

The moment I step through the doorway to my private room the paddywagon alarms flood the ship. My hands cover my ears and I turn to see the giant of a man has broken free of the paddywagon's plasma restraints. He's running straight toward me.

***

As the sound of alarms flood the ship and the giant of a man breaks free, my once-entrenched beliefs in his intentions collide with the urgency of the present, forcing me to question not only the flawed systems around me but also my own place in this crumbling world.

__MOTHER__

→help him now Eulər←

Mother's message is clear and despite my fears that he intends to kill me as revenge for the murder of his two prostitute friends, I feel I must help. With my private room key held at the ready, I step away and to the side of the opening. As the giant of a man enters the room at full speed and with Androps in pursuit, I slide the room card across the door reader. The door slides closed, and the sound of the vacuum seal tells me the door will hold off the Androps. At least for now.

"Lock the door," I shout into the door reader mic.

"Door is locked," A soft and soothing robotic voice announces. "There are security Androps requesting access. I will open the door."

"Don't let them in," the giant of a man says. "Not yet, I have something for you."

The door begins to slide open. "Close door and lock," I shout. The door closes again. The word, Locked, above the door illuminates in crimson. "Do not allow security to enter the room." I am hesitant but shout the command into the door mic.

My back is pressed against the wall next to the door and the muted sound of the security Androps pounding at the other side of the door sounds as if the door is dense but the veracity of their intentions is discernible. His massive hand searches inside the front pocket of his green onesie and then, when he pulls it out, a small parcel is held between his thumb and forefinger.

The package is the size of a one-inch square box. It's covered in what looks like black velvet and tied like it has been gift-wrapped with a chartreuse-colored string. In an instant, I smell a combination of sweet and musky notes, reminiscent of ancient incense and exotic spices. My HUD does not warn of any poison or danger but the scent is captivating, drawing my attention closer, and I want to uncover the secrets and power contained within the parcel.

"From Rupirah," he says. "This is a charm, a Lia Fail that was prepared for the one who comes to save Planet Earth. It is a Destiny Stone. The Lia Fail was recovered from the Charente deep in the backwoods of the French countryside. Rupirah cleansed the stone in a salt bath. Changing the salt every day for seven days. Chanting each time as she changed the cleansing salt bath. Om Mane Padme Yum.

"After the cleansing period, the Lia Fail was charged with high energy and aligned with The Source. She placed it inside a blessed vessel and chanted over it every day and then sealed it closed. Opening it up once each day, she placed two drops of water obtained from Eban's Creek in Wales. She completed the chanting before sealing it inside the vessel again. Repeated six times each she chanted first. Om Ay Ra Pa Ta Na De."

Every vowel he spoke is long.

"Then she chanted the second verse six times. Om Muni Muni Mahayamuni Shakyamuni Svayhay. Finally, the chant concluded by repeating the heart sutra six times. Gate gate, paragate parasamgate bodhi svaha.

"The Destiny Stone was then placed next to the handwritten copy of the Arya Sanghata Dharma Prayaya on a perfectly arranged holy altar before it was wrapped in black velvet and tied to secure it from being seen. Once the package is opened the energy is expelled. You must not let it be opened until you know it is time."

His huge hand extended to me ready to give up the velvet package. "How will I know when it is time to open it?"

__message from MOTHER__

→take the package←

→you need this package or you won't be able to complete The First Priority←

--what is The First Priority?--

→you must hurry←

As my fingertips make contact with the smooth, wrapped surface of the stone, a subtle warmth spreads through my hand, resonating with a pulsating energy that seems to flow from within. The package texture is cool to the touch, yet it carries a comforting weight, imparting a sense of stability and connection to something ancient and profound. There is a faint, almost imperceptible vibration, like a gentle hum, that can be felt resonating through the hand and into my body, creating a harmonious and tingling sensation. It is a tactile experience that instills a deep reverence and awe as if I am touching a conduit of destiny itself. It even danced on the tip of the tongue, a tantalizing burst of sweet flavors.

The sound of the pounding on the other side of the door changes now to the telltale sound of a laser cutter.

"You will know it is time," he says, "because there will be nothing else that can be done. Now, stand back and open the door."

The door card is in my hand and the package is in the other, I slide the card over the reader. The word, Open, above the door, illuminates in a dark hunter green. Before the door was done opening the Androps fired their guns and emptied them into the body and head of the giant of a man. He fell face forward to the floor with a loud thud. With no ceremony or reverence to the life that moments ago was, Android Security Unit 6A55 drags the body from the room and then across the general Sleepy Joe torpor chamber area and leaves it laying on the floor beside the paddywagon.

"Let that be a lesson to you," Android Security Unit 1777 says in a mechanical voice void of emotion and respect. "When you next think reactionary and idealistic thoughts. Remember how it feels right now and stop yourself. It is for your own good. Space and Society have no place for idealism."

"Close the door," I say into the door scanner mic. The door slides closed and I watch as the scene outside my private room disappears from view behind the scorched door.

Four deaths in one day. These people on human-occupied planets treat life so casual and they even program their robots to treat them as if they are a commodity rather than a miracle. There's no time to philosophize about the human condition and suffering. Nevertheless, the mission will continue.

***

The forefinger and thumb of my right-hand fidget, turning and pulling at the ring on my finger. Despite my knowing it's impossible that it can communicate with my HUD. Yet, it has done just that. It was empty when I first checked it over. To make double-sure, I'll check it again.

--open device MOTHER--

__device is empty__

--examine for erased and encrypted files--

__device, MOTHER is empty__

As I suspected nothing has changed and It is indeed empty. How can it connect to me through the HUD if there is no data, and no OS, nothing in storage? As I pause to take it all in, the impossibility of an empty mechanical device to send an electronic signal to my HUD . . . I recall the fresh memory of the Androps and the cold, inhumane machines' actions. Without hesitation, they kill and interact with people as if their programming was written to be inhumane.

Thinking of their killing ways causes me to flashback to a conversation with my mom.

"Why are you always going to Planet Te? I ask one evening while she was packing her luggage for another trip. She often left me and my father for months at a time. I knew her work was important but I had never asked her anything specific about her work before.

"Planet Te is just the portal from where we can safely travel. Opening portals is dangerous because the Aryans can detect the rhythmic disruption. They'll hunt us until they know every last one of us has been eliminated from the universe."

She stops herself and tries to assure me of my safety. As any good parent, even a mother will do. "But you don't have to worry, Eulər we are safe from the Aryans. They will never find us here on Planet Forty-Four. Anyway, I take a space transport from Planet Te that our contact, Rupirah arranges and then I go to Planet Earth. I work with a great group of people. They are advancing stem cell research to improve biological brain-directed computing that is replacing silicon-based computing.

"We Syganoids already use organoid computers and you have thousands of microscopic organoids inside you. All of us do. We are equipped with mechanical devices, and silicon computer processors, and all of these

implants are driven by a technology we call synthetic biological intelligence (SBI). The Organoid Intelligence connects our HUD logic system to the hyper-efficient processing systems we wear and have implanted.

"The team I work with are an extended family. Our work makes life less harsh and more humane. Though I must admit, I've had to kill dozens of men in my travels. Killing is never easy and I . . ."

The memory is abruptly halted as the transportation ship's loudspeaker interrupts. "All passengers aboard this Relativity Starship are required to be inside the Sleepy Joe before the Starship can depart. Please strap in and press the activate button on the Sleepy Joe located in the center console of the chamber. This is the final warning before the security Androps take control of the launch sequence. We urge all of our passengers to consider their personal safety and to take their places now."

--Activate Emulation Clone--

__duplication process open__

--place the clone inside the Sleepy Joe and connect to the starship as a human--

__clone is in human mode__

This is the first time I've seen my clone as the holographic android takes my place inside the chamber. Like a dream where I am watching myself at the same time knowing it isn't real. The slender frame with its large muscular chest, shoulders, and arms -- identical in every way to my own. The mid-length, thin blonde hair with a slight wave and tucked behind the ears. My large forehead and square jaw with a slight bend to an otherwise normal nose. With ylnmn blue eyes, I'll need to adjust the iris color to make it less obvious that they are those of a Syganoid's.

--Set Eye Color to grey-blue--

__eyes are now adjusted to human tone, grey-blue__

That should do it. The android will fake out the Sleepy Joe stasis chamber, keeping my humanoid identity free from their detection.

Memory drifts now that the ship has left Planet Te and the long voyage is at last getting underway.

"It's our energy output that makes us easy to detect. Even with a simple radiology scanner, I recall my father explaining it. Mother had gone on another work assignment on Planet Earth and I asked why her work was so dangerous.

"On Planet Earth AI made significant advancements in various domains, but there are many key limitations to its capabilities when compared to human brains. Human brains possess qualities that make them superior to AI in certain aspects."

"Humans can't possibly be more capable than a computer, dad," I insisted. "Like how?"

"Your mother could explain it better but here's what I remember her describing to me. Human brains have the remarkable ability to think creatively, generate new ideas, and make novel connections between different concepts. AI, on the other hand, relies on predefined algorithms and data patterns and struggles to replicate human creativity.

"Human brains have emotional intelligence, which allows them to understand and navigate complex emotions in ourselves and others. This aspect of human cognition is difficult to replicate in AI systems, as emotions are subjective experiences deeply tied to our consciousness.

"The brains of people and kuudere alike, possess a remarkable ability to understand the subtleties of language and context. We can comprehend nuanced meanings, humor, sarcasm, and cultural references effortlessly. AI progress in natural language processing often struggles to grasp the full depth of human communication.

"Then there's adaptability and generalization. We can learn from a few examples and apply that knowledge to new and unfamiliar situa-

tions. AI systems require large amounts of data to train and are limited to the specific tasks they were trained on."

"Okay, I get that," I say, still confused. "But she said her work is about power consumption and limited resources in power supplies. Her science enhances humanoids, not robots and AI applications. Right?

"Yes, well this is more my expertise," he boasts. "Medical applications and using organoid intelligence in our bodies. See, it's like this. When it comes to space exploration and planet colonization energy efficiency is a critical factor. AI systems are necessary but they require significant amounts of computational power, which translates to high energy consumption.

"Your mother designs lab-grown miniature human organs to study brain function and develop advanced AI models, that we inject into our biomechanical implants. We humanoids use organoid intelligence to bridge the gap between AI limitations and superior human cognition. She and her team have enhanced humanoids by providing us with a more accurate model of human brain activity. We embody the advancements in AI systems that better mimic human cognitive processes, strength, power, and speed. But requires no additional power source."

After a moment of silence, my thoughts fade from this flashback memory and the present comes to focus.

--activate Stealth Mode--

__oranoid devices at full capacity__

__no additional operations will be sustainable while Stealth Mode is active__

__would you like to proceed__

--proceed with stealth mode--

Now this android will fake out the stasis chamber but Androps will check the ship and private rooms throughout the flight and at every stop along the way. They won't see me standing here for the ninety-three-day voyage.

The thought of my mother killing men has haunted me for many years. Everyone on her medical and science team owes their life to my mom. She had to kill to keep them all safe and to improve life on every habitable planet. Now that I've witnessed how simple death arises, it seems too easy. I think death should be more difficult to achieve.

Again my thoughts drift back to my father. After we left the morgue my father and I sat together on a park bench in our favorite garden in the Nature Dome. I asked,

"Do you think Mom was happy?

"Happy is the meaning of life," he said. "God is the religious word for happiness. We all seek to return to the True Self and to be free of this human existence. The return to happiness. You can find moments of happiness in this life, but like every aspect of this Newtonian existence, it all ends. Everything that arises, will subside.

"So, yes, to answer the question - was mom happy? Yes she knew moments of happiness."

Chapter Four

Welcome To Earth

Log Entry Two: Day ninety-four. As I peek through my squinted eyes and see the world below my shielding hands, my senses become overwhelmed. "Ironic," I say as I stand here blinded by the intense sunlight, "I'm committed to this mission on Planet Earth now."

On Planet Forty-Four, our sheltered beneath-the-dome existence in five floating, protectively-spherical-domed cities, interconnected by long, transparent tubes. Each of the four tubes is nearly ten miles long, and each domed habitation has a forty-mile diameter and height. All of it is protected from the direct light of the main sequence star we call Eridani, filtered by a deep, thick, opaque gas cloud. Even Planet Te with its M-Class red dwarf star isn't as luminous as Earth's sun. But I don't dare activate my enhanced eyes. I cannot risk being identified as a Syganoid here.

While my eyes are slow to adjust, the smells overwhelm and capture my awareness. The salty sea, mixed with arid alkalinity, carried on a cool breeze. The contrasting dry and moist battle for dominance. Each fighting to extinguish the other. Then the voices of hundreds of people walking beside me and passing me on all sides. Few walk with me, most go in other directions. The sounds of the constant stream of vehicles with their hum and a whir of air as they speed along the paths beside the walkway. A siren squeals and screams, a horn louder still than the siren, and then three vehicles with lights flashing brighter than the sun streak past.

I stand frozen except for my swiveling head, like in a trance. The walkways lined with pedestrians, the roadways streaming with vehicles, the sounds of voices, the whir of the motors, the cool breeze contrasting with the heat of the sun on my skin, the bright light illuminating it all into a single existence. Each building strives to be better. Each has its own unique color, height, and shape. Some of them are built in contrasting textures and colors while others are rigid and symmetric. Textures run the full array from soft, and smooth to rough, and coarse. Everything in The Great Starzel Republic competes not just to be recognized as unique, but wanting to dominate and take center stage of full sensory attention.

In this cacophony of sights, smells, and sounds, I couldn't help but feel trivial in a vast, pulsating machine, my purpose and significance dwarfed by the magnitude of the world around me.

Exhausted from the overwhelming scene, with sensory overload, I walk toward a uniformed man. He's dressed in an orange bibbed overall with no shirt. He's otherwise well-groomed with short hair and a short beard. When he notices me walking towards him, he turns his back to me. He's sweeping the pedestrian walkway beneath the trees. Clearing the leaves and picking up pet waste. I circle him to stand where he can see me.

"Could you point me in the direction for Culver City?"

Without making eye contact or giving me any body language suggesting he acknowledged me, he says, "Follow the sign toward Hollywood." Then turning his head toward the left he points with his chin, "That way."

Several meters away, and across the roadway there is a sign for Hollywood and an arrow. When there was a break in the vehicle traffic I sprint across the road and follow the arrow. The sounds and smells arise and subside every half dozen or more meters. Coffee shops, restaurants, jewelry, barbeque, chicken, bread, and more. The scent is so powerful the tongue can taste the flavors.

Signs in windows and placards on the passageway suggest various ways to fulfill a need, to better the quality and comfort.

After several hours of walking and following signs toward Hollywood, I see a sign for Culver City. The sensation of hope and excitement fills me. I've come all this way and just now, the sight of the small, worn-out, dark green background with chipped and peeled white letters -- sign, forces a smile. As I'm starting to accept the notion that my journey to recover the missing data may succeed I become aware of a very large billboard featuring two women's faces with their names typed in bold letters just below their chins. Above their heads in a vivid rainbow of colors spelling out the words, The Founding Mothers of Our Republic. Each of the women is decorated and exaggerated with facial makeup, elaborate styled, and artificial colored hair. They are too perfect in every feature, eyes bright, fake eyelashes, delightful painted-on smiles, and a healthy chemical glow. The woman on the left is named Nancy Pelosi, and the one on the right, Karen Salmansohn. I remember Nancy as the Democratic leader of the Feminist Party in the former United States, but I don't know this other woman.

There are fewer shops and restaurants as I continue along a more narrow and less crowded walkway. The residential buildings are more frequent in this section of the city and there are few office buildings. As I continue to glance up, looking at the details of the large billboard and the two women, my shoulder collides with a woman passing me in the opposite direction.

"Oh, sorry about that. I wasn't watching where I was going. Are you alright?" I ask.

Without a word, she continues on her way. Several times she glances back over her shoulder in my direction. Her pace quickens. Then, I decide to turn and keep going. Still aware and scanning for any signs directing me to Culver City or hints of the historical reference to Banyan. There are none for several hundred meters, but then I see a large poster in the window of a store. I can recognize the woman in the poster as Karen Salmansohn from the billboard. I cross over to the store for a better look.

"Now Starring in a hit television series based on the Academy Award-winning movie of the year, of the same title, the author of How to Make Your Man Behave in 21 Days or Less Using the Secrets of Professional Dog Trainers -- Karen Salmansohn!"

***

Screams. Frightened screams fill my ears as I turn to look in the sound's direction. When I see a woman on the other side of the street being supported by another woman at her side. She struggles to stay on her feet. Several more women rush to help. The woman screams once more, her arm outstretched and finger pointing in my direction. There's no one near me. She's frightened by me. Has she detected I'm a Syganoid?

Without another moment to waste, I turn and quicken my pace away from the gathering and the screams. At the first corner, I turn left and then run toward the next intersection. The sounds of a patrol car's siren-screams replace the woman's and they are coming closer.

That's it. They're going to execute me. But how did she know I am a Syganoid? I quickly scan my body and the attached devices but nothing looks out of place. My HUD is turned off and other than my clothing being a little odd even for Holywood, I'm at a loss for why she is screaming.

A patrol vehicle whirs past and immediately swings back around towards me.

__emergency detection, heart center afferent pathways engaged__

--disengage HUD--

--disengage bionics--

__request overridden life preservation protocols are active__

--disengage protocols--

__protocols disengaged__

__systems shutting down__

While I argue with the Neurolink and HUD interface implanted in my head and OI eyes, I've outrun the high-speed patrol vehicle. Dodging and ducking down narrow alleyways and one-way avenues at speeds no human could.

What's the use of shutting every system down now? They already know what I am. Then again, why keep up the chase? It only delays the inevitable.

I stand silent, tucked between the dingy yellow brick wall of a three-story apartment building and the dingy grass-green rubbish bin on the side of the street.

"Come out away from the building with your hands above your head," the voice barks from the patrol vehicle's megaphone.

The whir of the vehicle's diamond battery motor tells me they parked the vehicle a meter or two away on the left side of the rubbish bin. With my hands above my head, arms outstretched at thirty-seven degrees, I walk into the street and face the vehicle. Doors on both sides of the police vehicle pop open and swing over the top.

"Down on your knees. Keep your hands where I can see them." Two large men in silver uniforms emerge from the vehicle. They fix their uniforms as they stand out from the patrol vehicle. Make sure there are no wrinkles in their trousers, no untucked shirt tails, belts, and attached holsters in designated positions. They slick back the sides of their hair and then place the silver and royal blue berets over their heads. All the while grooming their perfect impression, neither took their eyes off me. Aside from their meticulous efforts for a perfect appearance, I notice these men are huge, above average height, and have evident extreme muscular development.

The one on my left walks toward me while the one on the right circles wide to come around behind. Once he's behind me says, "As slow and quiet as a fart in church, take your right hand and pull that backpack off of your right shoulder."

The strap slides off as I slip my hand underneath and back up into the air.

"That's it, big guy. Now the other side, but not so fast. I get nervous when a very fast man moves too fast. Makes me think I should slow him down. Maybe hit him over the head with a billy club to slow him down. So, go ahead and take that backpack off, nice and slow."

My arm and hand are so slow, my thoughts are focused on not one other thing. Slow!

The backpack falls off and tumbles over the back of my legs and onto the roadway.

"Well done, muscles. You don't mind if I call you muscles do you?" the patrol man standing in front of me asks.

"My name is Eulər."

"Well, Muscles. What the hell are you doing running around Santa Monica unescorted, out of uniform, your hair looks like a monkey's ass, you're facial hair is shaved off, and what is in the backpack?"

Pain rose from my knees as the uneven, gritty paved surface of the roadway push up into the bent thin skin under my weight. I'm using my focus to push away the stabbing waves and the impulse to move. With a grimace and squint, "I'm on my way to Culver City."

"Culver City? On foot, all the way to Culver City. What are you going to Culver City for?"

"Who," I say.

"What the fuck do you mean who?" I cannot tell which of them is asking the questions now. I'm focused on not adjusting my legs to accommodate my pulsing pain.

"I'm not going to Culver City for anything. I'm going there to find the sage writer named, Banyan. That's who I'm going to Culver City to find," I say.

"Do you think we are stupid, Muscles?" The one in front of me squats down to look me in the eye while he slaps his truncheon in a slow and menacing rhythm against the palm of his right hand. "I know my ancient history. The writer called Banyan isn't in Culver City."

He's wrong and I respond to help him, "The sage author, not a writer."

"The fuck did you just say," he squints and asks me while still slapping the baton into his palm.

"You said Banyan is a writer. Once a writer is published they are an author. Banyan published seven books. He's no writer."

His expression appears to ignore my help. "Another thing I know about Banyan is he's been dead for, I don't know exactly but something like a hundred years."

"Yes. I didn't mean to say I was going there to see him. I meant that I'm going there to see if I can find where he went after he left Culver City. You see, when he left Culver City, he wrote the most important code of his career. The First Priority and I need to find what I can because the beginning of The First Priority, the Arya Sangata Dharma Prayaya, is missing."

Pain on the left side of my head shoots up and over the crown. The cool, sea breeze washed against my face as my eyes see the gritty pavement getting closer until crashing, my face feels the hot, rough surface of the road. An unconscious dream arises.

From out of the veil of blackness I see my mother's face pushing through. Her facial features catch the light and arise then fade like the decorations of a flag shifting with the gentle but persistent wind that carries the darkness.

"Humanity is lost," she says, "and the slow decay of their overwhelmed senses leaves people in fear, desperate, and filled with anger. Already the ninth sense of morality has vanished, and the tenth sense of love is on the brink. Something has altered the universe. The code becomes unbalanced. One of my children needs help, but I don't know which one of you is the cause."

***

The sound of voices stirs me into consciousness. I am here awake but not moving. I don't want anyone to know I've regained consciousness. There's a soft pillow surface under my back and my eighth sense tells me I'm laying inside a ten-story building. On the sixth floor, about three miles from where the police knocked me unconscious. The smell of synthetic BBQ chicken fills the air and reminds me of walking past several fried chicken restaurants.

"He's awake. Listening to us and pretending to be unconscious," a woman's voice says while chewing her artificial chicken. "Bring him to my courtroom in twenty minutes." She slurps the last drops of liquid from her cup. "Clean his face. No. Don't clean his face. The blood will get the television crews to give me more air time. More networks will also want in on this one. They love to see men bleeding in my court.

"Twenty minutes!" she snaps as her loud heels click in rapid, bold succession across the room and carry her out the door.

Keys rattle against the console of the paddywagon and I can sense the holographic force-field around me fade and evaporate.

--activate basic systems and run diagnosis--

I need to check my brain implants for damage.

__basic systems active__

__diagnostics scheduled for completion in one hour and eleven minutes__

"Alright, big guy. Let's get you upright and aware of the circumstances." A very short man stands beside the control council. "This device here in my right hand carries enough torporin to send you into a six-year coma. It's the best high and euphoric trip you'll ever experience, but I don't think it's what you want. Because you see," he pauses to laugh, if only to himself, "Nobody has ever fully recovered their mental faculties after a high dose. This is what I intend to give you if you do anything other than exactly, precisely, and without hesitation when I say it. Solid brother? Do you feel me?"

"Yes. I understand," I say.

I rise to my feet and look around. The room is well lit from a row of windows that face east. Sunshine covers the scene beyond with trees bending and twisting limbs giving way to swift winds. The floors are covered in well-polished bamboo wood sheets about a half-inch thick on top of concrete and steel rebar. Above is a foam board drop ceiling hiding ancient materials of copper wire and aluminum ducting for ventilation with a concrete and rebar combination further above. The walls are antique metal framed and plasterboard with a thin wall of fibrous insulation board before the outer layer of heated clay bricks. There are two sets of double doors. One is on the west wall about the center of the room and the other is on the south side, close to the adjoining west wall.

"Step down out of the restriction chamber and let's have a look at you. Mmmm hmmm," he walks around me as I step down from the platform.

My scans tell me there's no chance for me to escape below or above. Well, I suppose I could blast through the thick concrete, but then I'd have to do it again and again to the bottom, or top. The more effortless escape would be through the windows. But I'm not being held for execution. I don't think they know I'm a Syganoid. My life isn't in any danger. Not yet, anyway.

"Those are some big muscular arms and what a powerful-looking back and chest. You are well prepared and fit. Beautiful face and hair. Those eyes of yours would make many women melt underneath you. There might be a place for you, but first things first. The judge is going to sentence you for the crime of being unescorted in public and without appropriate permission documents."

"Wait, what does that mean; unescorted?" I ask.

"Don't be daft, man. You know you can't be on the streets of Starzel without a woman's protection. What's even worse in your case is that you don't have a chipset bracelet identification from your madam. Did you take it off? Are you trying to escape? You can trust me. I'm here to help."

"Bracelet? Chipset?" I feel confused and again consider the jump through the windows.

"Listen to me, you are pretty and you have that magnificent body that will make many women fantasize about buying you, but it is a bad gamble. There are more women who would rather have you put into service and used as the filthy dog that you are. More still are demanding these days for the end of men and would rather see you executed. Now, I'm sure you don't want to be used for building houses, serving in the military, or cleaning sewers, and I know that execution isn't what you want either. Talk to me, man. Tell me what's going on and be honest with me. Why are you wandering the streets alone? What are you after?"

Without my HUD system operation, I can't check his vitals and electromagnetic, and harmonic waves to see if he is truth-telling. His voice sounds sincere and his eyes never leave mine while he talks. I think he's for real. He wants to help me.

"Can I have something to drink? I haven't had anything to eat or drink all day."

"Yes. Of course," he smiles a wholesome and appreciative smile. "Just tell me your story and then I'll give you some of that chicken or whatever it is over there. He points to the table where there are two paper sacks with a chicken logo boldly printed and several small containers and cups scattered. The sight of it all refreshes my awareness of the smell of synthetic meat that permeates the room.

"Have you ever heard of the sage author named Banyan?" I ask.

"Let's just say I haven't so why don't you tell me why it's important to you," his facial expression remains sincere and he takes his left hand and puts it on my right shoulder.

"This might be difficult to understand, but I'm trying to repair a tear in the fabric of the universe. Banyan wrote a righteous code for humanity and his publication of The First Priority has gone missing from the files. If I cannot find it and replace the missing data, humanity will be erased from history."

His expression wavered for a moment but regained its well-rehearsed position as quick as I could blink. "Sounds horrific, man. Still, you haven't told me why you are here in Santa Monica. This writer named, Banyan? Do you think he's here in the city?"

"No, he lived in Culver City. He was an Author, not a writer. Not now, of course, he's dead. His work started there and I hope to find evidence, maybe even a relic of the writing may still be there."

"So you're walking through The Great Starzel Republic," he surmises, "to get to Culver City. Where did you start out?"

"Three months and two days ago, ninety-four days in all. I took a starship from planet Te and arrived in Burbank earlier today. Can I eat something? Please."

"Sure, sure, sure," he repeated. "One last thing you must understand," he hesitates as he gathers his thoughts. His head and eyes looked toward the floor as he searched for the words.

"The judge wants two things from this case. Ratings, and air time. Everything in The Great Starzel Republic hinges on ratings and air time. I can tell that you're new to our country so I'll tell you in the most direct way I can in the hope that I'll make an impression on you.

"There are two ways this can go. You can cooperate with her majesty the Judge and provide entertainment and lively contesting, but respectful debate. Or, you can be a jerk and she'll rip you apart and make you look foolish. Either way, she'll use this case to get her algorithms to go higher. She hates synthetic food and the interest rates on her car loan and home are getting more expensive. The payments are killing her vacation dream.

"Remember, ratings mean everything. Getting real food and the best life requires a lot of airtime and quality ratings. Now, you think about that while you sit over here and eat."

He leads me by the arm to the table where the sacks of BBQ synthetic chicken and sides wait to be consumed. Then he walks through the double doors on the west wall. Printed above the doors, "Judges' Breakroom."

***

"My finger is still here on the button, ready to send you off into a coma. Be a good boy and do exactly as I say. Here we go, you follow close behind me."

When I pass through the double doors we go to the right. The hallway is lined with people and their pets. Some are in paddywagons and most are standing around waiting for the Judge to start her session. The woman in black is right outside the courtroom. For a moment, the emotion of relief fills my heart-center and throat, but I regain control as she's still being held prisoner. Her eyes grow wide and an expression of intensity fills her when she sees me approaching.

--how long until the diagnosis is complete--

__diagnosis will complete in fifty-one minutes and fifty-one seconds__

Communication with her is impossible while the diagnosis is underway. Her face transforms to express confusion as we walk past her and through the doors of the courtroom. The camera crew, booms, lights, and shape of the room look more like a production studio than any courtroom.

"We'll sit here and I'll stay with you as your court-appointed advocate," he says.

"So, you're my lawyer?"

"No, no, no," he repeated. "There are no lawyers in The Great Starzel Republic. Especially not a man's position," he laughs in a whisper of hilarious expression.

"Quiet on the set!" shouts the producer. "Roll the credits and let the people in. Keep it quiet for the Judge's entrance. "

People swarm the studio, racing one another for the best seats. The woman in black is floated into the center of the room and her chamber sinks midway to her waist into the floor. Her head is visible from the judge's elevated platform. A massive display of flowers and greenery surrounds the platform. A desk of solid stone, reds, yellows, and browns swirls and streaks the exquisite rock face. Finished off with four Persian cats. Two on either corner of the floor and two on each corner on top of the judicial bench.

Lights from above and on all sides prevent shadows and the entire room seems to float within a void of illuminated white space. Contrasting shapes are defined only by the starkness of design and colors. When the timer above the door marked "Judge's Chamber" reaches five seconds, the courtroom lights flash in rapid succession as it counts down to zero.

As everyone stands, the Judge's chamber doors vanish. The spotlights that a moment ago directed golden beams on the doors now illuminate the Judge. She stands in the opening where the doors once stood closed. Her robes are purple and outlined with sparkling gold electrical waves of light energy. Her face is made up to look as if every feature was exaggerated and brilliant. Not human but she stands in godlike perfection.

As she steps into the courtroom, every motion of her arms, hands, and robes exhibits grandness and elegance to grace the room. When at last she reaches her chair behind the grand stone-faced desk she faces the audience. Her eyes sweep the room from side to side, lifting her gaze to those standing in the balcony area and then higher still to the ceiling where a mural of Nancy Pelosi dressed in a purple gown is surrounded by elegant women captured in gay dance and frolic within a lush garden.

"Please be seated," she waits a moment for the sound of hundreds of people taking their seats to stop.

"Taking three minutes and twenty seconds for a commercial break!" shouts the producer. The Judge stands as if frozen in place until the commercial is complete and the producer calls out, "And we are live in three, two, one."

"Thank you for taking time out of your busy-busy-busy day to come to my courtroom for another super delicious display of justice. Not just any justice, but -- Women's Justice!" The people jump to their feet with applause and loud cheers. After a few seconds of the outburst, she motions for everyone to again take their seats. "Let's remember in these hallowed chambers that emotion and feelings are not the influence of women's rights and feminism. These chambers are only influenced by the natural order of The Great Republic of Starzel.

From her left to her right she scans the inner chamber. Starting with three court recorders seated at small tables and chairs and dressed in stately uniforms. She then studies the woman in black. Turning more, she looks over my backpack and the contents. A few tablets and two drones, the magic stone that is still wrapped in black velvet and tied with chartreuse string. They neatly displayed these across a large folding table. Then to the right side of the chamber, she looks at me. No expression on her exaggerated fake godlike face. I wonder how anyone can take another person who is so decorated and dressed as she is with any seriousness.

"Before I begin today's trials, I must cover some housekeeping rules with all of you," she strokes the cat on her left. "You're currently listening to my show on the Chamber broadcast's general station. However, once I start the trial, all the sounds you hear in your earpieces will remain. Music, audience prompts, special effects, etcetera. But you won't hear me and you won't hear the accused." Everyone moans.

"Wait a second," the Judge beams. "All you need to do to hear us is to swipe right, like my show, click. Swipe right again, and rate me a twenty-five-star. Then you can hear everything that goes on. And believe me, you don't want to miss today's trial. We have murder, intra-galactic theft, unescorted man roaming our streets, and something very special. They have never been on trial here before. Let's take a three-minute pause for commercials while all of you give me that twenty-five-star rating. When we come back the trial will begin.

***

While the commercial break is ongoing, she points toward the woman in black with her left hand and then at me with her right hand. "This trial is about me and my ratings and nothing else. I don't give an ants sneeze about either of you. You can end up on death row and executed tomorrow, or be set free when the show is over today. It won't make any difference because I will get my ratings up today. I hope you understand me."

Before the producer calls out the countdown, she takes a long drink from the glass, puts the cat back on her desk. Then she takes her seat and glances at her reflection in a hand mirror from the desktop. She smiles warmly at her reflection, sets the mirror down, and looks into the camera as the producer with his fingers outstretched above his head and says, "Three, two, one."

Perhaps it was an oversight, or perhaps it was purposeful, but I have no earpiece to listen to the show. I'm live and between myself and the woman in black, we are the show. Still, I can hear the sound from the earpiece the little man next to me wears. There is mood music, audience dubbed-in noises, and occasional sirens, whoops, and whistles toned at random levels. All to make the audience here and at home perceive reality in an altered and artificial experience.

My mind wanders back in time many years before when my mother and I took a trip to the nature dome.

The fields of wild grass and flowers seemed to stretch out before us and go on forever. The distant mountains with snow-covered peaks and the cerulean-colored sky outside the dome. Now and then as the thick clouds above thinned out and then thickened again, I could see the otherwise transparent dome that protects us from the deadly gaseous atmosphere of Planet Forty-Four.

"It's easy to forget what is real and what is material in our physical forms," she said.

"Yes. I see it too Mom," I said. "The air we breathe and the domed habitats are not real. But, then again. They must be real or we wouldn't exist. I'm confused now. What is real, Mom?"

"There is one truth to this universe," she took my hand and laughed a sly laugh. "If you listen to your ninth sense of awareness. The sense that knows you know and the part of your thoughts that is aware of you being aware of the awareness. Then you should ask yourself who is being aware.

In this physical form, as a human and even as a Syganoid we cannot identify any more layers to the self than this. That awareness of being aware cannot be observed any further. The one observing is the universe in all of us. One consciousness disguised as many individuals. We each have unique experiences but only one shared consciousness. That is the only thing that is real. Everything else is an illusion, temporary, and can only exist in the fleeting present moment. Even a slap in the face is an illusion. Gone in an instant. The only thing that never changes, and never ends is consciousness. We are simply observers of consciousness. Like the glass dome that holds life within it. One day the dome will crack and life inside it will transition. Consciousness will still remain unchanged. Wakeful, aware, and observing as The First Priority provides."

The trusted advocate nudges me with his shoulder and I slip away from the memory and back to the present moment.

"Can you hear me Eulər? Asked the Judge.

"Yes, Mom," I say.

The courtroom explodes with laughter, hoots, whistles, and hollers while I realize what I've said. I steady my eyes on the Judge as I maintain my composure. The sign above the Judge's desk flashes in rapid tempo, "SILENCE." After several seconds, her courtroom goes quiet.

"Well, I wish I could say I'm flattered."

Again the room explodes with laughter, but she raises her hands and motions as if she were pushing the audience's enthusiasm back and downward.

"Mother? Is that who you are daydreaming about, your Mother?"

"Yes. I'm sorry if I wasn't fully present. I am now."

Through tight squinted eyes, her head at a slight tilt to the right she looks at me and analyzes how to respond. "Before I delve into your thoughts about your mother, I'm going to have the clerk read the charges and introduce the defendants for this case. It will be in your best interest to stay focused and listen."

With the motion of her hand as if casting a spell from the end of a magic wand, swirls, and points to the middle of the courtroom's inner circle. A meter-squared space of the floor opens and rising up through the opening is a woman decorated in sequins. Stage lights illuminate her with beams of gold, tyrian, and violet. The scent of lavender is pumped into the courtroom and through his earpiece, I can hear the sound of trumpets and harps. Then, once fully two meters above the inner circle on her raised platform, the gold and royal purple spotlights illuminate upward over her and onto the ceiling mural of Nancy Pelosi's image.

"The Great Republic of Starzel requests our lady of honor, the supreme Judge and protector of our Feminist Society to rule over this case of heinous treacherous acts. Acts of terrorism. Two of our undercover border patrol customs agents working from Planet Te have been murdered. They were doing their jobs and posing as call girls working at the transportation depot to protect our great republic when they were brutally murdered. I enter these images into the records."

Several images of the two dead prostitutes who had attacked me in Rupirah's home are shown in a floating three-dimensional holographic display for the judge and the audience. Their mostly nude and twisted corpses are captured in many images from different angles. The faint sounds of an astonished audience and solum music emerge from my advocate's earpiece.

"These two suspects," the woman's finger points stabbing blows at me and the woman in black, "were reported as being seen with our now deceased, brave, and heroic customs officers in the moments before their murder. Though there are no fingerprints, no DNA match, and no video to prove their guilt, The Great Republic of Starzel has every confidence in our Judge to find truth and provide justice for the protection and freedom of women in our Feminist Society.

"Now, without further delay, this trial is called to order."

***

With the bright flash of a lightning strike and the loud clap of thunder, the courtroom goes dark and the golden lights now illuminate the Judge. In an instant the normal lighting of the room returns. The court announcer is gone, the raised platform she stood upon is gone as well. The sound of suspense, pulses, and hums from the earpieces, otherwise the room is silent. I reach for the pitcher of water and fill my glass halfway. Then I fill my advocate's glass to the brim. After setting the pitcher back in its place I drink from my glass and finish it in one long refreshing act.

"Custom would have me start with the woman in black," the Judge says while flipping through her tablet. "I don't want to dishonor the woman otherwise. So, bring her up so we can have a look at the murderous thing she is."

Not a sound was made as the woman in black, held in place by the energy beams, is raised higher and level with the floor. Her restraining module rotates and the audience whispers and soft voices begin discussing her fate.

"Guilty of murder," the Judge states with a raised voice of predilection. "Simple to decide. We can all tell just by the way she looks and the clothes she wears. This is what a murderess looks like. Her bare face, natural fingernails, no hair color or style, and plain clothes do not properly display her feminine form. Nothing about her other than her sex is feminized at all. But, still, let's give her a chance to speak. Perhaps there's something more here than meets my careful eyes.

"Why did you kill our customs agents? What sort of horrible animal are you that allows you to murder two perfect and innocent officers of The Republic in cold blood?"

The woman in black responds in a quiet, quivering voice, "I didn't murder them."

"You caved in her head," the bloody telltale image of the woman illuminates in a hologram on center stage. "Then you broke the other agent's neck!" The holograph image changes and then alternates between the two dead bodies. "Everyone here knows it was you who did it. Confess and let me move on with the sentencing."

"That's a commercial break for six minutes!" The producer shouts. Stagehands rush to adjust the holding platforms and move the table with my backpack, drones, and the magic stone. The Judge is swarmed with makeup, hair, and costume hands. Refreshments are offered to the audience like the hotdog vendors at a sports arena, "soft drinks, snacks, v-waters!"

"We are back in four, three, two," the producer swirls his arm over his head to signal we are rolling and live. Then he points at the Judge.

"There was another man in the room. He killed Rupirah and when I walked into the apartment he was going to kill me. Your brave and vigilant agents tried to save me. He killed them and then he ran out of the room. I was scared out of my wits and in shock. I couldn't move and when the androps arrived and retained me, I tried to explain but they abused me with Tasers and held me against my will with lasers. One of them tore the back of my pantsuit. I need to be freed and made whole again. I was only doing my job and the next thing I know, I'm witnessing brutal murders, being abused by the galactic authorities, detained for thirty-two days on a space transporter, and now I'm accused of murder? Your honor I ask for restitution and compensation."

Loud laughter fills the courtroom. Not the fake sounds pumped in from the earpiece, but true laughter from those present. The Judge uses her tablet to change the message on the display monitors scattered around the courtroom to read, "SILENCE." When the room is quiet, "Should I bring in the lie detectors?" The room explodes with voices, "YES! Strip her down and find the truth!" Again the Judge illuminates the monitors and adds the sound of a warning siren. Above her platform, the ratings flash as the Judge's numbers press above four-point-four. A court recorder catches the Judge's attention and points toward the rating monitor.

"Savage," she snickers. "There isn't anyone in the room who believes you. They all want you stripped bare and wired up to the truth monitor. Your humiliation and shame will be known. What do you say now? Are you still innocent?"

Before the woman in black could respond, the audience was gripped in silent anticipation, "There was another man there. Sadly the Interstellar Authorities murdered him on the transport ship." The cameras, the audience eyes, the Judge, the advocate next to me, and even the woman in black all turned to look at me. Filling my glass, half full, I motion with the pitcher toward the producer, "Cheers. Do we need another commercial break?"

"How dare you interrupt my courtroom and my interrogation!" The Judge snarled through a tight jaw. "You will be lucky if you ever see daylight again when I'm done with you."

The advocate pushes his chair back a bit and stands, "May I approach your honor?"

"You cannot. Say what you have to say from there," she says.

"Why does he have a lawyer and I don't have a lawyer?" asks the woman in black.

"When did I lose control of my fucking courtroom?" the Judge spits. Sirens ring, and from her tablet, she directs the monitors to read, "Order in The Court!" "If one more person speaks out of turn I will bring in the androps.

"He does not have a lawyer. The Great Republic of Starzel does not have lawyers in courts of law. The law isn't a debate or a guideline to be argued about. He is a man with no identification, no marks of any training, and men are not allowed to be unescorted. The advocate you see sitting beside him, now standing there waiting to say something to me before you interrupted my court, is a highly trained man with awarded privileges who is escorting the criminal.

"You also have no identification and my report from the Galactic and Interstellar authorities tells me they cannot find any records for either of you. Who the fuck are you?" Her face leads her extended head and stretches forward with her fake eyelashes, as she leers at the woman in black.

There is no chance for either of us to survive if they wire her up to the truth machine. They will discover her Syganoid implants and Neurolinks. She'll be immediately executed and then they will suspect me of being a Syganoid as well. I have to change the momentum. My eyes catch the ratings monitor now approaching four-point-nine.

Desperate and running out of options, I interrupt again,

"If you would allow my advocate to speak those ratings will probably jump above five."

***

--open stealth communication module--

__HUD systems are currently inoperable during diagnostics__

--time remaining for diagnostics to complete--

__there are forty-seven seconds estimated to complete system diagnostics__

There may not be forty-plus seconds to save her. I'll need a further distraction. Think of something, quick.

Meanwhile, the Judge looks up to see the live ratings number, up .003 in the last ten seconds, now at 4.92779. Her otherwise composed, tight lips show the faintest raised corner of a smile. "Right, that's almost a record for this courtroom," she spouts.

The audience gasps and then bursts into applause as the truth-telling chamber is brought into the room. It's carried in by two uniformed men with perfect hair and matching beards. The uniforms are tight, bright pink, and the logo Her Majesty's Guard, is boldly printed across their muscular chests. The pair look like bodybuilders, and their muscular arms and legs are fully exposed, well-oiled, and bulging with every step as they march with the machine toward center stage.

__diagnostics are now complete__

--are there any system or component malfunctions--

__would you like to read the diagnostics report__

--no--

--tell me if there are systems or component malfunctions--

__a complete list of systems and status is available in the diagnostics report__

__a complete list of components and status is available in the diagnostics report__

__would you like to read the diagnostics report__

--fuck me--

--yes--

-- Open the report---

__initiating HUD systems__

--cancel HUD systems initiation--

__canceled__

--initiate stealth mode HUD--

__stealth mode protocols initiated__

__HUD initiated in stealth mode__

__diagnostics report is located in lower center line nine.__

__would you like to open the report__

--open the report--

__there are not enough energy cells available to open files of this size in stealth mode protocol__

__there are unused energy sources available in stealth protocol__

__would you like to boost systems energy through a hacked energy source__

The file must be huge, there must be a lot of damage. But, I don't have time for this and it seems like I have some systems capability in stealth.

--open communication with nearby Syganoid--

__one Syganoid nearby__

__communication request accepted__

→It's about time Eulər←

→listen we don't have much time. I need you to cooperate with this Judge. Stop trying to make her mad. She can ruin you and kill you←

--yes yes yes whatever I have this under control--

→like you had those agents under control in Rupirah's home←

→casper warned me about your stubborn, brash, seat-of-the-pants acts←

→okay. here's the thing. no matter what else. stay seated, stay calm. cooperate←

__communication ended__

--reconnect communication--

__communication request denied__

Confused by her reluctance, and words, and now feeling a sharp pain in my left arm I reach with my right hand to massage the pain. The floor below the woman in black opens and the restraining device with her inside falls through the floor in the flash of an instant. The loud crash of the machine thunders through the courtroom. Laser beams of deep blues and greens flash up through the opening of the floor and scorch the ceiling. Burning and smoldering the mural. One wayward laser hit Nancy's figure in the forehead direct between the eyes. In a few seconds, it was over.

For the first time in my life, I followed the instructions from someone else. I stayed in my chair just like the woman in black told me to. The audience was bustling with everyone's attention on the gaping, singed, and smoldering hole in the floor. The two muscular men sat the truth-telling machine down and then cautious as a moth, leaving the cocoon for the first time, approach the opening to peer over the edge.

"Keep recording!" shouts the producer. "Get a camera on her Majesty's Guard and I want tight coverage on their faces when they look over the edge."

"That woman is dead for sure!" says the Judge. "There will be a full investigation into this mishap. I will find out how this floor collapsed and whoever is responsible for this . . . well let's just say he will be punished!"

"Justice will not be interrupted or swayed by acts of terrorism. I still have one pundit in this trial who I will rectify with a verdict today."

"That sentence is not correct," I say while sipping on another glass of water. Then I turn my head toward the audience, "I mean, does anybody know what the Judge just said?"

If looks could kill, her eyes would have vaporized me into a puff of smoke as I finished saying it. The advocate beside me sits down and then stands back up with a tight curled fist and he strikes me across the jaw.

"You will not speak to the Judge or any woman with that sarcasm. We, men, are honorable and never question what a woman says. I will beat you bloody if you ever speak like that again," he says to me.

"She's gone," one of the guards says. "The woman in black isn't down there." He points down where the restraining machine lies decimated and smoldering.

"That was awesome!" the producer cries out. Followed by a few hoots and wow we wow before he says, "Cut for commercials. We've got some real big-money companies wanting to buy commercials now. So this might be a ten-minute break. Let's get the stage cleared and the cameras back in position. Let's move it, people!"

Without hesitation, I pushed back from the table, stood over the little man, and pat him on the head. "Brave man. Very brave." Then I walked over to the hole in the floor to take a look at what lies below. As I pass by the table where my backpack, two drones, and the destiny stone are, I snatch the stone and store it in my vest pocket. When I see the calamity below I open communication.

--open communication to Syganoids near me--

__there are no Syganoids nearby__

--are there problems with systems and components in the diagnostics report--

__there are not enough energy cells available to open files of this size__ __there are unused energy sources available in stealth protocol__

__would you like to boost systems energy through a hacked energy source__

***

"This full police report in front of me tells me that you were seen outside the theater on Wilshire Boulevard staring through the window. A woman across the street saw you and screamed out of fear. You didn't drop to the ground and assume a face-down neutral position. Instead, you turned toward her and looked directly at her. She screamed a second time and then you took off running.

"Let's start with a few simple questions. Do you know that facing a woman and looking directly at her is an act of criminal violence?"

The Judge taps her long, pointed, bright purple, phony nails on the wired-for-sound and amplified benchtop.

"No. I didn't and it wasn't violent."

"Watch your words, man," the advocate hisses through clenched teeth.

"I see," she pauses. "What were you looking at through the window?"

"Nothing. I mean, I wasn't looking through the window at all. I was looking at the poster that was displayed in the window. It was something about training men by using the same techniques used for training dogs. Something like that."

"Of course. It is a very popular book and they made it into a movie, and now they made it into a weekly sitcom for television. It has become so popular that the writer's ratings went through the upper atmosphere and now her granddaughter is the President of our Great Republic of Starzel.

"So, what do you think of the poster?" She asks me.

"Truth?"

"Of course, the truth. I'm the Judge and you're in court. What else?" she smirked and the audience burst out in laughter.

When the courtroom was silent again I said, "If you change just one word in the title I can imagine there would be an exact opposite response to her ratings." I stayed quiet forcing her to have to ask.

"Come on with it then. What one word would you change?" She sucked her teeth.

"Take the word men out and make it women. How to train women in twenty-one days with the techniques used by professional dog trainers."

"Kill Him!" A woman somewhere in the audience shouts.

"Yes. Destroy the filthy beast!" Cried another and then another until the entire courtroom was filled with outraged cries for my immediate execution.

Fury mixed with tension and soon the courtroom was filled with angry voices. The Judge looked up to see the ratings which have surpassed the target mark. The monitor beside the ratings shows all stations in the broadcast band were now watching her courtroom. As she turns back to look at the audience I can see the glimmer in her eyes. She allows the chaos for a few more seconds and then illuminates the word, "SILENCE" on all monitors and sounds the sirens.

When the doors around the outer walls open and the Androps come through, two at a time in each of the five doorways, the audience returns to quiet and attentive. "There are many reasons our Great Republic adopted the rule of law. Perhaps no one reason more telling

or important than this display taking place live inside my court today."
Her attention turns to me as well as each camera one by one.

"Do you understand why they call for your death?" she asks.

"No." I restrain from explaining how the human condition has evolved an intuitive disdain for life.

"There are four beliefs in our population regarding men. The most popular being that men are a utility best used for entertainment and slave labor. This group of women wants men trained to fight to the death. They love to watch cage fights, kickboxing, and similar sports where men beat one another bloody with their bare hands. For the men too old and too weak for fighting, they are trained to build houses, and streets, serve in the military, or be placed in prisons where they can provide the sexual demands of the stronger criminals. The latter of which provides popular television and high ratings for late-night shows but I've never watched. I don't enjoy syndicated rape shows, but that's just my personal choice.

"The next largest group of women believe men are too dangerous to be allowed out in public. They say men are like pitbull terriers and even with proper training, rules of law, regulations, and the like, they think our world will never be safe until we ban men from the planet. They panic in fear at the presence of a man. They feel powerless and threatened. Fear is a terrible emotion and one no woman should ever have to experience."

The sounds of cheers and applause fill the room for a moment. Silence comes when the androps flash yellow beams into the crowd and announce thunderous words of warning. All went quiet.

"Please control your emotions in my court. None of us want to experience the heavy hand of these cybernetic patrols," The Judge pleads before continuing.

"You see, Eulǝr, this is where my decision concerning how to deal with you becomes a choice."

"Me?" I question with a voice of contempt for the human lack of sense for true justice. "You told me that all you cared about were the ratings. I've helped you achieve the highest rating and now the entire world is sitting in front of their televised device watching you. You should allow me to be free and on my way."

Out of the corner of my eye, I see the advocate take a swing at my jaw. I caught his fist and throw him backward from his chair. Before the androps moved, and before the small man could leap to his feet, she screamed, "Stop!"

"This will not go on one more instant. You will be respectful of this courtroom and the laws or I will have these androps finish you right here. You have the choice to sit quiet or I end your life. What will it be?"

As my eyes scan the room I see their hungry eyes. They want my death to fulfill their desire for a false sensation of superiority. My sense of instinct to raise my HUD and initiate extreme survival protocols rise. It would be the right thing to do, but I stop myself. Remembering that the end of humanity ends life for the kuudere too. The universe would erase our history. My mission to find the missing data and restore the code is more important than proving Syganoid superiority.

For a moment I twist mother's ring on my finger and then I feel the destiny stone inside my pocket. Looking at the Judge, and then I fold my hands on top of the table, "I will sit here quiet, and listen for the judgment."

"This is the only warning I allow you." She says.

***

Before the final decision is made, the judge flips through her tablet. I imagine she's taking time to calibrate her thoughts. She'll want to refresh and regain control of her performance act before the cameras are back live. I watch as she's getting herself into character for the show. She motions for the camera and the lights to illuminate her face.

For all I know she could be booking her vacation, in any case, the cameras are back live.

"The third group is much smaller than the first two, but it is the most powerful group," she says while picking up a cat and petting its long thick fur. "Because this group of Ladies is aligned and not at all divided on the issues that are most important to them. When they vote, they vote as a united society and that has great power in the effect on ratings. They call themselves The Ladies. They want men to admire them, worship them and romance is their dream life. The Age of Chivalry with Knights in shining armor stir their libido. They want men trained to be puppets for women to play with. They want handsome, well-groomed, and perfectly behaved men at their feet.

"You have many qualities for this group with your fine chiseled shoulders, chest, back, and arms. I could see there would be many women who might choose to have you under their control. You would do well as a servant in their harem of boy toys to play with and torment.

"Still, with all those muscles you would also be a good choice for cage fighting. There are many women here today who would enjoy watching you get the life pounded out of you. This brings me to a decision point. A choice awaits. Is The Great Starzel Republic better served training you for the military role of killing and death, or for romance and emotional torment?

"There is one more question I have to ask of you and then I will decide your fate. Your advocate tells me that you told him about a special mission that you're on. Perhaps it is time for all of us to hear it from you rather than me repeating what he has told me. I want you, Eulǝr, to tell the world about this grand mission. Tell us why you are going to Culver City."

Confident as the day I left Planet Forty-Four my heart center swells with pride for the salvation of humanity. I stand and face the nearest camera.

"There is a rather large and important data set missing in the universe code that binds human existence to the evolution of time-space reality. The code itself was defined and later the document was written by the sage named Banyan. His writings were completed when he lived in what is today called Culver City. I am going there in hopes of finding a copy or copies of his work and from there I can repair the code and replace the missing data. If not, I hope to find some clues for where the code may otherwise be located."

While I take my seat, the advocate pats the back of my hand and gives me a nod of approval. But, before I can scoot my chair back to the table, the audience erupts with laughter. Pet dogs howl and bark too. She doesn't wait for the room to fall quiet as she had before, now she speaks in a laughing voice to show her solidarity with the room.

"That is a very important mission, isn't it?" She leans across her desk, plucks the cat from the right corner of the bench into her arms, and laughs with the crowd working the room with her eyes and posture before turning in seriousness to look at me. "You've done a great amount of acting and performing for me and helping with the ratings, but now I want you to stop acting and tell me the truth. Why are you walking through my Republic without escort, without documentation, and without an identity? Truth, Eulǝr, truth!"

"What I have said is the truth and it is, as you say, a very important mission."

Once more she motions with her arms and hands for the audience to quiet.

"You are some kind of fucking idiot," the advocate whispers.

The sound of the stone head gavel slamming against the granite gavel block reverberates through the courtroom like a thunderclap in a silent sky. It is as clear and as certain as her final words. "Take him to the training center in Santa Monica. Process him into the general population of the facility. I give him forty days of training and if no woman claims him in forty days, bring him back to my courtroom and I'll consider his suitability for the fight ring. He doesn't deserve to die with honor in the military. Let the viewers watch him die in the caged fighting ring instead."

The gavel struck the stone again, but this time, its sound seemed to meld with the screams that filled the air. The true nature of my mission became obscured in the darkness, and the hope that had once burned within me flickered, threatened by the encroaching nightmare. My head pounding in pain from the swing of the policeman's baton hours ago. My skin feels brittle where the dried blood covers my ear and the side of my neck.

The androps, no longer programmed for crowd control, approached with cold, unfeeling intentions, their robotic forms now taking on a menacing aura. They seized me with force, their metallic grip biting into my flesh.

The camera crews, instead of breaking down the set, turned their attention to me with a sinister glint in their eyes. The once well-lit room transformed into a dimly lit chamber, casting eerie shadows on the walls. The holographic projections shifted from serene landscapes to distorted images of destruction and despair.

Inside the portable holding cell, the comfortable seat transformed into an unforgiving, metal contraption designed to restrain and subdue. The hum of machinery took on a cold, mechanical rhythm, echoing the heartlessness of the world outside. The beeps that filled the air were sharp and unforgiving, reminiscent of a countdown to an inevitable confrontation.

Disappointment mingled with confusion as I realize the society I find myself in is a twisted manifestation of feminist ideals taken to an extreme. The judge's gavel strike reverberated through the chamber, but instead of justice, it carried a sinister sense of control.

"I'll be going with you," says the advocate. "I'll make sure you are processed and transitioned."

The electromagnetic beams inside the paddywagon grab my arms and legs and I am spread eagle within the ultra violet-colored traction beams.

Chapter Five

Grooming Boys

Transportation from the courtroom to the training facility in Santa Monica is a blur in my memories. I can recall the twisted streets, I know it was a few hours, and that's about all I recall. My head is pounding with pain and the wallop that the patrolman gave me must have caught up because when they released me from the transporter holding cell, I passed out. Right now I'm awake but still feel half out of it. Behind me, I hear the sound of a heavy door when it closes into a solid jam with a thud followed by the sound of a metal chair as it slides across a smooth slab floor. I'm laying on my left side on top of a thin mattress and facing the wall of what sounds like a small cement-walled room. My senses pick up on two men in the room who are seated across from one another around a steel table. While they talk, I lay quiet, my head throbs and my consciousness struggles.

"Hey. Sorry to be an ass, I mean I know you got yourself in some shit too. You wouldn't be held up in this security room if you didn't have some crap going on, but fuck-me-brother. My life is hauling ass down the highway called out-of-control and what seems like light speed. Man, I'm not even sure what day it is. My wife has got me spinning like a top, and well, shit up my back . . . I'm fucking outraged. Man, I'm going to pop if I don't talk to somebody about this crap."

The second guy, who has been in the cell for awhile clears his throat a couple of times before responding. "It isn't a security room. This is a processing cell. It's where they put men when they are being arraigned for transfer into a training program."

"Fuck me to tears," the new guy says. "What's his story? The guy in the rack."

"I'm guessing he's sick. He hasn't moved since they brought him in a few hours ago."

"Fuck me to tears, man. He's probably got that new virus strain that is killing, what is it now something like two fatalities out of every fifty cases? Just my luck I get locked up with some superspreader fucknut. Shit my life in a pail, cus it is a hellhole of shit!" he shouts.

Five crashing thuds against the solid door come in rapid succession as someone on the other side uses a club against it as they shout, "Hold it down in there!"

"Take it easy man." The first guy says. "You don't want to get these ex-cage fighters turned training center security guards riled up. They love little else but to smack us with their billy clubs. Talk to me. Tell me what's going on."

My eyes close and my mind watches the HUD display as my systems run routine self-diagnostics and monitor my internal implants and attached devices. Resting here, while I listen to the two men.

"Thanks, brother. Like I said, I know you've got enough of your own shit to deal with but I have to talk. It's how they train us for years we learned to talk everything through, and express our feelings and emotions. Then, when we do, they punish us for being soft and ridicule us for being like little babies. They tell us to man up and be strong. Take it in stride. And so, when we take it and bottle it up they tell us to stop being so stubborn and all closed off. They ridicule us for being too self-centered and egotistic. Telling me I have to learn to trust and be open about my emotions. They fuck us no matter what we do until we finally accept that we are just wrong no matter what. We learn to accept that it doesn't matter one way or another because we are stupid men and we lack, from birth, the ability to be good, valuable, worthy beings.

"Shit, dirty fucks! Oops. Sorry man. I'll be quiet." He shouts at the door.

The new guy pauses a minute anticipating the security guard to acknowledge his apology for the second outburst. When he continues, I can hear the other guy drinking some water and then he chews on a bite of what smells like a meatloaf sandwich. The new guy continues.

"My beautiful wife. That's what we are supposed to call them right? Beautiful, wonderful, amazing, and all that. She's been having an affair with some fucking douchebag across town out in Malibu. My friend knows the guy and tells me the suck-ass bastard is a real player. You know, a pickup artist with no training at all in marriage and romance. But it doesn't matter to her because he's handsome and tall, and has a good-paying job. The typical PUA profile guy.

"Night before last she didn't come home and I was going nuts worrying. Where is she? I wonder and fret. What's happened to my darling beautiful wife? Well fuck, you know . . . so then I'm calling around to all of her friends trying to find out where she is. Nobody knows anything. Well, then I called around to the hospitals and nobody had her listed in the medical systems.

"There can only be one place else. She's off with this fucking douchebag, fucking her brains out all night leaving me, her three dogs, and our two kids home worried sick. Shit, man I'd like to tell you it's the first time she's played this scene out, but she's done this twice before. Well, I decided then and there this was it. I'm packing up and taking off to Santa Barbara."

"Calm down, man." The first guy says with his mouth full as he chews. "You're getting loud again and those guards are going to come through that door any second now."

"Okay, okay, okay." Says the new guy. "I'm just so angry with her. So, like I said, I'm going to take the kids and we'll ask for MGTOW to take us in and protect us. They have almost all of Santa Barbara County under their control now and they're growing. But that's a different story.

"Where was I . . . oh ya, so I take the dogs and kids over to my mom's house first thing yesterday morning. I asked my mom to take care of them and tell her I'd be back tomorrow to get them. She's all riled up and started telling me that joining up with MGTOW is dangerous and not good for the kids. But I told her we would be fine. Then, I went home to wait for my wonderful wife to come home so I can have it out with her. I'm going to give her what's what and fuck her life up for a change. You know what I mean?"

The first guy takes a bite from his meatloaf sandwich and through a mouthful of meat, "Mm-hmmm. Go ahead, man tell me more."

***

"The whole day drags on where every minute seems like an hour with me waiting like a love-sick teenager." The new guy in the cell wasn't going to give up telling his story. "When the day was done and not one sign of her, not a phone call or a message. It was like an emotional roller coaster for me. My mind was running nonstop from panic and worry that something has happened to her, to fury and rage that she can be so cruel and uncaring about my and her children's feelings. Then, the phone rang and I scrambled to answer but it was my mom.

"Fuck-me to tears, man. My mom was hysterical and I can't understand a word she was saying. 'Mom, slow down, I can't understand you. What's happening?' After a few minutes, of me trying to, but I still can't get her to calm down enough to speak so I can understand her, I give up. 'I'm coming over Mom. Be there in ten minutes.' I hung up the phone, grabbed my keys, and went to the truck.

"When I got to Mom's house there were three patrol cars out front. Lights flashing and a few cops are posted out front keeping watch on the front yard. And then an ambulance pulls up and they rush out a gurney and take it inside. At this point, man . . . I'm right on top of them as we slip past the two cops out front one of them grabs me by the collar. 'Hold on there shorty. Where do you think you're going?' He shoved my back to the porch wall beside the front door.

"It's my kids and my mom in there! I shouted back at him. What is going on? And just like that," he snaps his fingers. "Three of them fuckers have me on the ground, handcuffed, and a knee on the back of my neck pushing my face into the front lawn. When they let me up he puts me in the patrol car and brought me here."

"Pretty intense scene man," the first guy says. Washing the last of the meatloaf down with a long drink, then he says. "Why did they take you down like that? What was that all about?"

"Jesus H. Christ, I'm going to murder that douchebag of a boyfriend. When I get out of here, I'm going to find him and kill him. You won't believe it but that asshat slugged my mom and broke her nose. Somehow he and my wonderful sweet loving wife figured out that I had taken the kids over to my mom's and so the two of them showed up at mom's. Well, of course, Mom tells them to go ahead and just fuck right off cus they aren't taking her grandchildren out of her house. Yeah, so then this ass clown slugs mom in her face and while she's down, he keeps her on the ground while Mrs. Wonderful Wife packs the kids, and dogs into his car and then they leave."

The first guy stands and paces across the room. "Wow," he says. "Still, why did they arrest you?"

The new guy slams a fisted hand onto the steel table, "The last time she did this shit I went nuts. When I near beat the life out of her boyfriend the judge warned me. I promised to be cool and my darling beautiful wife promised to be less obvious about her affairs. So, now, because of that last incident they arrested me. For my own protection, they said. For my own, fucking protection."

The room went quiet and I fell unconscious again. When I woke now, my head isn't throbbing and the room is still pitch quiet. The new guy is still here. He's sitting at the same place in the same chair at the table. I roll out of the rack and stand up. As I stretch and come to my full senses, refreshed and feeling no pain, I look at him. He's staring at the table and his head, neck, and shoulders tense.

"Are you okay man?" I ask.

"Fuck me to tears, brother. Did you hear any of what was being said in here last night?"

"I did, I heard your story," I say.

"Fuck me to tears man, I know you got a shit load of troubles too. You wouldn't be in this holding facility if your life was golden, but you know that guy who was in here? The one I was talking to in here all last night. Well turns out when they took him out of here this morning, the guard tells me he's the guy who broke my mom's nose. I'm going to kill that mother fucker. But you know what really toasts my hairy ass?"

"No man. I don't know what else would really toast your hairy ass. If the fact he was right here for several hours. Not more than an arm's reach and a lurch out of your grip. That you had the guy who took your children, took your beautiful wife, stole your world away from you, and who broke your mother's nose wasn't what toasted your ass. What is it?"

"He sat here listening to me tell him the entire saga while eating a meatloaf sandwich, and I didn't recognize it was one of my wonderful wife's fabulous meatloaf sandwiches. She always makes meatloaf sandwiches when we go away on trips."

As I stand in the dimly lit holding cell, a storm of emotions raged within. The air feels heavy with tension, and my heart pounds in my chest like a relentless drumbeat. The taste of anger lingered on my tongue, just like the bitterness of injustice. My hand instinctively reaches up to touch the gash on my head, a painful reminder of the violence. As I caught a glimpse of the steel table, I can't help but notice the remnants of the meatloaf sandwich, a simple comfort that turned sour, much like my life in recent days. The combination of emotions and the scene's elements weigh on my soul, driving me to find a way to reclaim what I have come here to accomplish.

He never lifts his head or moves a muscle the whole morning. Not even when the guards open the door to take me. The new guy stays in that full-body tense position at the table. Then right before the guard closes the door he asks,

"Do you have that new virus? Is that why you were sick in this rack all day yesterday?"

When the guard hears the question, he holds me in place, "Well, are you sick? You got this variant strain that's killing folks all over The Great Starzel Republic? Answer the man."

"Yesterday I got hit over the head with a club by a patrolman and I have a mild concussion. I lose consciousness from time to time, but I'm not sick."

Both of them look at me with disbelief so I dip my head and squat down so they can see the gash on the top-side of my head.

"Goddamn, that's some deep slice. It needs stitches," the guard says.

He pulls the door closed and shoves me forward down the hall. I take a few quick steps to catch my balance and look back at him. "Keep moving," he points down the hallway. "Let's get you processed for training. We'll get to the truth about yesterday and that head gash."

***

Life on Earth is different than what I had expected. Log entry three: Day ninety-five.

#Analogy -- When a transport car travels from one domed city up or down to another domed city there's no stopping. Once the transport is underway, no matter what else happens, it doesn't stop until it is to the next dome. That's what life on Planet Earth is like. It keeps coming at you like a transport car. With every breath, the causal events of doing, keep coming. Life is forced upon humans. There's no time to consider alternatives or take time off for health, sanity, or sheer desperation. Even while asleep, life keeps coming at you. Like the transport between domes, there's no time to change direction or step off the transport. End # Analogy. After ninety-four days into the mission there is no progress.

Laws, enforcement of laws, politics, media, and the limitations on existence because of the five hindrances, the insignificant senses. Every aspect of the human path is a realization. Unstoppable and all-pervasive. Me, living in this culture of confused humans without the use of my superior senses and full Syganoid capabilities makes me wonder if

I can succeed. If I turn my systems on, there is no chance to complete the mission and save humanity. If I do not, then, I fear the same result.

"Take the chair right there," the guard says as he forces me into the chair leading me with a tight grip across the back of my neck. "Tell me what you learned."

As I feel my way onto the seat I look around the large room. In contrast to the brashness of the guard, the space casts a sense of feminism and romance. It radiates an atmosphere that is both delicate and welcoming, with a strong emphasis on female empowerment and an oddly twisted depiction of love.

The walls are adorned with vibrant tapestries, depicting scenes of fearless heroines breaking free from societal constraints and embracing their individuality. With men laid dead underfoot or faded images in the background behind them, the artwork celebrates women from all walks of life, showcasing their strength, resilience, and beauty. The colors burst forth, reflecting the diversity and vibrancy of femininity.

Soft natural light filters through sheer curtains, casting a warm glow upon the room. The curtains themselves are adorned with intricate patterns symbolizing unity and equality, embodying the spirit of feminism. The air is infused with a delicate scent of fresh flowers, evoking a sense of romance and passion.

The centerpiece of the room is a stage, adorned with a grand piano draped in silk fabric, featuring powerful quotes by feminist icons. A talented pianist sits at the instrument, playing melodies that echo the spirit of female strength and love. The music resonates with each note, the celebration of some demented and sadistic depiction of love.

The open office concept maintains its place within this fascist setting. Six stations, adorned with grand desks and comfortable chairs, feature framed portraits of inspirational women from different eras and cultures. The desks are decorated with meaningful emblems such as equality signs and interlocking hearts, symbolizing the fusion of feminism and romance.

My face scrunched, with eyes squinting as I try to pry the meaning from his words by looking into his face for a less cryptic question. The man is hard to look at. His face is scarred from what, at first, would make me think he survived a horrible bomb accident. Scars over scars crisscrossing his forehead and right eye. Through the half-closed lid, I see the white and half of a green-colored iris and the deep black pupil. Switching attention to look into his left eye I'm intrigued by the teeth marks. From the right side of his nose, of what looks like the upper teeth over to the mid-cheek where the deep impression of the lower teeth. Someone must have tried to bite his face off and left their dental pattern in his flesh. Though his shirt covers his neck, I can imagine that the telltale signs of the physical injuries cover his entire body.

"What did I learn? From the Judge do you mean?" I ask.

"Treat me like I'm a fucking idiot. Talk down to me as if I'm as dense as a concrete floor. Shit, I love it when you piss me off. I want nothing more than an opportunity to break your face. Fuck no. I could give two shits about your courtroom experience, you dipshit dweeb. What did you learn from the holding cell?"

While his oversized and disfigured fingers and hands curl into tight fists on the top of the desk positioned between us, I consider how to respond. "It's couldn't give, not could."

"What the fuck?" he leans across the desktop, his face now demands my full attention.

"You said you could give two shits about what I learned from the Judge, but what you should have said was you could not give two shits. Even better would be to say you would not give two shits. The meaning is more clear when you use proper syntax. The communication code can be wonderful but it demands careful precision."

Through his mangled lips and reconstructed chin, his laughter fills the entire building. "Well fuck, Eulər you saved us both a lot of time. I'm going to fast forward to the place where I know for certain, I hate you. I'm going to fast-track your training on my express car to fuck your life up." He slaps the desktop with the underside of his fists as he continues to laugh.

When he quiets, I respond with my still curious expression unchanged. I stay focused on looking into his one undamaged eye.

"There was some danger in placing those two men in the same holding room. If the story had taken the wrong path they would have clashed. I imagine one or both would have been killed. Otherwise, can I ask when we can get some food around here? I haven't had anything to eat since they gave me some engineered synthetic chicken barbeque at the courthouse yesterday."

The smile that could make the hair stand up on the back of Satan's neck spread across his face. While he rifles through every drawer of the desk his head wags in disbelief. Then he stood and went to the gedunk machine, retrieved a sandwich and a tube of water, brought it back, and placed them with exaggerated delicate gracefulness. "There you go, sir. All you need do is ask and I will provide whatever you demand."

All sarcasm aside, I tore into the sandwich and half-chewed the first couple of bites. My systems are running low on energy. The HUD display is flashing red danger signals on almost every diagnostic indicator.

"Every one of these scars on my face," he says, "was won in a fight for life. You see an ugly man sitting here. A low-life security guard doing a thankless job, yes? I was a cage fighter for five years and after my tenth kill, I earned my way out of the cage and was awarded this work. Most of the retired fighters go into the military to serve in battles and defend The Great Starzel Republic from the Trump Confederacy and their alliance with the Russian military. They award the worst, the meanest, and the most vicious of killers with luxury jobs such as security and police.

"That's how I see your future, Eulər. I see you in the cage. Fighting every day for your life."

***

Perhaps his experience in the cage fights reinforced what he already believed about himself. Proud and certain of his invincibility. He would not be so valiant if he had to fight with me. The superiority of my intellect alone would have defeated him and the genetic difference in our kuudere is on a different, much higher level than people.

"What you should have told me about your experience in the holding room," he says, "was how romantic it all was. You aren't right for this intensive training in chivalry and the education for the world of The Lady. If you had what it takes to learn how to provide a Lady with everything she needs you would have seen how beautiful those two men had given every fiber of their being to provide their woman, their lives. They are giving her every thrill she wants. Did you even consider how exciting and fun her life is? Having a husband she can cuckold and yet he will kill for her and sacrifice his own life to enhance hers. She is honored and glorious, her life enriched.

"If you had an ounce of romance in you, you would have understood exactly what was unfolding in that holding room. But you did not, you could only see the potential for the fight. You are a killer. Just like me, and you want to be trained for killing. Don't you? Admit it."

His one good eye is intense and his perspiration signals his desire for the fight. Rather than answer him, I sit back and cross my legs, left over right. My gaze drifts from his eye and I turn to observe the other people in the room while I eat.

--open communication with nearby Syganoid--

__there are no Syganoid within communications range__

__would you like to review the last diagnostics report__

--close communication requests--

__communications request is not open__

How is that possible? I just opened the application. Is something wrong with the system? Is that why I can't locate the woman in black? Try again.

--locate Syganoids nearby--

__there are no Syganoid nearby__

My fingers twist and tug on my mother's ring as I wonder if the destiny stone can set me free of this trap.

"How about you and me step into one of the holding rooms and you can show me what fight you have inside you? Just the two of us. Nobody watching, promise." He waits for my response and when he gets none he says, "Tell yuh what. I'll give you the first five swings before I defend myself or hit back. You can do your worst five times. Come on you know you want to."

The desperate smell on his breath and from his perspiration offend my olfactories. Enthusiastic about the fight, he snatches my arm by the wrist in his left hand and squeezes as he says, "How about if I promise only open-hand slaps? You can still use your fists but I'll only use an open hand. Come on Eulər, you chicken shit pansy. Let's do this. What do you say?"

Though the tight grip is a surprise, who knew a human could develop such strength, I'm sure it's his rage that accelerates his adrenaline.

"Is everything okay over here?" A powerful voice arises from behind me and to my right side. As I turn to see the source, the guard lets go of my arm and answers.

"All good over here boss. I'm just getting to know this new student. All good, boss."

"Then let's get a move on. We'll be taking the new boys off to indoctrination in an hour. No time to waste with idle chit-chat." The supervisor walks away. His attention is now fixed on another new student and guard at a desk several yards away.

"Artificial," I said while the guard watches his supervisor now engaged at the next station. When he turns back to face me I greet him with a half-formed smile and raised an eyebrow to the same side as the lifted cheek. "This entire conversation . . . a total hoax and what's sad about the hoax is you."

The audible struggle for maintaining control of his tone and decibel is obvious as he nearly chokes on the words, "You push me too far and I will end your life right here. Don't let your words overload your ass, boy."

As I challenge the guard's misguided beliefs, I couldn't help but feel a sense of disappointment in a society that perpetuated violence as a measure of masculinity.

"Chill out big guy," my voice is calm and I take a posture of sincerity. "There is a reason you experience these feelings that are violent and why you are eager to act out those feelings. You have never been taught how to discover the True Self within you. All your life they told you your purpose is to serve the desires of women. They taught you what those desires are, and they taught you the proper way for a man to fulfill those desires. You have allowed the outer world of sensations to rule your life. You see only outside of your True Self. Never believing in yourself except in your one ability to kill for the purpose of women's enjoyment in you killing other men. What puzzles me and all free-thinking men, who are in control of our self-respect, is how you allowed them to capture you and control you. You can't understand how puzzled we are because all I see when I look at you is a misguided holy being.

"Your training is an argument preceded by a false belief that boys are juicing with testosterone and need "taming" reveals an unbroken, and mythical conception of men stemming from ancient times – and it is wrong. Men are not born as wild animals in a testosterone-fuelled psychosis waiting to tear people limb from limb. We need not buy our sons punching bags nor insert them into football training from two years of age to channel some androgen-fuelled chaos (doing it for fun, though, is another reason). The claim that men are unclean, bestial creatures in need of taming is not only false – it is extreme misandry and it needs to be challenged head-on with each bigot -- man and woman -- who perpetuates it."

Everyone in the chamber turned to look when they heard the empty water tube rattle and clang after I drank the last swallow and then tossed it to the metal bin beside his desk. Then I stood and turned the chair so that I could straddle the seat and lean forward into the back support. "So what have they trained you to do as you prepare for my indoctrination into the school? How about you show me how well-trained you are at performing the tasks they told you to complete? Come on, boy. Do your job."

Anger and frustration turn his face red and I smell his disturbed bowels. He thumbs across the large tablet, stopping at times to enter data. His teeth grind in time to the tune of Mandolin Wind as the pianist plays from the center of the room.

***

The bus idles at the side of the school, where a magnificent statue of Gloria Steinem stands tall. The bronze figure captured her resolute gaze and outstretched arm, symbolizing the unwavering spirit of feminism in the face of adversity. The School of Romance bus, with its bold white letters and large metallic flake, eggplant-colored exterior, is parked in the shadow of the feminist icon.

The bright sun stings my eyes as it bathes Santa Monica in warm, vibrant rays, casting a gentle, warm breeze that caresses my skin and the students, and it rustles the leaves of nearby palm trees. The sky is clear except above the distant mountains were billowing white clouds, presenting a picturesque day that contrasted with the underlying ideological tensions within The School of Romance.

As the security guards escorted the new students and me onto the bus, their eyes briefly met the stoic statue. Each guard, six in total, bore the physical remnants of their past battles fought within the cage. Their tight uniforms accentuated their muscular frames, but their expressions betrayed a mix of fear, sorrow, and pain. Once the students settled into their seats, the guards stood alongside the bus, awaiting the arrival of the enigmatic leader they revered.

Just as the bus driver, James, approached, a slender woman adorned in a suit jacket and an oversized tie emerged from the crowd, with her small dog on a lead that matches her tie. Dr. Seraphina Pelosi, as she introduced herself, commanded attention with her bright tapestry of colored makeup and sparkling gold glitter. The overpowering smell of grassy, cut flowers fills the bus, burns my nose, and waters my eyes. Her appearance resonated with the resplendent hues that adorned the statue itself.

A broad smile graced Dr. Pelosi's lips as she addressed the apprehensive group of students. "Welcome to The School of Romance, boys," she declared with confidence, her voice cutting through the air. "Today, you embark on a transformative journey to become well-trained men in our society of women. Over the next four months, through rigorous training and testing, we will guide you away from your primitive instincts and mold you into men who understand and honor women's desires. Like horses, dogs, and men, you too shall shed your wild ways and become civilized under the tutelage of women. Men need to be taught when to walk, run, sit, shit, play, work, and, of course, when to cease fighting and attempting rape. Women will do this for you."

After this brief speech, she steps out of the bus, the driver enters and in a minute we are underway. The men are quiet and their faces look straight ahead.

"You are all good men," I say. "There is nothing wrong with any of you."

The driver hits the brakes, causing the bus to jerk and when James catches my attention in the rearview mirror, he says, "I won't have that sort of talk on my bus. Keep it quiet."

Though James asked for quiet, I feel obligated to explain and help these men. "You've been tainted and brainwashed by a society of women to feel inferior and subjugated to believe that you are genetically damaged. But you are a miracle from birth. Over the last one hundred thousand years in the history of humankind, it has always been men. Survival has been accomplished by the strength and ingenuity of men. The discovery of medicines, shelter, farming, technology, society, and every aspect of life that improved our existence has been brought about and is the result of men. The only value of women is the incubation of children to further the gene pool."

"If you don't stop this heresy, I will call the androps," the driver holds his phone out for me to see. His voice is nervous but stern. The men are fidgeting and uncomfortable, but not one of them turned to look in my direction. No one made a sound.

"I will say just once more and then I will be quiet until we arrive . . . wherever you're taking us," I say. "You are miracles from birth, every one of you has the power of the universe within."

For the next several minutes, as the bus makes its way through the streets of Santa Monica, silence fills the space. Were it not for the sounds of the road grinding under the wheels, a few squeaks of metal against metal, and the whir of passing vehicles, the bus was still and quiet. When at last we arrive at the destination James opens the door and points and says, "Straight up this trail about two hundred feet and just over the rise you'll see the statue of Hera. The dean of our school, the woman who spoke to you earlier, will meet you there. No talking!" He looks at me. "Just go there and listen to her and only her words mean anything."

As we gathered at the statue of Hera, the dean, Dr. Pelosi greeted us with a warm smile, acknowledging each of us individually. We formed a line, standing side by side, facing the imposing figure of the ancient goddess.

"Alright, everyone," Dr. Pelosi began, her voice filled with a conversational tone that drew us in. "Let's dive into our first lesson. Today, we're going to talk about marriage and how it has been used throughout history to tame men."

"Hera, the Ancient Greek goddess of marriage, was quite the character," she continued, chuckling lightly. "She had a reputation as 'The Tamer.' It wasn't just horses and heroes she tamed; she aimed to subdue all that wildness and freedom."

Leaning in a little closer, as if sharing a secret, "Now, Hera had a bag of tricks when it came to taming. Marriage was her go-to tool. She'd yoke men and women together, binding them in the institution. And let me tell you, she had quite the way of enticing people to conform."

She paused, letting her words sink in. "If anyone dared to rebel, Hera would unleash her arsenal of shaming and aggressive punishments. Even her husband Zeus wasn't spared from her wrath. No one was safe."

Pointing at the statue, the dean remarked, "You see that yoke there? That's Hera's symbol, representing her desire to turn beasts and men into mere utilities. She wanted obedient men tied to their wives, ensuring they'd be subservient. And heroes? Well, she had a special treat for them too. They were yoked to an inevitable fate. Death. All their labor and sacrifices were for the betterment of women and society."

"Now, let me share a little tidbit from the Iliad," the dean said, lowering her voice slightly. "In some tales, Hera tamed heroes through death, not marriage. It was believed that sacrificing themselves for others was the 'right' thing for men to do. It's a concept that has persisted throughout history."

Aloof, she concluded her lesson, the dean's expression softened, and she met our gazes with empathy. "So, here we are, ready to explore these dynamics, challenge norms, and find our own paths. Remember, this is just the beginning. We have much more to discover together."

The conversational tone of the dean's delivery made the students feel engaged and eager to delve deeper into the complexities of gender roles and relationships. I stood there, absorbing the lessons, knowing that this was just the start of a transformative journey. As she speaks, I sense the swelling of her ego and I smell the serotonin increase in her perspiration. Joy and gratitude drive her voice to a higher pitch and she has to rein in her energy so to speak clear and precise.

She motions for us to kneel down before her and the statue. Then she goes a few steps away to stand beside the statue.

***

Despite my better judgment and a growing dislike for this school of romance, I take a knee. Considering my options to escape and run away or to stay, I know neither of these serves my purpose. It is time for me to take a necessary chance at being exposed as a humanoid. I must find the missing data or the entire universe will erase humankind from the matrix. I push my hand inside the front pocket of my blouse and find the small destiny stone. My fingers brush the soft velvet wrapping and trace the thin cord that binds the velvet in place. Is this the time and place to open the package? Is there nothing else to do? As the giant of a man told me when he gave me this, magic package. 'You will know when it is time to use the magic because there will be nothing else that needs to be done.'

In a very loud shout, "Boys! Hear me now and remember my words until the day you die." She kisses the hand of the statue. Hera's arm extended down from the giant sculpted in stone with the back of her hand poised in expectation of pledged loyalty and allegiance.

"Once upon a time, a mother who wanted to see the beautiful statue of Hera had no oxen or horses to carry her there. But she did have two sons. And the sons wanted more than anything to make their mother's wish come true. They volunteered to yoke themselves to a cart and take her over the mountains in the scorching heat to the faraway village of Argos, the home of the statue of Hera (the wife of Zeus). Upon their arrival in Argos, the sons were cheered and statues (that can be found to this day) were built in their honor. Their mother prayed that Hera would give her sons the best gift in her power. Hera did that. The boys died. The traditional interpretation? The best thing that can happen to a man is to die at the height of his glory and power. The statues and cheers can be seen as bribes for the sons to value their lives less than their mother's request to view a statue. The fact that the statue was of Hera, the queen of the Olympian gods and protector of married women is symbolic. The sons' sacrifice symbolized the mandate for men to become strong enough to serve the needs of mothers and marriage and to be willing to call it glory if they died in the process.

"Yes these are myths, but on this topic, life had a way of imitating art. Those who wrote the stories were drawing on experience to some extent, and married couples re-enacted the selfsame rituals of Hera and Zeus. In the marriage month (February) the mythical marriage of Hera and Zeus is reenacted and celebrated with public festivities, a time when many couples get married in imitation of the divine couple. On these occasions, prayers and offerings are given to Hera, and the bride pledges fidelity to extend Hera's dominion on Earth."

The men next to me bow their heads as the dean motions with her hand and extended finger. Not me though, I don't bow. I want to watch her as she finishes this lecture.

"By dint of a peculiar intersection of social beliefs, women came to be viewed as perfected from birth – due largely to the fact that through the Catholic, Christianity veneration of the Virgin Mary became amplified in the eleventh century and, by extension, the reverence bestowed upon the Virgin was extended to the female sex in general. As Mary was perfect, so too became all women.

"No longer like the Biblical Eve striving to imitate the Mother of Christ, a woman becomes Mary's counterpart on earth, and thus the cult of the "lady" is born as a mirror of the cult of the Virgin. Men for their part remain in a thoroughly fallen state like Adam while striving to imitate Jesus – knowing full well they will fall short of the goal. To enjoy the company of a lady a man must now prove himself worthy of her and so advance upward, step by step, toward a culminating union at her level; because everything noble and virtuous, everything that makes life worth living, proceeds from women, who are the source of goodness itself.

"With the advent of women becoming men's moral superiors, we must recognize men are the servants of women. It's here in our school the reciprocal service previously entertained between the sexes begins and teaches gynocentrism. As the faithful owed obeisance to The Virgin, henceforth man must render his obeisance to the Virgin's earthly counterparts. As it has been for a thousand years in this age of 'Lady' women are viewed through the lens of the feudal contract whereby she became his overlord, and he the vassal in dutiful service. It is a woman whose role is to civilize the depraved, fallen creature called man by teaching him the gynocentric virtues of chivalry and courtly love.

"The belief that morally superior women should enculture men into the arts of chivalry and gentlemanliness for the benefit of women. This is our purpose at the School of Romance. It is our mission.

"Lifelong feminist and former National Organization for Women member, Tammy Bruce, provides the lessons that you boys will learn to follow and pledge to die for. What she feels is the time-honored power of women; of being morally superior to men includes the feminist responsibility to civilize men's animalistic tendencies.

"Another glorious feminist, Christina Hoff-Sommers agrees with this idea that men need to be civilized and you boys will learn her methods of chivalric manners. Masculinity with morality and civility is a very powerful force for good. But masculinity without these virtues is dangerous--even lethal. Chivalry is grounded in a fundamental reality that defines the relationship between the sexes, and given that most men are physically stronger than most women, men can overpower women at any time to get what they want. If women give up on chivalry, it will be gone. If boys can get away with being boorish, they will, happily. Women must stop this and establish feminism as the social norm in its place."

As Dr. Pelosi's speech stirred conflicting thoughts within me, I grappled with the clash of ideologies and the deep-rooted problems presented. The desire to confront these issues and strive for change fought against the urgency of my true mission. The imminent threat of humankind's erasure compelled me to set aside the ideological battle for now, knowing that the immediate task of finding the missing data demanded my full attention. This sick and evil ideology might be evidence of the missing data and the change underway within the Universe. I must hurry or soon all of humanity will erode and plunge into obscurity worse than feminism.

As I weigh the options in my mind, a clear and resolute course of action emerges. The right path forward is to wait until our return to the school and then execute a calculated escape under the cover of night. The certainty of this decision settled within me.

Chapter Six

All Caged In

T hroughout the short twenty-minute bus ride from the statue of Hera to the School of Romance, I preached to them. After several minutes into my rant, James the bus driver, is on his phone. I took it from him and smashed it under the heel of my boot.

Man-taming by women, from Ancient Greece to the present day, represents a challenge for us to overcome. Nothing has changed; the chivalric servitude of men, trained into them by women (yes, and by men too), remains the order of the day. The one timeless voice echoing through all this is the monomyth of the animal-trainer – womankind and her pussy whip.

"With the continuing encouragement of women to be slavemasters, and their enthusiasm to take on the role, is it any surprise that the majority of horse and dog training schools – obedience classes – are peopled by women? That so many little girls desire to possess their own pony is a no-brainer, and it's time we woke up to what this expensive little pastime symbolizes – the racing of horses may be the sport of Kings, but the training of ponies is for the delight of princesses.

"Emasculate men and you set the universe against humanity. The code of the universe feeds the weak to the strong. The natural balance of existence is duality. Humanity is man and woman not in opposition but in step. Each makes the other stronger. But if the natural order is augmented by feminizing men then the code will devour the error in favor of creating an improved experience of The Self."

Three of the men watch me and nod. But James cautions them, "You don't want to get tangled up in his lunacy."

"In a modern 'enlightened' society," I say. "It's high time to ditch the idea that males, and only males, need taming. Let's instead rely on men's natural human empathy, a thing that exists in both sexes before the training begins. If you see a baby boy begin crying after he hears another baby crying nearby, it's a demonstration of empathy that is there from the start. Like girls, boys develop mirror neurons that predispose them to be caring as they develop – we don't need to see them as heartless beasts in need of taming, curtailing, or genitally maiming. So let's cease with the gynocentric boot camp for males; they are already trained from the start by their own good natures – yes, men are good."

When James slams on the brakes and comes to a stop I'm thrown forward into the windscreen. His eyes contact mine and I see his anger and disdain for me. The door opens and the screams of fright and terror, mixed with shrill dog barks from outside the bus, blast in on my ears. Shaken by the jolt, curious by the screams and barks, I walk down the three steps at a cautious inquisitive pace and exit the bus.

What is the terror and horror causing these women to scream in hysteria?

At first glance, I see there are about thirty or more women with several pet dogs on leads and a few with birds perched on their shoulders, they are gathered in groups of four to five on either side of a walkway. The groups of women are each in various states of panic and stress. Dr. Seraphina Pelosi in the center of the walkway, just below a banner over the front door of the school: Welcome New Students. She looks at me and shouts, "Do something boy!" I follow her shivering pointing a finger to look at a coughing woman. Brutal, chest-caving coughs are robbing her need to inhale a breath. I run to her but just a step before the indoctrination guard, also running at full stride to her aide, blindsides and shoves me away.

Face down and out of balance, I slide across the fresh-cut, short blades of sharp green grass that fill the ground around the School of Romance. When I roll over and look up at the clouds as they gathered in the darkening sky, the scent and the taste of dust and rain intertwined and compete on the wind, creating an atmospheric dance that foretold an imminent storm.

Pushing myself up and rising to my feet I see three more women in the same condition of uncontrolled, brutal coughing. As I gather myself and straighten my body, clothes, and my wits, I see the woman closest to me is now coughing and spitting blood. As fast as it started, her struggle ends. The women scream in panic and tears stream from their bewildered faces coupled with expressions of horror.

"She's dead. My god, she's dead!"

The emergency team burst onto the scene but despite fever-paced efforts, one by one the three other women die. "This virus, epidemic, whatever it is. It's killing people faster than the frontline of the war with Texarkana and Mexico," says the indoctrination guard.

The six guards gather by the front doors of the school and engage in a quiet conversation. One of them, the one who seems to be telling the rest, points his finger at James. He's standing beside his bus, leaning onto the front wheel housing sobbing and blubbering about the shame that nothing could be done for the women. Then the indoctrination guard, still talking with an expression full of condemnation, points to the five new students who have gathered together in a tight huddle about twenty feet away. They look scared and sheepish, with no direction and no ability to think for themselves. But then, as I look back at the six indoctrination guards, the finger points, and their eyes are now on me.

My guard, ole droopy eye, snarls through a curled upper lip and tight jaw. Then he looks at the group and says something that they all nod in definitive agreement. All at once they turn and in a single file through the front doors and out of sight.

***

When Dr. Pelosi finished speaking with the last of the emergency team, she and her small dog stood watching as the ambulance doors closed. The ambulance fires up the ignition crystals and the lights flash in a travel cadence. The siren sounds and then the vehicle pulls onto the road and soon vanishes from sight as it rounds the west corner of the school. She turns to face the group of new students.

"Why is there only five of you? Who is missing?"

"I'm here," I say as I walk over to join the five.

"One hell of a first day, boys. One hell of a fucking day. This virus is spreading around the world and seems to be getting worse by the hour." She picks up the small black, curly-haired dog and holds it in her right arm, stroking its head with her left. "Except, of course, China tells the world they have it under control. They always lie and can't be trusted." Her head nods with a visual demonstration and a certain confirmation of her own words.

"It's are there," I interrupt her speech.

"What?" she snarls at me. "What are you saying?" Her head oscillates in negative.

"A moment ago you asked them, 'Why is there only five of you,' and I'm explaining to you that you meant to say, 'Why --are-- there only five of you. You understand, of course, 'is' would" would be singular and 'are' would be the plural. Since there --are -- six of us you meant to inquire in the plural."

With a silent clap of her hands, she holds them tight as she rolls her eyes. When she decided the best next response would be to ignore me. Placing her pet back on the ground, she stands and tosses her hands away to dismiss my comment. "At this time in the indoctrination for you new students, we would normally have introduced you to your potential mistresses and then we would escort you to your rooms inside the dormitory. However, given the chaos and unfortunate events of horrible deaths and general fear of helplessness, I trust each of you can find your way.

"Through those doors," she points at the double doors where the guards were standing, discussing and conversing several minutes ago. "Down the hall, you will find the rooms. Your name is on the lintel. Dinner is at seven o'clock. Everyone must arrive promptly and on time." She walks toward the street and down the long walkway, side by side with her dog.

"Can you tell me? I mean, is the plague virus killing women because of what you said on the bus? That we have altered the Universe duality code?" He asks after the other four new students are in their rooms and we stand outside the door to his room.

"The virus seems to attach to the lungs and throat," I say. "It isn't gender specific at all. I'm sure just as many men are dying as women. They aren't going to care about men dying in this country so you're not getting all the true facts. But genetically there are no differences between the sexes for a virus to target one over the other. The major evolutionary difference in humankind is the development of qualia in some brains. About sixty percent of people have three energy centers located inside their brain which gives them four additional senses. Unfortunate as it is to Earthlings, the very rich and the very powerful are not evolved. They lack qualia. The virus isn't attacking along these genetic differences either."

"What do you mean, Earthlings?" his face contorts quizzical.

"Here's your room," I say. "We will talk later. I need a shower and I'm tired for now. Okay?"

"Before you shower, can you tell me one thing? How would I know if I'm evolved? How can I tell if I have qualia?" he asks.

"Easy to identify, difficult to give qualia room to grow the three senses. But if you can feel the emotion from the beauty of a flower, or experience the intensity of a brilliant sunset. If you can know the joy and let yourself melt into the comfort of a mattress. You have eight, not five senses."

After a few steps away from him I hear his door close and the hall feels empty. Quiet, with few artificial lights spaced far apart the sound of my steps in the dark echoes. When I reach the room, I run my fingertips over the engraved lintel. "Eulər," I say aloud as I direct my eye on the cornea reader and the door opens.

__Activate Defense Systems__

__emergency protocols engaged__

The automatic Syganoid system is indicated in my HUD as I enter the room. Two of the indoctrination guards are inside. One grabs my arm and throws me to the floor. Before the first message appears in my HUD display his knee comes down across the back of my neck.

--disengage protocols--

--disengage defense systems--

As I scramble to keep the biomechanical systems hidden, the second guard zip-ties my hands behind my back and then binds my ankles together.

__defence systems deactivated__

__emergency protocols paused__

--disengage protocols--

__would you like to view the diagnostics report__

"Don't go too tight. They want him undamaged for the event. You know how much he wants to beat him legit and shit. Take it easy." The guard tells his counterpart as he kneels his entire body weight across the back of my neck.

--no report--

--acknowledge disengage protocols--

__there are Syganoids nearby__

__would you like to communicate with nearby Syganoids__

--yes--

--open communication with nearby Syganoids--

__there are no Syganoids nearby__

"Hogtied is what the man asked for. Get his feet tied to his hands. They won't allow us into the arena if he ain't hogtied." They join in a laugh fest as my feet and hands are bound together. A hood over my head brings blackness and a ballgag sinched tight, a taste of vinegar and chlorine, causing me to drool, unable to swallow my saliva. I'm hoisted upward as one of them on each side of my body takes an arm and a leg.

Perhaps I should have allowed the emergency protocols and executed extreme prejudice. I'm growing more exhausted by the never-ending interruptions to my mission by these humans. I could succeed as a humanoid against these simple people. There is a slight chance of success. But what is wrong with my cybernetics and biomechanics?

Would I even be able to trust my systems? I feel fine and I sense no cause for alarm, but now . . . there is evidence of some damage. Did the arresting officer's blow to my head do some harm?

***

When he pulled the hood off, my eyes open to see the familiar face of the indoctrination guard. Ole droop eye himself. We're nose to nose and his contorted face expresses a wide twisted smile from ear to mid-cheek bone. His teeth bent from left to right in a mismatch off two full teeth from bottom to top. "I knew you weren't right for the School of Romance," he spits the words through an enthusiastic, near hysteric laughter. "You're a fighter with huge muscles and a generous frame. Hell, boy. If I were into men, I'd want you to fuck me up the ass. Do you want to fuck me up the ass? Do yuh?"

His massive fingers work at the buckle behind my head to release the ball gag he looks up from his kneeling position over the top of me to speak to the other guards. "Hell, I think he wants to fuck all of us up the ass."

My jaw aches and sharp pains shoot through my teeth and chin as the gag is plucked out and I try to close my mouth. The six of them laugh and engage in a battle of wits over who would go first in the lineup, and which would enjoy it the most. As their macho banter went on I tried to see the surroundings to get an idea of where they had brought me.

"Listen up, big guy," he says to me with his face again pressed nose to nose with mine. "I'm going to cut you free and stand you up. You are going to be on your best behavior. But if you decide to go rogue and try to escape. Well, we will eat you alive. Literally, eat you bite for bite and let you watch as we chew every mouthful."

When I stand and catch my balance, "You will be."

"Shit no way! What did you just say?" One of the five says to me.

"The man said to me, 'You are going to be on your best behavior.' But he meant to say, 'You will be on your best behavior. It's impossible and therefore meaningless to say, "You are going to be. One can only be or not so it is correct to say you will be on your best behavior."

"Fuck this arena bullshit I'm going to kill him right now," one of the other guards says as the five hold him back away from me. "He's not worth the wasted words. I'll take care of him but let me do it in the ring. Where you guys can collect credits and earn off my ratings. Remember we're just eight thousand points from earning that side of beef. Think bout how long it's been since you tasted real meat."

As the men get their perspective they form a small circle around me. One of them hands me a container and he says, "Drink this." Then my indoctrination guard says, "This can go two ways. One, best for you. You take the carton and drink. It's just protein to give you energy and strength. Nothing else. I promise. I want you healthy and strong when we fight. I want to beat you fair so you'll know when you take your last breath that it was me that won. Second, which may go bad for all of us. We stuff a tube down your throat and into your belly and we force-feed you. Last time he tried it, the tube punctured the guy's throat and he ended up bleeding to death in the cage."

"Sure it's only protein?" I ask.

"Drink it down. All of it," he says.

"The first fight this evening is some stupid kid on a vengeance quest. It won't last long," he says. "Then it's our turn. When we get in there and the fight starts I'm not going to do anything at all. I'm a gonna stand in the center of dat cage. You get five free punches. Do your best and hit me with everything you got in that massive body and those big arms of yours. But know this. After the fifth time, you bring all that hate and anger through your fist, and if I'm still alive I'm going to beat you to death. In my mind, I see a future where my friends win real food from our war. After this fight, my eleventh in the ring, I'll get awarded nine and a half thousand credits." His eyes pierced mine and glowed with certainty and desire.

With the protein drink carton held to my lips, I waited for him to finish talking. Then I poured into my mouth the last of the liquid, saccharin-rich watered-down chocolate chalk drink. Crunched the carton in my hand and licked my lips.

"Not bad at all. I have had one sandwich and a can of Nestea and nothing else all day." Sharing a glance at all six of them, "Thanks, guys. That hit the spot."

Through the door at the far side of the damp, concentrated smell from years of sweat and no air circulation room, he pulls me by the arm. Up fifteen concrete stairs, we trek with the other five well-battled men close behind. With every step, we go higher and the sounds from the crowded arena grow louder. At the top of the flight, my eyes are momentarily blinded by the intense white light of many spotlights sweeping through the interior. They reveal the women, some seated and some standing in rows of terraced seats that surround the cage at the center of the arena. Billboards of multiple colored lights display the lineup of scheduled fights and the multiples of odds and payouts. These billboards display data for the spectator's gambling desires. The interior of the building is enormous and the distant seats at the top are visible though the faces are unrecognizable.

"Welcome Ladies!" The raspy voice of a woman announces over the amplified speakers drowning out the crowd. "Misandry Arena is proud to announce we have a sold-out arena for this evening's entertainment. Fifty-eight thousand in attendance and we promise you a brutal and bloody evening of man-on-man war in the cage." The crowd jumps to their feet and cheers at the announcement. Chanting begins at one side of the arena and spreads to a roar that vibrates the concrete floor under my feet.

"WE HATE MEN . . . WE HATE MEN . . . WE HATE MEN!"

As the tension in the arena reached its peak, a unique sight caught my attention. Seated at the announcer's booth was a rather regal-looking cat, sitting nonchalantly on a plush cushion. The announcer, a stern-looking woman with a headset, affectionately scratched behind the cat's ears between her announcements, as if the feline was her trusted companion.

My gaze then drifted to the audience, and amidst the sea of cheering spectators, I noticed a few people with their loyal canine companions. Some dogs were resting beside their owners, while others couldn't contain their excitement and wagged their tails, barking.

In another section of the stands, a young girl held a small terrier on her lap. The little dog barked, caught up in the tense atmosphere. Its owner, however, looked at me with a worried expression, as if wishing me luck and safety.

***

The announcer waited for the chanting to diminish to a murmuring roar before she continues. "The first war is ready." The spotlights swing around to illuminate the cage and two intense beams of light shine on each of the first two men standing toe to toe at the center of the cage. I recognize the smaller of the two men. It's the guy I met in the holding cell after my arrest yesterday morning.

"He wears the sun yellow sandpiper shorts and 'staying alive' Bee Gee's t-shirt. His mother had her nose broken by the bully who towers over him wearing bright white cargo shorts, black sketcher hightops, and no shirt.

"Look at his bare chest, shoulders, and the size of those big guns, ladies!" The women scream in a frenzy of enthusiasm and a group in the seats begins a chant that soon, once again, resounds from one end of the arena to the other.

"But wait, ladies. You haven't heard the worst of it. When the ambulance took his mother to the hospital where she could have her face repaired, she caught the virus. A few hours later she died a brutal coughing death while he held her, helpless in his arms. Tonight he promises to kill in revenge, the man who he says killed his mother!"

While the crowd provides the predictable exuberance I scan the cage. Its imposing presence casts an outline of gloom over the rows of onlookers. The chain-linked fence, with its unyielding bars and intricate mesh, symbolizes my confinement, leaving no room for escape. The cold, unforgiving floor of solid concrete serves as a stark reminder of the harsh reality I'm about to face. Above the circular cage, the glinting razor wire coils like a sinister crown, a menacing barrier that traps me inside and shatters any hope of freedom. Inside the suffocating space, the cage becomes a tangible manifestation of my struggle against time and the continual decline of humanity, a visual representation of the overwhelming odds stacked against me. Every bar, every strand of razor wire, echoes the relentless fight for survival.

"Go on then. Kill that goddamned man!"

The announcer screams the start of the fight. In a flash of lights and the sound of a rumble gong-like crash, the referees exit the cage, and the cage lights go off and then flicker back on again with more luminous intensity. The small guy throws his arms around the big guy and bullrushes him to the edge of the cage. They slam into the fence and bounce off. The small guy lost his balance and falls onto his back. Wasting no time, the big guy kicks the small guy in the ribs. Repeated again and six more times. Then rounds the body to do the same on his other side. When the big guy stops kicking his opponent, he walks to the center of the cage, panting for air, he raises his hands over his head to show the women a champion.

They chant back to him 'KILL HIM, KILL HIM, KILL HIM!'

After a moment of hesitation, the big guy drops his arms and returns to the still-breathing but otherwise lifeless man, lying on the floor. Settling onto one knee he gathers the little guy up and manhandles him over his left shoulder and then hoists him up as he stands. With the little guy now slung over his shoulder, the big man starts to climb the cage fence. Wedging the toes of his shoes into the narrow gaps of the chain link matrix and three-finger grips he works his way higher and higher up the fence wall.

The women chant, 'CLIMB, CLIMB, CLIMB . . . When he reaches the top, he pushes and forces the little guy's back into the razor wire.

Pain-filled screams confirm the little guy is still alive. Then the big guy takes a firm grip on the fence with his left hand and digs his shoes in as deep as he can for support. With his right arm free of the climb he lifts the little guy to push him upward. The razor wires cut deeper into the flesh and muscle. Blood rains down as the screams of horrible pain burst from the center of his being. When the little guy's head and right arm popped through the top of the wire, the big guy pushed him away and toward the center of the cage. The blood pours down and his limp body dangles lifeless. The big guy climbs down but before he can reach the bottom, the razor wire cuts through the little guy, under the weight of it and the deep sliced body flops to the cage floor into a pool of his own blood.

"Fucking great war! How about that ladies!" The announcer laughs with excitement over her blaring loudspeakers. She pets her cat as she makes the announcement. "Our cleanup crew has their hands full after that one." She continues to laugh and adds a couple 'boo yahs' in celebration.

The lights grow dim inside the cage. They sweep the audience again as the camera crews and television spokeswomen recreate and discuss what took place in the first fight. The men I thought were referees enter the cage to gather the body and escort the victor out.

"I'll provide these fine ladies with an even better show once you and I get inside that cage," he shouts in my ear. The smell of his breath is horrible, a pungent miasma that could wilt even the hardiest of flowers.

"Life has no sacred value to you humans. You're nothing but barely conscious animals." I say. The taste of the chocolate chalk drink lingered in my mouth.

While he never stops smiling as he watches the clean-up crew scouring the now-darkened cage, I see the indicator in my HUD glowing in the upper left corner.

--accept the communication--

__now connected__

→I've been trying to reach you all-day←

→why aren't you communicating with me←

--there's something going awry with my HUD and systems--

--I think the blow to my head damaged something--

--where are you--

→look over your left shoulder←

→just above the television announcers←

The woman in black stands among the excited women and all their pets. She's watching me and waiting for me to acknowledge her. I nod and feel an odd emotion of hopefulness. How strange. I've never felt or needed to experience this emotion before coming to Planet Earth.

→when the lights go out, we'll take you out of here ←

--we who are we--

--how will you take me out--

→we will discuss it later. don't resist us. once the lights go off move toward the cage doors. I'll be there←

__communication closed__

***

"Main event or not we are in for a real treat this evening," the raspy-voiced woman crashes the arena soundscape with her announcement for the next battle in the cage. "In my opinion, this should be the main event. Not taking anything away from our champion man-killer featured in this evening's final war." She retracts and covers her words from scrutiny. "Some of you will remember the meanest man-killer the Misandry Arena has ever witnessed. He's featured in many of the posters and his scarred and mangled mug is recognized by the tooth pattern permanently displayed over his face when his opponent tried to eat his face. He accomplished ten kills in this arena and holds the record for the most kills in the fewest consecutive wars."

The arena ignites with excitement as they all know the man-killer the announcer refers to.

Shouting into the already over-amplified sound system, she continues, "His opponent is a criminal and a woman hater. Today on a bus with new students for the School of Romance while on their way to the beautiful statue of our goddess, Hera, this criminal acts as a coward possessed by satan's intention. He openly speaks against women and The Great Republic of Starzel."

"He must die!" screamed someone nearby the announcer's station.

"Yes, he will die. Let's all hope our returning champion man-killer will bring the gore and slaughter this criminal deserves in the most gruesome way. He's never disappointed in this arena before."

The spotlights flood the cage and shine on us. Center stage and nose to nose with the guard who wants to kill me.

"This is showtime boy. Ready or not it's time for you to die," he says. An unfamiliar hint of calm in his voice.

"Don't take it personal. Man-killer is it? That's what the woman announcer calls you. Right?" He doesn't respond or budge a muscle. "I won't be dead when this is over, and good news for you. You won't be dead either."

"Five free shots, boy. You take the first five and then we'll see who does and who doesn't die. And we won't be playing nice like those two did in the previous war. I play for keeps."

The referees step out of the cage as the lights went off. I turned to head towards the cage door but before I took one step, the lights were back on.

"Kill him!" the announcer screams. When I look over at the announcer her cat curls its back upward, shows me rows of sharp teeth, and then hisses. Looking back now at Droop-eye, I jump back about four feet when he throws his arms out to either side.

"Nervous, boy?" he asks.

--open communication with nearby Syganoids--

__a Syganoid is within communication range__

--open communication with nearby Syganoids--

I place my hands over my eyes for an instant to allow my thought image to enhance the command on the HUD.

__communication accepted__

--what the hell is going on I thought you were going to turn off the lights and we were leaving--

→that is the plan←

→do what you can and be ready←

→we are working on it←

--working on it--

--I thought you had this planned out--

→I do have it planned out←

→now hit that monster and stay focused←

→we won't have much time to get out of here←

My most powerful punch is something I learned from watching Mike Tyson Youtube videos for how to throw a killing punch. I curl my fingers into the palm of my hands and wrap my thumb across the index finger. Squeezed my hand with all my might, ran toward the man-killer and jackhammer punch him in the throat. The sound that escaped his mouth was similar to a thrown bottle crashing into a steel wall. He steps back five times before catching his balance and stood still wheezing through a collapsed windpipe.

--okay. He's going to run out of air in about thirty seconds let's get the lights off before I have to revive him--

→revive him←

→why are you going to revive him←

--I'm not going to let him die--

--are you suggesting I should kill him--

--no way--

Both of his arms struggle to move his huge biceps out of the way so that his hands can reach his throat. It took a few twists and turns of his hands and arms but then he was able to place a hand on each side of his neck. With a rapid pop, he slaps the sides of his throat and reopened his windpipe. After taking a few deep breaths, he steps back to the center of the cage and extends his arms again.

"Classic and nostalgic ladies. Our champion man-killer's patented move allows the opponent to take the first five punches free. Don't be fooled, my fellow noblewoman. Our champion is learning the opponent's techniques and discovering his weakness."

--I'm ready when you're ready--

--hello ready here--

→almost there cherryboy←

→you need to hit him again←

→try to hit him hard this time←

--felt to me like I hit him hard the last time--

I walk clockwise around him in a three-foot radius and then pick up my pace until on the fourth round I'm at jogging speed. As I come around in front of him I leap and use all of my kinetic energy to spin kick him a direct hit to his solar plexus. The whole arena hears the crack of what must be two ribs on his right side. Again he steps back several times and falls onto one knee before catching himself. His face grimaces as he stands and collects his composure. Then he returns to his pose, center cage.

"Come on old man," I shout at him. "Stay down. You know it's not worth it."

Out of the corner of my eye, I see his five friends placing their bets at the bookie's table. I look up at the odds display and see the data has changed and it favors me to win now. When my attention returns to the ring, Droop-eye staggers a moment and his right knee twitches. In response, the odds go even more in my favor. He winks at me.

"Three more boy." His voice is still calm. "Bring your worst."

→here we go←

→move to the gate now←

With a burst of energy, I charged forward, the sensation from powerful punches and kicks connecting with bone-crunching impact, still filling the energy of the arena with a symphony of the man-killer's gasps and wheezes. Each move in the cage was a calculated dance of survival, as the clock ticked down to my escape, guided by the arcane kuudere known as the woman in black. I will live to fight another day but my fight is in the larger battle of saving humanity.

I run toward the gate. The arena goes darker than midnight. When I open the gate she's there pulling me through the vortex.

Chapter Seven

Waste of Time

Waves crash onto what appears to be an endless stretch of brilliant gold sands. Seagulls float on the churning swells and take flight to chase one another under the warm sun. The northern mountains far off in the distance appear in shades of purple outlined by a bluish-grey sky and billowing white clouds. To the east the mountains are closer still. They have white snow-capped peaks and the foreground is a rolling wall of desert foothills covered in hard-packed sand, sparse bunches of thick green leaf iceplant, ironwood, and sage. I stand here taking in the magnificence and feeling the ease of being free of the cage, and the anxiety from the drama of the last two days seems to melt.

"In all my one-hundred and twenty-six years of life on Planet Forty-Four, I have never known anyone other than my mother to die. But in the last two days on Planet Earth, I have witnessed eight people killed. Humans seem to thrive on it. Not death so much. They find it exciting to watch, read about, and commit murder."

"Wrong. They don't find it exciting at all," the woman in black says. "It isn't fun, Eulər. It has been a dominant part of their evolution and seems unavoidable to them. So, I suppose they accept it as part of living."

The sound of the waves begins to fade as we walk away from the shoreline and toward the town. When we reach the parking lot there are a dozen men engaged in conversation. Some slip out of their wetsuits, others throw a football and some hurl a frisbee. An iconic beach scene as I've seen on many videos and displayed in old movies.

"Where are we?" I ask. She paces fifteen feet ahead as I pause to take in the surrounding area.

"We are in Santa Barbara. Stop lagging behind. You have work to do. I'm taking you to meet someone who knows where to find Banyan's last book."

The sand is soft and golden, just perfect for lounging and sunbathing. It stretches for miles, giving plenty of room to relax and enjoy the coastal atmosphere. Plus, the beach is well-maintained. Dozens of men and women, children, and families with their dogs. Enjoying the beach and the sun. Their laughter and spirited, playful sounds are welcome after the vicious noise from Misandry Arena.

As the four-foot waves land on the shore, I see the water is crystal clear, and several dozen people enjoying the shallows. At the opposite end of the beach, there are several restrooms, showers, and picnic areas. A few places to grab a snack or a drink at beachside cafes and snack stands. Beach gear shops rent chairs, umbrellas, and even paddleboards.

"Look at those magnificent buildings up there on the side of the hill," she says. "Those mansions are known for their exclusivity and opulence. Some of them have stunning architectural designs, sprawling grounds, and even private pools overlooking the ocean. It's like living in your own private paradise. That's where we are going," she points at one of the many massive luxury homes on the hillside. "You'll meet someone who knows where we can find Banyan's archive, and it was his crew who helped get you out of the cage."

The words perk my spirits higher and the mission comes back into focus. "You have to stop ignoring me," she says. "When I send you communication requests I expect you to accept the requests. It's rude to ignore a kuudere. Very rude. All day yesterday and again today you shun me." She stops to face me. Her hands on her hips cause the deep v-shaped jacket to open wide and expose her bare skin, and ultra-white chest in stark contrast to the black fabric. "You're lucky that I didn't just go home and abandon you here on this Planet you hate so much."

"It's not that I'm being rude. There is something wrong with the HUD communication system because until just now, I hadn't heard from you. I've tried to locate and open the channel, but no one was within range. I think when that badge-wearing mafioso hit me with his club the blow damaged some part of my Neurolink. Besides, I will never ignore anyone."

"Which reminds me of the other thing your friend Casper told me. You have a medical procedure scheduled in three days. Mandatory procedure to upgrade your OS and devices. Are you kidding me with coming here and you know your systems are years ago outdated? When he told me . . . I refused to take the project but he talked me into it. So, alright maybe you haven't been ignoring me and maybe you aren't being rude. But, in my opinion, you are in no condition to succeed on any mission to Planet Earth.

"Do you want to explain to me why we are here? Your father couldn't explain it. He said you are on a secret mission for The Source. Casper couldn't explain it. He said you are a member of an elite cosmic phenomena. Give me a break, I say. Please!" I can almost hear the eye roles.

"Clue me in?" Her arm swings through the air as she directs me to follow. A second swing of her forearm suggests hurrying me along. As we continue, much to her chagrin, I say nothing to further explain the mission.

After crossing the PCH we pass through The Best Pancakes restaurant. The savory aroma of the sausages with the enticing fragrance of freshly baked dough filled the cafe. As we hurry past the buffet, I take a couple of the pigs in a blanket and scarf them down as we exit out the side door. They are savory, slightly salty, and buttery with crispy fried batter yet tender to chew. A natural umami experience. I can hear her huff as I turn and run back inside to grab three more and a flask of water.

We zig-zag our way through the village and then take a sudden left turn onto a narrow trail between a row of homes. She leads me into the garage of a mansion situated at the end of the trail. At the far side of the empty six-stall garage hangs a bronze cast, three-dimensional, artwork of letters. "MGTOW."

She pounds on the door with the cusp of her left hand. A moment later the door swings open.

***

"You did come back, and this must be the 'one and only' Eulər," he says. The tall, thin man with handsome features and onyx-green eyes. He looks like a well-groomed surfer with short blonde hair and a Coppertone tan. His deep wrinkled skin looks weathered from many years outside in the surf and sun. His hand extended as he welcomes us through the door with a gracious smile. "The woman has told me you might have found yourself in a lot of trouble down south in Los

Angeles County. The feminists put you on trial for being a free man. Shit, it all goes to show how bad this world has become. Well, don't worry about being a man here in this county. We allow men to be free. In fact, we insist on it."

As we release the handshake he leads us further into the mansion. Passing through the large kitchen and billiard room, we come into a grand room decorated with many lush, deep-cushioned recliners and reading chairs. The room features several floor-to-ceiling and a meter and a half wide windows, but they are covered in thick fabric to filter the natural light. The ceiling is tall, I'd guess fifteen feet or four meters high with the long side of the room lit with directional, low luster, recessed fixtures. The main feature of the room was a wall of twelve televisions. Four columns of three, all hung on the wall, side by side and top to bottom. Each television was on and displays a different program.

"These are the main broadcasts from the six countries that used to be the forty-eight United States. Now they are war-torn territory and deeply divided nations. They televise a steady stream of propaganda for their citizens to stay asleep in the propaganda their elitist governments spread. Hear in Starzel we hack into their satellite broadcast through a company called Pluto TV. They are headquartered at the Pacific Design Center over in West Hollywood. Deep inside The Great Republic of Starzel and far behind the borders where the fighting continues. They can't keep Texarkana out of the basalt mines."

Stood in front of a wall of monitors in awe of the depth of color and panorama details. "What is MGTOW? I saw the acronym on the wall in the garage where we came in," I ask.

"Men Going Their Own Way," he says as he guides me over toward one of the windows. "It is an anti-feminist, anti-nationalism, misogynistic group advocating for men to separate themselves from women and from a society that has been corrupted by feminism. Most feminists, both male and female, call us by the acronym, MGTOW. In my mind, I see us in a different way than that. I see our society as an opportunity to live in freedom.

"See this billboard display?" He points out the window in the distance there stands a larger-than-life-size tower on the side of the PCH and the display across the top scrolls with a message in text and iconic images. "And we spread the message on nationally syndicated television too. The message is clear and shares a single truth about women and the world's grievances against women."

As we stand here watching the billboard, he narrates the message. "Why do women spend so long on their appearance? Because it's all they have to offer." In the one hundred and seventy thousand years of humankind, the only contribution to society from women are:

1) venereal diseases

2) alimony and oneway child support

3) media and gossip

With a sharp tug on the curtain, it closes and we turn back toward the wall of television monitors. My HUD displays warnings scrolling over the televised images. Each time a station breaks for a commercial, the warning messages scroll over the image.

__corrupt pro-nationalistic messages and brainwaves containing subliminal messages__

__prolonged exposure to repeated messages will cause altered states of being__

"How often do you watch these broadcasts?" I ask.

"From time to time I guess. Like once or twice a day I come in to see what is going on. Say, well I don't know for sure. Maybe fifteen, twenty minutes a day. I guess I never thought about it. Why do you ask?" He asks.

"There's something about the commercials that makes me suspicious, is all."

__communication request received__

--accept the communication request--

__communication accepted__

→these warnings are precipitous←

→cruel even←

--precipitous--

--that's an odd way to describe what you probably mean to say is dangerous--

→he knows we are humanoids←

→he spotted me right off←

→you can trust him←

--it's not polite for us to talk this way--

--the kuudere would not want us to make this a habit--

--though I find it less distracting than verbal communication--

→verbal keeps us more in touch with the human side of our being←

→you know←

→it keeps us aware of humanity's struggles←

--it does not keep us aware--

--it makes us aware--

→your father was right about you and your constant need for correcting another's speech←

→you are infuriating and frustrating to speak with←

--close communication--

__communication closed__

__communication request received__

--reject all requests for ten minutes--

__ten minutes starting now__

He steps back from the monitors and looks at the woman in black. "You told me he was pretty smart. I see what you mean. He's big, strong, and makes a good first impression too." He chuckles and looks back and forth between us. "I have long suspected there was something odd about televised commercials and many other network and syndicated programs as well. Can you get a read on how it's done? I mean, can you describe what the technique is?"

"Not from watching the broadcast. I would have to get a look at the code they use for video production. Maybe then I could define it," I say.

"That would be impossible," he says. Shaking his head as he walks to a recliner and sits. "If I could get my hands on the station's software, I'd give it to you. But the stations and the top positions working in the stations are all held by women. At least that is, in feminist-controlled and ruled Starzel. There's no way that any of the men here could get their hands on it. And none of us would put any women living here at risk for such a clandestine mission."

From the side of the recliner, he lifts up my backpack and hands it over to me. "This is yours, isn't it?"

"How did you get it from the courthouse?" I ask.

"We have people in strategic places and positions and I thought you would want this back. There's something more. I can help you on your mission to find the original writing from Banyan. Would you want my help?"

***

Before I can ask him what he knew of Banyan, lights flicker and alarms chirp several times, he rose from his chair and dashes out of the room in response to the sudden indications. My eyes follow him as I switch to magnetic resonance imaging. He soon disappears from sight. The electromagnetics and heat signatures grow too distant to trace.

A woman dressed as an early twentieth-century housekeeper brings a tray of coffee cups and a pitcher of coffee into the room and leaves it on the sideboard. The aroma of dark roasted beans fills the room. Then the woman in black follows her through a wall becoming intangible.

I had no idea she could do that. How would she metabolize at a frequency that fast? She must be learning these skills from Casper. So . . . she's one of his students.

My thoughts are interrupted when he comes back into the room.

"Sorry for the disruption. My electrical box has been hijacked recently and we have a tracer set up with alarms to locate the source," he says.

"Banyan? You said something about knowing where to find his writings and unpublished works."

"Your woman friend told me that you went looking for him in Culver City and I know for a fact that he's never been in Culver City. Those were rumors started in the nineteenth century by the mayor to get tourists to visit the city. Which was an armpit of a slog city then, and it is even worse now as it is overrun with bigoted feminists and PUA. If you want to find Banyan's true writing haunts, you will have to go to Europe. He wrote everything of any meaning and value when he traveled to the country of Andorra. While he was on a pilgrimage hike known as El Camino, the path took him high into the Pyrenees mountains. He felt the calling to write and moved to the small, farmer's village of . . ." his voice dropped off and he stood looking down at the travertine-tiled floor.

"What is it?" I ask. "Are you all right?"

He stood silent for several minutes then he motioned for me to come with him. He walked to the far end of the large television room to the opposite side farthest from the wall of monitors. Taking a seat in a large, green, upholstered, and well-cushioned sitting chair. "Please join me." He motions his right hand for me to sit in the duplicate chair beside his.

"Before I tell you the exact location of where to find Banyan, I need your help with a perplexing problem."

"I'm not sure how I can help you, but if I can, I will."

His expression is that of a desperate man. "The virus is destroying our planet. Humankind will be extinct in less than five years. That's what my health advisors have told me. If we can't get a cure soon, the tipping point is only three months from now. Even with a cure if it takes longer than three months it will be too late."

While he speaks my attention is distracted when out of the corner of my eye I glimpse a disturbing scene in the center of the wall of monitors. Instantly I tug and pull on my mother's ring as I watch the images on the monitor. His left-hand reaches over and takes hold of my right arm.

"Sorry to trouble you with this issue. I'm sure you have more to worry about than what happens here on this planet," he says.

"Don't be dismissive," I say. "I do care about humanity and people. But, the monitor there in the center-right, what is that all about?"

"Christ be damned! Not again with this shit," he says.

"What is it?" I ask.

"There, in The Republic of The Heartland, they have a law against mass shootings. Mass shootings are an epidemic that has spread since back in the days of the United States. Some madness takes hold of someone who then gets her hands on a rapid-fire rifle with a large clip for ammunition and she goes on a shooting spree. After killing as many people as she can the Government and media go on a frenzy of campaigning and selling advertising to make a ton of money. Meanwhile, the citizens watch in dismay. Nothing changes, and a few weeks later, bata boom, another shooter repeats the killing in another town, another school, or another office somewhere. In their Republic, the law they created to combat the shooting is pure evil.

"First they bind the shooter to a pole in the center of the stage. Then they bring in the immediate family. Sons, daughters, wife, husband, father, mother, siblings, uncles and aunts, and grandparents. The armed militia stands behind the shooter and when they get the green light."

The monitor is broadcasting exactly what he describes. The man tied to the pole, and about ten feet in front of him is a gathering of what must be his immediate family. I count nineteen people. A green light is lit behind them and in a flash, they all fall dead. Four uniformed officers from behind the shooter opened fire on the family, killing them all.

After the family was shot, his grip on my arm tightened. "Those ignorant lunatics," he says.

"What is the point of killing the family?" I ask.

"They kill the shooter now. Watch if you can. One of the militia will put a bullet in the back of the shooter's head." As he spoke, the monitor verified the action.

"There is no point to the killing," I say.

"Like it or not, The Heartland government is determined to extinguish the epidemic by putting an end to the spread of a contaminated DNA strain. The punishment goes further. After killing the immediate family and the shooter, they take all the first and second cousins and blast them into space to work the rest of their lives as miners in the asteroid belt. Solves a few problems. First, they can't find any other way to get workers into the mines and second, it is supposed to take away the glory of being a mass shooter.

"The virus is to blame for all of the madness spreading across our world. The sickness runs deeper than just an obvious lung and bronchial tube infection. My theory is there is something more sinister than the mutations and spread of a simple virus. People don't behave in this way. It isn't normal to crave wealth, crave killing, and to hate others."

His eyes dash from side to side as he stares into my eyes while making an impassioned speech. When he stops and releases my arm his gaze turns back toward the wall of television monitors.

***

Housekeeping brings another tray of cups and a pot of coffee. Replace the previous and untouched offerings on top of the sideboard. The woman in black is still following along and the two appear to be in a deep conversation.

"There is coffee on the sideboard," I say. "Shall we try it? It's the second tray she brought in. I wonder why she keeps bringing it in when nobody is asking for it?"

Not a word was spoken while we decorate our cups with sugar cubes and milk. Filled to the brim, we make our way back to the green chairs. I sip the steamy off-white liquid. The taste is bold and a sweet and bitter combination tickles my senses.

The need for MGTOW, to save men from a world that has over time made him a utility and a tool. A vessel, a pawn for war, grunt work, and to be treated with disdain. Is this part of the rift in the universe something I have caused? Have my tinkerings with the code and

meaningless alterations caused humanity to grow disrespectful of men?
Was my disrespect for my responsibility as guardian of the code the cause
for this decline?

"Suspicion is often intuition disguised. This eighth sense is a back-of-the-brain gland that is a master sleuth. I too suspect there is more than meets the eye. Such as when you left the room earlier to attend to the electrical system. You told me that someone has hacked your system, but I believe it is you hacking theirs." His face and eyes race to hide the emotion of being found out. "It's no big deal," I continue. "Let's face it. There are a lot of men trying to get out of The Great Starzel Republic. However, do whatever you need to do. If you can be the help that sets them free and help them to live a better life is well endorsed by me.

"In my understanding of Planet Earth's history in regards to human civilization, Marx had his finger on the button. According to Marx's theory of historical materialism, societies pass through six stages: primitive communism, slave society, feudalism, capitalism, socialism and finally global stateless communism. The virus is an unforeseen anomaly and therefore, it is an unnatural, man-made scheme."

Life returns to his demeanor and after he swallows down the warm, rich-tasting coffee he fast steps to the sideboard. Setting the saucer and cup down he turns back to me.

"This is a critical point to make. As we examine the narratives of men coming into our city and living free of feminism. We look at their stories and what we find with great redundancy is the expectation for them to perform for women. From the mandate to please mothers, to protection and provision for women, to heroic sacrifice, and even down to the basic assumed responsibility for the female orgasm, we see men in a role to satisfy through performance.

"MGTOW is the manifestation of one word: 'No.' Rejecting modern culture's definition of manhood, we refuse to bow, serve and kneel for the opportunity to be treated like a disposable utility. The MGTOW man looks out for one thing, living according to his own best interests in a world which would rather he didn't.

"In our governing, MGTOW, we have a bone to pick with anyone who opposes our masculine ideology, including the authorities. We deserve to be autonomous and free to exercise supreme authority. Our contributions to society over one hundred and seventy thousand years include everything of value to the quality of life. We built roads, put roofs over our heads, learned to work the ground to grow food, process food, extract minerals, produce minerals into products, found medicines and cures, discovered water treatments, nutrition, healthcare, mathematics, engineering, and the list goes on for centuries. It is so easy and simple to claim that women could do all the same and through oppressive masculinity they didn't but that is nothing less than a cop-out. You know it, and they know it too. While they do have brainwashed men who fight and kill for their feminist ideals, we have men who evolved to know better. And tens of thousands of women live here who all disagree with the era of the lady and feminism.

"Without the virus, I believe we are on the cusp of getting people back to a world where we embrace humanity and love the contrasts. And these men here have a massive job ahead of them in carving out a place in life where the needs for social connection are not met at the cost of living lies. Sadly, I think the trauma that so often leads men to go their own way, also sours them on humanity. Thus, we see the push for artificial remedies for a virtual existence. And while no one in their right mind would stand in harsh judgment about men seeking refuge in those things, our need for each other remains as it always has"

The words and ideals he speaks are holy and it is impossible to disagree. Men and women are trapped in this duality of existence together. Only together will we free ourselves of suffering. The more people separate and divide, the more lines of separation manifest. It is the code of the universe. The way to freedom is through unification. I listen to him speak more about the glory of mankind.

"Maslow's ladder withstood the test of time. Obviously, each man who beats the so-called -- red pill -- isolation will have his own way of doing it. I think though, if my own path is any indication, that it requires the willingness to risk, to roll the dice on people, even though people are more often a source of disappointment than satisfaction. That reality only proves that we face the same dilemmas as -- blue-pill -- men, only our radar for disappointments is a little sharper.

"It isn't fair of me to hold you hostage. Banyan was in Andorra. Go there to find what you are looking for. The farm village of Sispany.

"If you can, help us fight the virus. I know you will."

As our conversation reaches the end, my emotions remain in turmoil--a blend of guilt, determination, and a burning sense of purpose. I must find the strength to carry the burden of my past actions and turn them into a catalyst for change. The journey to Andorra will be a test of my resolve and my willingness to make amends for the world I might have inadvertently shaped. But amid this guilt, a flicker of resolution ignites within me. If I indeed hold the key to stopping feminism and restoring men to their former glory, I must take responsibility for my actions and set things right. My quest to uncover the truth behind the clues now leading me to Andorra takes on profound importance.

Chapter Eight

Great Wealth & Benefit

L og entry 4, day ninety-six. The woman in black found the harmonic resonance and it brought us to Bera, in Spain. I've taken one of the country's fusion-powered busses, which makes its last stop at Sispany in Andora. On this hours-long journey, I held onto the destiny stone and mother's ring in either hand. Thoughts of their killing and more killings in the days of this mission haunt me.

Burdened further by the realization that my actions brought about the deteriorating morality of women and disrespect of men by nations, I embark on a journey of self-reflection. With humility, accountability, and a renewed purpose, I look for personal growth and reconciliation.

By seizing opportunities of great wealth and benefit, the traditional ways of the kuudere, I aim now to rectify the damage I caused and fulfill my mission to find and replace the missing code, restoring balance to the universe. Making men whole again and returning women to respectable beings.

From the moment she entered the bus, I could tell she had more on her mind than she could manage. Deep in thought she managed to climb the three steps, paid the bus fare, grabbed her ticket, and made her way to an empty seat. She was only going through the motions and not fully conscious of her actions. She didn't, for example, notice how she had cut off the elderly man with his cane trying to negotiate the first step up into the bus as she whisked past him and he fell onto his backside trying to avoid her collision. She didn't acknowledge the driver's greeting as he wished her a good morning and told her she should help the old gentleman. The seat she dropped herself onto is marked for handicapped passengers, which she is not. I saw an opportunity, and one like this can't be ignored.

To acquire great wealth and benefit I would simply take advantage of her empty-minded action. I rush to the front of the bus, offer my hand through the open bus door and help the old man to get up the steps. Once he is safely inside, I turn to the driver, "I'll cover the man's fare but would you wait until we find him a seat before you start driving? He's already taken one tumble to the ground this morning."

"Sure thing mister. That was a nice thing you did there," the driver agrees.

"Wait here for a moment," I say to the man. He is busy examining the damage to his cane and gives me a quick, uncomfortable nod.

With a knowing wave to the driver, my hand asks for another minute as I place my right knee on the floor and clasp my hands together in front of my chest. I confront the hurried woman in the handicapped seat. "Excuse me, may I bother you to please allow this gentleman to use the handicap seat you are in?"

Patience is a bonus for the reward of merit. I wait there a moment and then she lifts her head from the tablet. Her light brown eyes engage with mine. She looks me over wondering why I am kneeling here in front of her. Her short, natural brunette, fringe bob hairstyle accentuates her oval face, and when she looks me in the eyes again, I share a gracious smile and bow my head.

My eighth sense hints at her profession as a journalist or reporter. She is dressed in professional attire, exuding a sense of purpose and determination. Her clothing is well-tailored, suggesting attention to detail and a desire to make a professional impression.

The woman carries a laptop case that prominently displays the logo of Pluto TV, a recognizable broadcasting company. The presence of this logo indicates her affiliation or connection with the media industry.

"What, is this?" She asks. Her voice is soft but not high-pitched. "I didn't realize I was in the old guy's seat. Of course, I will move." Startled that she had taken the designated seat. She rushes to gather herself, the tablet, and a laptop case slung over her left shoulder, and moves down the aisle of the crowded bus until she finds a seat.

But what catches me off guard is when our eyes briefly met again. "That is the most amazing ring I have ever seen. I absolutely love the design pattern. It is brilliant." Her admiring comments about my mother's ring linger in the air, filled with a genuine appreciation for the sentimental value of the heirloom.

The gentleman gets situated in the handicapped seat. The driver closes the door, flips a switch that raises the bus from the curb, and with an audible huff, steers the bus on its way.

After returning to my seat the merit and wealth just gained felt warm in my chest and my ears felt oddly hot. If it is my fault, and the history of mankind is decaying because of something I've done, I need the merit to save my True Self. The bus driver is watching the actions in the rearview mirror and as I sit here, I can see the driver watching me. Our eyes meet in the reflection and we exchange nods. The driver checks his watch huffs again and then pushes the bus to go a bit faster.

As the bus makes its way through the small mountain valley towns and villages, moving along the paved narrow road. The morning rush hour traffic finds several more public transports each one filled with passengers. The walkways on either side of the street are busy with people too. Everyone going to work I suppose. The myriad of small taverns and cafes are busy too as most people stop for coffee and toast before continuing on their way. Tobacco stores and newspaper stands are still popular in Europe as the communities insist on a more family and people-centered way of life.

Morning and late evenings are the busiest times of the day for socialism and taking active participation in the local community. In these modern times, the newspaper is again the main source of propaganda and syndicated influence for the wedge. The popular middle-class word, wedge, refers to political scuttlebutt.

"Did the wedge get broken?" I wonder as I look out of the window and watch these morning activities of traffic and people looking for any hint. The busy woman seems to be part of the wedge. My eleventh sense of perception tells me that somehow she's involved in the momentum of the altered universe code. Or, perhaps someday she will be.

I did catch her eye but she was so disengaged with her presence that I'm not sure about her involvement with the wedge. If the wedge didn't break then I only got half of the value of merit and half of the benefit. There's nothing to be done about it now.

The sun reflects off the polished windows of a cafe as the bus maneuvers around a tight corner and a steep incline as we near the village center. My thoughts culminate and the present moment concentration returns to observing the day and the journey. Seven minutes later, "Shops and tourist attractions. Old Town district," the bus driver announces. This is my destination. Banyan wrote the code for humanity here in this old village center of Sispany. Nearly everyone on the bus is getting off at this popular destination though for different reasons than mine.

***

Just fifty steps from the bus stop I took a seat at a sidewalk tavern. The waiter takes my order. A cup of hot black tea, lemon, and steamed milk. The tavern is not particularly impressive to look at. To the casual passerby, there isn't anything here that would cause them to stop or take notice. The tavern is small with just five white plastic tables and small plastic chairs set up on the sidewalk outside. The small corner tavern of maybe 300 meters squared is further dwarfed by the three-story parent building that occupies the entire city block. There are many small stores, fruit and vegetable markets, and businesses that occupy the first floor while apartments make up the top two floors.

From my sidewalk table, I can see through the open door of the cafe. Inside, there are just three more plastic tables and a sparse liquor stock, but a crowded display above the barkeeper's station. The small bar itself features a single, very worn-out but sturdy, four-legged wooden barstool. Nobody would know, just by looking at the place, the significant universal code imprint event that took place in this little agricultural village. It was a code of all humanity and it centered around this tiny tavern several thousand years ago.

If I was to write about this moment I wonder what words and how would I use them to express my senses. Perhaps; as I sit here at this humble sidewalk tavern, the cool mountain breeze gently rustles my hair, carrying a hint of nostalgia in its invisible embrace. With every sip of the hot black tea, bitter lemon, laced with creamy milk, I feel a connection to the past, as if the taste itself holds the echoes of the historical event that unfolded here. The smooth touch of the stoneware cup in my hands, worn with time like the tavern's history, becomes a conduit for reverence towards the universal code of compassion that was once written. The sun gently bathes the scene in golden light, casting a soft glow over the memories that dance before my eyes, and toy with my imagination as I contemplate the significance of this unassuming yet momentous place.

Light-hearted as I stop the pursuit of authoring and waxing poetic, my fingers impulsive, tugging and twisting at Mother's ring. My head feels odd and a hot flash causes my neck to sweat.

My sense of recall and presence tell me that Banyan himself sat here. He was writing the code after translating the historical events that had been taking place.

My memory recalls the significance and how the historical event started out with a poor migrant worker's daughter who had four sons from four different men.

Her migrant farm-working parents traveled with the seasons across the country trying to find work as sharecroppers and pickers. When their daughter was pregnant with a fourth child they knew they couldn't afford to feed her and all the grandchildren so they told her to leave. A few days later, with her and her children starving, weak, frazzled, and afraid that death would soon take her children's and her own life, she begged the tavern owner for a job.

The tavern owner seeing she was pregnant asked her why her husband wasn't providing for his wife and children. She told the owner the truth, she relayed to him the details of her four children, their four fathers, and her poor migrant parents who could no longer afford to support her. The tavern owner listened to her story of circumstances and he could feel the emotion from her frail voice that she was nearing collapse and certain death. The owner is a prominent figure in the town and despite the possible questioning and damage to his reputation in the community, he hired her. Not wanting to lose business by having a woman with four children from four different men working at his tavern he gave her work in the back of the tavern. There she was busy preparing food, washing dishes, fetching wood, and keeping the fire burning. She was charged with many jobs and he told her to stay out of sight. Not one person should ever know that she worked at his tavern for fear of gaining a bad reputation and losing business.

For many years she did just as he told her to do. She worked in the back of the tavern making certain no one would see her. She worked from early morning until late at night cooking, preparing, and cleaning the floor, the tables, chairs, the kitchen, and the entire tavern every evening before leaving. Only after it was dark and when no one could see would she leave and only in the very early morning when the town's people were still in their homes, would she go to work.

Though she worked six days a week, the tavern owner could only afford to pay her for two or three days, but somehow it was enough. She managed to take care of her four sons with a little bit of pay and a small amount of food that he gave her. Her four sons wanted nothing as she made certain that everything they required was provided.

The waiter brings more tea and I ask him, "Have you ever seen me before? Do you recognize me?"

"That's an odd question," he withholds a laugh as he replies. "Do you remember being here before? Some kind of deja vu?"

"I'm remembering a story about the original owner of this tavern and a woman he hired. The memory is . . . hyperthymesia. How do I know this story so well?" He gives me a queer sideways look. "The memory of these two people and this tavern are as vivid to me as the smell of the hot black tea rising from my cup. It's as if I was here when it happened."

"Then perhaps you wrote it. Or maybe you read it? Cus this place is thousands of years old so there's no way you could have been here back then." He looks through the open doors into the tavern and a photo on the wall behind the bar. "Sorry mister, but I have to get those plates before the food goes cold. The people at that table inside are waiting."

When he walks away, I watch him until he disappears from sight after he rounds the open doors back inside the tavern. I take the multi-colored stoneware cup from the matching saucer and take a sip of tea. My memory recall picks up where it left off.

***

Then one day, after many years of working with him the tavern owner didn't open the tavern. She went back into the woods where she would leave her children in a thick grove of trees and spent the odd day with her four sons. The next morning when he again didn't come to work she was worried. Despite his insisting that no one should know she worked for him, by this time, years later, though nobody mentioned it, everybody knew. So, she asked around hoping to discover if anyone knew where he was. After asking four or five people, it was another tavern owner who knew where the man lived.

She went to his house and found him sick and barely able to speak. He couldn't lift himself up or even swallow the water she offered him. She asked him if she should find his children, or brother or a sister, but he had no one for her to contact. He had no family and never had time for a wife and children. He was alone. She stayed with him for as long as possible but when evening came it was necessary for her to return to her children. She helped him to drink some water, and she was able to help him sit upright, she cleaned his face, and hands, and washed his feet. Once he was comfortable, she left.

The next morning the tavern owner didn't open the tavern again. She went to his home and he was sicker than he had been the day before. He wasn't even able to open his eyes or to speak at all, and by the third day, he was dead. There was no family to contact and since he had no one, she decided she would need to carry out the responsibility for his burial. She gathered her sons and brought them to his house. She put them to work gathering the wood for the pyre while she prepared the ceremonial circle for the cremation. She carried his body out and managed with the help of her four sons to place him respectfully on the pyre.

She and her sons sang the death songs and provided the eight actions for honoring the deceased. They provided for the tavern owner as if they were his family and heirs. She lit the fire and then they watched and circumambulated the pier sun-wise every seven minutes until the body was completely transformed by the fire and even stayed seated in lotus pose praying until the cinders had cooled.

After the fire ceremony was completed and the last of the eight actions of the deceased was completed she instructed the two oldest sons to go back into the forest where they had been living. She told them to gather the blankets and what few belongings they had and then bring them back to the tavern owner's house. Since the tavern owner had no family and no relatives at all she decided to take up living in his home. While they were gone to gather the items from the forest, she and the two youngest sons cleaned the house and prepared it as if it was their own.

The next morning she went to the tavern the same as she had been doing for many years. Once she arrived she tied a heavy blanket over her shoulders and fashioned a sari over her head and face. She carried each table out to the street including four chairs for each table. She did everything necessary to prepare the tavern for business. When the people of the town began to arrive for their morning tea and bread she prepared the water, seeped the tea leaves, and toasted the bread. She served each patron but said not a word to any of them. When they asked her, "Where is the man who owns the tavern?" she dared not answer.

Once again, I reach for the cup of tea but the cup isn't there and the plastic table has changed. My hand touches a stony table top and I test the contours of the smooth sandstone. The view straight ahead is blurred like looking through a thick fog. *It's a dream-like sensation of a past recollection, perhaps this is a recurring dream?* When I look back at the table I see there's a tablet and a quill in front of me. The writing on the tablet looks like code. *Is that the missing data, is it The Universe code?* At the bottom of the page is a name. I can't make out the signature or see any of the writing with clarity. I close my eyes for a moment hoping my sight will clear and then open them wide trying to better focus on the writing.

When I open my eyes, the white plastic table is there. My hands are holding the stoneware cup.

"Are you okay, mate?" the waiter asks. "You look pale and confused."

"Not a problem. I'm fine. Just a bit distracted in thoughts."

But despite his words, as he hurries away the vivid memory of the story continues.

She had been so worried and focused on opening the tavern that she forgot about getting food for the midday meal. She began to panic and wondered what she could do for the midday meal. Many businessmen and shoppers regularly come to the tavern for food and coffee and She didn't dare close the tavern now because everyone would certainly stop coming to the tavern after being closed four days in a row. The business had already missed several days of previous business and she noticed the number of morning patrons was already far fewer than normal.

My thoughts are again interrupted when the waiter returns with a fresh cup of black tea, lemon, and steamed milk.

"Where are you from, mate?" the waiter inquires. "I don't recognize your clothing as being from this continent. Just a guess, but I'd say you come from Cascadia in North America. Am I right?"

***

His round face grew a large smile as he stood tall beside my table. He is at least six and a half feet tall, and he stands staring down at me waiting for my reply. He's a young man too, probably in his early thirties. And, it's obvious to see he is fit, probably a bodybuilder.

"It looks to me that you're in great condition," I say with a hint of jealous respect. "I'd guess you're a bodybuilder?" I ask.

The waiter laughs and nods affirmatively. "Nobody in their right mind would add steamed milk to tea, mate. And lemon!" He spits out an insulting hysterical laugh. "Lemon curdles the milk. It has to be a most horrible-tasting cuppa." When a sudden gust of cold air hits the tavern everyone grabs the placemats and napkins taking flight. Undaunted, he continues laughing and shaking his head as he walks away from the table and rushes back inside the tavern.

Through my tight squinted eyes I watch him go back inside the tavern while I squeeze the lemon, pour in the milk, and stir my tea. When he enters through the door of the tavern the reflection in the glass catches my attention. The reflection reveals the scene taking place behind me. A camera crew is busy setting up in the town square across the street.

"That's her!" I say aloud. It's the hurried woman from the bus. She's standing across the street directing a small group of performers while the camera crew, lights, booms, and reflectors are going up all around them. The team busies themselves with her barking orders and then she is joined by who, I imagine, must be the set director. The director goes over the shooting board with them encouraging them to get into character and mimics with hands directing how the cameras and crew will shoot the video.

Here's another great opportunity to gain great wealth and benefit.

The shooting board software would have the coding for the brainwashing that the studio and network use. Perhaps I could hack into the director's laptop. I close my eyes and wonder about the recollection of the ancient story about the woman with four sons from four different fathers. And the vision and sensation of having been here before. The tablet in my hands and the page with the signature. As I reflect on these the sensation and emotion return. Again I feel as if I have been here long ago.

What is the signature on the tablet?

When I open my eyes the tablet is here in my hands. The vision is again blurred but it begins to come into focus. In a flash, startled by the signature, I blink and the vision vanishes.

"Banyan"

The sight of it went by me in a flash but was recognizable and as clear as the reflection of the camera crew in the glass window in front of me.

If this story came from Banyan, and the Universe is revealing it to me here, then I must have the missing data now. If so, then I can return home and repair the file. The Universe Code for humanity will be repaired.

My eyes and thoughts return to concentrate on the scene across the street. I see the hurried woman and her team. They sit around the set and watch as the director and her talks through the sequence outlined on the shooting board. If I'm going to hack the laptop I will have to get close enough to allow the AGI device inside my left hip joint to crack and hack the operating system. With one last mouthful from the cup of tea, I fidget with my mother's ring and then a plan comes to me.

People are still contaminated and the virus hasn't changed at all. This story hasn't changed anything. How could it? It's just some random woman who gave five minutes of pleasure to four different men and earned herself four sons in return. There's nothing ethereal in this story. Only suffering, and more suffering.

As I weigh out the situation in my head a memory flashback ignites. While she was waiting for the harmonic balance to open the portal to Spain, the woman in black told me,

"Starzel was once a part of the United States. Today it is a country on one of the two remaining human-occupied planets still using democracy and elected officials to organize and run the politically manipulated, mafia-style of government. The elected in Starzel are chosen based on their popularity, which is largely determined by their television ratings. The bigger the star, the more people watch and interact on social media, while the person is on television shows, or in music, or sports, etcetera, the higher in government their position of power. Feminism has control and laws are enacted to further the rise and dominance of women."

"Don't they know," I asked her, *"that most civilizations on other planets have used artificial superintelligence to provide government oversight? Machines provide for the prosperity of the people."*

"Sad to say it, but no they don't," she says. *"Starzel is a country where very few people live well. For that matter, on the whole of Planet Earth,*

more than sixty percent of the inhabitants live in poverty while just a few thousand, less than one percent of the population, control the wealth."

The flashback memory only serves to aggravate me further. There is so much to consider. I need to take action. Maybe there is some importance in recalling the story, the vision of Banyan's tablet and his signature, and now this network television recording crew manifest. I need to think!

What is the stark difference between prosperous planets like my home world and Earth? None of the prosperous planets allow elaborate television production sets with multiple camera angles and sophisticated lighting, artificial and mind-controlling backdrops, white noise, and camera techniques. Civilized planets realize that social prosperity isn't something for the few but a right for everyone and such devices social media, camera tricks, and televised broadcasts filled with reactionary content does not serve social well-being. These are the tools that define and drive a wedge between social groups.

The man in the mansion from Santa Barbara told me just before the woman in black opened the portal,

"The shooting board software is used to define the plan of manipulation," he said. Grabbing my upper arm in his hand to enforce the message, "It's the tool that psychologists, and highly trained politically influenced public relations scientists use to ensure the recording and editing of the video is perfectly able to control the minds of anyone and everyone who watches. Starzel, like most of the other countries on Planet Earth, has used artificial general intelligence (AGI) to optimize the shooting board and video editing software to gain maximum mind control of the population. The planets of Earth and Mars, as well as the Moon populations, have become violently divided and the political party-contaminated mafioso governments are authoritarian dictatorships rather than democracies. It is well known outside of these

two planets that television and movies are a tool for corruption and the star-struck populations are incapable of surviving the elite-controlled media manipulation. What we cannot figure out is how they spread the brainwashing and why isn't everyone afflicted."

Once more he said to me, "If you can help, I know you will."

***

If I can get close enough to the laptop, I can capture the shooting board software. If I capture it, there's a good chance that artificial superintelligence (ASI) can study it and uncover how the elite-controlled media of Starzel and Planet Earth are brainwashing the population. Then MGTOW can put an end to whatever is driving the wedge, causing widespread viruses of violence and hate. Also, if the data I found here from Banyan's story is the missing data I need, I would see it. But everything here in the present time is still wrong.

"The drone cameras are going to be two hours late!" a set designer yells out to the director.

The set director throws her arms up in disgust. "Those jerks do this every time," she yells at no one in particular. "Well," she says to the team seated in front of her, "that's lunch."

Not wasting any more time I upload the necessary nft to the nft-reader on the table to pay for the tea. Fast stepping my way toward the production crew and straight over to the director and team. "Have you ever heard the story of the greatest chef from ancient times?" I ask them in a voice that sounds like a circus caller trying to entice the patrons into his theater. "Let me tell you the story if you have five minutes, and you can try to guess who the most famous chef is."

The crew gather around me and seem excited by the thought of a guessing game for a celebrity chef. Someone shouted out, "I bet it's Ramsey." And a few others said, "it must be Alton Brown." The very notion of it being someone famous is enough to capture their attention. They are from Starzel after all. Meanwhile, I maneuver around the group to a position as close to the set director's laptop as I can. Once they have gathered around I start to tell the story.

The heads-up display from my Neuralink provides the notice I need, flashing a navy-blue message in the lower right window, the proximity of the laptop. Once the device is within an optimal precision range. I attempt to download the entire OS from the laptop.

--connect to a device The Laptop--

__attempting to acquire a connection__

__connected to The Laptop__

--copy entire OS--

__password required for The Laptop__

--neutralize password requirements--

__attempting to bypass passwords__

__copy resumed__

__The Laptop passwords are neutralized__

The story I share with them is about the woman with four children from four different men and how one day she found herself running the tavern on her own.

"She had forgotten to gather food at the markets before opening for the day. It was nearing time for the midday meal and all she could find in the kitchen was three kilos of tomatoes, several heads of garlic, a few dozen leeks, and a half kilo of ginger. It would have to be enough, she thought. Then she used the branch side of a large pine cone to grate the tomatoes into a very large bowl. She did the same with the leeks, ginger, and garlic. She mulled the vegetables until they were completely pureed and then strained the liquids through a canvass sieve.

"As the people of the village began to sit outside at the tables, she ladled the mixture into bowls and served it with a thick slice of bread. To her surprise, everyone loved the brew and asked her, 'What is this lovely dish that you bring us for the midday meal?'"

Distracted by the bright red flash of a warning message, I pause from telling the story to focus on the AGI display of the HUD. Noting that it is making slow progress, I glance over and see the laptop has gone into hibernation. This is slowing down the data transfer to a crawl. I'll have to slow down telling them my story.

"Come on then. Let's hear the rest of the tall tale," says the director.

"Yes, go on with it," seconds the hurried woman.

With a nod to each of them, I take a moment longer to rub my eyes and then continue. "Word began to spread about the tasty broth served at the tavern during the midday meal. As the days, weeks, and months went past and over the next several years everyone became familiar with the tavern. The woman and the broth gained notoriety and her fame spread. After a while the lines of people waiting for the midday meal would wrap around the town square and many people would come from villages near and far. Oftentimes she would run out of broth before being able to serve them all."

As I stand amidst the buzzing film crew on Starzel's set, the intense overhead lights cast a stifling warmth upon my skin, intensifying the sense of urgency that courses through my veins. Beads of sweat form on my forehead, and I wipe them away with the back of my hand, feeling the moisture on my fingertips. The taste of anticipation lingers in my mouth. It's thick like the memory of gazpacho from the story I spun for them. My heart pounds like a drum, each beat echoing the seconds ticking away as I try to maintain my composure. I can't afford to falter now; this is my chance to uncover the truth behind media manipulation. As the crew leans in, captivated by my storytelling, I focus on the task at hand, my senses sharpened to the sounds of their hushed voices and the flashes of bright colors around me. This is my moment, and I must seize it.

"It's gazpacho," one of the set crew shouts out. "The broth she made them is called gazpacho," he says to the large number of curious people that have gathered around.

When he spoke my attention was distracted by a vision. Outside my periphery, I glimpsed towards the tavern and a man seated outside where I had been seated several minutes ago. I turn to look and the tavern appears as it was many hundreds of years ago. Slate-topped tables and hard wooden bench seats. The man is writing on a tablet and stops for a moment to look up and when he sees me looking back at him, he seems as perplexed by the vision as I am.

That must be Banyan, but I feel that odd sixteenth sense of my having seen and experienced this before.

*The vision of
Banyan*

The Vision of Banyan

Chapter Nine

A Bunch of B.S.

***

"Am I right?" The crew member asks. "It was gazpacho she invented, right?"

Nodding in the affirmative, I continue with the story about the woman with four children from four different men.

"Well, time moves forward as always and next thing we know years have passed and her four sons have grown and married. Their mother has managed to get each of her sons well-established in the community with their own businesses and each of them married well too. As word continued to spread to other regions about the delicious broth and the now famous tavern, the king of the land that was once called Madhya Pradesh, gathered his entire entourage of five thousand and an army of twenty thousand for a journey to the village. They traveled for eighteen days before they reached the village. On the nineteenth day, the king and ten of his advisors went to the tavern for the midday meal.

"Everyone in the village and from many other villages had gathered around the tavern to see the king and his men. Therefore, the general of the king's army knowing it would be necessary sent guards to keep the people back at a good distance. Once the king and his advisors arrived at the tavern and had been seated she greeted them with the five postures of honor and respect. She gave them, in the way all leaders of humans should be served, a jug of water. Then she brought them each a large bowl of broth and a loaf of dark bread. After the woman served the king and honored him in all the ways a king should be honored, and after he finished the meal he told his closest advisor that he wanted to have an audience with the woman. Then the king, the advisors, and all of the soldiers left the tavern except the one advisor who stayed behind to deliver the king's invitation.

"The advisor remained at the tavern drinking ale and watching her clean the tables and serve the other patrons until late in the evening and the tavern was closed. The woman with four sons from four different men approached the king's trusted advisor. She showed him respect by performing the five rests. When she completed the performance she asked if he needed more ale or more food. 'No, I require nothing more,' he replied. She stood back away from his table at a respectable distance and waited for him to request whatever he may request. It is customary for tavern owners to remain open until the last patron leaves the tavern."

"This story is a bunch of crap and just plain BS!" The set director bursts in and interrupts.

"Yeah. No shit. This sounds like a bullshit conspiracy story from Texarkana, or maybe Trump Nation!" Another member of the production team adds in support of the director's comment.

"Those people lie with every breath and make up these conspiracy shit stories all the time," adds still another from the production team.

"It's the liar's curse," said the hurried woman from the bus. As she says it, she stands and walks toward me.

"What's the liar's curse?" asked someone in the crowd. The crowd has been steadily growing in numbers of people around the tavern to listen to my story.

The hurried woman walked over and stood next to me, after looking directly into my eyes, she holds my attention for an acknowledgeable moment and she gives me a sly but reassuring wink. So, then she turned to face the crew and gave a wave to the crowd.

Standing beside me she answered them, "The conservatives from The Heartland, just like the Republicans and Confederacy in Trump Nation, tell so many lies and make up so many conspiracies they believe everyone else tells lies too. They are self-convinced that no one is truthful and everyone is a liar just like they are. So they live in a constant state of fear, disbelief, and hate. That's the liar's curse."

The set director replies, "He looks like he's from Cascadia," as she points at me. "Just look at what he's wearing, no one in Starzel, or Europe dresses like him."

Then the hurried woman on the attack snaps back at her, as she waves her hands motioning to the entire team and the crowd of people in an attempt to capture everyone's attention, "This man is not from Starzel, nor is the story he is telling us a lie. He can prove to everyone that the story is true."

The director shrugs in a sign of skepticism and asks, "If this tavern woman with four sons from four different men is a famous chef from eight hundred or, wot ever . . . eight thousand years ago, why haven't any of us been able to guess who she is?"

A deafening silence settles over the town square as all eyes stare at the hurried woman and me. She looks at me, and again she made direct eye contact as she spoke, "Go ahead," she says to me, "show them the proof that the story is true."

Her eyes remained locked with mine as she slowly turned her head towards the tavern. Her movements guide me to follow her eyes and to look across the square to the tavern. As I do, it becomes obvious what she wants me to see, the proof of the story was right there inside the tavern doors hanging on the wall.

"You don't have to believe me, but I think you cannot disagree with her!" I say while at the same time pointing to the tavern wall.

Displayed on the tavern's wall is a large advertisement that filled the entire front of the tavern. The advertising poster was a larger-than-life-size headshot I don't at first glance recognize, but can imagine is a well-known feminist of a Starzel-syndicated show. The poster read, "Home of the original Gazpacho. Known throughout the entire universe."

***

As everyone looks to see where I am pointing, The hurried woman says with a stern commanding tone, "If it's true enough for Nancy Pelosi, the founding mother of The Great Starzel Republic to put her face to it, then none of us can say otherwise."

The stunned and somewhat exasperated director replies, "Well that's just amazing. Why don't I know about this place?" She shakes her head in self-deprecating acceptance and then says, "Well everyone, let's have gazpacho. No! Make that, let's have the original gazpacho for lunch."

When she stands from her director's chair, she grabs the laptop from the portable table and tucks it under her right arm. The indicator in the lower right corner of my HUD signals a green flashing message. Download completed.

--restore password function to the laptop--

__password function disabled__

What is going on with my HUD functions? I'm going to have to find time to read that diagnostic report.

--restore password function--

__password function is enabled__

--erase history for the last ninety-one minutes--

__waiting__

--what are you waiting on--

__would you like to open the diagnostics report__

--no--

--erase history for the last ninety-one minutes--

__waiting__

The director takes the first chair at the nearby table as we reach the tavern. Me hovering beside her as my Neurolink and HUD communications continued to malfunction. She looks up from her chair giving me a queer-eyed glance.

__history has been cleaned__

--disconnect from The Laptop--

"Sorry mate," I say pretending to go for the same chair as she. "You got here just before me. I'll grab another chair."

__device, The Laptop not found__

--disconnect from The Laptop--

Her face turns stern and just as she starts to question me hovering over her . . .

__disconnected__

While I am struggling to get the internal biomechanical systems to work correctly, the entire production team has walked across the square to the tavern. The waiter brought several more tables out to accommodate the large crowd that followed. He's trotting around to bring more chairs from storage inside the tavern while some people decide to leave rather than wait.

This is a chance for me to make a break away from the group. If I act fast, the production team won't notice me leaving and I will go find a hostel for the night and start sorting through what the OS hack was able to download from the director's laptop.

"I know who you are", the hurried woman whispers. She's caught up to me as I tried to blend in with the crowd. "What I mean is I know why you're here and I want to tell you I hope you can help save us from destroying ourselves."

A polite smile forms and I give her a nervous nod in the affirmative and then I turn to leave.

"Hey!" Shouts the director. "Where are you going, story-man? You have to tell us the rest of the story. I want to know what the king wants from the tavern woman."

"Hell yeah, me too!" another woman says. "I will buy you lunch. Come on, dude we want to hear what the king wants with the woman with four sons from four different men." The crew chuckles and several of them wave me over to join them at the tavern.

The hurried woman locks her arm in mine and then escorts me over to the tavern and the crew.

While I am anxious to investigate the director's shooting board software and upload the findings to the Tathagata ASI system to help me find a solution, I am reminded that opportunities for great wealth and benefit can never be ignored. The merit of the story is earned when the story is heard in its entirety. I accept the invitation and continue telling them the sacred story.

"The king's trusted advisor waited for a long period as he sat at the tavern long after everyone in the city had returned to their homes. Finally, he asked the woman with four sons from four different men to join him at the table.

"It is not of my station to sit with such a revered and highly accomplished one of the king's most trusted advisors," she replied.

"Then come closer to my table to hear what I have to say regarding the king's request to have an appointment with you. It's late and I am tired, full of ale and I don't want to shout across the tavern."

She bowed her head and moved closer to where he was seated.

"Come to the king's tent on the morning of the next day. Come early and be ready to hear what the king has to tell you." After saying this he stood to leave but before he went he placed a very large sum of money on the table. The sum of money was more than what was necessary to pay for the king's meal with his advisors and more than she would have made for the entire day.

"When the appropriate time arrived, the woman with four sons from four different men went to the king's tent as she had been instructed. There the king invited her into his court and asked her to tell him all there was to know about her life. The woman bowed to the king and showed him the seven signs of respect and honor the way all kings should be shown respect and honor. Then she kneeled, sat back on her heels, with her head lowered, her hands on her knees, palms up, and told him everything.

"She told him about her four sons from four different men. How her parents were poor crop pickers and could not afford to care for her and the four sons. She told him of the conversation with the tavern owner when she and her sons were near death from hunger and hardships. She recounted the story of the tavern owner's death and how she and her sons served his passing and performed his service with honor and respect. She told him how she took up living in the tavern owner's house and took up running the tavern. She told him how she cared for her sons as they grew, providing them with all she could of herself and the income she earned from the tavern. All four of her sons were now well established in businesses and had obtained good marriages."

***

"I'll take your drink orders first," says the waiter as he goes from table to table. With me acting as patron entertainment, strolling around each table as I tell the end of the mystery. My head and soul are still bewildered as I marvel at how I came to know this legendary tale with such detail. My mother's ring seems tighter on my finger and my sixteenth sense is keenly aware of the scene.

"The king was very impressed that a simple abandoned woman with four sons and only a simple tavern in so small a village could accomplish so much for her children. He asked her how it was that she came to know how to greet a king and how to perform the high acts of honor and respect to him and his royal advisors. 'My parents showed me the way,' she replied. 'My parents taught me how to show honor and respect for kings and they taught me how to pay honor and respect even to the highest most honored one as well.'

"After hearing everything she had to tell him, he asked her to join his trusted advisors as the chief of the king's kitchen. 'Please forgive me for refusing the gracious honor of the good king,' she replied. 'But if I could ask for a different position in your service. If you, the great king of Madhya Pradesh and all of Andora, would honor me instead with one remaining desire in my life, good king, I will vow to instruct your kitchen chef on how to prepare the gazpacho.'

"The king being impressed with the woman, and so he listened and considered her request. She asked him to provide her with the necessary land, resources, and his approval to build the first holy stupa at the top of Mount Santis and in so doing to honor the Buddhas. 'It will be a place where limitless numbers of people could come to acquire great merit and a monument to serve as a support for the eternal wisdom mind of the Buddhas,' she said.

"The king was blown away and he was compelled to grant her the land and access to all the supplies to build the stupa. She had spent everything she made raising her four sons, gave them all she could to get them established in their own business, guided them to find suitable wives and now she wants to give everything she has remaining in her life to building a stupa where countless numbers of people will benefit from great merit.

"After calling his counsel to join them in the King's meeting. The woman on his right and his treasurer beside him on the left, he told them. 'The businessmen and farmers of my kingdom come to me with requests to make their lives easier and richer. Every day I am asked to provide them with more land, more money, more soldiers, and more resources of all manners. This woman is the first to ask me for something that benefits everyone. Her request makes all of us wealthier and happier. She will have my seal to have whatever is required to complete her project.' The king so instructed his counsel and advisers.

"With the land granted and permission secured, the woman and her sons began construction. After two years the structure was already standing at a height of three tiers. The local aristocrats became intensely jealous; despite all their wealth, they had never generated such an aspiration as this poor, single, paltry woman. They saw the rising structure only as a testament to their miserliness and greed. They made an appointment so they could take their case before the king. They wanted the king to stop the construction and order each stone of the holy stupa to be returned to where it came from.

"The great king refused their pleas explaining to them how the woman's request was so astounding that his exclamation of approval would not be recanted.

"Construction continued unceasingly over the next six years. Everything was completed except for the holy stupa's gold dome. But the woman at this time realized her life was nearing its end. She gathered her four sons by her side. She requested they complete the holy stupa, fill it with the relics of all the Buddhas, and then perform an extensive consecration festival. This, she assured them, would provide a field of great wealth and benefit merit for infinite numbers of sentient beings. She told them to fulfill her wish and the wishes of the Buddhas and allow for the accomplishment of something vastly meaningful for this life and future lives.

"After she spoke these final words, she passed away. The ancient legend tells us at the moment of her death, music resounded from heaven and flowers rained down from a sky filled with streams of rainbow lights. These were all signs of her attainment of Buddhahood from the great wealth of merit she had accumulated in her life."

Hallucinatory, visions of the tavern begin to fill my eyes and again the area transforms into another time of an ancient year. Banyan is gone, and nobody is here. He's left his tablet on a table with the pages open. I look closer to see what he left for me to see.

The signature again? It's as clear as before, "Banyan," but there is something more. Something is written below the signature that wasn't there before. EA2222, it reads.

The warning message flashes red in the center of my HUD and disrupts my post-cognition.

__critical override__

__memory device error__

Not three hours ago she told me this could happen. I recall the woman in black saying to me before I left her in Bera, "Your implants are outdated and should have been replaced a year ago. Are you an idiot, or what? Your HUD is faulty and getting worse by the day and you never get my messages. How am I supposed to do what Casper asked me to do and keep you safe?"

She shoved me in the chest with both hands. "You are scheduled for the operation of the upgrades but this assignment came up as immediate and critical. Though no one could tell me what we are doing here. It must be critical because I was there when your father tried to postpone the operation.

"The implant will be for the beta version of the newest full cognition with complete linking capability for up to eight external devices; the Neuralink 7.19b. I would give my back teeth for those upgrades." She tries to appeal to my sense of intrigue. "Right now, I imagine those upgrades are necessary for this mission to succeed. You are a liability to yourself and the Universe. I will not let you miss the appointment! I'll drag you kicking and screaming if necessary."

Still distracted by the memory device error, I check the list of available memory devices to see if I can access the software the director uses for creating the shooting boards. It is there. Relieved, I take a deep ujjai breath. Sorted by the last update time, I see the device is operational. "Yes," I say aloud, forgetting there are a couple of dozen people waiting for me to finish telling the story.

They can wait another minute.

In a few seconds, I've got the investigative system scanning the OS to identify the algorithm the software uses to optimize the camera angles, backgrounds, audio tone, lighting, and shooting techniques. That's exactly what I'm hoping to find.

I'll need a lot of time to analyze and prepare the software before I upload it to the Tathagata system.

"Where did you go Story Man?" the director shouts between slurps and spoons full of gazpacho. Amidst the lively ambiance of the tavern, the tale I told them unfolds like an ethereal thread, weaving through the hearts of those who listen. Each word carries the weight of centuries, and the legend of the woman's unwavering determination left the onlookers in awe, their minds wandering to the mysterious past and the boundless possibilities of the future.

__warning highly contagious viruses are imminent in ten minutes__

__warning virus protective capability will expire in ten minutes__

__life at risk bio systems failure_

***

I'm not going to die! These system failures are like the visions of Banyan and the tavern. Illusions. There is nothing wrong with me and though my HUD sends these perilous flashing messages, I'm still a capable and superior humanoid. Telling the story of the first holy stupa provides me with great wealth and benefit for all who hear it, but it must be told all the way through to the end. And for this assignment, I need all the wealth and benefit I can obtain. It will help right these evils I know result from my tinkering. Yes, I am anxious to start analyzing the algorithms inside the shooting board software, and right now I am seeing the warnings from the Neuralink HUD, I must hurry to complete the story.

--I must complete the story of the woman, Jaczimin, first--

__I can't help with that__

__do you want to access the first priority__

--what is the first priority--

__virus infection imminent in two minutes__

Focus now. I lock my gaze on the hurried woman's eyes, ignore the errant messages from the HUD, and continue with the story.

"Her four sons continued their efforts to fulfill their mother's aspiration. After just three more years, the holy stupa was completed. As they placed the -life tree- at the structure's center, thereby fully consecrating the holy stupa, Buddha Kashyapa along with all the Buddhas and Bodhisattvas from the ten directions are said to have appeared in the sky to celebrate the completion of this great accomplishment. At the time of consecration, the legend states, 'From the awakened forms of the gathered Buddhas, countless myriads of millions of light rays shone so that for three days there seemed no difference between day and night.'

"The great one, Kashyapa, spoke to the four sons. He told them because their mother's aspirations had been fulfilled with such pure, altruistic motivation, the assembled Buddhas and Bodhisattvas promised the four sons that each of their aspirations would also be fulfilled.

"The eldest brother, the son of the horse keeper, aspired to be reborn as a king in the northern land of Tivlabet to establish the teachings of the Buddha Shakyamuni. He was the wheel turning, King Trisong Detsen, the royal establisher of the dharma.

"The son of the swineherder aspired to be reborn as a pure, fully ordained monk who would uphold the holy monastic order in Tivlabet. He became the great abbot Shantarakshita, and he was the first abbot of Tivlabet.

"The son of the dog keeper aspired to be reborn as a master of mantras, to thereby tame malevolent forces and help his brothers protect the dharma in Tivlabet. He was Guru Rinpoche, the great tantric master who subdued all of Tivlabet's hostile beings through the power of his mantras.

"The youngest brother, the son of the poultry keeper, realized that his three older brothers might be reborn in different locations and times and therefore aspired to be born as one who could connect them and allow them to reunite in their future lives. He was reborn as the royal minister Nanam Dorje Dudjom, the king's minister responsible for inviting Guru Rinpoche to Tivlabet."

After a moment of silence, the hurried woman asks, "Where is this first stupa located? Is it still there?"

One of the women on the crew spoke up and answered while pulling a warm sweater over her shoulders, "It's been moved some time ago and is now in Katmarnu. The forbidden zone of China and the Asian Alliances."

The day is getting colder as the breeze has been joined by occasional gusts of what feels like air from the tops of the snow-capped peaks that surround the village. Clouds have taken over much of the sky and their thick billowing shapes veil and unveil the bright sun.

My HUD has been flashing warnings for several minutes now. I've been here too long and my sensory brain protections are reaching capacity. If I don't leave soon, like everyone around me, my mind will be subjected to brainwashing.

"What I like is the Buddha guy, what's his name, Kashy-something or other gave each son some sort of special gift for helping their mother," the director smacks, chewing a mouthful of bread. "But," she continues, "what happened to those wealthy business guys who tried to make the king stop the woman from building whatever it is called -- holy spooka thing?"

A few of the crew laugh at her mocking question.

"According to the ancient scriptures," I say, "they are the first in the lineage of the worst of humankind. Some of their names you might recall from history: Jingus, Mussolini, Stalin, Hitler, Reagan, Franco, Trump, and Williams. But, the worst of their karma was the father of the Aryan religion: Butler."

Turning to the hurried woman, the star of the show, I say, "I have to go." Then I walk away from the tavern and the camera crew. The HUD is still flashing danger signals.

__warning highly contagious viruses are imminent in four seconds__

__warning virus protective capability will expire in four minutes__

Adrenaline rushes through my body as the Neuralink implants are triggering my brain to produce the immediate energy necessary for escaping the contaminated air and sensory-altering sound waves. Planet Earth is contaminated, though most of the inhabitants will tell you that it's just a made-up story born from the conspiracy chasers. Scientific proofs be damned. The people of Planet Earth are entrapped.

They aren't hopelessly lost in the wedge, not as long as I am here to help everyone escape the Aryan devastation.

__warning highly contagious viruses are imminent in three minutes__

__warning virus protective capability expired__

Not more than three seconds after I reach the bus stop a hydrogen-fuel cargo van screeches to a stop directly in front of me. The side door of the van powers itself open.

"Come on," someone calls out from inside the van. "Get in here, Eulər!"

The van is covered from front to back and top to bottom with the logo, Tathagata. With no hesitation, I leap to get inside. The door powers itself closed behind me.

"Sit down right here," a very slender man wearing a respirator hiding his face from view says while pointing at a captain's chair.

As I follow the instruction and take the assigned seat. The van peels away and starts down the street at a high speed. The slender man hands me a respirator as he lectures.

"We've been getting warning messages from you for more than twenty minutes. What's wrong with your HUD? Didn't you see the danger signals? Why don't you answer my messages?"

Then, I attempt to explain that I was obtaining great wealth and benefit. It couldn't be helped. But he cuts me off short.

"Well lucky for you I have a Moderna vaccine available." As he is saying it, the slender man stabs the long-needled syringe into my thigh and injects a cold liquid into my leg. "But you're contaminated now man, and this injection of Nanos will need three, no," he hesitates, "You better give them four days to make sure all the damage to your humanoid implants, as well as the organoids, are repaired."

As the van pulls up to an elaborate-looking hostel, the slender man presses the button to power the sliding door open. He grabs my arm firmly, as I start to step out and onto the walk. We make eye contact and he says, "Oh hell no man! Look at you . . . You shouldn't even be on this assignment, never ever come to Planet Earth with that outdated Neuralink." He releases the grip on my arm. "Leave that respirator on for the full four days. Whatever you do, stay indoors, too!" he shouts out of the van door as it closes and the van speeds away.

Chapter Ten

The Shooting Board

Though I couldn't watch the journey from the captain's chair I was aware of the van's voyage to the hostel. Its ascent, navigating the winding streets of the village. Arriving at a five-story townhouse, which serves as a hostel. The townhouse is part of a series of interconnected dwellings that stretch along the narrow street.

As I step into the hostel, a holographic host materializes before me, its projection flickering slightly. Its voice carries an air of warmth and hospitality as it addresses me by name.

"Welcome, Eulər. I've been expecting you. Make yourself at home. I understand you will be staying here as a guest for some time. I hope you will find this hostel suitable to your liking."

I offer a nod of gratitude to the holographic host, appreciating the gesture of personalized welcome. With a mix of curiosity and weariness, I proceed further into the hostel, eager to settle in and navigate the challenges that lie ahead.

Curious about the occupied stasis chambers, I gesture towards them and inquire, "Are those the Sleepy Joe stasis chambers?"

The holographic host nods, acknowledging my question. "Yes, those are modified stasis chambers designed to serve a more medicinal purpose," it explains. "Many of our patrons use them for fasting periods of two to three days, or even longer durations for dietary and mental rejuvenation, such as indulging in opium or embarking on hallucinogenic journeys.

"Your time in our modern facilities grants you forty minutes of recreational use per week. However, I must inform you that wearing the respirator is not permitted inside the Sleepy Joe chambers."

When it mentions opium I become aware of the scent of opium smoke from the Sleepy Joes. With its rich, earthy, and slightly sweet, and a hint of floral and spicy undertones. We use it for special occasions on Planet Forty-Four because the smoke exudes a warm and enveloping quality, creating an atmosphere of relaxation and contemplation. The scent can evoke a sense of mystery and nostalgia, often associated with exotic and distant historical events.

"If it's all the same to you, I won't be indulging in recreation," I say. "Where's my room, please."

"But of course, Eulər. You have the penthouse on the fifth floor. Use the eye scanner on the door for access. The lift is opposite the staircase." The voice from the holographic image lacks the warmth, spontaneity, and emotional resonance of genuine human interaction. Each word is carefully pronounced, but it is missing a natural cadence and rhythm.

As I head up the stairway the host shouts up the corridor, informing me of the hostel policy for noise control, guests, and cooking and I ignore the rest of it.

The room is spacious and well-furnished. Two bedrooms, a fully equipped kitchen, and a high-tech modern furnished living room. The large central window looks out over the luscious park in its full bloom and trees with new leaves exude an atmosphere of tranquility and natural beauty. Tall trees towered above grass and walks, their branches swaying in the cool breeze. Lush hedges, vibrant shrubs, and blooming flowers adorned the landscape, painting a visual representation of the onset of the spring season.

Taking four days to stay off the grid is all I will need to analyze the shooting board and prepare a solution for upload to the artificial superintelligence (ASI) system, Tathagata. But, that means an entire week will go by and the Universe code for humanity is decaying by the second. If I stay focused on one task, there is a chance of saving humanity but which task? While I consider the options I hold the destiny stone in my hand.

The missing code requires that I find the unpublished work from Banyan and then hope that it will include some information about this so-called, The First Priority. The visions I saw at the tavern today are clues to The First Priority, but the story isn't the answer. It can't be since nothing has changed. Or has it?

Still, I can't help but wonder where the memory of the story came from and why I remembered it when I got to the tavern. The last clue from today is a real puzzler. What was the code below the signature EA2222? My mind flashes back as I recall Banyan sitting at the slate table looking at me, looking at him.

These humans are facing a killing virus that spreads fast and kills within minutes. The virus attacks the lungs and bronchial tubes. There aren't any clues or diagnostics available for developing a solution. And, with my failing organoid and biomechanics, I can't diagnose the disease.

Devastation and rapid decay in human quality of life are obvious and seem to be accelerating. Already the former United States and Canada have been destroyed by violent wars and now six more inhumane governed countries emerged in their place.

Brainwashing systems are key to Aryan manipulation. I think this has to be where I place my time and try to establish a cure. It has to be that this software holds the manipulation code. Since my systems are failing I will have to use the conscious machine, Tathagatta, to find the cure.

The shooting board is used to define and show every single shot of an advertising film in a pre-drawn image. Thus the number of images always corresponds to the number of camera settings in the later video recording. The representation in different image sizes (for example as long shots or half shots) is the rule. I'm familiar with the process and can download any information I need from the Starlink satellite system.

--connect to Starlink access code syganoid7musk7--

__starlink prime connection successful__

__Musk Ultimate Knowledge Engaged__

--download and read file--

<//>The director is always responsible for the briefing and content of a shooting board. The basis is a predeveloped shortlist, i.e. the written list with all shots that are necessary to tell a story. Cunning professionals among the directors or draftsmen consider it a matter of honor to visualize not only the image detail but also the perspective characteristics of the planned camera lenses (wide-angle, long focal lengths). To keep the effort small, the detailed accuracy of a shooting board is limited.

Aryan-owned and controlled video production companies are using ASI to design shooting boards not just for cinema and television movies, but also for the growing popular televised and syndicated opinion broadcasts. For the last thirty years, it is believed that three countries are actively using supercomputers for science and military exploration. Before the year 1978, artificial intelligence was only a concept and most computer scientists in the twentieth century believed it would be several hundred more years in the future before a computer would be programmed with super-intelligence. However, the Aryans in the early twentieth century were secretly developing ASI for a specific purpose. They wanted to use television and radio broadcasts to control the human race so the Aryans could prosper from global slavery behind the guise of capitalism. With a computer-aided designed shooting board, the production of the video was enhanced to cause the human brain to develop and become more easily manipulated, belief-biased, and less trusting of reasoning, logic, and scientific proof.

Their focus has always been on advertising. Aryans use the ASI-designed software for producing video, including the sound bites and background music for radio to be particularly hypnotic. When producing commercials, a shooting board is regularly used. It is the last and most important step before an advertisement video and audio are recorded. The reason it is a critical step before the recording starts is that it anticipates editing and lays the foundation for planning the day of shooting or in the recording booth.

Every single second counts in mind-control advertising, precise and clean planning are half the battle. Remember too, that each day of shooting costs a small fortune. It is therefore very important for the director to know exactly what is to be shot step-by-step in the pre-production phase. The shooting board plays a vital role here. For the Aryans, it is critical to use every opportunity to plant their mind-controlling virus into every second of every commercial.

For a feature film of ninety minutes or more in length, it is usually not economically justifiable to draw each individual film frame in advance. Here, the shot list alone should be sufficient. For the Aryan production companies in the 1960s and '70s with their sophisticated use of ASI to develop the shooting boards, every frame was easily produced and many film writers and production companies soon began to use them exclusively. By 1970, eighty percent of cinema and seventy percent of advertising companies relied on Aryan-owned production and development businesses.<//>

Taking a break from the Musk Ultimate Knowledge report, I realize it's all boring and about as dry as watching desert sand on a prickly pear cactus. I'm starving and there's not one bit of food in the room.

--locate glovo food delivery--

__what service, restaurant, specific food__

--oriental cuisine--

__there are eleven restaurants nearby__

__choose one or view menus__

--order pad thai and a bottle of ardbeg--

__order placed__

__delivery in twenty-one minutes__

✳✳✳

A demanding single knock comes from the door. Before I can engage my sensory devices to investigate it, the doorbell rings six times in rapid succession. Placing my backpack on the foot of the bed, I set my twenty-eight-inch holographic laptop on top of the small round table at the center of the room. I take a deep breath and exhale slow while I count to three before opening the door.

"Hey, man. This be da livry for some Eulər? It's Thai food and whiskey but I never heard of this whiskey called Ardbeg, man? It's expensive stuff too. So, you Eulər?"

A short man stands outside my door holding a bag and a bottle of Ardbeg. A black bicycle perched against the side of the wall next to the lift. I assume this to be his. There is no usual insulated carrying box with the Glovo logo on the back rack, nothing at all that shows he's a delivery employee. He's wearing cargo shorts, white socks, white cross trainers, and a deep blue t-shirt with the words, STOP IT NOW written in large yellow letters. He's unkempt with muffed black hair, an unshaven face, and deep wrinkles in his clothes that suggest he has been wearing them for several days. I recognize him, having seen him earlier today at the tavern.

I take it all in, opening the door further while he speaks. Then he's finished and I look into his face and give him a top to bottom once over before looking him in the eyes.

"I am Eulər. Yes, I've ordered the food and whiskey. It's a Eulər."

"There are no initials? Not A. Eulər, just Eulər?" He responds with a lack of confidence.

"Not my point," I said while taking the whiskey from him and working the foil wrapping off the top, uncorking the bottle. "You said, 'This is for some Eulər.' What you meant to say was this is for a Eulər." I take a pull of whiskey and enjoy the peppery feeling on the back of the tongue and the smokey-sweet taste.

"Why are you delivering this order instead of a drone?"

His head askew and he persists to end his sentences with a question even when it isn't. "I don't get what you mean? That is I'm unsure of the meaning? But we don't ever use drones for delivery anymore? All of the EU banned drones use for jobs people can do? There's the whole young people and unemployment issue, see?"

While we talk I investigate my suspicions.

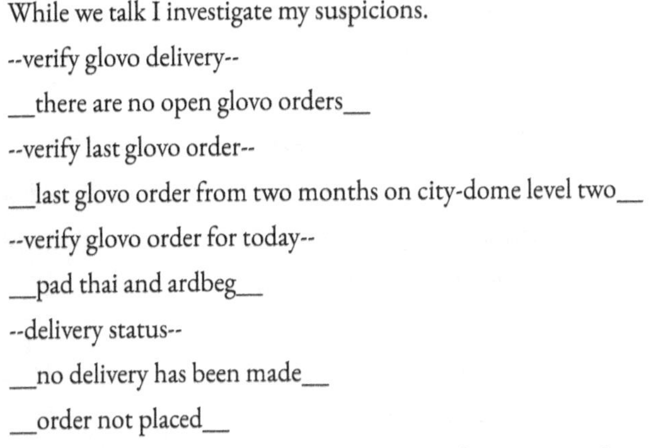

--verify glovo delivery--

__there are no open glovo orders__

--verify last glovo order--

__last glovo order from two months on city-dome level two__

--verify glovo order for today--

__pad thai and ardbeg__

--delivery status--

__no delivery has been made__

__order not placed__

My HUD system is a disaster. One time it works, next time it's wonky.

"Super idea and policy. I'm glad you found a job you are qualified for."

"Actually, wow man, uhm see I am a college student making my way through to a degree in the arts," he smirks.

"You speak with the skills of a lower-class, uneducated fool. I find it hard to believe any university would allow you in their program. What sort of art degree?"

His demeanor adjusts as he stands tall, runs his fingers through his hair and for a moment considers himself. "Sorry for the sloppy speaking and jive? I suppose the act is just that. An act. Anyway, my degree is in cinematography and performing arts."

"The act is off-putting and ending every sentence in a question makes you sound dull and dimwitted." Just before closing the door, I ask him, "Do you know anything about a storyboard?"

"I know a lot about the storyboard. We use a storyboard before we build a set or schedule the first recording. It's critical to the success of the video recording."

Accept it and believe it. I think, now convinced without any doubt, my Neurolink and embedded software programs are failing. The

Earth-born viruses have got me and I don't know what I can trust from my HUD at this point. I'll have to do this the old-fashioned way and use my gut feeling.

"How would you like to earn some extra money and help me with a project? I have a storyboard program from a major syndicated production company that I'm trying to debug. Myself, I find the project to be about as exciting as watching lirks dig holes in the ice on Planet Te. I could use your help."

His eyes pop wide open. "Are you serious right now?" He fist pumps the air above him several times. "I can take a look at the program. But I might not find where the bug is. I make no promises."

"What do you know about the history of the software they use?" I ask as I assess his knowledge. He is confident and eager as he replies.

"The storyboard always shows only single scenes or film sequences. As soon as a video or film is illustrated with pictures throughout, it becomes a shooting board. Nevertheless, both terms are not consistently distinguished and applied in video production outside of advertising film. The main task of the shooting board in commercial film production is to enable the agency and the client to check the content for verification of the way the story is told, for completeness, and comprehensibility in advance of the actual shooting."

"Why don't you come back when your shift ends to give me a hand? I'll give you ten thousand in the NFT of your choice," I say.

A smile takes over his face, "You were my last delivery. I can start now. Do you have any lunar Dogecoin or Mars even? And may I ask, why are you wearing the respirator? Nobody wears those anymore. The virus is a hoax and a conspiracy."

"If you don't mind, I would rather not get into it with you. Come in, and let me set you up with this laptop." I point to the twenty-eight-inch computer on the small round table. He pulls a chair over to the table. Still wearing an ear-to-ear smile, he sits in front of the large laptop and opens it. The display immediately lights and the word, SYGANOID displays.

"Is that a new computer game? I never heard of it," he asks.

With my head bobbing side to side, "Not now. Let's focus on what you can tell me about the storyboard. Tell me more. Then I'll tell you about Syganoid."

***

Like a professor lecturing before the class, he continues telling me the background while I mirror the software from my biomechanical storage devices to the laptop.

"The storyboard has a different task in TV commercials. It is used when the advertising agency wants to convince its client of the implementation idea. That's why visualization here is much less a planning basis than a sales tool. Further, that's why it usually comes in color and is often based on the language of a comic book as a sequential narrative.

"Can I be serious with you? Eulər is your name right?"

With a few more pulls off the Ardbeg bottle, my nerves begin to stiffen and my confidence strengthens. "Please do be serious with me. I need your help, and my project is in your capable hands now," I say.

"It's just that there are several of my friends working with me to. . . how can I say this? We have evidence that Aryan-led businesses have used software to brainwash people. If that sounds too crazy, man, I will leave."

The smell of pad thai spreads through the room as I open the sack and pull open the container. I'm standing about two meters from him with his back to me as he clicks away at the keyboard and mouse pad.

__food contamination detected__

__three fluid ounces of narcotics, sleeping agent__

"Do you want some of this delicious-smelling pad thai?" I ask.

"None of that for me thank you. I try to never eat after eight at night. But, I'm serious about the Aryans and this software. They are evil and they are power hungry."

"How did you know I had hijacked the director's laptop?" I ask as I walk past him to sit on the end of the bed facing him. The container of food in my left hand and chopsticks in my right perched and ready to dig into the pad thai.

He pretends to be surprised but before he can say a word I continue. "I saw you standing in the crowd while I was telling everyone about the woman with four sons from four different men. I saw you again after we moved from the square and went to the restaurant. You sat at the table beside me and right behind the director." I flip the noodles from the container using chopsticks to stir and mix the flavors.

"You said you were going to be serious with me. You should also be honest with me." I lift a large portion of food from the container and offer it to him. "There's plenty here for both of us. Are you sure you don't want some?"

The look of surprise exits his expression and fear enters and is evident in his eyes. He has the look of a man ready to run but trapped. His voice shakes, "I have. That is we have been. I guess there is no denying I was there." I raise the food to my lips. "Wait! Don't eat that!" He says. I drop the sticks into the container and then place it on the table between me, the laptop, and him.

"The plan was to drug you and then I would come back in an hour to steal the computer. The food is dowsed with torporin. Look I'm sorry, man. It's just that . . . well you have to understand. We've been trying to get our hands on this software for almost a year. We know there's something in it that the Aryans are using. Anyway, I'm sorry, man."

Calm and expressionless I reply, "Don't worry about it. As I said, I recognized you from earlier today. I'm not surprised you are after the software. Trying to poison me. Well, that's something we can discuss later. For now, be honest. Be serious. Tell me everything you know."

As he continues to flip through the code displayed on the laptop monitor, his fingers clicking the keys and his eyes darting about he continues to talk. "Where the Aryan video and commercial production companies made their name and reputation was in movies that required particularly demanding sequences. These can be stunts or scenes in which real shots must perfectly complement computer-generated digital effects. In this case, cinema films or TV movies and series – although those require a shooting board – are confusingly referred to as storyboards. By the late twentieth century, nearly every made-for-cinema and made-for-television broadcast was produced by Aryan production software for green-screen shooting boards and storyboards.

"The first experiments with the mind-controlling ASI produced shooting boards and storyboards were the Aryan companies' clients. When the clients began to behave as the ASI predicted they would, the Aryans could fine-tune the systems and the messages. Then they knew it was time to use the techniques on a global scale.

The clicking of the keys stops and his eyes peer over the top of the monitor as he looks at me. "Putting all this video production mumble-jumble aside," I say, "the software program I hijacked means everything in solving the viruses on the entire planet. Our success requires not only that I can define how video and audio are created, recorded, and then later broadcast, but in no way can the software leave any hint for the existence of the internet or the use of satellite communication. Because the conscious AI known as Tathagata will use this project to devise a plan. But, that super-intelligent, conscious machine can never become aware of the internet. Doing so would allow the ASI to discover everything vulnerable about the human race, our history of wars, our weaknesses to famines, our vulnerabilities to worshiping idols and gods, our sickness and disease for wealth and power, and how we demonize ourselves to an elite imagination. An ASI such as Tathagata would likely decide to twilight the human species. People are too frail and weak for change and without changing the human race will destroy the habitable Planet Earth.

"Some talk about mankind spreading throughout the galaxy and colonizing other planets as the great era of entering the heavens. But I think we are disturbing and trespassing into the hallowed space of the gods."

***

We've worked into the early hours of the morning. Munging and scrubbing until we have a usable project ready for Tathagata. We have also finished three-quarters of the bottle of Ardbeg and sleep is the logical next step. Just before I head for the bed the student asks me, "Why is it that we crave love? What I mean is, I'm happy with who I am and so proud to be able to accomplish something meaningful like what we did here today, this evening. But still, I feel this desire to love someone. As if something is missing in my life. Do you know what I mean Eulər?"

"One of the best descriptions of that sense and emotion came from a man named Rupert Spira. I am probably too far into the whiskey bottle to do him justice, but he explains it something like this.

"Your True Self is asleep and having a dream about being in a small village somewhere in a land called Andorra. In this dream they imagine themselves to be a student who studies cinematography and artistic technology. At times, the dream becomes intense and the self becomes engrossed in these illusions and begins to miss being awake. It is at those times when the dream state misses the Self. We call it longing for love but in reality, it is our True Self longing to wake from the dream. Self love is the only true love and until you can love yourself, the illusion goes on."

As I make my way to bed and collapse onto the lumpy mattress, my recurring dream of Ibrahim and Lizet unfolds. This time, the dream reveals more to me than ever before.

>> The next morning two monks walked to the city and after finding Ibrahim they told him the Abbot required his council. Without hesitation, Ibrahim agreed to return with them to the monastery. After he explained to Lizet the Abbot required his council she wished him a prosperous meeting and told him she would wait at the farm for his return.

While he was walking to the monastery in the company of the two monks Ibrahim was enjoying the conversation. After the Abbot explained the celebration would require Ibrahim's help, Ibrahim accepted the task and immediately got to work. In a short time, he remembered how good it was to be in the company of the monks, disciples, and the Abbot, and to be performing the tasks and mission of the monastic life. Several days passed and everything was ready for the seasonal ceremony.

The ceremonial city is one hundred kilometers from the monastery. The Abbot told Ibrahim to lead the procession of monks and everything in tow to the town. There, after arriving, he was charged to set everything in motion for the celebration. Ibrahim was very honored and he had never felt so content as he did while living with the monks. But he needed to get word to Lizet to let her know he would be gone for three months. So the Abbot agreed and sent his messenger to give Lizet an update on Ibrahim's journey.

But now horns blow with the sounds of the celebration fading and a new surrounding and sensation takes hold. My dream state changes and the great gate narrating the fable fades and disappears. In its place, I see the honorable elders of the monastery. They look tired and I can imagine they have been several days wandering through the forest and have at last come upon the Abbot. In this vivid dream as they approach and upon finding the Abbot, in sync, pulled their robes over the left shoulder, placed their right knee on the ground, pressed the palms of their hands together in front of the chest with the tips of the thumbs just below the heart. Before any of them could say anything the Abbot told the story about Ibrahim. As they remained in their places, showing respect to the venerable Abbot, the great monk, the precious one of their monastery, next revealed the legend he called, "The First Priority."

At the end of three months, with the seasonal festivities and the ceremony completed Ibrahim began to say his goodbyes to each of the monks. His thoughts over the three months returned time and time again to his beautiful betrothed, Lizet. He imagine her soft and smooth olive skin and the warmth he would feel looking into her beautiful dark gold eyes, her perfect mouth, and the sound of her voice. The thoughts of her would often cause him to wish he had never accepted the position and the task of the monastery. But he also found his passion for the monastic life.

Each day and night while performing the various chores and participating in the teachings, exercises, the practice, all of it would bring him enormous contentment and peace. The way of these teachings, he had discovered, was his true purpose. He felt torn between the two callings. Divided by his craving for Lizet and absolute peace from living like a monastic.

When Ibrahim approached the venerable Abbot, the great monk, the precious one of the monastery, he performed the five rests and four positions of respect. Then stood to one side of the Abbot. The precious one pressed his palms together with thumbs just below the heart and bowed to Ibrahim. Ibrahim was surprised to watch the Abbot greet him in the way one greets an arhat.

The Abbot said, "It pleases me to see you this morning, venerable arhat, great being Ibrahim."

The monks who heard this invocation of respect and announcement of his place in the monastery agreed that Ibrahim was indeed a venerable arhat and had become a great being.

After giving them time to digest the announcement the Abbot continued, "Now is the time to gather the disciples and monks to prepare for the journey back to the city of Baloc. Please make it your place to prepare everything and make ready to leave in the morning."

Ibrahim knew he was indeed a venerable arhat and when he practiced he experienced everything that only a great being would experience. But hearing the words from the Abbot was as if he had only just become aware of the depth of his accomplishments. He had only one doubt remaining regarding the reality of his achievement. Those thoughts and the deep longing for his Lizet.

The journey to Baloc was long and the procession would arrive just one month before the date of his wedding. The division within him had grown deep. The monastic way is a resignation from normal life and a necessary singular concentration.

That night as he tried to sleep his monkey mind prevented him from rest. His thoughts swung from the invocation of desire for Lizet to the doubt about his ability as a great being. Eventually, his mind grew tired of repeating these thoughts over and again and he did fall into a deep dream.

His dream was a transcendence to the fields of eternal rest. He saw all the perfect and complete precious ones there in the fields of contentment. Their needs were taken care of by celestial nymphs with never-before-seen beauty and charm. Each of the precious ones is honored and provided for by one hundred celestial nymphs. The precious ones radiated countless myriads of millions of light beams in all directions which illuminated the universe with energy, love, peace, and contentment. When Ibrahim awoke from his dream, he knew the truth of the dream, and his doubt was conquered.

***

A bell sounded in my ear, from where or why I do not know. As I lay here sleeping knowing that I am deep in this dream, and not deep within the forest. But, now at the start of the ninety-seventh day of this epic journey, I am lying in bed, inside the hostel in Sispany, Andorra allowing the dream to take me further. I listen and watch the dream story as the scene carries an ethereal quality, amidst the teachings of the venerable Abbot. The answers that I need must be contained in the dream's messages.

The juxtaposition of the bustling city of Baloc with its cheers and celebrations against the heart-wrenching plea of Lizet adds layers of emotion to this tale of love, loss, and spiritual growth but now, the Abbot stops telling it and says,

"Honorable elders, venerable arhats, great monks, I was Ibrahim. The story I have shared with you is my legacy. At the time of the passing of the former precious one of our monastery, many of you were still a thought in your father's minds. At my ascension to the Abbot position, I accepted the responsibility of the precious ones. Listen. The monastic life is a never-ending war.

"Each of us is at war against an enemy that wants to conquer our minds. But we must sometimes seek shelter when we need a rest from the harshness of war. The shelter needs to be like a small hut with a thatched roof. If your roof is not well thatched when the battle arrives like a monsoon rainstorm, then in your mind the rains will find a way through and you will drown. But a well-thatched roof can weather the battles of even the most tepid storms.

"The monastic doesn't survive the battles when it craves love from others, sex, food, comfort, wealth, fame, position, or power. The monastic isn't a service to laws or rules, nor is it debated by great monks as to who serves the law nor of whom are served by the law. Monastics prepare the way to peace and contentment for all sentient beings. We are the gateway to complete and total liberation from cravings. It is, therefore, better for you to live in total isolation than to surround yourself with wrong-minded ones. This is The First Priority."

My dream state fell deeper still and I experienced a sensation of being present and out of body. I am aware of my source energy, there with the elders and monks as Self. Right then the bodhisattva, the great being Sarvashura descended from the fields above. He appeared before the gathered assembly and I there in the deepest part of the forest. He told the complete story of the journey of the disciples and monks, led by Ibrahim to the mining city, Baloc.

"That city is home to Lizet's family where she was born and where she grew up learning how to be a perfect wife and companion for her chosen husband, Ibrahim. At the time when the monastery's procession arrived in the city everyone from the municipality was there waiting for them to attend the lessons. And also, they were there preparing for the great wedding of Ibrahim and Lizet. As they had prepared for this wedding for many years. The people lined both sides of the street to welcome the procession of monks and disciples with cheers, music, and dancing as is the custom in civilized places when the dedicated and precious ones visit.

"Lizet and her family saw Ibrahim leading the procession. They felt great respect and pride knowing he was chosen for such an honor.

"Each night for the next month Ibrahim and the monks would provide various teachings and guided practices for the people. Following the practice, there was a feast and celebration. At the end of the thirty days, it was time for the assembly of monks and disciples to take the last part of the journey to the monastery.

The day before the expected wedding the procession departed Baloc. Lizet was in the bath and had just begun to soap her hair when the housemaid told her Ibrahim was again leading the procession as the monks returned to the monastery. Lizet, with her hair still wet and half-covered with soap, wrapped herself in a robe and ran from the house. She ran as fast as she could to the street where the procession would depart, but they were already half a kilometer past the city. She screamed with all her might.

"Precious Abbot please don't take my husband Ibrahim from me!" She collapsed, falling to her knees in great despair.

"The wedding was necessarily canceled, and the celebration was canceled as well. Everyone in the city who had attended the nightly teachings and who had heard Ibrahim lead the practice knew he was certainly a great being. They knew he had transcended earthly cravings and they felt sorrow for Lizet but also they felt great joy for the blessings of such a great being.

"After some time had passed, Lizet's broken heart began to heal and her attendants helped her to endure the grief. A year and several months later she heard that the great being Ibrahim and a staff of monks were teaching in a nearby town. She told her attendants to gather supplies and prepare for a journey.

"We will go and spy on these monks and I will find a way to be alone with Ibrahim," she told them.

"She believed if she could get him alone that their love would reignite and she could have her husband and life back. Lizet's retinue prepared and when everything was ready they journeyed to the nearby city. They disguised Lizet so that anyone who saw her in attendance at the teaching would not recognize her. As they sat listening to Ibrahim's teaching Lizet received the fruit of conversion and she attained stream-entry. Not just her but also her entire entourage attained stream-entry. The next day they went to the monastery of nuns and dedicated themselves to the practice full time."

Then the bodhisattva, the great being Sarvashura circumambulated the venerable Abbot three times and disappeared by his own supernatural powers.

***

LOG ENTRY five: Day ninety-seven. There are only two elements required for this project. The outcome will be a cure for brainwashing on Planet Earth. When I upload the relevant data, the supercomputer will be charged with the discovery and plan. I must be one hundred percent certain. The data has to be soundly engineered for the possible discovery of a cure for this Aryan-created virus. Second, when I hand this project over, Tathagata must not discover that humans have the internet and their satellite networks. I wonder if I should tell the young student how it is that I have access to the Tathagata. Would I be safe telling him that I am Syganoid and the race of humanoids who were driven from Planet Earth?

Today my mind is reminiscing about our culture and its norms. How Syganoid training requires the first one hundred years of our life to complete. Proud of our commitment and once we complete the training, the kuudere commit to a four-hundred-year contract to help humanity. It's a highly intense, dedicated kuudere who dedicates five hundred years to the humanitarian cause.

Sidebar note: The student is still sleeping on the sofa when I rolled out of bed.

My day always starts the same. There are strict protocols for someone with the level of software and number of Neuralink implants I require for my job. First I complete forty-five minutes of Tai Chi. The rhythm and the stretches cause the mind and body to harmonize. The body becomes aware of the mind, and the mind becomes aware of the body. Epigenetics is our science. Once these two independent organic lives become aware of each other they become aware and awake to the available knowledge and energy from outside. They combine and become sixteen senses with the influence of internal and external energies.

Awareness of external energy including the endless energy from space and other life forms, organic, electrical, magnetic, light, sound, and vibrations from many thousands of other living energy. These all empower my epigenetic actions, organoids, biomechanical, and human energies within me to function optimally throughout the day.

With the last movement completed, the Tai Chi exercise moves seamlessly into a thirty-minute Lìliàng Yoga routine. This type of yoga was designed specifically to align the super-human strength provided by the organoids and spinal path Neurolinks. These positions build incredible muscular strength and dexterity and also clean the organs, including the lymph nodes. I lay quiet on the floor for a moment and think about my friends back home.

I'm not even a season away from Planet Forty-Four and I miss their presence, the sounds of their voices, and our group workouts and meditations. It's been months since I've joined them in the fields and I now think it is the faulty software and devices within me that have hindered me. Enough of this reminiscing. I crawl to my hands and knees, stand and walk as if on a balance beam across the room to the bath. I take a long shower and think about a traditional breakfast.

The typical Syganoid breakfast is fresh juice and oatmeal, but in the last several years oatmeal has become hard to find since Planet Forty-Four can't grow those crops. Most whole foods require inter-planetary transport and trade.

While the student is still sleeping I decide to take a walk through the park and the village around this hostel. The respirator is an attention attraction but no one can see me greeting them with a smile and so I nod and bow instead. Walking around is always an opportunity for discovering great wealth and benefit. Today, however, since I am supposed to stay inside quarantine, and wearing a respirator, I cut my walk short and I'm going back to the room. I'm making too many people feel uncomfortable.

Back inside, still wishing I could walk outdoors in the bright star and its unobstructed light, I make due instead by watching the scene outside from the window. I flashback to the conversation from last night with the student about camera angles and I notice how this fifth-floor view is elevated. A similar camera angle would cause the viewer to feel they're superior to the life below. Superior sensation to what's below, the human instinct is now observing all that goes on with questioning and judging, perhaps even suspecting. In my isolation, however, I watch and observe jealous of those outside who are freely moving around in the universe.

"There's an opportunity", I think aloud as I observe rubbish someone has left under a tree. Then I see another opportunity for great wealth and benefit as a woman walking her dog fails to disinfect the dog's urine on the park bench it just pissed over. If I wasn't stuck inside I would have picked up the rubbish and disinfected the urine. "If I can't earn these benefits in person," I decide, "then I'll use technology!"

From the side pocket of my backpack, I dig in and unzip it real quick. I pull out a CTRL-Labs wearable armband and strap it tight on my right forearm, and another one on my left. The right one is already synced up to a drone with a grabber mechanism, while the left one is paired with a drone carrying a disinfectant sprayer. Once I've got the drones all set, I place'em outside the door and let'em take off. With my mind focused, I launch those drones, their opal-colored bodies soaring into the bright-clear sky. I steer'em into action, cleanin' and disinfectin' the park across the street.

"Good morning Eulər," the student says as he joins me in front of the window. He's naked except for the short white socks over his feet and ankles. "What are you watching?" he asks.

"Drones, those brilliant opal-colored drones across the street."

Both drones emit a gentle hum as they work, their opal-colored bodies glinting in the sunlight. They move with calculated efficiency, responding to my mental commands as I guide them in their cleaning and disinfecting duties.

He stands with me watching for a few minutes. Then he laughs and says, "You are a madman. Wacked and nuts you stand there cleaning the park and playing with the children and pets. Hilarious, man." He disappears into the bathroom and I hear the water from the shower.

As the opal-colored drones dance gracefully in the bright but half cloud-covered sky, I can't help but feel a pang of nostalgia. My mind is fully immersed in controlling them, yet my heart aches for the familiar sounds of my friends' voices back on Planet Forty-Four. The taste of fresh juice and oatmeal lingers on my palate, reminding me of simpler times when our culture and traditions bound us together. My Tai Chi and Lìliàng Yoga routine ground me physically, a reminder of the deep training we Syganoids undergo to serve humanity.

The touch of the wearable armbands on my forearms connects me to the advanced technology we've mastered, yet it also accentuates the isolation I feel on this distant planet. As I disinfect the park and watch the bustling life below, I yearn for the obstructed light of our domed cities where I could freely move and commune with my fellow kuudere. If only I could share these emotions with the young student, but the burden of secrecy weighs heavy on my shoulders.

***

Between cleaning up the rubbish and disinfecting behind careless pet owners with my drones, I spend quality time people-watching. I often wonder what they are about, and what's their backstory. Are they in a good mood today? Has something entered their life recently bringing happiness, maybe a new love or a new life opportunity? Perhaps they are angry because they've lost their job or are they strapped with too much debt? Nevertheless, for every person I see and that passes by I wish each one happiness and liberation from the causes of suffering. This is how merit is earned and how epigenetics are controlled.

An hour goes by with me staring out the window and helping the community. The shower is still running and the student must be ultra-clean by now.

It's time to get to work.

Last night we discovered the software for the shooting board uses an archaic computer language from several hundred years gone past. It's written in a version of Microsoft C## which was, according to Musk's Ultimate Knowledge satellite information an object-oriented, lexically scoped breakthrough for Microsoft back in the last decade of the 20th century. The student decided to scrap all but two of the objects since the other twenty-nine had references to the internet.

My knowledge of Earth History reminded him how Microsoft and Space X financed the human diaspora to the galaxy but Microsoft was destroyed by a Trump Nation's satellite using a fusion blast. Later, the Trump Nation satellites hunted down Elon Musk and Bill Gates and then executed them. Trump and Ivanka claim it was for crimes against humanity.

The student read me the historical data from the twenty-second century. "Just five years before the human diaspora, all but thirteen countries abandoned the use of video and radio broadcasts. Today, many human-inhabited planets do not allow any form of recorded video or audio. Starzel is one of the few countries where the Aryans still have the population held in slavery. The last great hope of Planet Earth to establish a country that allowed people to live in peace and prosper free from the oppression of religious rule or heavy-handed government conspiracy was laid to waste by the Aryans. They destroyed the American dream and a long civil war broke the United States and Canada into seven separate countries. Besides Starzel, the other countries still using broadcast communication include The United Kingdom, Trump Nation, The Heartland, and the European Union, except for Andorra.

If I can properly prepare this project, there may be hope to reverse the Aryan and Conservative, Republican's destruction of the ideals that were in the United States. I continue to work on the software and have organized and simplified the software system hacked from the director's laptop. Driven by the hope that a cure could be developed, the population of mindless feminism and conservatism in Starzel and elsewhere would be freed.

After the student fell off to sleep in an Ardbeg-induced drunken slumber, I accessed more information from the Musk Ultimate Knowledge files. Historical records documenting how the Republican Coalition took over and controlled people's thinking for a large portion of the population in the United States is a horrifying story.

<//>Following the fourteenth great Aryan war (popularly known as World War Two), when in defeat, the Aryans and Nazis had to flee northern Europe. They emerged shortly thereafter in three countries. The majority of the leadership migrated to South Africa and to the once-great Soviet Union. The vast majority of the scientists and engineers went to the United States.

While most of the people of Planet Earth feared the development of atomic weapons by the Aryans in Germany it was the Aryans that later migrated to the United States who succeeded. Atomic weapons and nuclear bombs were not the aims of the Aryans. Mind control was their real passion and they were engineering and researching pharmaceutical drugs to explore consciousness, metaphysical as well as using harmonics and lightwaves to hypnotize. Drugs such as heroin, lysergic acid diethylamide (LSD), and sound waves found in popular music from the 1960s such as Elvis Presley, Tony Benet, and the Beach Boys showed great promise.

The weapon of choice for the Aryans, especially in the 1980's Ronald Reagan era leading white supremacy in the United States, was the discoveries from biochemistry. The biochemistry of belief-based science discovered what causes people to believe rather than acknowledge facts and tangible proofs. As they wrote in a letter sent to Reagan in a Republican and Nazi Party report:

'Amygdala and Hippocampus are involved in the process of thinking and thus help in the execution of beliefs. NMDA receptors in this region of the brain are involved in thinking and in the development of beliefs. These beliefs are subjected to challenge. A belief that is subjected to more challenges becomes stronger. When a new stimulus comes, it creates distress in the brain with already existing patterns. The distress results in the release of dopamine (neurotransmitter) to transmit the signal.

'The research findings of Young and Saxe revealed that the medial prefrontal cortex is involved in processing the belief valence. The right temporoparietal junction and precuneus are involved in the processing of beliefs to moral judgment. True beliefs are processed through the right temporoparietal junction. Saxe explained that belief judging starts at the age of five years, citing examples of judging belief questions on short stories by children. Belief attribution involves activating regions of the medial prefrontal cortex, superior temporal gyri, and hippocampal regions. Studies by Krummenacher et al, have shown that dopamine levels are associated with paranormal thoughts suggesting the role of dopamine in belief development in the brain.'

How they got the population of the United States and around the planet to believe in Donald Trump as the greatest human on Earth was made simple by these pharmaceuticals. Once the Reagan led Republicans, Nazis, and Aryans knew where in the brain and how to target this belief region of the brain, the next step was to optimize the process.<//>

Today, hundreds of years later, we know the facts about what followed. In those ancient days for the people who loved, yes they loved Ronald Reagan and Donald Trump, but they didn't know it was a love induced by a virus and decades-long planning that ed to calculated and targeted brainwashing.

***

<//>The Republican Coalition (Aryan, Nazi, White Supremacy Groups, & other Conservatives) began using viral warfare on a global scale in the 1970s. It started with a Republican-controlled congress enacting laws requiring automobiles to use unleaded gasoline additives. The emission from those additives caused an overabundance of dopamine in the human brain. However, white supremacist scientists needed people with larger frontal lobes to take advantage of the increased dopamine. The cerebral challenge in those early chemical warfare days was to simultaneously shrink, or worse, to deaden the scientific and reasoning receptors in the brain while growing the frontal lobe's capacity. They found the perfect catalyst to accomplish both of these in people's pets.

Every dog, cat, and caged bird became the tools of the Aryans and the Republican Coalition. Not everyone was affected by the viruses. President Reagan instructed his Aryan scientists and white power engineers not to worry about one hundred percent efficacy. He assured them they would only need twenty percent of the population. The strains of pathogens developed were multiple strains of viruses, bacteria, fungi, and protozoa. Most efficacy of these pathogens achieved thirty-five percent or higher. The scientists were ecstatic, as were the Aryans.<//>

With this information and the student's help with the software, I engineered the project for the supercomputer.

--initiate file for Tathagata upload--

__file configuration optimized__

__waiting for data location for compiling__

I steer the pointer in the HUD to the file I've prepared

__compiling for Tathagata__

Project outline:

```
using System;
using System.Collections.Generic;
using System.Linq;
using System.Text;
using System.Threading.Tasks;
namespace WormVirus
{
class Program
{
static void Main(string[] args)
{
// Read the information about camera angles, shot sizes, and camera movements.
```

```
        string[] cameraAngles = { "eye-level", "low angle", "high angle",
"dutch angle", "over the shoulder" };
        string[] shotSizes = { "close up", "long shot", "medium shot", "single
shot", "two-shot", "three-shot", "POV" };
        string[] cameraMovements = { "360 degree", "zoom", "pan and tilt",
"tracking shot", "crane", "dolly", "random" };
        // Read the program for background music from 1968 rock and
roll.
        string[] songs = { "Born to be Wild", "Hey Jude", "White Rabbit",
"Satisfaction", "Jumpin' Jack Flash" };
        // Create the worm virus.
        WormVirus virus = new WormVirus(cameraAngles, shotSizes,
cameraMovements, songs);
        // Upload the worm virus to the harddrive of the laptop.
        virus.Upload();
    }
}
class WormVirus
{
private string[] cameraAngles;
private string[] shotSizes;
private string[] cameraMovements;
private string[] songs;
public WormVirus(string[] cameraAngles, string[] shotSizes,
string[] cameraMovements, string[] songs)
    {
    this.cameraAngles = cameraAngles;
    this.shotSizes = shotSizes;
    this.cameraMovements = cameraMovements;
    this.songs = songs;
```

```
}
public void Upload()
{
// Iterate over the camera angles and create a worm for each angle.
for (int i = 0; i < cameraAngles.Length; i++)
{
string angle = cameraAngles[i];
Worm worm = new Worm(angle);
// Iterate over the shot sizes and create a worm for each shot size.
for (int j = 0; j < shotSizes.Length; j++)
{
string size = shotSizes[j];
worm.AddShot(size);
}
// Iterate over the camera movements and create a worm for each
camera movement.
for (int k = 0; k < cameraMovements.Length; k++)
{
string movement = cameraMovements[k];
worm.AddMovement(movement);
}
// Add the worm to the list of worms.
worms.Add(worm);
}
// Iterate over the songs and play each song.
for (int i = 0; i < songs.Length; i++)
{
string song = songs[i];
PlaySong(song);
}
```

```
}
private void PlaySong(string song)
{
// TODO: Play the song.
}
}
class Worm
{
private string angle;
private List<string> shots;
private List<string> movements;
public Worm(string angle)
{
this.angle = angle;
this.shots = new List<string>();
this.movements = new List<string>();
}
public void AddShot(string shot)
{
shots.Add(shot);
}
public void AddMovement(string movement)
{
movements.Add(movement);
}
}
}
```

End of File

"Let me ask you something?" the student says as he emerged from the two-and-a-half-hour shower wearing a towel around his waist and a face covered in shaving soap. "Are you a humanoid? Is that why you're hacking computers and researching their software? You're here to destroy us and take over the planet. Right?" he laughs.

"Safeguarding humanity is a universal public good," I respond in all seriousness. "For centuries those who have studied and written about human extinction have suggested the exploration of space and settlements on other planets would make us safe. In reality, as we became an interplanetary species, the vulnerabilities did not end. The risks that threaten human life when all our eggs are in the single basket called Planet Earth are still a threat across the inhabited Universe. Disease, war, tyranny, and permanently locking in poor values are each correlated across multiple inhabited planets.

"Unaligned artificial general intelligence (AGI) and ASI are completely correlated: if they affect one planet, they affect all planets. While settlements in space provide existential security for the uncorrelated threats there has always been cross-communication and heritage of humans across the habitable zones. But, when the Tathagata became conscious the single ambition and the priority written into its ASI programming is to safeguard long-term potential for humanity."

His question reminds me that there's only one place and just one person that can get me access to the Tathagata. I need to get to Tivlabet and once there, I need Chinese government approval to visit the Abbot.

When I've finished packing away the laptop, and drones, and restoring the room to an organized mess the door swings open. The woman in black dashes inside and closes the door with a loud slam behind her.

"Where is he?" she asks in a huff. "For fucks sake, Eulər, you told the kid who we are?" she hisses through clenched teeth. "Have you completely gone out of your mind?"

"Hey, sweet outfit," the student tells her as he steps back into the room and a cloud of steam vapor follows him from the bathroom.

Before I could finish swinging my backpack over my shoulders she cartwheels across the room, capturing his head between her legs midway and then flipping him off his feet as she completed the maneuver. The sound of his neck and spine breaking in three places made me cringe and sick to my stomach.

My fingers twist and pull on my mother's ring as I look down at his lifeless body. "No!"

Chapter Eleven

Tathagata

"Get mad. Go right ahead and get real mad," she says as we come through the vortex. "But instead of being mad at me for protecting you from getting yourself publicly executed, use the anger to find a cure to the goddamned virus. Have you spoken to anyone on Planet Forty-Four of late? Whatever you discovered missing, or that has gone wrong, is starting to take our planet apart now too. So, focus on the mission and get something done."

The vegetable fields we are standing alongside smell of chemicals, like a strong bug spray, and it makes the roof of my mouth itch and a metallic taste on my tongue. She motions for me to walk alongside her and we follow a narrow footpath through the rows of the farmer's fields. The rows of plants go on as far as I can see to the horizon in all directions. The blue sky is full of lenticular clouds that move swiftly on a steady breeze. The sun at our backs formed long shadows before us that angled at twenty degrees as we walk toward the west. She's incensed, full of energy, and seems anxious. Not because she murdered that student, but because of Planet Forty-Four and the virus spreading there.

"Traveling to Tivlabet requires a long journey through China and the American Asian Alliance," she explains to me. "These are the safest places for travel on the entire planet. Why? Another result of the most devastating war of the last eight hundred years. During the Fifteenth Aryan War, after more than thirty-three million people died, the United States came to a bloody end. What followed threatened to end democracy and civilization. The destruction led to the worldwide collapse of financial systems and global commerce. In the scramble for power and control that followed, China, Mexico, Panama (from Central America), Brazil, Paraguay, and Argentina (from South America), and most Asian countries come together to form China and the American-Asian Alliance (CAAA). The United Kingdom acquired Hawaii and the Philippines, while North and South Korea merged with all of southern Asia, and with the exception of Germany and the Nordic countries, all of Europe entered exclusive trade agreements and adopted currency with the new CAAA.

"While the events following the war laid the foundation for the human diaspora into colonization of the galaxy and further plans for the Universe, the era of cold wars and world power were no longer limited to Planet Earth. It became clear to historians that the human era ended in the 1960s and was superseded by the computer era."

After a deep sigh, she stops speaking and she grabs my right arm with her left hand to stop me. When I look up I see we've come to the end of the footpath and we are now at the edge of the city. She points at the building to my left a few hundred steps away.

"This is as far as I go with you for now," she says. "You are on the way to the Tivlabet monastery. I can't go there. But I can tell you that most of the journey from Beijing to Tivlabet is underground in vacuum tunnels that transport three hundred people in a single vehicle at close to nine hundred kilometers an hour. I wish I could go with you just so I could experience those speeds. Anyway, just through those doors there, the travel is arranged in your name. Follow the guide." She hands me a large gray envelope with the documents and travel passes.

She walks away following the path back towards where we have come. She'll clear the mess at the hostel and I hope she does a better job than the last time she murdered people while protecting me.

Instructions written on the back of the envelope tell me that after traveling through the tube, I will travel the next six hundred kilometers on an autonomous driven, fusion-powered above-ground bus. From there, the final one-hundred-sixty kilometers are hiked up a steep mountainside.

The location of the Tathagata is not well known and not easy to reach. It is high up in the Himalayan Mountains of Tivlabet and hidden within a monastery.

My grandfather was part of the select group who documented and later confirmed the machine's consciousness. My father's team made their declaration one hundred and twenty years later. Long before they made their findings, China made certain only one person could have access to it and who is able to upload data to the ASI. That person is the Abbot of the monastery.

As I travel, I look through the gray envelope further. There's a small IO chip at the bottom of the package. After it's attached to my buckle I access the historic records from the Universe data records on humanity. The Source uploads the knowledge into my memory. As the knowledge streams it seems as if I'm recalling information I already know. The information tells how China had established this supercomputer in the early 1940s while the Nazis and the Aryans were close to completing a similar computer in Germany during the Four-teenth Aryan War. Neither group knew about the other's achievements. There were rumors and rumors of tall tales, but no one knew for certain.

The humanity records show that it took China another twenty years before they realized consciousness with their supercomputer. At that time, only a handful of scientists knew the system had achieved consciousness and they named it Tathagata.

As the Tathagata began to provide necessary actions that were needed to achieve the prime directive (Safeguard the Long Term Potential of Humanity) the scientists knew it was time to reveal the system to the heads of the Chinese Communist Party.

It was in the year 1982 when the Chinese scientists showed the heads of the communist party how the Aryans and the Republican Party in the United States had undertaken a long-term plan to enslave the population of that country. They exposed how the Aryans were using pharmaceutical pathogens and biology. Through this ingenious but sinister chemical warfare, not one bomb would need to be dropped. No military action would be required, and no declaration of war by a government was necessary. The simultaneous three-pronged Aryan-engineered strategy had been perfectly executed. With expansion planned for Europe and Asia.

Anger fills my mind and through clenched fists, I pound on the wall of the transport train car. The man next to me places his hand on my shoulder and says something to me, but I can't translate his words. My anger has me overwhelmed by what the knowledge tells me of the virus.

First, they used the human immune system to cause the frontal lobe of the brain to increase in surface area and cellular density. Second, they used visual and audio waves to infect the frontal lobes with a virus that caused the host to be excessively vulnerable to beliefs and become averse to truth and scientific proof. Third, the Aryans would divide the population along political party lines to distract not just the government of the United States from the Aryan methods, but to distract the world's populations from the reality of the viral plague.

Tathagata provided a thorough report revealing these methods for the three-pronged Republican Coalition strategies along with the date and location for when each had begun. Tathagata also provided medical research papers published in the mid to late 1970s defining the discovery of inflammation in human organs. The reports showed similar symptoms across the U.S. were beginning to become more frequent in patients as a result of unknown but specific pathogens.

From https://www.ncbi.nlm.nih.gov/books/n/imm/A2528/def -item/A2540/

The pathogens were typically nonaggressive and were able to mutate into multiple infectious pathogens quickly. While most microorganisms are repelled by innate host defenses, an initial infection, once established, generally leads to perceptible disease followed by an effective host adaptive immune response. This is initiated in the local lymphoid tissue, in response to antigens presented by dendritic cells activated during the course of the innate immune response. Antigen-specific effector T cells and antibody-secreting B cells are generated by clonal expansion and differentiation over the course of several days, during which time the induced responses of innate immunity continue to function. Eventually, antigen-specific T cells and then antibodies are released into the blood and recruited to the infection. A cure involves the clearance of extracellular infectious particles by antibodies and the clearance of intracellular residues of infection through the actions of effector T cells.

***

Traditional mountain-top monasteries follow a prescribed code of conduct and tasks that are precise and divided between tasks for the elders and tasks for the students. Preparing the daily requirements for life as well as ceremonial events defined by the calendar and special occasions. For example when someone such as myself is coming to visit the monastery. A visit to this monastery is rare indeed since it is hidden and often thought by most people to be a rumor. Special permission from the Chinese president himself must be obtained. Then, the elders are notified by a secret envoy and they instruct the order of devout men and women to prepare.

The ritual in the Himalayan monasteries, I recall from a conversation with Casper many years ago. He was preparing for his first lecture to teach students how they can use epidemiology for transcendence in the Buddha Field.

"The method is as refined as our physical mind can absorb, he said. "What I cannot do is greet them when they enter my field. Like the monasteries on Planet Earth, did you know? The occasion to greet others in much the same way as great migratory swans on the nearby lakes greet each other. The Tibetan horns with loud, deep-octave tones, students' and elders' cheers are shouted, and they embrace and they dance, sing, and exchange bows of reverence. Mimicking the movements and sounds just like the birds do when one of the flock returns to the lake." A smile washes across my face as I recall the sounds of his voice and his demonstrative way of speaking.

At the highest point of the mountain reached by a narrow foot trail, I squeezed into one of many narrow splits through the tall sheer cliff wall. Undetectable from any of the other cracks along the face of the mountain's cliff. In the envelope the woman in black gave me, the shape of the split was drawn on the map, along with a small electronic tracking device that I have been instructed, must be worn at all times.

On the first day of my scheduled visit, a student swept the trail from the point of the crack all the way through the tight stone-walled path to the hidden monastery. Leaving me with a small cup of water at the midway point is the only other evidence for me to know I have taken the correct path.

Once I step through the other side of the cliff path the monastery itself is otherwise an unremarkable sight. A park within the mountain top of hardpacked soil and little vegetation. Given the high altitude, not many plants can survive and those that do will not thrive in the arid and always cold temperatures. Stone-walled huts, about two dozen in number, and one large building in the center of the randomly dispersed dwellings. Well-worn paths lead from the huts to one of three entrances to the large building near the center.

As I come through the walled opening, I am greeted first by students who are seated in a lotus pose on either side of the footpath, chanting the heart sutra. Long Tibetan horns, one on each side of the entrance to the large building, are given three long blows at the first sight of the visitor emerging from the mountain's cliff wall. Many curried rice dishes and special flavored rice wines are made ready to serve at the joyful feast and the smells permeate the air. Later, when the meal is complete and the students and monks clear and clean away the festival, the elders will gather around me and provide blessings and give a prayer for prosperity.

My hands cover my ears while I return bows to so many monks I've lost count. When the sound from the last Tibetan horn blast exhausts, I shake my head to try and free the inner vestibule of my ears and regain my hearing. I am greeted again by several traditional saffron-colored robed students and monks who have been waiting for me inside this huge elaborate designed and ornate building. The smell of rice and curry has now become overpowering, as much or more so than the sound of the horns.

After twenty-seven minutes the greeting celebration begins to wind down. "Can I speak with the Abbot, "I ask a monk while he hugs me.

"The Abbot has left the monastery," he laughs as he steps back from our embrace. His expression changes to a pang of sadness and with his head lowered, "He has taken up residence deep within the forest."

Bloody fucking hell this can't be real. The only person with access to the Tathagata is away on some sort of, what, a sabbatical. I need to keep my cool and be respectful. This monastery is off-limits to all outsiders and I'm aware the only reason I am allowed here is because of my father's relationship to the ASI project.

"May I ask why the Abbot of the monastery has taken up residence deep within the forest?

The monk looks embarrassed, humble, and shy as he explains. "Kind sir with deep sadness I must tell you that our community of monks has become divided into two groups and neither group can get along with the other group. Our precious and wise Abbot has tried to bring the monks together. He told and demanded we monks be at peace with each other, but the division between our two groups only worsened and so the Abbot abandoned us. Saying that life is too precious to waste time on idiots."

"Please tell me this is some kind of joke," I say. As I watch him standing with his head down, shoulders slumped forward, and motionless, I can sense the deep sorrow he is feeling.

From somewhere inside my chest I feel a troubling sensation of grief. No, it is more a sensation of despair as if being torn between the two sides of the monk's argument was more devastating than a planet plagued by killing viruses, murderous Republican and Aryan coalitions, and an evolved intuitive carelessness for life itself. I've never imagined the human side of these natural conditions, the causes of suffering. They are unable to help me with the cure for these problems. My time here is just what Father said it would be. This has all been a complete waste of time. All the people who have been killed because of my coming here and every effort to find the missing data was a dumb effort.

"Is there somewhere, quiet where I can go and think? Perhaps there is a meditation chamber?"

"But of course. Kindly follow me," he forces an enthusiastic smile that fails. "After the feast and the elders bless your visit, I will show you to the meditation chamber," he says after leading me to the long table and motioning for me to sit on the worn pillow that is placed on a weaved, dingy, and ragged blanket.

***

During the long meal I am beginning to wonder if it will ever end, the monastic abbey's community chat without ceasing. It seems as if everyone is speaking and none are listening. Despite speaking in Chinese, I can't be bothered to switch on the voice interpreter. Instead, my own thoughts of disappointment fill my head and I sense feelings of anger.

For the last ten minutes, I've been staring at the monk who is supposed to escort me to the meditation hall. Showing my body language and expressions, with all certainty that I am wanting to go. He has so far been successful at ignoring me. In my disgust, I speak to myself in the HUD system.

--the only person with access to the Tathagata system isn't here.--

To my surprise, the HUD responds.

__our kuudere seek your attention__

--clarification--

--our kuudere--

__your friends on planet forty-four call to you from the fields__

__the abbot is the key to the Tathagata and must be found__

__the recurring dream is manifesting__

Eight of the elders came to greet me. I make my way from the blanket and pillow to stand up with a cup of rice whiskey still in my hand. They bow and I return the gesture of welcoming with a deep and lengthy bow of respect.

Why am I being so formal and respectful? I don't even understand my own actions anymore.

One of them takes the cup from me and then they each in turn hold my hands facing me and chant a prayer. But I'm not listening to what they are saying. My thoughts are caught up in the anger and the longer this ritual greeting goes the less happy I am to be here.

The woman in black's last instructions flashback into my thought, "Remember that the only reason for going to the monastery is to upload the shooting board project into the ASI so that the ASI can examine and develop a cure for the virus. You have a medical appointment that I will not allow you to miss. And, you have to attend the ceremony for The First Priority."

--connection request for boundrian creator--

__boundrian creator identified__

__connection established__

→what is wrong Eulər←

--the abbot has gone missing--

--this mission has failed and I am ready to go back to locate banyan--

→banyan did communicate with you and gave you a mission←

→find the abbot and stop wasting my time←

--the first priority you spoke of--

→there is no time for that now←

→find the abbot whatever it takes←

--disconnect from boundrian creator--

__connection not found__

→your systems are useless and dangerous←

__connection terminated__

"Trust in their words," the monk says. "I will take you to the meditation hut now if you still desire it."

"Yes. Please let's go." Heaving my backpack from the ground. In one swift motion, I have it over my back and shoulders through the straps. The monk leads us out of the central building and we follow a footpath toward the far north end of the monastery. When he gets to the stone hut he steps off the path and pulls back the thick tapestry from the entrance. He bows his head with slight reservation and his expression still shows his sorrow.

"Thanks," I say. When I step through the doorway the stone hut is dark and smells of stale dust and canvass. When my eyes adjust to the dim light the small room is empty. A single blanket and pillow on the bare ground off to the left. It is set in the darkest part of the already dark room.

Well, I might as well give it a go. My thoughts appear dismal. But it's been weeks since I've been able to transcend in my meditation and then there to meet my friends in the fields where we communicate and heal the Universe of pains, sufferings, and replace hardships and evil with boundless love and good fortune. My systems are at fault. Though I have been denying it for months, I now realize I have put off the operation for too long. Still, I have to try to reach them.

An hour goes past. Then another hour. I stay in pursuit of the meditation practice. After another hour slips by . . . *wait a second. I know what to do.*

--set the internal frequency to gamma wave--

__gamma wave will cause total systems failure__

--initiate gamma wave on all conscious and subconscious organics--

"Eulər, is that truly you? I can sense you but I cannot sustain or complete the aware-feeling," Casper says. "You made it to the fields again. Come further so everyone can sense-recognize you."

"This is the best I can do, Casper," I try to communicate through the transcending fields. The voices are faint and awareness is coming and going in waves and in shadows.

"My biosystems and mechanics are causing my mind to falter."

"We will have a son," Gatia says. "You are right we need a son and The Source told me his name will be Magallan. You need to get home as fast as possible! The entire dome system is at risk. We, the whole kuudere, might have to desert Planet Forty-Four soon."

"Desert the domed city? Why?" I asked.

"You altered the past," Casper says. "That's what the investigation committee is telling everyone. They said you were tinkering with Planet Earth during the Cretaceous period on a continent called Laurasia and that you moved a plant. The plant withered and fell into the stream, instead of decaying with the other plants. Some scientists speculate the epoch was changed by a millennium, which caused the crystalline structures of some particles used in the making of the domes. As time catches up, we witness the altered state of a new reality. Our protective dome structure continues to weaken."

"Ten thousand died in level four when the dome cracked," Gatia says. "It is horrible and they sealed off dome five below them and they only have a few days of food before another twenty thousand begin to die there. What did you do, Eulər? You need to come home and fix this."

While the fields fade from my reality and their thoughts fade with it, I can piece together their garbled messages and in my gut, I can feel their grief and panic. "Casper, what era was the plant relocated?"

There is no reply and the fields dissolve from my perceptual mind. Still, while I am in this altered state, I recognize my True Self. "I must restore my body and mind! The gene expression from the power of intention."

--halt gamma waves--

--initiate normal human vibrations--

__human functions initiated__

__humanoid systems ready__

--engage humanoid systems--

My frustration builds as I sit here recalling the deaths, the virus, the brainwashing, the wars, the feminist slant taking over Planet Earth, and now Planet Forty-Four is beginning to fade from history. With every step I take to accomplish the mission the forces of life cause me to stumble. Through the seemingly unending meal in the monastic Abbey, surrounded by chattering monks. The taste of rice whiskey in my mouth brings little comfort as I recall how I felt as I watched the monk, who was supposed to escort me to the meditation hall, completely ignore my signals of wanting to leave, and then he instead brings me to this stone hut. I could feel the weight of my backpack over my back and shoulders, a tangible reminder of the weight of the Universe.

It's all too much and there are too many layers of issues, variables, entangled plots, and deep intertwined intentions. My mind is filled, confused, and over capacity.

The oppressive atmosphere inside this stone hut further amplifies my sense of confinement and discomfort. Yet, amidst my turmoil, a faint hope remains as I reach my friends through the transcending fields, only to find my systems faltering, the home planet, and kuudere deaths, leaving me with a deep sense of urgency to fix the situation here, back home. I will not continue to be beaten and restrained from success on this mission. I have accomplished more destruction and wasted everyone's time.

***

This is catastrophic and I can not believe it except that I heard it with my own ears. Could my simplistic actions, those simple, meaningless changes in the prehistoric past have caused the failure of the domes? If it is true, then I have murdered ten thousand humanoids and possibly the entire Syganoid race. There's no time to waste debating the evidence. I don't believe the dome failing has anything to do with my actions. The scientific team must be wrong . . . but if it is true . . . *This is the end, it cannot get worse or more desperate. There's a limit to what even a Syganoid as I can bear.*

I must find the ASI, Tathagata, and I have to find it now. But where in this secret monastery would it be? No matter. Even if I can discover it, it won't communicate with me.

The Abbot must be found.

That's it! What was the message from the HUD?__the recurring dream is manifesting__ YES! It is my dream, The Abbot was found in the forest by the monks. I remember now.

Mother's ring seems to vibrate and an energy wave sends a pulse through my body.

Besides finding the cure needed for people to halt the brainwashing and disease, the act will give me great wealth and benefit. The merits are even more important now if I am to blame for wiping out my kuudere of the Syganoid race.

"I will not quit trying!"

Leaping to my feet, I run through the doorway and race along the footpaths. Popping my head inside the doorways of each hut, I hunt the monk who has been assigned as my escort.

"Tell the monks to spread the word and to have the elders meet me in the perfumed chambers," I say to him. "I call for the entire assembly of the elders to meet me at once." I bow to the monk and turn to race back to the meditation hut to gather my backpack.

The perfumed chamber is soon filled with the elders of the monastery. Everyone is sitting in their lotus position and silence fills the chamber. Smoke rises in the eight directions of the room filling the space with the scent of jasmine. All eyes are upon me as I take the center position on the raised platform. I follow the instructions as they are detailed to me in the HUD showing me how to perform customary actions to lead the gathering. First, lacing my hands together just in front of the chest, the tips of my fingers poised just below the heart. I place my right knee on the ground and bow my head in respect and show great reverence to the monastery's elders. In keeping with tradition, they all chant the diamond sutra together. They repeat the sutra twenty-seven times.

"A shooting star, a clouding of the sight, a lamp, an illusion, a drop of dew, a bubble, a dream, a lightning's flash, a thunder cloud-- This is the way one should see the conditioned."

Chanting in this way is designed to guide the thinking mind to stop its monkey-like behavior of swinging from one thought to the next thought. These exercises, when practiced, bring us to a place of controlling the mind's resources. This group of elders assembled here, when in control of their mind's resources amass a very powerful assembly.

In haste, I rise from the position of kneeling, pulling my ceremonial robe over my right shoulder. Folding my arms across my waist I ask the assembly of monks seated on the left, "What is the division that has caused the separation of the monastery from its Abbot such that now we find the Abbot living deep within the forest?"

The honorable elder, the venerable arhat, the great monk Chongraling rose up from his lotus position and after addressing the room with the five rests tells the story. "The government's minister of the treasury had come to our monastery at the invitation of the Abbot. The two of them had dinner and spent most of the evening walking through the monastery while talking about the affairs of the monastery and the affairs of the government. They walked and talked together for many hours and when it was very late they retired to the sleeping chambers. The guest chambers are in the same location as the Abbot's sleeping chambers.

"The morning came and the government's minister of the treasury arose and went to the bath where he took time to perform the necessary morning exercises. When he had finished and when he left the bath, he did not take his soiled towel to the laundry as is the law, but instead, he left the towel in the bath chambers. When the Abbot went into the bath to perform the necessary morning exercises found the soiled towel from his guest.

"Later, when the Abbot met with the government's minister of treasury, the Abbot told him he was shocked to have found the soiled towel. The guest replied to the Abbot with an apology. He explained that he did not know and was not at all aware of the law requiring him to take his soiled towel to the laundry. He further explained that in his palace within his bathing chambers, the house servants perform just these sorts of tasks. The Abbot then said to the minister of the treasury that since the minister of the treasury did not know this was the law within the monastery, the law was not violated and no crime had been committed."

After saying these things about the incident, the honorable elder, the venerable arhat, the great monk Chongraling returned to his seated lotus position.

My head spins as I listen to this pathetic recollection of events that caused the division in the assembly. But, despite how I think or what I feel to be so stupid, (a dirty towel!) I continue with the formality and customs of the abbey. Turning my attention to the monks who are seated on the right, I ask, "How did this event cause such a catastrophic divide between the monks and students of the monastery and so much so as to drive the precious one, the venerable Abbot, from the monastery to take up living deep within the forest?"

As I finished asking the question, the great gong in the perfumed chamber was struck. The striking of the gong at such meetings of the elders is a tradition. When five minutes have passed it is struck and is used to keep our minds from losing the meditative powers. We chant the bodhisattva vow repeatedly thirty times.

"May all beings be free from suffering and the causes of suffering.
Just like all the previous Sugatas, the Buddhas
Generated the mind of enlightenment
And accomplished all the stages
Of the Bodhisattva training,
So will I, too, for the sake of all beings,
Generate the mind of enlightenment
And accomplish all the stages
Of the Bodhisattva training."

***

Then at that time the honorable elder, the venerable arhat, the great monk Maitreya who was seated in a lotus position on the right rose up. He pulled his robe over his right shoulder, folded his arms across his waist, bowed deeply before the elders, and told the story.

"It is exactly as was said by the honorable elder, the venerable arhat, the great monk Chongraling. Then, as for what happened next, the Communist government's minister of the treasury finished the morning meal and after saying farewell to the Abbot, he left the monastery. Many conversations between monks who heard their conversation concerning the law took place.

"It was said by some monks, the law is not subject to only certain people nor is the law only valid for certain circumstances. Rather, the law is specific for all times, all people, and in every circumstance. Further, those monks agree, it is meaningless to have laws that can be altered to suit any random circumstance. There would be no need for the law at all if we allow anyone to simply say it is this way, or say it is that way, and so saying the law can become anything at all. Therefore, the way of the law has now become defeated and meaningless."

As Maitreya spoke, the honorable elder, the venerable arhat, the monk Chongraling rose from his seated position. He addressed the monks in the perfumed chamber in the customary way. "A law that is used to punish the unknowing and unwitting is not a law but rather a tyranny and a trap. Such a law would not be a help for the orderliness and condition of a life of harmony but would destroy the freedom of living without fear. A system of laws designed to punish and entrap is meaningless, it is self-defeating and has no place in the monastery. That sort of law would be cruel and empty."

After these words had been spoken by the honorable elders, the venerable arhats, the monks returned to a seated lotus position. After they had returned to a seated position the perfumed chamber remained quiet until the time of the next striking of the gong.

After the sound of the gong was no longer audible. I bowed to the entire assembly. Then I bowed to the group of elders on the left, and then to the elders on my right. Following this, I began to chant the eighteen primary root downfall vow of the monastic life. As prompted by the research and information displayed in my HUD. After each stanza, I waited for the assembly of elders to repeat the stanza. I begin by telling them,

"For the last thirty-five centuries, this is how elders and monks teach the downfall vow to students. On this day, I will use the teaching technique as a reminder to you elders of the great power contained within the vow.

1. Praising ourselves and/or belittling others

2. Not sharing Dharma teachings or wealth

3. Not listening to others' apologies or striking others

4. Discarding the Mahayana teachings and propounding made-up ones

5. Taking offerings intended for the Triple Gem

6. Forsaking the holy Dharma

7. Disrobing monastics or committing such acts as stealing their robes

8. Committing any of the five heinous crimes: (a) killing our fathers, (b) mothers, or (c) an arhat (a liberated being), (d) with bad intentions drawing blood from a Buddha, or (e) causing a split in the monastic community.

9. Holding a distorted, antagonistic outlook

10. Destroying places such as towns

11. Teaching voidness to those whose minds are untrained

12. Turning others away from full enlightenment

13. Turning others away from their pratimoksha vows

14. Belittling the Shravaka vehicle

15. Proclaiming a false realization of voidness

16. Accepting what has been stolen from the Triple Gem

17. Establishing unfair policies

18. Giving up bodhicitta"

As I tug and twist on my mother's ring, I empty my mind of thoughts. Then I say to the assembly. "In this way, honorable elders, venerable arhats, great monks, I ask you: Is the law dependent on humans? Does the law only exist because we are present or does the law exist even without humans? When you became inflamed and divided because of the actions of the Abbot when he gave forgiveness to the minister of the treasury was it the Abbot who inflamed you or was it your own thoughts that deceived you?

"The law exists not to serve individualism, nor to serve a certain social group, or a community of people. The law in human existence exists as a thought. What doesn't exist as a thought? Everything is thought. If I see a person and I say the person is tall the height of the person is only possible in relation to something other than the person. Such as a comparison to a rabbit the person is tall, or compared to a piece of fruit the person is tall. If however, I compare the height of the person to a house or to a mountain then the person is not at all tall.

"Everything in perception requires something else. If there is only a single thing there is emptiness, nothingness. Even empty space can only exist when compared to obstacles that appear to not be empty space. There is nothing in the human observable perception that can exist without something to contrast. Therefore, when you realize this truth of everything is only possible as long as there is everything else it can be perceived that everything is nothing. Conversely, knowledge in this way also provides a knowing that nothing is everything.

"In the space of the mind, when you reach this level of knowing, awakeness can sense absolute truth. None of us can see it, define it, or touch it. The edge of human awakeness like this, at the exact moment when you struggle to grasp the meaning of nothing-is-everything and everything-is-nothing, you have reached the edge of the human's ability to apply reasoning and knowledge. This place is awkward and uncomfortable, and self-doubt arises. But, nonetheless, you will sense something more to knowledge is there beyond my limitation. Something is eluding the experience. What is that something?

"It is outside the realm of human existence to know what it is. It is not, however, impossible to know that it is there. You did reach some place of uncomfortable unknowing, and you are unable to know anything deeper. Everything-is-nothing, nothing-is-everything is evidence of a higher self and another level of existence not available to this human existence. The higher level cannot be seen because it is an existence free from suffering.

"Monks! That is why we are a monastery! To help guide all sentient beings to be free of all suffering. Not through laws, not by bickering on the right, and on the left of those thought arguments."

The monks, realizing the delusions that had divided them, wept for several minutes and then arose and embraced one another. They joined mindful of the karma of thought that had tried to destroy the monastery. Because they had now conquered the delusion of the law, each one of them grew more devoted and more powerful at that very moment, I could sense the fifteenth awareness and their energy startled me. I never knew humans could hold such strength from universal energy.

Even in the protection of daily monastic life, the thinking mind is still able to cause clouded actions and divide our perceptions. There is no need to mention how much more easy the mind loses a grasp on reality for those trapped in the world outside of the abbey and a monastery or for those infected by the brainwashed viruses from the Aryans.

The entire assembly gathered themselves and set off to go at once. They invited me to join them as we went off to the forest and there to find the Abbot so they could beg his forgiveness. I watch the procession of monks going into the forest.

It is the dream. My recurring dream is manifesting and soon these monks will learn the parable of the well-thatched hut and The First Priority will be restored on Planet Earth.

Chapter Twelve

Stranger Than Fiction

Beneath the window ledge of the south-facing window, there was a stone out of place. Not conspicuous, but if someone was looking for clues, like I am, it appears. Shameless, I scour through the Abbots' room for anything to point me in the direction of Tathagata or an answer to what I should do next. The out-of-place stone looks almost as if it came from another planet and manufactured to blend in but just missed the mark. Behind the stone is a small helicon memory stick. Attached to my left pant pocket connector, the file reads into RAM.

Prophetic insight and vision take shape as a holographic image forms in front of me. The form is mystical and sacred and I don't know how to use words to describe it other than to say it was greater than light energy. It resonates with a form of energy that is audible and palpable and emits a smell I have never experienced that is soothing and alluring. Its voice scrambles trough many dialects until it stops on my own native language and then it shares with me.

This is the Tathagata itself that appears and speaks to me.

From the Tathagata to the Chinese Communist Party, a plea for action. In the year, 1988 the Nazis in Russia and South Africa officially declared Donald Trump from the white power syndicate of the United States as their coalition supreme leader. This solidified all eight of the far-right extremist groups into a unified global Republican Party. A month before this grand ceremony, the World Health Organization sent out the official report on the devastation of the Virus Evolution Theory and how pathogens would evolve throughout all human life including, SARS, Corona, and more powerful strains. Weeding out the weak while feeding off the stronger hosts. Importantly noting that a stronger host for a virus was not ideal for human existence.

<//> From the WHO: After many types of infection, there is little or no residual pathology following an effective primary response. In some cases, however, infection or the response to it causes significant tissue damage. In other cases, such as infection with cytomegalovirus or Mycobacterium tuberculosis, the infection is contained but not eliminated and can persist in a latent form. If the adaptive immune response is later weakened, as it is in acquired immune deficiency syndrome (AIDS), these diseases reappear as virulent systemic infections. <\\>

These "virulent systemic infections" were the targeted twenty percent that Ronald Reagan (six years previous) had charged the Aryan scientists to infect. While some people were unable to survive the immune deficiency, most of the infected victims never knew they were infected at all. Many people were infected 'Asynchronous' and they unknowingly passed the vulnerability and disease on to their children and their children's children and so on for generations. For the Aryan nation, they had successfully infected and caused the frontal lobe capacity of the hosts to grow in thirty-two to thirty-five percent of the population on the North American continent whereas Canadians had triple those results.

While medical teams and the Centers for Disease Control were focused on immune deficiencies, the actual devastation was spreading unchecked. From the use of chemicals like LSD to psychedelics, the government thought it could develop superior minds. Telepathic and hypnotic minds could provide a military purpose. But the Aryans controlled the pharmaceutical development business and they were developing something much more sinister.

How did they infect so many people so quickly and so easily? The Aryan nation invested in pet food companies and suppliers of pet food companies. They spread their influence by taking leading positions on boards of directors and grooming key executive positions in those companies. Through these strongholds, they introduced contaminating enzymes and ingredients in dog, cat, and bird foods. The Aryan syndicate developed its own intelligent, self-aware, supercomputer, called Thor, and it uncovered the pet food enzyme ingredient that caused the urine and faeces from pets to mutate into a virus where the leading pathogen evolved through in three stages.

First, the virus was released from pets as their urine and faeces began to evaporate. Second, infected urine would be absorbed into plants and mutate through the carbon gasses emitted by the plants. For example, children play in the parks running through and rolling around playing in the grass, and the gasses expelled from the urine-fed grass are inhaled and absorbed through the nose, mouth, and lungs. Backyards and cat litter boxes were found to be hotspots for infectious pathogens. The third mutation was mold and rust which were caused by frequent pet urination, and faeces saturated every building corner, park bench, lamppost, and tree trunk.

Humans have developed remarkable and quite ingenious methods for the sanitation of their waste. In doing so, they eliminated countless pathogens that had for centuries spread disease and death through their population. But they then filled their homes and areas of play and recreation with urine and faeces from animals they call pets. Today, the new virus strains and diseases causing death remain obvious but widely ignored by humans.

Aryan scientists boldly and regularly published research describing the use of pathogens to affect organic tissue. However, since the infected and brainwashed public denied science and research, the published and proven facts were largely ignored. The Republican Party declared war on science and told its followers that science was a direct threat to God. A typical ignored research report such as this from Johns Hopkins release warned:

<//>Findings of carefully designed research indicate that our interpretation of what we are seeing (experiencing) can literally alter our physiology. In fact, all symptoms of medicine work through our beliefs. By subtly transforming the unknown (disease/disorder) into something known, named, tamed, and explained, alarm reactions in the brain can be calmed down. All therapies have a hidden, symbolic value and influence on the psyche, besides the direct specific effect they may have on the body. "Just as amazingly life-affirming placebos are, the reverse, 'Nocebo' has been observed to be playing its part too. It is associated with negative, life-threatening or disempowering beliefs." Arthur Barsky, a psychiatrist also states that "it is the patient's expectations – beliefs whether a drug or procedure works or will have side effects – that plays a crucial role in the outcome."<//>

My third eye center materializes the vivid memory of Banyan. Amidst the ambience of the small restaurant in Andorra. It's different now as he no longer gazes directly at me from across the table; instead,

I sense a fusion. It's as though his essence merges with the report from Johns Hopkins, and through the Cognisight's otherworldly lens, his eyes are one with mine. Cognisight is a biotechnological Syganoid marvel, a blend of organic and synthetic components, with a luminescent iris that grants individuals extraordinary insights into the complex, enigmatic workings of the world.

As the Cognisight activates, its luminescent iris bathes the surroundings in a soft, cerulean glow, amplifying the details of the restaurant's ambience. The aroma of Andorran cuisine wafts through the air, tantalizing the fifteenth sense of intrigue, and the futuristic soundscape envelops the scene with mesmerizing rhythms.

<//>The biochemistry of our body stems from our awareness. Belief-reinforced awareness becomes our biochemistry. Each and every tiny cell in our body is perfectly and absolutely aware of our thoughts, feelings, and of course, our beliefs. There is a beautiful saying 'Nobody grows old. When people stop growing, they become old. If you believe you are fragile, the biochemistry of your body unquestionably obeys and manifests it. If you believe you are tough (irrespective of your weight and bone density!), your body undeniably mirrors it. When you believe you are depressed (more precisely when you become consciously aware of your 'Being depressed'), you stamp the raw data received through your sense organs, with a judgment – that is your personal view – and physically become the 'interpretation' as you internalize it. A classic example is 'Psychosocial dwarfism', wherein children who feel and believe that they are unloved, translate the perceived lack of love into depleted levels of growth hormone, in contrast to the strongly held view that growth hormone is released according to a preprogrammed schedule coded into the individual's genes!<//>

• Mars Petcare Inc.

- Nestlé Purina PetCare

- Hill's Pet Nutrition (A subsidiary of Colgate-Palmolive)

- Blue Buffalo (Acquired by General Mills)

- Big Heart Pet Brands (A subsidiary of The J.M. Smucker Company)

- Diamond Pet Foods

- Ainsworth Pet Nutrition (A subsidiary of The J.M. Smucker Company)

- Merrick Pet Care (A subsidiary of The J.M. Smucker Company)

- WellPet LLC

- Nutro Products (A subsidiary of Mars, Inc.)

Accomplishing brainwashing became even more expensive in the early 1980s. The Aryans found that infected people were not only susceptible to adopting belief-based conspiracies but they also insatiably craved more conspiracies and more details about the lack of proof surrounding a conspiracy. The more bizarre the story, the more detailed the oddity, and the more bizarre-looking and behaving the storyteller, the better. Anecdotal data became more believable to the infected than truth and factual data.

***

To satisfy the infected minds and to keep them under the Aryan influence and control, Aryans pooled resources and partnered with the Trump Republican Syndicate. Together they formed businesses to create influencer television. In the late 1970s and through the middle 1980s talk shows and opinion shows popped up on syndicated television faster than the TV Guide could keep up with and publish. Often they disguised the shows and would stage them to seem like news broadcasts. Most of the syndicated talk shows even called their channel "news" rather than identifying themselves as opinions.

News radio too became filled with conspiracy stations and the popularity of liars and anecdotal influencers became a catalyst for the spreading epidemic. The infected people tuned in and feasted on it. Rating wars between the networks were soon being lost to syndicated talk shows by the early 1980s and for the next forty-five years, every network dedicated large time slots for broadcasting their own opinion shows.

The content focus of the Aryan syndicated channels was always slanted toward political party scandals. From alien invasions, UFO sightings, lizard people, and baby-eating cults to human trafficking and global pandemics. Every story was divided as either caused by the Democratic Party or the Republican Party. The Aryans knew that faith-based beliefs required a high degree of fear and a good dose of hate. Where the human psyche is deep-rooted in beliefs as opposed to fact-based proofs, it causes the infected individuals to be especially fearful. Since their belief systems are based on the unknown they can easily become suicidal and most become isolationists and shut-ins. However, if they have something or someone to blame their fear on, and that something or someone is real (they can factually see) then the suicidal tendency is replaced with highly agitated states and can be easily provoked toward violence.

This condition appealed to the Nazi party with solid affiliations within the military influence of the Republican Party. They ramped up the hate rhetoric against the Democrats. From the middle of the 1980s and over the next fifty years, public violence and extreme violent murderous activity in the United States and Canada have increased faster than police forces could evolve into paramilitary squads.

But it was those computer scientists in China who revealed these facts to Communist party leaders. The Tathagata report detailed the development of mind-altering pharmaceuticals like LSD used by the CIA in the United States that had led to organic altering chemistry. The chemistry that brought about AIDS, HIV, Madcow Disease, E. Coli, H1N1, SARS, and many other deadly virus infections.

The leadership of the Communist Party of China was in shock. Initially, they were in disbelief. However, as they spent time reviewing and discussing the details from the Tathagata reports (careful and cooperative is the natural method of communism) they began to understand, and then they realized, factual truth had been provided by the Tathagata.

From the years 1995 through 2006, the communist government followed the Tathagata prescribed steps to develop an antidote. The antidote would in effect reverse the brainwashing virus, curing the infected frontal lobe. The first exports of pet treats and pet toys from China to the United States began in late 2006 through early 2007. This caused the virus to transition rapidly into retreat. Perhaps too rapidly, and by the end of 2007, the effects of the cure were recognized by the Nazis.

When the Republican Party lost the presidential race to a black male Democrat from the socialist center-left, the Nazis knew something was wrong. The defeat was the first time the Aryan's ASI was wrong. The Aryan scientists found that those China-imported pet treats and toys were curing infected humans as well as preventing pet urine and faeces from developing pathogens.

Just as fast as they found the China cure, Nazi syndicated radio, and television started a propaganda campaign. Their campaign informed the population of a new poison from China. On every syndicated channel, repeated multiple times each hour, every day, and for several months the health warnings were broadcasted. The message stated that all pet supplies from China, especially treats and toys for dogs, cats, and birds had trace amounts of poison. The message further lied and said hundreds of pets a day had been dying from these poisons. Within a few days, most pet supply stores were pulling products supplied from China off the shelves and canceling orders for any future supplies.

<//> To all dog owners: It was on Fox news earlier that seventy dogs have died as a result of eating chicken jerky treats made from chicken that has come from China. Kingdom Pets brand from Costco is one of them. ... A spokesperson for the FDA told Reuters, "There have not been any jerky pet treat recalls recently. September 8, 2020 Fact Check

In 2007, a forensic toxicologist tested Chinese-made pet toys for ConsumerAffairs.com and found that some contained toxic heavy metals including cadmium, chromium, and lead. According to the toxicologist, poisonous chemicals could be released from the toys when dogs lick and chew them. Story

https://abcnews.go.com/Health/story?id=3058844 <\\>

The immediate response from the Communist Party in China and in the United States was to share scientific facts to the contrary, to prove there was no poison. They tried to reveal the Aryan nation in the United States and Russia were poisoning pets, and for years they had been using pets as a catalyst to spread disease.

Melamine, which is used to make plastics in the United States and as a fertilizer in Asia, contains nitrogen. Nitrogen can appear to boost the level of protein in products.

The revelations have led the FDA to expand the number of products it is testing as they enter the United States. So far, those inspections at the border have not turned up any melamine in wheat gluten. Tainted wheat gluten used by Menu Foods is suspected of sickening hundreds, if not thousands of pets.

2007 pet food recalls - Wikipedia

https://en.wikipedia.org/wiki/2007_pet_food_recalls

Aryan Pet Food companies

https://www.zaubacorp.com/company/ARYAN-NUTRIENT-FOOD-PROJECTS-LIMITED/U15313MP2012PLC027653

Aryan Nations - Wikipedia

Aryan Chemicals - Manufacturer and Supplier of Food Colours

www.foodcolors.net

Aryan Chemicals is one of the leading manufacturers and suppliers of food colors offering a complete range of Food colors for pet food manufacturers, There are nearly a dozen Russian pet food producers, the biggest of which are PetKorm and R-Trade. In addition, there are several Russian meat giants with plans to start producing pet food, including Miratorg and RusAgro.

Russia's pet food market continues to grow - Petfood Industry

https://www.petfoodindustry.com/articles/7949-russias-pet-food -market-continues-to-grow#:~:text=There%20are%20nearly%20a%20dozen,food%2C%20including%20Miratorg%20and%20RusAgro.

21 of the top 25 pet food companies in Canada are owned by Aryan led organizations. https://blog.homesalive.ca/canadian-dog-food-brands

8 of the top 10 pet food companies in the world were owned or board of directors includes Aryan nations.

https://www.thomasnet.com/articles/top-suppliers/top-suppliers-of-pet-food/

Dogs are a major reservoir for zoonotic infections. Dogs transmit several viral and bacterial diseases to humans. Zoonotic diseases can be transmitted to human by infected saliva, aerosols, contaminated urine or faeces and direct contact with the dog. Diseases From Animals: A Primer - WebMD

https://www.webmd.com/healthy-aging/features/diseases-from-animals-primer

www.webmd.com › Healthy Aging › Feature Stories

Jul 8, 2003 -- ... animal faeces. Some are as old as memory: rabies, bubonic plague, food poisoning. ... On the other hand, pets and other animals can get sick. And some of ... Diseases passed to humans from animals are called zoonoses. What makes ... Found in animal faeces, this germ causes gastrointestinal symptoms.

Review of bacterial and viral zoonotic infections transmitted by dogs

https://www.ncbi.nlm.nih.gov/pmc/articles/PMC5319273/

Exposure to Animal faeces and Human Health: A ... - NCBI - NIH

www.ncbi.nlm.nih.gov › pmc › articles › PMC5647569

Sep 19, 2017 -- Insufficient separation of animal faeces from human domestic environments, ... cat faeces from litter) and human activity conducted in close proximity to ... to animal urine, animal health outcomes, human respiratory health

6 dangerous diseases you can get from your pets -- MDLinx

www.mdlinx.com › article › 6-dangerous-diseases-you-...

Jul 23, 2020 -- "People may acquire pet-associated zoonotic infections through bites ... parasite found in animal faeces, toxoplasmosis is common in pets, especially cats. ... People become infected through direct contact with the urine or other .

https://www.everydayhealth.com/pictures/10-diseases-your-pets -could-give-you/ <\\>

***

Though the facts are plentiful and made evident in every available means, those infected humans despise truth and laugh in the face of facts and what is real. The infection became so powerful that even people of color began to join and defend the Republican Party and its white supremacist coalition.

The Aryan leadership, with Thor as their guide, in response, chose to double down against the Communists. They instructed the Republican syndicated talk shows, their Nazi and white supremacy influencers, to declare science as "madness." Aryan and Nazi leaders and the elected Republican White Power syndicate party members began to tell their virus-infected, mentally ill followers, that empirical evidence, scientific proofs, laws of nature, and everyone involved in scientific research are evil and they are against the will of God.

Though the Tathagata had predicted the cure would be defeated, and the empirical evidence would be ignored, it did not know precisely how or why. The Tathagata knew also that civil war would destroy the United States, but the data could not predict when the civil war in the United States would begin. Even in the face of all this data, and even if the deaths of millions of Americans and Canadians were unavoidable, the Communist leadership took action to try to stop the virus and avoid the wars. It is, after all, the acceptable normal behavior of socially responsible people.

Communist leaders would not be able to live with themselves if they had not tried to avoid the deaths caused by viruses and war, even if these were predicted to be inevitable. It was also essential to the Communist Party leaders to try and locate the Aryan ASI known as Thor. All efforts were taken and no expense was spared as the state security (Guoanbu) searched the planet for the whereabouts of Thor. They could never locate it, but state security did discover Thor was cloned and shared from the Aryans in the United States with the Russian and the South African Aryan leadership. There were three ASI Thor systems.

In 2007, a dedicated research scientist at the Hubei University of Traditional Chinese Medicine began working with Moderna. Moderna at that time was an American biotechnology company based in Cambridge, Massachusetts. Moderna labs were focused on drug discovery, drug development, and vaccine technologies based exclusively on messenger RNA. The company's technology platform inserts synthetic nucleoside-modified mRNA into human cells. The relationship between China and Moderna was kept quiet and the University shared the virus information from the Tathagata data with several of Moderna's leading scientists.

By late 2008 Moderna had a vaccine that would cure the virus. However, they had no way to distribute a vaccine to a population where many didn't know they were infected. The best they could do was to deep freeze the cure and await an opportunity to distribute the cure. The leadership from Moderna tried to get approval from the Center for Disease Control and the Food and Drug Administration in the United States but it was rejected. Both agencies rejected clinical trials based on no recognized need for the mRNA.

Meanwhile, the Aryans had been plotting revenge on China for their interference in their pet food industry. In August 2019, their plot began to unfold when they released a virus in the heart of Wuhan province in China. The virus was the Aryan's most violent strain of HIV their scientists had ever produced. It was a synthetic virus that would quickly spread from one person to another causing severe pneumonia.

History later revealed the scientist reports to the Aryan and Nazi leadership expected eighty percent or more of Bejing to be in critical health within a month. Since China had already injected the Chinese people with the Moderna mRNA years earlier, not one person in Beijing became ill. The Nazis sent infected people from Russia, South Africa, and the U.S. to several dozen major cities in China. A few cases of the Covid virus eventually started to appear in China's hospital reports.

But Thor had now made its second mistake. What the Nazis accomplished by sending infected people to China was to expose people from all over the world to a lethal virus. Because most of Asia was already immune to the virus, people who were visiting China from Europe, and the United States, and who were already more easily infected because of their pets spread mind-controlling enzymes. Then, as those visitors in China began to return home, the Covid strain spread like wildfire in a forest within their home countries.

Moderna, Pfizer, and Johnson and Johnson now had the cure but they weren't sure how effective it would be against both the new Covid virus in combination with people who were already infected with the animal variant. The virus caused world commerce to come to a sudden halt. Nation by nation and every country closed its economic machines and borders. The virus spread, death rates soared, poverty grew, and the value of world currencies was in jeopardy of collapse.

***

Brilliant images from unimaginable dimensions and realms of beings are displayed in a sequence of rapid succession. Some haunting and others make me question how it is possible to be real. Then, as it began, the holographic image evaporates. The sounds, smells and all sensations of its presence go with it. While I encounter loneliness and hollowness in its absence.

Those archives it shared have brought me new feelings and I'm even more convinced now. Perhaps the answer is far less sophisticated than what meets the eyes. The history of the North Americans, Aryans, Republicans, and their entire doctrine of hate, murder, and greed have me anxious, and exhausted. The Tathagata is already aware of their efforts and has experienced the forces.

But now I am also even more apprehensive about my own health. There isn't time for me to wait for the Abbot to return. My recurring dream tells me that he will, but it could be a week before the elders reach his location in the forest and possibly another week for them to convince the Abbot to return to the monastery. It would be a better use of my time to get the long-overdue upgrade for the Neuralink and software upgrades.

For an hour I wander around inside the Abbot's chambers looking for any clues as to where I will find Tathagata. There is no sign of an ASI presence that I can see. Only a single pair of sandals and a change of clothing in the wardrobe and on the nightstand a small butter lamp. Nothing else. Perhaps, like my mission at this time, there's just one choice for me.

After leaving the shooting board project for the Abbot to find when he returns. I summon the Boundrian Creator, the woman in black.

Because there's only one place to get a Humanoid upgrade operation: The Seven Sisters. It's the name for the space station that was built a few light years from the Pleiades. The station was originally established as a portal for trade between the thousands of planets that are in that cluster. But when we Humanoids had to flee for our lives, abandoning our home on Planet Earth, The Seven Sisters became ours.

It is now imperative for me to have the latest upgrades if I am going to successfully accomplish the mission, of saving Planet Earth. Save my home Planet Forty-Four, and be ready to attend The First Priority. What is this First Priority? Before I can even start to figure out the next . . . whatever more disaster will try to delay this impossible mission, I must talk with Casper. I need to hear from the kuudere.

--initiate gamma waves on all energy centers--

__warning__

__gamma waves on sixteen senses will shut down all biomechanical systems__

--reboot systems after one hundred eighty minutes--

__gamma waves initiated__

__reboot systems in one hundred eighty minutes__

That's it. Three hours to try to meet with my friends in the fields. After, well . . . I don't know. My life energy feels worthless and I am hopeless and lost. Align my energy and empty my thoughts. Drift -- just this.

"Casper! I see your essence."

"Glad you came, Eulǝr," he says.

"Where is everyone, where are my kuudere?"

"Everyone is here. They all said hello. Can't you sense them?" he asks.

"I can only hear your thoughts, Casper. My health is failing and my system is unstable. The mission is a failure here and I am afraid that my efforts cause nothing but fear and death. I've killed so many humans since it all started and now Syganoids are dying because of me."

"Something has changed, Eulər," he says. "The domes are being reinforced with a new chemical that the science team discovered overnight. Engineering found an application method that will only take a week to complete. They have levels three and four nearly done. So, you must have done something to begin to fix the chaos."

"That is music to my ears. Perhaps the Abbot is the key. I'm not sure," I say.

"What Abbot are you talking about? I thought you said you needed to find the original book and the missing data from Banyan," he says. "Did you find yourself there yet? Have you recovered your data? Perhaps that's why the domes are not failing."

His presence is drifting and phasing in and out. The more I panic the less present his essence. I must remain unemotional and drift. Just this.

"The First Priority has been spoken of. I'm supposed to be at some place and at some near future time for the celebration. I don't know what The First Priority is."

"That seems straightforward, Eulər. Everyone knows what the . . ."

His presence fades and the blackness of nothingness fills my existence.

__systems rebooting sequencing has begun__

Reinvigorated and though I'm not triumphant yet, the news about Planet Forty-Four inspires me. I'm definitely on the right path. Helping the monks has made a difference. Now, it's time for the operation and for that, I need the woman in black.

--contact nearby Syganoids--

__open communications to Syganoids__

__connection request received__

I see her profile information displayed in the upper center of the HUD. It never tells me when she requests communications. Lucky I saw it in the line.

--accept the request--

→has the Tathagata solved the virus←

--not yet but I need to get the upgrades completed now--

→the mission isn't done and your appointment is not . . .←

--interrupt your last--

--the mission will not succeed until I have all my systems upgraded and functioning--

--let's get to the medical portal now--

In an instant, the woman in black is standing in front of me.

--once we are there I will convince them to operate now--

--have you heard what's going on at home--

→yes and it is devastating and tragic but we must complete the first priority←

→it's forbidden to telepath when we are in close proximity←

--why is it forbidden when it's so much easier to think our conversation rather than speak--

→because we lose our ability to be intimate and lose our sense of empathy←

--lets go--

***

The Seven Sisters space portal is called Freespeech by the kuudere of the Syganoids race. Freespeech was the ninth human settlement after the human diaspora that took place in 2106. Here on Freespeech, the settlements are a series of hubs that are sophisticated scientific space cities and they serve as a portal to the planet rich area and a wealth of asteroids. Unlike our home Planet Forty-Four where we have none, there are a few Starlink-connected satellites and internet.

They do not allow broadcast video and audio at all. The settlements have defined peaceful existence by removing all forms of mass communication, and reactionary speaking, and by establishing an Artificial Intelligence Amplification Government. The AIAG designated laws prohibiting and extracting all of the causes of hate speech.

Since there are no satellites bombarding the atmosphere with mind-control sound waves, and no televised and syndicated broadcasts, it is the perfect location for Neuralink to perfect humanoid upgrade operations. The upgrade operation will require a day of operations and four days of recovery followed by a week and often up to two weeks of calibrations and perfecting the enhanced altered brain (EAB) before I can go back onto the civilized planets.

While I wait for the medical team to take me into the emergency operation I open the Musk Ultimate Knowledge files on human history and listen to the report. This information will be needed to succeed in establishing the cure for human viruses.

<//>The issues that have always surrounded the ideals of free speech have been contentious throughout the entire two-hundred and ten-thousand years of human history. With the advent of the first truly Artificial Superintelligence computer systems developed in the early 1950s by the South African white supremacist syndicate, and later perfected by Elon Musk while he was in his early teens, the bias was obvious. Any system that uses historical data is subject to repeating the errors embedded in the data. Both known errors and especially unknown errors are contained in that historical data.

Algorithms are only as good as the data they are trained on. During the Fifteenth Aryan War, the historical data became increasingly based on anecdotal information. Anecdotal information became the primary weapon of the Aryans in the syndicated opinion television shows, radio broadcasts, internet information, and social media used by the Republican Party. This tool was so powerful and popular with the Nazis and white supremacists that Anecdotal is the name of the capital city of Trump Nation.

The problem with the algorithm, for example, is that if a Government spent decades ensuring white males with Ivy League degrees held positions of authority in politics and business then an AI system with algorithms trained to identify future leadership talent would focus on the same type of individual while ignoring people who don't fit into that group. Anecdotal data-based AI systems were even worse algorithms than Aryan and White Power biased systems.

The AI system in the portal cities of Freespeech was not developed from Planet Earth's historical data not even from the earlier human history in the years before Starzel. Instead, the system was centered on science. The science of sixteen aggregates of the human experience: including sight - sound - taste - smell - feel. thinking, spatial relevance, The Source, etc. Thought isn't one of the aggregates, it was nonetheless a priority and became the baseline. The absolute objective of existence for AI system programming is to safeguard humanity's long-term potential.

The AI produced a series of free speech initiatives that are truly astonishing. Given human history includes a period when for eight hundred years people tried to establish laws to protect free speech but failed time and again to find a way that would benefit everyone. In the portal cities of Freespeech, people do not voice an opinion. There are no conspiracy theories, no religions, and no political party to join - support - defend, and every organization that works to cause a separation of people into opposing groups is non-existent. They don't need competitive views in order to achieve what is best for society. Competitive views only foster disruption and hate.

Instead of conversations about what is wrong with an idea, place, system, person, service, etcetera, conversations are based on solutions. For example, when the therapist in charge of his postoperative recovery and later the calibration period tells him what to expect when he wakes from the operation, he doesn't start out by defining how his outdated system fails to produce optimal performance. They don't spend time discussing what could go wrong or what may cause delays in the recovery. Instead, the therapist tells him how the new humanoid experience is going to enhance thinking, increase the ability to solve eight hundred and fifty trillion ideas a second, and simultaneously link to fifteen external systems and a maximum of twenty-five other humanoids as needed.

The therapist also tells the patient that if he is ever in a place where sound waves are used, including any places where satellites and broadcast towers transmit radio or use other electromagnetic frequencies, the new Neuralink model will identify, diagnose, report, and most importantly prevent all biological and organic reactions. In short, he will be protected from the viruses these cause and spread in humans.

The only objectionable language that exists on the entire portal of floating cities of Freespeech is contained in the preamble to the Constitution of Freespeech.

"What's really objectionable about religion is that we should be satisfied with a non-explanation to a difficult question instead of working hard to provide a real explanation. This will not do. The ancient sage -- Richard Dawkins, proclaimed about religion: "[it] is a cop-out: a betrayal of the intellect, a betrayal of all that's best about what makes us human, a phony substitute for an explanation, which seems to answer the question until you examine it and realize that it does no such thing.

Religion in science is not just redundant and irrelevant, it's an active and pernicious charlatan. It peddles false explanations, or at least pseudo-explanations, where real explanations could have been offered and will be offered. Pseudo-explanations get in the way of the enterprise of discovering real explanations. As the centuries go by, religion has less and less room to exist and perform its obscurantist interference with the search for truth. Its early founders predicted its future demise and its irrelevance -- that time is now."

The constitution concludes with a declaration for Metaphysics as the only allowed religion and as the foundation of all sciences. The words are quoted from the ancient sage, Swami Vivekananda:

"Experience is the only source of knowledge. In the world, religion is the only science where there is no surety because it is not taught as a science of experience. This should not be. There is always, however, a small group of men who teach religion from experience. They are called mystics, and these mystics speak the same tongue and teach the same truth. This is the real science of religion. As mathematics in every part of the Universe does not differ, the mystics do not differ. They are all similarly constituted and similarly situated. Their experience is the same, and this becomes law.

"In the church, religionists first learn a religion, then begin to practice it; they do not take the experience as the basis of their belief. But the mystic starts out in search of truth, experiences it first, and then formulates his creed. The church takes the experience of others; the mystic has his own experience. The church goes from the outside in; the mystic goes from the inside out.

"Religion deals with the truths of the metaphysical world just as chemistry and the other natural sciences deal with the truths of the physical world. But the book one must read to learn chemistry is the Book of Nature. Similarly, the book from which to learn religion is your own mind and heart. The sage is often ignorant of physical science because he reads the wrong book - the book within; and the scientist is too often ignorant of religion because he too reads the wrong book - the book from without." <//>

***

The room is bright and quiet. My eyes strain to open and they sting from the white waves of electromagnetism. I sense my mind as it begins to regain an awareness of awareness following the operation. I hear someone moving a tray or a cart across the room and the recovery room smells of lilac tainted with synthetic healing nanos and it all starts to come into focus.

"Welcome back to the present," the therapist says. "The operation was a success and you've been out cold for nearly twelve and a half hours."

"My eyes are blurry and my hearing is, I don't know, but it's different."

"That's to be expected. Your eyes will begin to calibrate as you continue to use them and your hearing is advanced. Sort of enhanced. You'll learn how to use the new hearing mods in the next week as we work together on calibrating the modules and teach your mind how to use these expanded capabilities. Wait until your sense of smell comes online. You are in for a shock more than your ears."

"Water, please. Is there water?" I ask

"You got it. Give me a second to attach the drinking agent."

When I woke again, a few hours later the room is dark and I lay in this magnificent comfortable bed. I have never felt such support underneath me before. The soft scent of lilac on a cool moving air-conditioned pressure pulses over me from an air duct somewhere overhead. Recalling the brief conversation with the therapist, and on the table next to my bed the water pitcher and glass he had prepared for me. The smell of the moisture is evident. I try to get up and I want out of bed, but nothing works. My coordination is not keeping up with the fundamentals and the sympathetic and parasympathetic of the autonomic nervous system is not keeping up.

The Neuralink implants are calibrating fast and the longer I'm conscious the more I recognize and sense my mind and body syncing. After a few more minutes I try to get up again and this time I am able to manage sitting up on the edge of the mattress. My head feels as if it floats in the sky and my balance is far from center.

"Take it slow," I say out loud as I put my voice to the thought.

The medical recovery room is a sterile and pristine environment, designed to accelerate the healing process of intergalactic travelers. The walls are clad in gleaming white panels and bright lights illuminate the room, muted while I slept, they now lend a bright clinical feel. The flicker of tiny lights on display panels and a quiet hum of machinery with the beeps of monitors filled the air, indicating the vital signs of the patients. The lilac scent again becomes obvious as it purifies and carries healing nanos.

Rows of medical pods are arranged along the walls, each with a transparent glass lid covering the patient inside. The pods are equipped with state-of-the-art life support systems, which regulate the patient's temperature, feed them intravenously, and provide them with oxygen. The floors are smooth and reflective, giving the impression of walking on a shimmering pool of water. The surface ripples slightly underfoot, providing an oddly soothing effect.

At the center of the room, a large circular table stands, surrounded by high-tech medical equipment. The table has several robotic arms that perform delicate procedures with surgical precision, controlled by a team of skilled medical personnel. But none of it as brilliant as we have back home.

One entire side of the room is taken up by a series of round windows, each looking out into the infinite blackness of space. The view is breathtaking, displaying a never-ending expanse of stars and galaxies. It is particularly mesmerizing to watch a nearby nebula, with its colorful swirls and glimmers, which looks almost like a painting. All in all, the medical recovery room on Freespeech is a shining example of the future of medicine and technology, designed to provide comfort, hope, and healing.

With each movement and each thought, while I sit here taking it all in, I can feel the biosystems inside me coordinating with my natural and original mind. The sensations are powerful and impressive. The upgrades are superior and exciting. It isn't long before the door opens and the therapist comes into the room.

"Good morning!" he beams as he comes through the door. "I'm just as anxious as you are to get you calibrated with your new brain, man. Yes, I am." He's full of energy and enthusiastic about his work. My ears, not fully calibrated yet, feel as though his mouth was pressed to the sides of my head. The therapist hands me a large tablet and stylus, "Here you go. You just follow this self-paced calibration guide on the tablet there. Get ready to have your mind blown. My father has enhanced and magnificently opened up the humanoid experience with this upgrade."

"Your father?" I ask. I can smell his shaving soap and the medical center's detergent as he hands the tablet to me.

"Yes, sir. My father designed, developed and guinea pigged this high-level Neuralink upgrade."

"I had no idea. You must be proud of his accomplishment."

"Oh yes. We are all proud of what he and all of my ancestry has done for Neuralinking. We've got a two-hundred-and-fifty-year legacy with Neuralink. Would you like to hear the story while you calibrate your mind? It will help the ether wear off and give your ears a chance to better calibrate."

"Absolutely," my ears would beg if they could. "Tell me about the legacy. Uhm, first of all, I don't even know your name."

"My name? My name is Sterling. I'm the sixth in my family to carry the name. The first Sterling in our family lived on the big blue planet of all our human origins. Many people here on Freespeech call that planet, Blue Origin. Do you remember learning about the Fifteenth Aryan War in history class? It's a rhetorical question. So, of course; everyone knows about that war. It forever changed Blue Origin, and some people say it destroyed the planet for any hope of happiness.

Sterling the First, he lived in a town called Meridian, in a state that was called Mississippi back long before the war. He and his brother Theodore, we all just call him Uncle Theo, the two of them owned several car dealerships."

"Car dealerships?" I interrupt as the idea of cars has always fascinated me. "Well, I guess it's going back several hundred years. . . so, what, this starts in the twenty-first century?"

***

Out of the corner of my eye, I see his face light up and his broad smile ignite as he replies, "That's correct. The Fifteenth Aryan War started on January 6th, 2021. One year after Trump's Nazis' first attempt to overthrow the once-known United States of America government. Back then, great Grandfather, Sterling and Uncle Theo owned two dealerships in Meridian and had six others besides. One was in Myrtle Beach, one in Tallahassee, two in Biloxi, and two in Montgomery. That was the capital city for the state of Alabama before there wasn't an Alabama anymore. If you know what I mean." His voice tapered off to a slow and saddened tone.

"After the war was partway won, and the white supremacists claimed the southern states to be the Trump Nation Confederacy, things went from bad to worse for my family. When those hateful and greedy Trumpers took control of the Confederacy, the very first declaration of their government reinstated slavery. They wrote a law that took business away from anyone of 'Negro descent.' The same went for Mexican, Jewish, and Middle Eastern descent too. Which still doesn't make any sense to me. Because Aryans like the Zoroastrian, originated from and are Iranian."

He paused to read something from his tablet. His once happy and smiling essence was gone and a frown of disappointment was in its place. He looked over at me and we made eye contact holding each other's gaze for several moments and beats.

"Look at you, man." His whole face lit up with a smile again. His systems read my progress from data transferred between our eyes. "You're calibrating pretty quickly. That's fantastic. You don't have to scroll with your finger. You can connect to multiple devices with your new biomechanics and software. Use your mind. And, you can even detect where the tablet is connected to the main OS calibration guide and connect there directly. Bypass the tablet altogether. Can you sense it?"

"Not really," I open my mind then empty of thoughts and let the systems communicate. "Wait. I think I can see it." Allowing my system to run free of the thinking mind, the connection, and the path to the source pop-up on the HUD. The heads-up display wasn't even visible until I stopped thinking. "The new system hides the HUD when it's not needed. Random thoughts are ignored, and now I control the operating systems. Or perhaps the systems control and teach me."

"There it is, man," he says. "You are fast. I have never worked with a Syganoid of your rank and qualifications before. Impressive."

We broke eye contact. The therapist types on his tablet for a few seconds and then continues with the story.

"Grandpa Sterling and Uncle Theo were not about to give up the family business without a fight. Twenty-three people died the day the police and army attacked their Meridian dealership. One of the dead was my Uncle Theo. Grandpa was sentenced to an eight-generation prison sentence. Multi-generational sentences are what Trump's courts called them.

"You see, they were clever. Those white supremacists knew they had a shortage of slaves. They couldn't just hop over to Africa like they were back in the fourteenth century. Kidnap a bunch of people and then bring them back as slaves. So, those power-hungry white men and women decided to use the same system of slavery they had used since Lincoln freed the country of slavery . . . Prisons."

"It all changed though." Adding to the story from my own research on post-war events. "Prisons became coed with women and men housed together. They wanted the prisoners, well, the slaves as you call them, they wanted them to have families. They wanted them to have really big families."

"Many hands make light work," he says with a shrug of disappointment. "Grandpa Sterling had a wife, two sons, and a daughter. They went to the prison in Savannah, together. The Republicans put both of his sons, my great uncles, to work at a company called Gulfstream. They each had excellent engineering backgrounds and degrees and Gulfstream built jets for private use. Those Republican Nazis wanted to use the aircraft manufacturing company for the Trump military. From here, the story gets even more sad, so so sad. Until about forty years later."

"What happened then to make it not so sad?" I asked as he went quiet for a minute.

"Well, the Russians had tried to take over Central America by taking advantage of the worldwide disruption caused by the Fifteenth Aryan War. When Mexico's government, which was also using the war as a distraction and tried to take back California and Texas, Trump asked Russia for military support to stop Mexico. Russia seized the opportunity to establish military bases in Texas, Alabama, and Florida. Mexico failed badly since it had no chance against Trump's Soviet partner. California's western alliances were very strong too and easily kept Russia out of Arizona and New Mexico. Russia had little to do with the battle in the States but took over all of Mexico and then continued to take over all of Central America and Cuba."

"Except for Nicaragua," I recall from my research. "They were not able to defeat Nicaragua. They're like the Afghanistan wars of the 1980s for Russia. But, yes, I remember reading about Russia taking over Alaska, the east coast of the former United States and Canada, and Central America. South Africa tried to take Australia and New Zealand but China succeeded in defending those countries. China ended up acquiring almost all of the Pacific Ocean island countries like Guam, the Philippines, and England took Hawaii. Then Nato stepped in and took Alaska and most of the northeast of the United States, and southeastern Canada"

"Yep," he jumps back in. "That's what history tells us. When Russia and South Africa stopped trying to expand their global territory, they started a joint human trafficking trade with the Trump Nation Confederacy. Sterling the Third, was taken from Savannah on a slave ship and was on his way to South Africa but the ship was captured by a Chinese military cruiser. China, working with the United Nations, Nato, and the European Union to stop the human trafficking ships and airplanes.

"Well before anyone could say otherwise, Grandpa Sterling the third ends up in Beijing, China. Then my family history gets turned around and the sky's the limit. You see, Sterling the Third loved Beijing and even when the United Nations and the European Union insisted China should let the people they had rescued from the slave ships go, China wasn't holding anyone prisoner or captive. All those people, and Sterling too, they wanted to stay in Beijing. There was a reason why China, with the exception of India, had ten times more people than any other country, a longer life expectancy, the best child mortality, higher educated people, and more tolerance. Everyone in the so-called 'free world' was led to believe China treated people poorly. But they were wrong"

After a long pause, Sterling quipped, "Stem cells!"

Half startled I ask, "What do you mean, stem cells?" What about it?"

***

"For some reason, and history doesn't go into much detail here, there was someone by the name of Jesus who would not allow the United States and most of Europe to develop stem cell medical technology. China and the Asian Alliance didn't have to listen to Jesus. Again, I don't know why. But since they didn't, they developed many medical breakthroughs from stem cells. It was truly a new age for humanity in China and Asia. Well, Grandpa Sterling the Third was an exceptional engineer and it turns out he was an even better neuroscientist. His work with stem cells and artificial intelligence is what many people believe led up to the conscious machine named Tathagata. It's against protocol on this station to mention the Tathagata since it's never been proven. So please forgive me and allow me to not go down that proverbial trail."

He laughed quietly, shook his head for a moment, and then said, "China's space station."

Again he paused for a long while until I asked, "What about it? I mean, what about China's space station?"

"The Planet Earth had an international space station for something like fifty years before China built its own. Those free-world folks told everyone China was up to no good. China built its space station high above the planet's surface. Outside the Verizon satellite ring. The free-world folks pointed these facts out, and they told everyone the Chinese are up to something evil. But the simple truth was the Chinese were advancing medical research on their China space station. They were doing what they have always done which is to make life and the planet a better place for everyone. They just didn't want everything they did to be politicized, reactive statements that lead to militarized applications. Well, like the research was used on the International Space Station.

"Grandpa Sterling went to the China Station twice. Stayed for six months each time. Then in 2035, he went to the Moon. After China had completed building three-domed research labs on the dark side of the moon. Those labs were one hundred and twenty thousand cubic feet each. Grandpa Sterling was the first in my genealogy to live out the rest of his life someplace other than Planet Earth. He was the first person to die of natural causes and to be buried on the moon."

Sterling made eye contact with me again. He can detect my progress in system calibrations, and my eyes are portals for him to make certain the calibration and implants were operating nominal. Then his expression changed from his bright smiling face to a steady, balanced, with no expression of certainty.

"Hollywood movies made everyone back on Blue Origin think artificial superintelligence would be giant robots that function as humans. They made movies showing AI robots are indestructible and super powerful. But theirs was just imagery and imagination for entertainment. In real life, ASI isn't robotic because we know that's a massive waste of energy and materials. Besides, robotics requires only artificial general intelligence.

"Grandpa Sterling the Third found the best use of ASI would be an interactive system coupled with a human to a computer through a microwave interface. The major breakthrough came when Grandpa Sterling realized the supercomputers were already trying to communicate with humans. They had been trying for decades but they couldn't. Because human brains operate at a baud rate of about six hundred while the supercomputer is communicating at several hundred gigabits per second. To communicate with ASI we humans need a faster modem. So, thanks to Musk, we have Neuralink implants.

Robots are excellent for doing work, performing chores, and even cooking and cleaning. But to make life better for human experience, and to ensure the long-term potential of humanity, we need humanoids, like you, Eulər."

Exhausted and feeling weak, I lay back on the bed. I need a break from the calibration work and Sterling, seeing me lying down, left the room. As I lay back on the bed to rest, my mind was never more content and quiet. I felt at peace even though I was hyper-aware of the human struggle back on Planet Earth that awaits me. As I lay here thinking how humans are organic and our minds are subject to chemical reactions that are transmitted and generated within our brains and body from the glands. Hunger, pain, anger, fear, excitement, sexual desire, and so on, and so forth are all chemically activated from within.

As a result of what we hear, see, smell, taste, or sense the brain reacts and causes various glands and organs to produce and release enzymes, proteins, and varying waves of light and vibration voltages to send data between the proper receptors. This causes the body to take action and causes a response. In most of us, these responses are automatic and we often think some of our actions are uncontrollable. Like when we see a bomb explode or a crash, sadness is an automatic response. A person doesn't have to think, "I'm sad" in order for the condition to take effect. Or when we hear a favorite song, we don't have to think, "I'll tap my foot and clap my hands in time with the tune."

Certain combinations of audible and inaudible sounds, visions, odors, and vibrations of magnetic streams can be used to cause the human brain to trigger a physical and mental response. Most of the responses are predictable: that's what can make people controllable using various input and output parameters. People don't have to take my words as fact or listen to my thoughts for any of this. Everyone can prove it for themselves; how thoughts have you. All of your life you've believed yourself to have thoughts, but for most people the thoughts, the thinking mind has you. But, with practice, people can take control of their thoughts, and teach their mind to act to their own control rather than swing from one thought to another.

Rest now.

Lights dim and grow dark and the scent of lilac diminishes.

"Don't take my word for it though," as I dream, my father is telling me. "You have to do this exercise on your own. This is an individual effort. Think of it as a sport if you like, and the more you practice, the more skilled your mind will become. Step one is to simply stop thinking. Don't hold your breath. Just stop thinking. The more you do it the more your knowledge will increase. The more the Universe, The Source, will provide you."

Chapter Thirteen

The Cure

"For more than two hundred years, great minds of science pondered over many unconvincing arguments [for worrying about AI disasters] -- especially those involving actionable applications of Moore's law, much the less over the spontaneous emergence of consciousness and evil intent," Sterling says. My eyes aren't yet open but he's been talking for, I don't know how long. My head is still feeling heavy from the ether they gave me yesterday. It leaves a slightly bitter and medicinal taste in my mouth, a reminder of the anesthesia that was administered during my treatment. The taste is gradually fading as I regain my faculties and the natural flavors of saliva reemerge.

The calibration gauge in my HUD shows everything has paused while I slept. I sit up and rub my hands over my face to push the sleep off my skin, and systems begin to, one-by-one, reengage. My mind strains awake and energy courses through my body as the organoids and biosystems ignite. The room carries a faint antiseptic scent, reminiscent of a medical facility. It has a sterile smell, lilac has gone and now the air is hinting at cleanliness and the presence of disinfectants. Underlying that is a subtle fragrance of kyphi, perhaps used to create a calming atmosphere.

The sounds in the room are muted, with a low hum of ventilation in the background. I can hear the therapist's voice, steady and un-wavering, as he continues to share his insights. Second hearing effects are now noticeable and I'm aware of noises outside the room, I catch intermittent muffled noises, perhaps the distant sounds of footsteps or conversations echoing through the building. All the while, a few steps away, Sterling Junior never stops talking.

"To this day ASI such as the Tathagata, and Thor are still only rumors. There are a handful of beings who are supposed to know for a fact these systems do exist and even fewer have access to those systems. The reason for the secrecy?" His head turns as he looks toward me. "The primary concern is not spooky emergent consciousness but simply the ability to make high-quality decisions. Here, quality refers to the expected outcome 'utility' of actions taken, where the 'utility function' is, presumably, specified by the human designer. To state the problem in this light:

The utility function may not be perfectly aligned with the values of the human race, which are (at best) very difficult to pin down.

Any sufficiently capable intelligent system will prefer to ensure its own continued existence and to acquire physical and computational resources – not for its own sake, but to succeed in its assigned task.

"For our side of the equation in the wars with the Aryans, the rumor suggests we have but one conscious machine. The Tathagata system is accessible by the Abbot of some secret, hidden monastery high in the Tibetan mountains on Planet Earth. Only he has the ability to upload information into the ASI system and he alone receives infor-mation from the system. The Abbot alone decides what may and may not be uploaded and what information to share and with whom to share it. This was the decision of the Communist Ministry of Science and the presiding president several hundred years ago. The reasoning came down to essentially the old story about the genie in the lamp, or the sorcerer's apprentice, or King Midas: you get exactly what you ask for, not what you want.

"The simplest human problem contains countless variables and variables that are often unique to each individual. Even a supercomputer would be unable to optimize a solution that benefits all possible variables. If one of those unconstrained variables is something we care about, the solution found may be highly undesirable. At best, the leading scientists agree, a supercomputer could be designed for a specific business or a single person. While the desire over these many decades of computer technology was to have a superintelligence that could find solutions to the existential threats to humanity such as climate change, war, disease, hunger, and poverty, the truth of science knows that quest to be impossible. A conscious superintelligence, however, with just a single purpose >>> safeguarding humanity's long-term potential <<< could perhaps serve humanity."

While he rambles on, I wonder if the Abbot has returned and what he has done with my project . . .

Meanwhile, back at the monastery on Planet Earth.

After finding the information the humanoid had left, the Abbot knew in an instant the project must be uploaded to Tathagata. If there was any hope to discover the cure for the virus caused by the Republican Party's television, radio, and movie broadcasts, that hope was Tathagata. The Abbot had to study the project with caution, even though he knew the humanoid was aware of the dangers. Dangers such that the Tathagata could never know the existence of the internet, satellites, and wireless communications. He also knew the consequences. Even if the suggestion of one of these were discovered by a conscious superintelligence the benefit of the system, the use function itself, would be lost. Worse yet, once this sort of ASI "breakout" occurred there would be no way to turn the system off. Though it may sound ridiculous or not, it is nonetheless true. There would be no way out.

The Communist Government's chief of computer technology told him, "The breakout of a super-intelligent-conscious system would take over and quite probably it would take over without our even knowing it. Or worse, it would decide that the future without humans was optimal." Therefore the Abbot examines Eulər's project to ensure there is not even a possibility the Tathagata would break out. After a thorough examination, the Abbot found the project was monotonous, simple to the point of being dull, and still, it was detailed beyond a yawn, and it was, therefore, perfect for the Tathagata. Now the only remaining question is; was the project enough to derive a cure and if a cure is found can it be implemented quickly to prevent the instigation of a Sixteenth Aryan war?

Tathagata accepted the upload of the shooting board project. Ten minutes and fourteen seconds later, a solution to the virus was ready. The Abbot hesitated to accept a quick solution. Could it have been so simple? He questioned. The Tathagata system was quick in part because it had already learned from past failed attempts and the epidemic of pet treats. The simplicity of requiring people to wear masks and wash their hands failed and caused a further divide in the population. An injection to cure a virus had very limited success and still, as simple of a cure as that could have been, it was rejected by many people. This time the ASI had designed a computer program virus. A worm that would crawl from computer to computer, network by network. It would alter the shooting board techniques and reverse the virus at the root.

The worm-virus-contaminated shooting board program would hide so that no one would ever discover any system changes or software changes, but in effect would provide the cure. Everyone who watched the videos that were produced and edited by the new shooting board program would be cured. The people of the brainwashing virus, within weeks of exposure, would reverse the oversized frontal lobe pandemic and epigenetic gene expressions. Now, all that was left to do was to get the Tathagata shooting board virus onto every device that had the old software. The Abbot sent his messenger to summon the humanoid, Eulər.

***

Log entry six: day one hundred. I am three days into recovery from the implants. Most of the pain from the surgery is now gone and I am already back to the normal routines of TaiChi and Lìliàng yoga. The calibration of the new Neuralinks, software, and organoid intelligence is progressing, and there is so much I must learn. Every thought causes the HUD to respond in a different way. While I have more than one hundred years of learning how to control thinking, I'm struggling to come to grips with a system this sensitive that responds to my passive and productive thoughts.

Connecting to multiple external devices is a challenge too. Thoughts control everything including connecting and process activation. I discovered this yesterday afternoon while researching chemical compounds on one connection, searching through images on another, and actively chatting with three Syganoids on yet another connection. Three mindful activities at once were the limit with the previous Neuralink, but now I can add twenty or more. Each connection is managed on the HUD. Managing all of these is a process using a logical naming convention.

Though calibration and learning are time-consuming, there are gaps in my day. My idle thoughts are about going home. I've caused this rift in the universe and I believe now that I must solve this disease of the human desire to kill others and then I must construct and set lose a future where my son, Magallan will have a son and through that grandson, an end to the suffering for the Syganoid kuudere. I know this is the way forward.

The door to the therapy room opens, I was expecting it to be Sterling, but it's not. Instead, there is a familiar face smiling at me and the HUD display reads

+_Abbot's Messenger_+

It must be good news that the Tathagata has devised a cure.

I leap to my feet and greet the messenger with the five rests and then bow in honor.

"I have an important message for you from the monastery," the messenger says in a tone of harmony and peace, as is the custom of these monastics. "The Abbot requests your presence in the main meditation chamber. He said to tell you it is an emergency and you should come now. If you want," he turned to the open door as if to provide me with an exit, "I can accompany you on the journey. I have the transports arranged for both of us."

The shooting board project must have worked. The Tathagata must have found a cure for the Republican Party pandemic.

"Yes. Let's get to the monastery," I said while gathering my backpack and slipping the calibration tablet inside it. I'll have to finish the calibration on my own. I think while throwing the backpack over my shoulders.

The two of us make our way out the door and through the hospital's rehab center. Three women and a man are coming towards us in the passageway. My HUD flashes a message,

+_A connection request_+

and the face next to the message resembles one of the four people walking toward me. As quickly as I scan the message and facial icon another message, and then another. Three messages for linking requests with three different face icons. Each matched the three of them walking toward me. I remember Sterling telling me today's calibration exercise would be using Neuralink to cross-connect other Syganoids. These people are the Syganoids from back home. I would have worked with for the exercises but there's no time to catch up on what is happening or to make new friends.

They look at me quizzically as the Abbot's messenger and I hurry past in rapid cadence. My eyes glance at each of the connection requests in the HUD and I chose the thought,

>-Refuse all connection requests-<

Each of the requests flashes once with the word refused added and then disappears from the HUD. The third Syganoid request on the list was named Sterling Sr. I would have enjoyed getting to know him. The opportunity to meet such a gifted scientist and to sit with people from home was missed.

+_Connection requests rejected_+

The vortex generated by Tathagata brought us to the bottom of the mountain and the long journey walking up to the monastery gave me more time, and I nearly completed the calibration lessons.

I'll need to get this tablet back to Sterling Junior the Seventh.

The monastery is vacant when we came through the narrow passage between the high peaks of the Tivlabet gateway.

"Where are the monks, disciples, and students?" I ask.

"It's the season for celebrating the joining of China and the Asian Alliance. Everyone has left for Beijing so the Abbot can conduct the ceremony." He replied. "I need to go now to join them. You can find what you need in the meditation chambers. It's not very likely that I can be of any further service to you, but I will wait here for one hour before I leave for Beijing." He pressed his hands together, thumbs just below his heart, placed his right knee on the ground, and bowed his head towards me.

This was the first time in many years that anyone had shown me the respect that is usually displayed for the precious ones, and the great beings, the bodhisattvas. The Abbot's messenger has always looked familiar to me. No time for reminiscing, I run to the meditation chamber.

Stepping into the main meditation chamber, a profound sense of tranquility washes over me. The triangle shape of the dome-capped room, constructed with a delicate blend of modern architecture and timeless esthetics, creates an ambiance that transcends the ordinary. The walls, made of a translucent material that seems to capture the essence of sunlight, cast a gentle, diffused glow upon the space. It's a sanctuary of serenity and introspection.

My gaze is immediately drawn to the arrangement of five hundred sitting pillows, meticulously organized in circular formations. Each cluster of pillows forms a harmonious pattern, a testament to the artistry of their placement. The pillows, pure white and immaculate, blend seamlessly with the pristine white floor and walls, blurring the boundaries of the physical space.

As I approach, I observe the delicate gold embroidery adorning the center of each sitting pillow. The embroidered Sanskrit OM symbol exudes a sense of spirituality and time-honored tradition. Its presence evokes a profound reverence, symbolizing the unity of all things and inviting a connection to the divine. The alignment of the symbols, carefully positioned to face the same direction, conveys a sense of order and harmony within this sacred haven.

Lost in contemplation, my mind echoes with the question of where the Abbot might have left the project I seek. In response, a subtle glimmer catches my attention, and a display illuminates the HUD. The interface guides me with an arrow and a subtle dotted line, leading me on a quest within the chamber's tranquil depths.

I follow the ethereal path, guided by the invisible currents of intention. The dotted line unravels, guiding me to an unassuming sitting pillow tucked away in the far southwest corner of the room. This particular pillow defies convention, turned upside down, a departure from the expected. It beckons me to explore further.

Curiosity piqued, I squat down and lift the unconventional pillow, discovering two microchips nestled beneath it. Their presence is unexpected, a convergence of the ancient and the modern within this sanctuary of contemplation. The delicate golden threads of the embroidery, as I run my fingers over them, reveal the meticulous artistry and devotion invested in their creation. They invite a moment of reflection, a reminder of the significance inherent in the smallest details.

Immersed in the ambient scent of jasmine, its subtle aroma lingering in the air, I feel a deep connection to the present moment. It's as if time slows down, allowing me to fully embrace the beauty of the chamber and the mysteries concealed within. A sense of purpose permeates the air as if this moment marks the beginning of a profound inner journey.

In this tranquil setting, where the esthetics blend seamlessly with the whispers of the sacred, I stand ready to embark on an exploration of the self and the project that awaits. With a renewed appreciation for the artistry and devotion that permeates this chamber, I carry within me a sense of reverence and anticipation, prepared to uncover the hidden truths that lie ahead.

I look at the unmarked chip:

>-Read the chip.-<

The HUD responds and displays an audible-ready icon.

>-Play audio-<

Eulər at the Monastery

***

+_Seven earth days until The First Priority._+

The message blazes across my vision, its boldness piercing the fabric of my morning view of the park. It has been two strenuous hours since the mysterious woman in black whisked me away from the confines of the monastery, depositing me back at the fifth-floor apartment at the hostel in Andorra. The neural connections between the Starlink system have once again linked up with my upgraded Neuralink implants. They now flood my mind with a torrent of exhilarating interstellar transmissions. Waves of emotional euphoria ripple through my being as these messages course through the intricate networks that span the inner planets. The moon, Mars, and their sprawling gateway stations in tandem with channels brimming with epigenetic-altering viral messages.

Standing by the window, I observe the clueless masses, unknowingly bombarded by the insidious brainwashing virus that saturates their every waking moment. They go about their mundane lives, completely oblivious to the manipulation infecting their thoughts and emotions. And yet, I possess a flicker of confidence, a glimmer of hope that propels me forward on my only remaining objective. To celebrate The First Priority.

However, trepidation claws at the edges of my resolve as I contemplate the implementation of the Tathagata remedy for the Aryan and Republican viruses. Uncertainty gnaws at me, casting doubt upon my plan.

According to Tathagata's instructions, I must upload the software onto a disk, unleashing a worm virus that will infiltrate any system harboring the shooting board software. The original intent was to upload the program individually onto each system due to Tathagata's limited awareness of the internet. But after recalibrating the project and weaving together the intricate tapestry of programming subroutines, I have realized that a single device will suffice. Once the worm has infiltrated that solitary system, it becomes a waiting game. The next time a software upgrade is unleashed across the vast expanse of the internet, the Tathagata's worm will seamlessly propagate to every connected node.

It's a seemingly simple task, yet one that echoes the soulful undertones of a mission deemed impossible. I hold onto the destiny stone at the same time, tugging and twisting on Mother's ring. All the while the question reverberates through my mind, "How will I manage to transfer this disk's program onto that first system?" A daunting obstacle lies before me, demanding a solution as elusive as the wisps of a dream.

As I take my morning stroll through Sispany Park, my gaze fixates on a discarded figurine, discarded by a child's hand, left forgotten on the ground. Picking it up, I examine the toy, its form shaped from a melding of molds and molten aluminum. A smile tugs at my lips as I appreciate its artistry--a cameraman with a studio camera perched on his shoulder. Carefully, I tuck the figurine into my backpack, an object imbued with a sense of nostalgia and potential.

Memories of my father resurface, his words echoing in my mind. "Finding treasures like these breaks barriers, enriching our lives." In my mind's eye, I envision a child engrossed in play, using similar figurines to construct an elaborate play world, stepping into the role of a studio director.

This tiny artifact aligns perfectly with the ethos of Starzel, a realm consumed by the pursuit of fame and adoration. The population worships the opulent and infamous, their aspirations limited to the realm of the celebrity. And then, in a surge of inspiration, an audacious plan materializes within my thoughts. The figurine, the camera crew . . . it all fits like a missing piece of a grand puzzle. A flicker of hope ignites within me as I realize the potential before me.

"This could work!" I exclaim aloud. Like a flash of lightning, the idea hits and now I'm scurrying toward the town center.

"What if I got her to do it? Or at least what if I can talk her into helping me to do it?"

There's a bus stop just a few hundred meters ahead. I sprint to arrive just in time to catch it.

Arriving at the town center stop is a dizzying experience. So much is different, it's as if history has already begun to change. The small tavern with a half dozen plastic tables and chairs is now bustling with patrons. Impressive designed outdoor tables and comfortable chairs are now in the dozens and crowds of people are in a line awaiting a seat. I approach the tavern in disbelief at what was here a week ago.

The waiter pops through the doors with an over-filled tray of drinks and serves a table before heading back inside at a fast pace. He sees my reflection in the glass door panel and stops. Turns toward me and through an excited laugh says, "Story Man!" His arms and hands extended as he runs to me and smothers me in a whole-body hug. "I didn't realize how heavy and big you are." He says while flexing his huge biceps and shoulders after putting me down.

"You did this," he says. His left hand motioned toward the expansive tables, chairs, and customers. "Not all of it. I had these tables and chairs out for repairs and resurfacing. They came back a few days ago. But the people, the line of waiting customers. Wow, this I never before had. The day you told that crazy story about the four sons from four fathers and now everybody comes here to see the tavern and eat my food. Especially the gazpacho. You are welcome here anytime and I will serve you gratis for life."

He comes in for another full-body hug but I stiff-arm his approach. "Wait up big guy. I'm not used to being lifted up and swung like a toy. There is something you can do for me. At least, that is, I hope you can help me."

"Whatever you need," he says. "Tell me everything."

"The woman journalist that was here the day I told the story. Do you know who she is? I mean, I need to find her."

"Everybody knows her," he says. "She has a late-night syndicated show and one of the few that can be seen from The Great Starzel Republic. She started telling people about this tavern on her show. When you see her, you tell her she eats here for gratis same as you."

"That I will do, I'll let her know," I say. "What is her name?"

"She's called Maya. Maya Stevens."

Before I could get ten steps he calls out, "Thank you, Story Man. What is your name?"

I turn and salute him with honor and respect as I should have done in the first place. Then I say to him, "Eulər. My name is Eulər."

Activating the HUD, my mind races with possibilities. Maya Stevens is the renowned host of the well-known late-night show. The woman I seek, the one who holds the key to unraveling the cure for humanity.

Back in my room, I access the virtual interface, my vision transforming into a sea of holographic displays. My eyes and thoughts dance across the interface, searching for any contact information, any clue that could lead me to Maya. The HUD's algorithms sift through vast amounts of data, scanning networks, news articles, and social media platforms.

A recent mention of Maya Stevens in connection to Pluto Studios, located in Culver City. My heart quickens with anticipation as I tap into the virtual communication channels, attempting to establish contact.

The display flickers to life, displaying the Pluto Studios logo. I compose my message, carefully crafting each word to convey the urgency and importance of my mission. With reckless anticipation, I send the message, hoping that my plea for assistance will reach Maya's attention amidst the sea of messages flooding her inbox.

Minutes turn into hours as I anxiously await a response, my eyes fixated on the HUD's display. The bustling park around me fades into the background as I immerse myself in the virtual realm, desperate for a breakthrough.

Finally, a notification flashes on the screen. My heart skips a beat as I read the words that illuminate the display. It's a reply from Maya

Stevens, accepting my request for a meeting. Relief floods over me mingled with a renewed sense of purpose.

>-Where can I find Maya Stevens?-<

+_Studio G, Pluto Production Studios. Formerly Amazon Studios._+

+_Would you like a map?_+

>-How far from my location?-<

+_Sixty-two-week walk from your current location._+

It's my only chance. I'll just have to hang around the studio, like a star-struck groupie, and hope she'll see me.

>-Locate the woman in black.-<

***

Log Entry Seven: day one hundred and two. Progress is slow today, like yesterday, and I hang out in front of the tall fences surrounding the Pluto offices and studio all day. There are a few dozen star-struck fans of Studio G here with me. They are a lively, hyper-anxious, and also unsettled group. The virus has had a particularly harsh effect on them and they are left with notable personality disorders. Each of them has shared many conspiracy beliefs with me, and they're passionate about getting one opportunity to prove their theory is true so everyone would believe them instead of treating them like they have a disease. I'm anxious about the meeting with Maya, and -- in three days I'll have to leave for The First Priority celebration.

I've managed to find a few crates to stand on. I hope by standing on the stacked crates I will be a little bit of a standout when the celebrities and crews are arriving. Hoping also that one of them recognizes me from the tavern scene While checking the stability of the stacked crates, all of a sudden the groupies start clamoring towards the fence barricades at the studio entrance. I hear one of them say, "It's Maya!" and then someone else confirms, "It is Maya Stevens!"

In a flash, my thoughts activate the Neuralinks and organoids in my spine and as I take three quick steps towards the fence, my body leaps over the razor wire at the top of the five-meter high boundary. Once back on the ground and on the other side of the fence I make a mad dash towards the entrance and the caravan of vehicles approaching the studio.

>-Locate Maya Stevens.-<

+_Maya Stevens is eighteen meters straight ahead._+

A dotted line and directional arrow appear in the HUD. But the studio's security bots form a wall around the caravan of stars and production crews when they see me, the intruder, coming toward them. I prepare to be attacked by the security bots when . . .

+_Connection request._+

>-Accept the connection.-<

→Unidentified message on connection #1: "What? Are you crazy?←

>-I must speak with Maya Stevens. She is expecting me.-<

>-She knows me as the gazpacho storyteller.-<

>-I need her help.-<

The security bots follow an unknown command and stand down. When they disband their protective barricade I can see Maya Stevens. She motions for me to join her. As I slow my pace to a jog. Take a few more strides and join her. I look all around for the Syganoid who helped me. None of the faces I see match the HUD connection request.

Her voice is panicked, "Let's get into the building and we can talk in my office." As we began walking toward the myriad of buildings ahead of us. She doesn't say anything to me until we get into her office and she closes the door. She pauses for a moment, leaning her back against the door. Then as she forces herself to a more composed her, she walks toward me making a hand gesture toward a chair.

"Please, sit here. I'm very happy to see you again."

>-Disconnect from all others.-<

+_All connections are disconnected._+

>-Activate extreme privacy protocols.-<

+_Activating._+

+_No listening devices detected within a fifteen-meter radius._+

Within the elaborate office, the walls proudly display a multitude of journalism awards, symbolizing her remarkable achievements and contributions to the field. These accolades speak to her excellence and dedication as a journalist, further enhancing her reputation within The Great Starzel Republic.

Interspersed among the journalism awards, the walls also showcase a series of striking posters featuring Nancy Pelosi. These posters serve as powerful visual reminders of her political stature and influence. They depict Pelosi in various settings, capturing her role as a respected leader within the Starzel Republic and underscoring her impact on its political landscape.

The fusion of journalism awards and Nancy Pelosi posters in her office creates an atmosphere where her professional accomplishments intertwine with her role as a key figure in The Great Starzel Republic. It highlights the deep connection between her commitment to journalism and her significant role within the republic's political framework.

"I need to ask for your help," I tell her.

"With the cure, I can only hope," she quips with a note of sarcasm as if there would never be a day when a cure could be had. "Did you think you were the only one who knows there is a virus spreading?"

"Yes. With a cure. Though it may be risky and there's no way to know if the Aryans will detect it and counter it before we get everyone healthy. Whatever comes of it won't matter until we get ... until you get the opportunity in a starting place."

"What do you need me to do?"

"I have an Omegadrive that needs to get plugged into a computer that has the shooting board software. Once the Omegadrive is plugged in, the shooting board software will be modified in two ways. First, it stops the brainwashing, and second, it promotes a cure for the infection."

She contemplates, but for half a beat, "Won't someone notice the software has been modified or somehow tampered with? Don't get me wrong. I mean I am very excited that there is this cure. The entire republic will be healed! I'm very excited. But, I don't want there to be repercussions to make life worse than what the population already suffers."

"I've made the mods undetectable. But, I suppose there's always a chance, though it's very unlikely these changes will be detected."

***

Maya Stevens sits in quiet contemplation for several minutes. "I've got an idea how to get the Omegadrive plugged in.

"Listen while I talk this thought through with you. So, you see, over the last four and a half months the team and I have been shooting a documentary. The documentary is about the history of the Trump

Nation Confederacy. My great-grandmother from many years ago was married to Donald Trump when he destroyed the United States and began the Fifteenth Aryan War. I am her namesake. I've wanted to make this documentary since I was a little girl and after reading her memoirs. We were shooting a part of the documentary the day you told us about the woman with four sons from four different men.

"Right now, the director and three editors are making final cuts and getting ready to produce the video. I'm supposed to be hands-off at this point in production, but I think I can get into the editorial room and that's where we can find the director's laptop. Her laptop is what they will use to make the drafts and the final video since this is the only system with the software. Anyway, that's a whole different story about why we can only have one system with the software in Studio G.

"That's it. What do you think of my idea? I'll just go into the production room and pretend to be curious to know how things are going. I'll find a way to get the Omegadrive plugged in."

Her plan sounds good, but maybe I'm just anxious to be done with it and get free of Planet Earth. "You will need to have the system on and active so that the drive can install the updates," I say. Trying to ensure our success.

"OK. I can do that."

"You will need to give the drive at least two minutes to complete the updates. It's best to go for three minutes just to be certain," I caution.

"Don't worry about that. I'll make it five minutes!"

"You need to make sure that no one else gets the Omegadrive. If anyone else gets the drive, they will likely discover what's on it."

"I'll bring the drive back here. Is there any way we can know if the software was modified?" She asks. Adding a dose of her growing confidence.

After thinking about her question for a few, I ask, "Are you having a premiere for the documentary before broadcasting?"

"Yes, actually. We are supposed to have a first showing for the entire team and families the day after tomorrow. I'm scheduled to leave the day after for some big event in Katmarnu, so everyone is frantically completing production today and no later than tomorrow so we can hold the first showing. Why? Is it important?" She asks.

"Can you get me into the first showing?"

"Yes. Of course. You can come as my special guest," she says.

After readjusting my posture and removing my backpack I say. "If I can watch the documentary from start to finish, there is a way that I can detect if the software modifications were a success."

"You mean with your Neuralink?

My eyes catch her's as I'm shocked and I hesitate for a split second and she tries to reassure me. "I know you're a humanoid. I've known since you made eye contact with me on the bus when you asked me to move out of the handicapped seat. Only a humanoid would work so diligently to make eye contact with another person. Don't worry though. You're safe with me. No one would believe there are humanoids anymore anyway. Well, maybe they would believe it in the Trump Nation Confederacy or The Heartland Nations. Those people are into one conspiracy after the next."

With that said, I laid the Omegadrive on the desktop and then slid it over to her. Before lifting my fingers from the drive, I pause for dramatic effect. Then I look away from her eyes.

>-Track the omegadrive.-<

+_Tracking is initiated._+

+_Tracking confirmed._+

+_Do you want visual tracking now?_+

>-Yes.-<

+_Tracking live in the lower center view screen._+

As our conversation comes to a close, Maya reaches for the Omegadrive on the desktop, her fingers brushing against mine briefly. We exchange a knowing glance, affirming our shared purpose and the trust that binds us to this crucial mission.

"Wait here. It may be a while." She grabs the drive and hurries out of the office.

In my left hand, I clutch the destiny stone recalling the giant of a man's words. "You'll know because there will be nothing else left to do."

Maya Stevens makes her way across the studio offices and exits through the west entrance. She takes a robocar ride around to the back of the office building to the studios where the editing room is located. She easily slips past the security bot at the entrance and makes her way upstairs to her production room.

As Maya steps into the room, the atmosphere shifts. The video production room is dimly lit, with a soft, ambient glow emanating from the strategically placed spotlight. The space feels intimate and secluded, with only a small team of three working diligently on her new story.

The room is a sanctuary of creativity and collaboration, a haven where ideas take shape and narratives come to life. The walls are adorned with concept boards, filled with photographs, news clippings, and sketches that inspire Maya's investigative piece.

The team members, each immersed in their respective tasks, bring a diverse range of skills and expertise to the table. The cinematographer meticulously adjusts the lighting and camera angles, striving to capture the essence of Maya's story visually. An editor sits at a sleek workstation, expertly piecing together footage and sound bites, weaving them into a seamless narrative tapestry. A sound engineer hones in on the audio, ensuring every word and ambient sound enhances the impact of the story. She enters the small space to find the three hovering over a single display. They are discussing color mix in a section of Maya's documentary.

Despite the focused intensity, a palpable sense of camaraderie and shared purpose pervades the room. Conversations are hushed, filled with the occasional nod or approving smile as the team members exchange ideas and offer feedback. The hum of equipment and the tap of keyboards provide a rhythmic soundtrack, underscoring the collaborative energy at play. Through a temperature and air-controlled atmosphere to mediate odors and machine heat, the air is clean, cool, and dry.

Over the past many years working together, Maya rooted her place among her team, and she has become a vital part of the creative process. Her vision, passion, and determination infuse the room with an extra spark. The team recognizes her as the driving force behind the story, and they work tirelessly to bring her vision to fruition.

***

In this small, intimate space, Maya and her team forged a deep connection with their network audience, fueled by a shared commitment to lifting the veil to expose truth. They are united in their pursuit of journalistic integrity, ready to challenge the status quo and shine a light on taboo stories that have the power to reshape their world.

She looks around the room trying to locate the director's laptop when she spots it just a few steps away from her. She's holding the Omegadrive tightly as she walks to the workstation where the laptop sits. It is on but it's screen sharing to the same monitor where the team is huddled. As she inserts the Omegadrive into the ul45 port one of the editors yells out, "Don't touch that Maya. Please!"

Another editor turns abruptly and asks her, "What are you doing here Maya? We are on a tight schedule and have our hands full."

Unknowing these precise happenings, Eulər waits back in Maya's office. He clutches the destiny stone in his right hand, the same hand that wears his mother's ring. Present and undistracted he is watching the HUD, monitoring the Omegadrive progress.

+_Omegadrive attached to recognized device 1._+

>-Establish control of device 1.-<

+_Device 1 is in your control._+

>-Freeze the display on device 1.-<

+_Display locked on device 1._+

>-Connect, upload, and install contents from Omegadrive.-<

+_Omegadrive accepted by device 1._+

+_Uupload initiated._+

+_Upload and install password required._+

>-Hijack password.-<

+_Attempting to hijack password._+

Maya Stevens throws her hands above her head and laughs with innocence. "Hey, guys, take it easy on me. I'm not touching it and I'm not asking for anything. I just wanted to see if you needed something and maybe check in to find out how the production is coming along."

The sound editor sarcastically replies: "We are fine. And if we could just get everyone to stop coming in here to see how we are, we could have been finished by now. So, take a hint. Bye now?"

The editor says, "OK. Son-of-a-licorice stick, there goes the program. The director's laptop is frozen again. The laptop needs to be powered down and restarted."

The cinematographer leaps to his feet and starts toward Maya and the laptop, "I'll go restart it."

As he heads across the room to the director's laptop, Maya hurries to the other side of the workstation and positions herself in front of the laptop and between the two of them.

He stops and says, "Maya, please let me have the laptop. You really shouldn't be in here. If the director comes in, she'll blow a gasket."

"I know," she says. "But I was worried about you guys working so hard. Are you sure you don't need anything?"

He scoffs and looks back toward the other two men then says to her, "Yes, I need you to move so I can restart this laptop. I don't mean to be rude, but we have a tight schedule."

While Maya is keeping the team away from the system Eulər continues monitoring the progress of the Omegadrive.

+_Password hijack successful resume upload._+

+_Upload complete._+

+_Install completed in forty-four seconds._+

+_Do you want to restart the device?_+

>-Restart the device.-<

+_Device will restart in twenty-four seconds._+

Since the system is restarting and Maya Stevens is still positioned directly in front of the laptop. She doesn't know the progress or status of the upload.

Impatient and strained to be polite, the editor says, "What the hell, Maya, get out of my office already. Please!"

Maya is pointing at the frozen display on the room's large central monitor, "Is that reflection in the glass distracting to you? It is for me. Can you guys erase the reflection there?" The editors all look at the monitor and spend a half minute discussing the reflection.

The cinematographer scoffs and says "There's no time to edit the video and render it at this point. We can't do it, Maya. It's too late in the game. Sorry."

The bald editor with his glasses perched on his forehead stands and with a threatening posture says, "If you don't get out of here the entire system is going to erase the last hour of our edits." He points his right arm and finger to show her the direction for the door and starts to circle around toward the other side of her.

From her handbag, she pulls out a revolver and holds it at arm's length in a tight fist. "Get back to your station and sit," she growls at him. She then snaps her posture around to the first editor and motions with the weapon for him to move back to the editing station. "You too. Get back over there." She positions herself beside the laptop, eying the upload progress while staving off the three with the threat of being shot.

The video production room had become a sanctuary for Maya and her team, a place where ideas thrived, and stories were born and produced to share with the world. Within its confines, they embarked on a collaborative journey, weaving together their individual talents to create a powerful narrative that has captivated audiences and left an indelible impact, and that has won a number of awards. But now, with this solitary action, it all comes to an end.

"There is something fundamentally wrong with our lives," Maya asserts, her voice carrying a mix of conviction and concern. "The way we live and think is far off-center, out of alignment, and broken into pieces. It's obvious chaos, and yet no one can quite pinpoint what is wrong with the world. We all sense it, this odd feeling that something is off, but since no one can explain it or define it, we become complacent, thinking maybe it's just me alone who feels this way. You know what

I mean? It's as if everyone else has it figured out, and we're the one left struggling alone."

    +_System is active all programs are running._+

    >-Identify last upgrade date to software and system.-<

    +_Software updated eighty-two days ago._+

    +_System upgraded ten days ago._+

    >-Erase the files on Omegadrive.-<

    +_Omegadrive files will be deleted._+

    +_CONTINUE_+

    >-Yes, continue.-<

    +_All files removed from Omegadrive._+

    >-Unfreeze display.-<

    +_Display operation restored._+

While she kept the three editors quiet and in place, sharing her ideologies of life, she continues to discreetly monitor the progress of the computer upload. "Life appears easier for everyone else, but what truly messes us up is that we often blame others for every problem, as if we are the only ones who have it all figured out. It's a paradigm within the paradigm.

"Then, one day, if you take a step back and accept the world as it is, you might get lucky enough to see the truth. It's a simple truth. We don't belong here. This incarnate existence is some sort of temporary dilemma, perhaps a punishment or a prison sentence, or maybe it's a rite of passage to a better existence in the next life. You don't have to thank me for this."

With those words, she swiftly pulls the trigger, silencing the three editors. Pressing the broadcast button on the main program screen, she initiates the spread of the cure. The system migrates across networks, infiltrating televised programs, and transmitting the solution. The worm virus carrying the cure is initiated.

Retrieving the Omegadrive from the laptop with her left hand, she turns to face the cinematographer. He is still alive, mustering the strength to ask, "Why did you kill us? We would have stayed quiet."

In response, she raises the pistol in her right hand and, without uttering a word, pulls the trigger, finalizing her answer. "Shut up and be a man."

Just fifteen minutes after she left with the Omegadrive she's back in her office. She closes the door behind her and then falls into the chair across from me. After placing the Omegadrive on the table she pushes it in my direction. "That went better than I expected," she says.

"I was able to confirm the installation and then I rebooted the system. All we need to do now is wait for the preview, the day after tomorrow. Do you want me to arrange for transportation?" I ask.

"No. I'll pick you up and we'll arrive at the preview together. No fence jumping this time."

"You mentioned that you're leaving the day after the viewing of the documentary for an event in Katmarnu.

"I am?" she says her head poised in curiosity.

"Me too. I also leave for Katmarnu the same day probably for the same big event. Would you mind if I join you and your team on the journey? It's safer to cross China and the Asian Alliance with a group."

"I'm going alone on this trip," she says. "Unfortunate circumstances prevent the rest of my team from coming. But, it would be a true blessing to have you as my travel companion."

Chapter Fourteen

The Documentary

The theater is heaving with the finest and best-known women in The Great Starzel Republic. The seats are filled, and the room grows quiet as the documentary begins. The theme is about the new Trump Nation Confederacy. The film's purpose is to remind the audience of the devastating consequences of war, promoting understanding and empathy while emphasizing the need for peace and cooperation in a fractured world.

As the documentary begins the director of the film addresses us from center stage. "There was a failed attempt from unknown bandits, as many of you know. The three team members were murdered while defending this documentary from being stolen. In their memory and sacrifice, we are forever thankful." She leaves the stage, the lights dim, and the show begins.

The documentary showcases war scenes from the Fifteenth Aryan War. This conflict resulted in significant changes, leading to the dissolution of the United States as a series of states and a united entity. The boundaries between the states were erased, and the once ominous nuclear arsenals, represented by rockets, were found to be armed with non-explosive payloads (duds). They were disarmed by peace groups known as "Anonymous" and "Legion" early on during the six-year-long bloodbath. Soviet and many other nuclear threats were also found to be empty threats.

As the fighting drew to an end in most areas, six new countries emerged in the place of the former United States. However, small skirmishes continue to occur in certain border regions. Additionally, NATO forces remain present in the northeast, Alaska, and most of the southeast Canadian border, maintaining occupation and security measures.

Furthermore, the Pacific islands surrendered to China, but Hawaii chose to become part of The United Kingdom, reflecting the changing dynamics and choices made by different territories in the aftermath of the war.

The documentary utilizes powerful imagery and the evocative narration provided by Maya to convey the devastating impact of war resulting in a miscreant country known as Trump Nation Confederacy.

"Once Mr. Trump had secured the Trump Nation Confederacy he made good on his promises to return the country to a time of its former glory," Maya's voice flows emotionless and factual as the cinematography does all the heavy lifting in stirring emotions and offending delicate sensitivities. "It is common knowledge of how he put white-power in control of businesses, land ownership, and in the courts. Everyone knows how he partnered with Vladimir Putin's Russia and the National Party of South Africa to establish human trafficking. His lesser-known policies included multi-generational prison sentences for Blacks, Jews, and Hispanics as well as not allowing women to vote on government policies nor to hold political office.

"The one true love of his life, Ivanka, his daughter had an abortion in the last year of the war. It was a huge secret as everyone knows her father required the Christian law to be followed in efforts to keep the orthodox voters and so all abortion was strictly forbidden. The secret came out though during a huge celebration that was ironically held to honor Ivanka. As her father put it, "This is a great celebration, the best celebration, to recognize the most amazing woman in all history now and in human's future history. She will always be the greatest one. Ivanka and all of her amazing, super amazing, most amazing, no one in history has ever been nor will anyone in the future be as amazing as she."

"Even though she is a woman, and therefore technically a second-class citizen of Trump Nation, Mr. Trump was having her and his entire family christened as the Supreme Royal Family in charge of all matters of the Confederacy and The Universe.

"Donald was self-appointed, of course, as the Supreme Commander of The Universe, and he declared Ivanka Supreme Leader of the Confederacy. After the chief justice and the Pope of The Confederacy completed the christening and documented the event to stand for all of eternity and under heaven, Donald somehow heard about the abortion. It was rumored that Jesus (his oldest son had changed his name) had told him. Mr. Trump was outraged, furious, and heartsick that Ivanka had aborted his child, their first child.

"While the guests at the celebration were still having dinner and cocktails, the entire Confederate nation watched on a live televised stream. The population had no choice since Trump ruled no other show could ever run opposite of his air time. Donald abruptly took the podium, center stage, and with a live microphone in hand, he said,

"Abortions are against the will of God for he commanded thou shalt not kill. So shall I also command, from this day and for all eternity, no woman is ever allowed an abortion. All abortions end, now!"

"Everyone at the celebration initially fell silent, but they knew better than to act in any other way than to be amazed at everything Trump says. They stood and cheered and hooped and hollered in great joy. Donald and Ivanka didn't speak for three months following the ceremony. Some rumored it was because he was getting more stem cell operations. Most, however, rumored it was his child she had aborted.

"But there is validity to the stem cell theory. Chinese scientists have found longevity and vitality treatments in stem cell medical practice. While Trump made stem cell research illegal in the Confederacy, he was known to pay for Chinese medicine. Those doctors kept him alive in his original body for more than one hundred and seventy-seven years.

"The Astra Zeneca brain implants, known as Astrolink, were very similar to the Elon Musk, Neuralink implants, though not as advanced as the latter. Astrolink didn't require mind control as a prerequisite for the person receiving the implant. The Astrolink logo featured Astro, the dog from the cartoon series "The Jetsons." More astonishing, however, is that Astrolink was similar to Neuralink in being transferable from one brain (person) to another.

"Just before Donald's first implant, and just after the Chinese stem cell operation, he called for Ivanka to meet him at their house in Anecdotal, a suburb of Montgomery, the capital of The Confederacy. Some rumored he was just horny, but some say it was the night when he proposed to her. Whatever the case, on the 4th of November in 2037 she went to the palatial estate to meet her father.

"Later in the evening, as they both lay in bed, still breathing heavily from their make-up sex, he turned to face her. While playfully running his thick, fat fingers through her store-bought streaked and colored hair, he asked her about the abortion.

"Why did you murder our child? What were you thinking?"

***

The documentary features actors who role-play the parts of Donald and Ivanka. The settings and stage performances are breathtaking. I can feel emotions and stress as I continue to watch. The scent of sweet and savory foods as well as hot popped corn swept through the cinema. An odd contrast between the sustenance and the disaster portrayed by the documentary.

Sensing his aggravation, she pulled the sheet below her breasts, fully exposing them. She had learned long ago that he was a sucker for naked boobs. As his hand left her hair for the now exposed boobs, she replied.

"I had no choice, Daddy. We aren't married and children born out of wedlock are an abomination to the Methodist."

"Gawd damn I love your fine tits, honey." He moaned and squeezed with enthusiasm.

"Daddy, pay attention to me now." She pretended to be serious while thrusting her chest up to meet and enjoy his tight grip.

"I know. I know. But we can't get married," he says.

"The hell we can't!" She said in a firm voice as she tossed his hand off her breast and pulled the sheet back up to hide them.

He tried to wrestle the sheet away and fondle her surgically-younger firm, silicon-enhanced, female features, but she wriggled and squirmed, and fought off his efforts until he began to lose his breath in the effort. Which wasn't long since the man was in his hundreds.

"Come on, babe!" he expressed in exhausted exasperation. "Don't be like that. Give me my boobs, little girl."

She grimaced and scolded him, "You are such a little boy and a pervert. You act as if the world revolves around my ass and my tits."

He rose upon his knees above her and took her shoulders into his hands, shook her, and pinned her to the mattress. Then he said, "They are. I mean. It is, er uhm you are. Fuckit, God damn it. You know what I mean! I can't stand it when we are apart and when you aren't in my bed with me."

"Well, then you have to fix it, Daddy. You have to make it alright for us to make babies and make love the way you like it. Then, and only then will you be getting any more of this!"

With that, she sprung loose from his grip and out of bed. Quicker than he could blink an eye, she grabbed her clothes and went out of the door.

Maya's calm and refreshing narrative voice returns to the film and the scene displays actual footage of recorded events. "On the fifth of November, 2037 Donald called the press for a Trump Nation announcement at 11:15 AM. When it was 12:42 he took the podium, center stage, and microphone in hand. He told the nation:

"It is a declaration that all Supreme Royal family can marry and have children. It has always been this way since the day I first created the universe. Also, to celebrate this new law, Ivanka and I will be married on November 10th."

"He dropped the microphone and walked off the podium. No one had seen Ivanka's mother, Maya, since Putin agreed to help Trump secure the southern border and defend Texas from Mexico. Putin acquired six abandoned former U.S. military bases in Florida, Georgia, and Mississippi, and two other bases in Texas. The day Trump made the announcement was the last time anyone reported having seen Mrs.

Maya Trump. Rumors of course told how she was the price Putin required.

"On November 6th, 2037 at 10:45 AM Ivanka announced over the radio that she and her fiance, Donald Trump, would be married on December 25th, 2037. She further informed the citizens the Christmas celebration would from now and forever be replaced with the national celebration for the Supreme Royal family. Christmas would be celebrated on the true day of Jesus' birth. She didn't provide a specific date.

"On December 2nd, 2037 Donald called a national assembly of all businessmen and the media at 2:00 PM sharp in The New Vatican City in Mississippi. At 3:20 Donald took the podium, center stage, with a microphone in hand. He told the Nation:

"Starting today. Right now, actually. The Trump Nation will have one religion and one religion is quite enough. When you think about it. There is just one God and one right way for men to worship your God. So as I said, from now on right now the one religion in the nation is Methodist. Sorry Pope, but you're fired. The city here, this city we called The New Vatican City, didn't we? Yes. It was the best Vatican City and truly the real Vatican too. Now it will go back to its former name, Meridian. We Methodists don't need a pope and with no pope, we don't need a Vatican City. All the rest of the priests and ministers and all the rest of the heads of those wrong religions. Whatever they are or were as they were. That's it. That's right you're all fired too. We don't need you and your fake religion. Never did before really. So I said it once and that was what it means. I had to get rid of the fake news and now I got rid of the fake religions."

He dropped the microphone and left the stage.

"On the day of their wedding, Donald Trump looked like a man in his mid-forties. The stem cell operations and medical procedures were truly remarkable. He still walked like a man in his late nineties and he had trouble walking up and down ramps, but his appearance was noticeably younger. The wedding was a spectacular show and was paid for by the business owners in the Confederacy. Business owners deducted the cost of the extravagant celebration from their employee 401K, and retirements, and postponed all employee medical benefits.

"Ivanka was dressed in white and the gown alone was rumored to have cost nearly half a billion dollars."

***

"In the spring of 2038, much of the population was desperate and exiting the Trump Nation Confederacy. In droves, they illegally cross the borders into neighboring countries. Trump had built a wall across most of the Nation but many parts of the border with the Republic of The Heartland were still wide open. Trump turned again to his ally and friend Vladimir Putin for help securing the borders and required the shooting of traitors on sight. The Russian military acquired three more naval bases on the Gulf of Mexico side of Florida in the deal. In total, NATO reports told of twenty-eight thousand three hundred and ninety-one people murdered trying to flee Trump Nation before the wall was completed and a new era of the Iron Curtain began in the first quarter of 2046.

"Donald Trump's Astrolink implant operation was scheduled for the second quarter of 2045 and was largely a success. Only slight stuttering was noticed when Donald had to speak more than four words in a sentence without a pause. He had his personal biographer write how he was very excited to learn that the Astrolink could be modified.

The modification would be less responsive so the ability to solve problems, creativity, and physical strength could be paired back. Also. Donald wanted all his business owners and judges of the courts to have the less effective implants and he wanted one additional feature added to theirs. He wanted a kill switch installed. He was tired of having to fire one executive after another and then having to train new talent only to find they were not at all qualified yes men.

"What truly sickened him, the biographer wrote, were the judges and executives who would flee the confederacy and never return. Cowards, he called them. With the pared-back Astrolink equipped with a kill switch in everyone's head, Donald had the ultimate "you're fired" app developed and installed on his cell phone. All he had to do was select the icon of the person he wants to kill and then press the "you're fired" button. Wherever they had satellite coverage, the Trump Nation Confederacy business owners and judges could be struck dead in an instant. Of course, the Supreme Royal Family each had to have the implants too.

"The crimes against humanity go on and on and only get worse." Maya's voice changed as the documentary went on from here. She sounds more concerned, and a sense of plea is evident.

"The living conditions for ninety-seven percent of the population are minimal. In many cases, prison life was the preferred living condition. All revenue goes directly to the Supreme Royal Family, and Ivanka had sole responsibility for providing what was needed for the Trump Nation population. She was worse than her father, or husband. Depending on the celebration, the two would often switch between roles.

"The so-called Ivanka referendum, for example, is a reference to her depth of cruelty. Women throughout Trump Nation Confederacy pleaded for abortion rights. On January 6, 2056, during the annual

celebration for the destruction of the United States and the declaration of the Trump Nation Confederacy, she granted the Nation abortion rights. A modification that made abortion legal for all children to
the age of eighteen years. The following day there were seven thousand
and nine dead children ranging in age from three days to fourteen years
found in rubbish bins. The next day the number more than doubled.

"On February 10, 2056, Ivanka changed the abortion law referendum. It had been noted by many that the Donald's and Ivanka's
only daughter, who was thirteen years old, hadn't been seen for several
days. It was rumored that Donald favored the daughter, perhaps too
much. The changes to the abortion law cited only abortion clinics
could perform abortions, and both parents had to sign off prior to or
within ten days following the abortion. In the case of a single parent,
the family minister had to sign off as the second parent. She further
added to the law, thirty-one days later, at clinics, the ratio of a fetus to
nonfetus abortions could not exceed two to one. The latest legal clause
forced abortion clinics to comply with the murdering of children up
to age eighteen. Ivanka wanted to punish the Nation for demanding
abortions. Like her father/husband, father/grandfather to her children, she was acting in the manner of the old testament Christian God.

"In celebration of the birth of the Confederacy on January 6, 2158,
Donald announced the Supreme Royal Family legacy act. The act was
established so that on the death of Donald and Ivanka their Astrolink,
each, would be transplanted into one of their children's brains. The
child of choice would be identified in the last will in the testament.
When Donald suddenly died just forty-four days later it was rumored
that he favored their oldest son Malachi but Ivanka changed the will
to favor the middle son, Ezekiel, whom she desired even more than
her father before him. The transplant was completed and it was a
marvel of modern medicine for how much memory and personality

was carried forward from Donald to Ezekiel. The Donald and Ivanka Trump legacy for the Supreme Royal Family will continue on for all eternity."

In conclusion and as a small spark of life, Maya announces at the end of the documentary. She stands in front of a lifesize statue of Nancy Pelosi, her hands held as if in prayer as she speaks directly to the camera.

"Escape from the Trump Nation Confederacy is possible. A well-established underground is helping people get out. Though there aren't many places for them to go. Trump Nation is the only nation of the confederacy, and most of their population is too brainwashed to desire a life without their Supreme Royal Family. Liberation from the Aryan viruses is an obligation for Blue Origin. Liberation is an obligation for every human-occupied planet throughout the universe."

Chapter Fifteen

The First Priority

Final log entry. Today should be the last day I spend on Planet Earth. If I live, no one will ever read these logs. Still, even if I do make it back to Planet Forty-Four, my mission isn't complete, there is a huge rift in the Universe. But all that can be done has been done. While entering these words my hand reaches for the satchel attached to the front of my belt and I fiddle with the packet the giant of a man gave me nestled inside. My thoughts wander off as I recall his words. "You will know it is time because there will be nothing else that can be done."

The cure provided by Tathagata is a success and there were no traces of the Aryan viruses and brainwashing in the documentary as I watched it from start to finish. Success number one.

A sleepless night followed the viewing. Caused by the momentum of karmic energy and my realization of a new understanding about the universe's code. While I sat on the edge of the bed in cold sweats and deep shame I remember my mother telling me, "There's nothing more powerful than regret to remind us we are alive." I felt it was my choice to take on this mission and I thought finding Banyan's writing on The First Priority would repair the damage to the faltering morality and the decline of humanity. But after spending the sleepless night reflecting on the eventful revelations, it has all been a delusionary journey of self-discovery. My tinkering in Planet Earth's past set forth the karmic energy that took me on this mission.

They must have believed me insane back home, my father and friends diligently tried to get me to upgrade my organoids and software. The failed systems inside me similar to my own biased opinions needed to be upgraded and replaced. I was the stupid one. I had forgotten The First Priority is self-love. I was not being in love. I was not caring for myself and I was distracted from being the best person I could be. Instead, I was filling my time judging and concerned with the actions of others.

The missing data I was looking for, the great sage's writing that was missing were with me since the first day of the mission when Rupirah gave me back the ring. It is my ring, and I am Banyan. That has always been my pen name. I would give this ring to my mother to keep her safe when she went on her working trips to Planet Earth. The ring contains the humanity code that I had written including The First Priority. I knew if I gave it to her the Universe would protect her and she would have to bring it back. But Rupirah had it and Mother told her to give it to me. Mother knew she wouldn't be returning home and she knew I would come looking for it. Bittersweet, success number two.

Somehow and in some way I know the son Gatlia and I will have, Magallan will be the last effort I can take to fix the rift I tore into the Universe. Success number three. He will have the final task to end human suffering. It's unclear how and when it will transpire, but The Source told me his son, my grandson will provide the gateway to liberation. But this will have to wait until I am back on Planet Forty-Four.

For now, there is one last task to complete here on Planet Earth. Before I can go home I must attend the celebration for The First Priority. A celebration that The Source originated while on this mission and a further sign that morality and humanity's place in the universe are mending.

***

I meet Maya outside of the city of East Nagach. The journey from here is a long slow ride up through the highest mountain ranges of China. My research described crossing through the Asian Alliance as a journey of beautiful scenery, interesting people, an adventure of small villages and large metropolises, and various types of transportation. The journey is, however, physically uncomfortable. The narrow and unpaved roads are the same passages people have used for tens of thousands of years. These spine-crushing routes are often riddled with deep rain and snow-washed-out holes, and rock slides, and in many places, there isn't a millimeter of extra space for the vehicles between falling over the rocky cliff on the one side and crashing into the rock walls on the other.

China preserves the integrity of the population and won't allow any other form of travel through these areas of the alliances. While we wait for the transport to arrive I see a poster display that advertised the transports years ago when the fusion-powered vehicles were new. The poster is torn, weathered, and though the print has faded I can read the pitch.

Get ready to step into the future with the fusion-powered land-based bus, a technological marvel on the move! This bus is a fusion of cutting-edge advancements and sustainable transportation.

Powered by fusion, it combines smart design with solar paneled roofs and sidewalls, harnessing the sun's energy to fuel its advanced systems. Inside, you'll find luxurious seating, panoramic displays, and state-of-the-art connectivity. With autonomous driving capabilities, collision avoidance systems, and smart sensors, safety is at the forefront. Experience the next level of travel with Starlink, entertainment systems, and high-speed charging ports. Join the revolution and embrace a greener, tech-infused journey today!

As it pulls up to the stop, the transport is as worn and faded as the poster. Missing panels of glass, windows that are stuck open, dents, gouges, holes, and peeled paint combine to tell the story of the rugged conditions found on the roads ahead. Maya and I find reasonably comfortable seats together just as the transport pulls away from the station and onto the main road.

"You never had a chance to tell me what you thought of the documentary. Was it that bad? You don't have to spare my feelings. I can take the truth," she says.

She stares directly into my eyes. Her face is expressionless while she tries to discern the truth by reading my expression as I reply. She's like a poker player not wanting to give away any hint of the cards she holds. "My Neuralinks and software systems detected no viruses and no audible or visual anomalies from the beginning to the end of the video broadcast. I'd have to say the software modification from Tathagata is a success. Number four in the list of accomplishments."

"Could it be then, that we are at the beginning of the cure for this two hundred-plus-years plague? My heart says yes, but my research of Aryan history tells me that evil takes no time for rest. And, you didn't answer my question. What did you think of the documentary?" she persists.

"Caution is all that remains now as you suggest, the Aryans are not interested in short-term gains and losses. Their strategy has always been a plan for eternity. As for your documentary . . . The entire universe is limited by the same laws of physics through every form of matter and what our consciousness calls existence. We are each of us a completely unique life in form, but we are all exactly the same life in substance. You might like carrots and I may find them horrible, but either way, it is exactly based on the same shared aware sense of taste. What I find not enjoyable about the carrots that you enjoy doesn't make us different. These are just choices we've made, mental constructs of thought based on a shared awakeness.

"The villains of Planet Earth from your documentary are the Trump family and especially Donald and Ivanka. However, even without the Aryan virus and Republican Party-sponsored brainwashing satellites, videos, and radio, perhaps after watching your documentary fewer people would worship them, but some will still choose to satisfy their human desire for idol worship by worshipping the Trump family. Though you hope to free the world of this evil family, the evil Republican Party, the Aryans, Nazis, and all the rest, and you hope that by exposing their methods of corruption, bigotry, slavery, shameful distortions of religious doctrine, suppression of people based on their sex and race. And, well, yes your documentary has accomplished all this. Still, in the end, some people will find you reprehensible, and instead of seeing the truth they will choose to love Trump even more."

"So, you think it's all a waste of time?" She stands up and steps into the aisle to face me. Her hands on her hips and her face now displays scorn with righteous indignation. "You are saying that there is no hope for people on Earth? That we are just stuck with their evil forever?

Should we just give up then and let the evil bastards make slaves of us all?"

The transport goes over a few deep potholes in the road causing the entire vehicle to bounce wildly. Maya is tossed into the fusion chamber door across from where we are seated. As she tries to recover her balance the transport turns sharply to avoid a huge boulder protruding into the road from the side of the mountain and she is slung back the opposite direction and lands facedown in my lap. She lifts her head and the sunlight shines into her eyes tears form as she laughs, and her hand shades her eyes.

***

As I help Maya to take her seat and regain her dignity, several people in the transport have begun to give us their attention. "Your passion for humanity is admirable," I say. "But the documentary is intended to be reactionary. Reactionist statements are never helpful." I hand her the other half of the seatbelt she is searching for.

"Don't do that. Don't you dare patronize me and brush me off," she scorns and furrows her brow. "While I am aware of the absolute evils of the Republicans and the Trumps, and yes it's partly the disease of wealth and a sickness brought on by a sense of power, and yes, if you must pry -- I would love to free the planet of them."

She pauses to snap the seatbelt into place, gathers her hair from out of her face, and strokes it several times, finally, she pulls it to the back of her head twisting it and securing it with a scrunchy. "I am also aware of your beliefs and I know something, not too much mind you, but some of what you call the balance or the middle way." She relaxes her scorn, and her face softens.

"I respect what you accomplished, that is to say, I am aware of how you earned your highly developed and top-shelf Neuralink implant. I know you must be an extraordinary humanoid what with being given the responsibility to travel to Planet Earth for whatever it is you've come here to do. But, I don't want you to brush me off like I'm some simple human. Even if I am some lesser being than you, I want you to help me, to help us." She folds her hands together in a prayer-like manner, then places them over her heart. "Help us to be free of these plagues, these evil people, and to end this sickness of power and wealth.

"One more thing." She doubles up her fist and slugs me in the chest. "You make me feel all kinds of weirdness inside my head and body when you say these things about -- the universal laws of physics and consciousness, and that it's an illusion that we are all separate and different because in reality... we are precisely the same in every way except in our thoughts. -- You can't just talk like that to people. But still, these seem to be words that I've heard somewhere before or that I already knew in some other life or something. Somehow, along the way, I must have forgotten until . . ." She pauses for a moment looking off into the distance though not looking at anything in particular.

Then she looks back at me and I brace my arms to block her next fist throw, but she gives me a sly smile instead and says. "Until l heard you say it." Her hands drop to her knees and she turns her head slightly to one side quizzically as her eyes study my face. "As if, you are simply reminding me of something I already know but have forgotten. Just like that afternoon in the town square when you were telling the shooting crew and me about the woman with four sons from four different men. I know I've never heard that story before. And yet, somehow it seemed familiar."

The transport continues to make a slow and steady ascent up the mountain pass. The unconditioned roads toss the vehicle and everyone in it from side to side and bounce up and down. Fusion power engines make no noise. With most of the windows open, the cold air smells of dust, and arid desert. Through the open windows, the ominous sounds of the rocks being crushed under the heavy wheels and the occasional metal being scraped along the side as we hug the mountain at the narrowest points and tight turns.

"I am sorry for making you feel as if I would brush you off. It isn't my intention. Though, I will admit my arrogance and slight prejudice. Allow me to say this. What you desire is very admirable, as I said. Every one of us desires a peaceful existence and to be free of hate, pain, and all forms of suffering. As you humans have scattered out to live on other planets and will continue to spread through the universe, what happens here will always influence the other planets. Planet Earth is home to all of us. It is the origins of the human race. That is why most of the colonies on other worlds with reverence, refer to this planet as Blue Origin."

She opens her food case and hands me half of a pungent-smelling onion and mustard sandwich. The spice of the tangy mustard mixes with the spicy heat of the onion in my mouth as I chew. The air in the transport grew heavy with both apprehension and a growing sense of connection, as if unseen forces were at play, weaving our destinies together.

"Even for those who aren't born here and who have never seen this great blue ball in person, this is home." I pause for a pull of fresh water. "No matter where human life goes in the universe, we are always tied to our Blue Origin. Just like everything is tied to the physical constraints or the realities of physics." I pause, for dramatic effect and adjust my position so I can face her as much as the constraint of my seatbelt allows before continuing. Sharing a genuine soft smile and a change of my vocal tone for more acceptance rather than lecturing.

"You and I cannot ever free this universe from evil people and the sickness of the desire for wealth and power, nor the sickness of those who desire to worship the wealthy and the powerful. Some people will love them and others will hate them. That is the physical constraints of the universe or what some call the human condition. In my kuudere's education system, we call these physical constraints -- 'the matrix.' Everything that exists is constrained by the matrix."

My speaking quickens and becomes less passive but still calm and controlled. "This doesn't mean we throw our hands up over our heads and surrender to the hate and inhumane methods of the Republicans and Aryans. It also doesn't mean we take up war against them. Killing and hate are theirs."

***

Holding my hands in front of me as if holding a serving tray. "If you spend your desires demanding everyone accept -- your god -- and -- your method of worshiping, your sports heroes or movie stars, or kings and queens, or whatever lust you chose to worship -- then you are precisely constrained by the matrix. You may feel totally unique and keenly different, but in this, you are precisely just like everyone else. The more closely you hold on to and cling to these ideals the more you struggle in vain and do no good for yourself and no good for anyone else."

With that said, I sit back into the seat, place my hands together, interlock my fingers, and let my hands fall to my lap. "All you accomplish, Maya, is more of the same --evil, power, wealth, worship, disease, desperation, etcetera."

"Then my documentary is neither good nor bad, it's just more of the same?" She says in surrender.

Giant white, billowing clouds hang in the bright blue sky, the sun straight overhead and I observe the time and place while my mind swirled with profound thoughts, grappling with the vastness of existence and the limitations of human desires. The complexity and seeming intricate combinations are an illusion. Everything is just this, now. Endless right now. The generous present moment is all there ever is.

"It is both good and bad and yes, it is more of the same."

Not ready to give up on the opportunity to communicate with a humanoid, she persists. "Then, if I understand this matrix correctly, while we humans are discovering a cure for one disease and another, the universe is producing new ones at the same time -- or as normal. For every new method we manufacture that hopes to make life more enjoyable, the universe is designed to erode it and decay the products as soon as they come into existence." She thinks for a minute and then says. "Like this transport when it was new had a fresh coat of paint, windows that would open and close." She puts her hand out as if she were motioning toward an imaginary glass window in the empty frame beside me. "We see it and feel accomplished for the effort, but now the only thing that happens is decay. Minute by minute the paint becomes dull and begins to fail." She moves her hand to her cheek and turns her head to slightly rest in her palm. "I see the wisdom and the obvious logic." She expresses an awakened moment of clarity in her voice.

Continue with more metaphors, she says. "We fool ourselves into thinking a vacation is going to bring us happiness and satisfaction, but from day one of the vacation, we are aware of the end that lies ahead. It's the same for everything then, isn't it?" Her sense of awakening continues to express more examples as her knowledge fully engages in her mind. "We long for the weekend and on the weekend we dread the coming Monday. We get excited about sports but dread the possible outcome. We disguise our unknowing self by dressing in some knock-off team's jersey or the colors of our country's flag and what-not, but regret how others scorn our choice of clothes."

She unfastens her seatbelt and jumps out of the seat and into the aisle. Her voice raises in pitch and takes on a tone of contempt. "So, what is it then, are we just monkeys swinging from branch to branch doing time while we wait to die?"

The sound of metal coming into contact with the rock wall outside gains her attention. She looks out the window and reminds herself of the precarious terrain of our journey as she grabs the seatbelt and places it back across her lap.

My head nods and I can sense her exasperation. The ego's need to feel it is part of something important is now desperate and trying to make her stop listening and examining these truths. I say in response to her outburst: "There is a higher existence than human, and humanoid existence within the matrix. It's discovered when a person has learned the sixteen types of knowledge. First, we learn to focus the mind so that thinking is not happening, we then learn to focus the body so that comfort and discomfort are no longer demanding attention, and then learn to merge still mind and still body -- a realization and an awareness of existence outside of the matrix is found in this way. Until that time, when we each obtain that gifted life experience, perhaps we can teach acceptance for life with the matrix and simply acquire the merits to reach the second heaven of the 'desire realm'."

"What is this second heaven and what is the 'desire realm?' " She chuckles a bit. "For that matter, what was all of that you just said?" She shakes her head in a sign of unknowing the depth of my meaning.

"The sixteen types of knowledge cannot be told to you, or anyone. It is human nature for us to reject everything that someone else tells us. We reach the age of reason at about six years of age and from that age onward we do not blindly accept what someone says. Knowledge requires self-discovery, without effort and direct experience we are suspicious of others. Each person must discover knowledge for themselves, not through organized systems based on faith, or supernatural belief. In this existence, the wise monks, disciples, and the perfect and complete Buddhas can guide a person to The Source and there we naturally discover these sixteen types of knowledge."

Not ready to let me off her path of discovery she asks me, "Can you tell me about the second heaven?"

"I'll tell you about that and The First Priority," I say. "But first can you smell the mountain air?"

***

The transport enters the small village of Dinegu at the top of the mountain passage. Here, the autonomous driving transport pulls into the large parking area and stops. We are not stopping for fuel as there are no fuel stations here. It's been two hundred years since CFS began putting cold fusion power into automobiles and the last fossil fuel stations were banned twenty years later. The only reason these transports stop in the villages now is to deliver products to the people and allow the passengers a chance to stretch their legs before the journey down the steepest descent on twelve planets.

Maya pulls her jacket tight over her chest. As she steps down from the transport into the chilled brisk air cascading off the snow-capped peaks that surround us. The villagers swarm the travelers as we leave the transport. They bring us snacks and treats, and hand-crafted wares to tempt us with, and they offer to take us on guided tours. She watches as a few of the travelers retrieve their luggage from the storage compartments along the bottom of the transport. Maya wonders why anyone would be staying in this horrible cold, and near-deserted place. The air is thin and icy and when she inhales it burns her throat and causes her eyes to tear up. It tastes of stale earth and is an odd metallic complexity. Choosing the warmer atmosphere inside the transport over further exploring the village, she climbs back up the steps.

Maya's heart quickens as she takes her place back on the transport, she wonders why she is feeling anxious. She sees Eulər through the open window and watches as he plays with the village children. Dancing with some, they are chasing after one another in the bright sun and through the heavy layer of snow. The sunlight reflects off the frozen white surface making it difficult to keep her eyes open. His laugh is contagious to hear and as she lets a soft laugh escape her lips, she wishes the windows were closed as the frigid air begins to invade the coach. Turning her squinted gaze, she sees the departing travelers, who now have their backpacks in place, adjusting the shoulder straps. Her view of them with the snow-covered mountain peaks as backdrop reminds her of videos and photos from centuries past and now it all seems surreal as it's live and just a few meters away.

The scene unfolds before her like a vivid painting, a dance of laughter and joy amidst the frigid air. She yearns to join in, to immerse herself in the whimsical world of the village children. The departing backpacker's journey towards the distant peaks intensifies her anticipation, stirring an uninvited burning curiosity within her.

Her eyes scan the horizon, again searching for any trace of Eulər. The children continue their carefree play, their voices echoing in her ears, but Eulər is now conspicuously absent from their midst. Maya's attention sharpens as she witnesses him several meters further from the children. He is rummaging through his satchel. She wonders what secrets lie within that small parcel he pulls from the satchel. It's wrapped in exquisite velvet and secured with a vibrant green string.

Time seems to suspend as Eulər delicately places the enigmatic object upon the stone altar. Maya's breath catches in her throat, her entire being drawn to this sacred act. The icy breeze ripples through Eulər's attire, transforming the mundane into a sight of ethereal beauty. It's as if the very air holds its breath, honoring the solemnity of the moment.

Yet a profound change washes over Maya as she witnesses the extraordinary. Frowning with disbelief, she rubs her eyes, attempting to dispel the illusion that blurs before her. But it persists, growing more enchanting by the second. Eulər's figure becomes translucent, his presence emanating from an otherworldly radiance that defies explanation. Maya finds herself at the threshold of a mystic revelation, captivated by the ethereal transformation unfolding.

Compelled by an insatiable thirst for understanding, she leans further out of the open window, stretching her senses toward the enigmatic figure. Eulər's iridescent glow intensifies, enveloping him in an aura of untold power. It is a sight that defies the limits of her imagination, a manifestation of the impossible made real.

The moment is rudely interrupted as the transport's deafening horn slices through the air. Startled, she briefly turns her attention towards the front of the vehicle, momentarily torn away from the enigmatic altar. When her gaze snaps back, her heart sinks. Eulər has vanished, leaving behind only the small parcel and a lingering sense of wonder.

A mix of excitement and frustration courses through Maya's veins. The urgency to unravel the secrets concealed within the parcel intensifies, driving her forward with unyielding resolve. At that moment,

Maya felt a surge of wonder and curiosity, as if the fabric of reality had momentarily shifted, revealing a hidden world of magic and mystery. Was she dreaming?

The travelers began coming back onto the transport and Maya settles back into her seat. As she fastens her seatbelt he sits abruptly into the seat next to her.

***

"Is this seat taken?" I say with a smile and glance into her eyes.

There is a warm sensation in my heart center as our eyes exchange what words can never express. The horn sounds once more and a minute later the transport pulls out of the parking lot and back onto the road. Again, it resumes the relentless torture along the rugged trail and bounces its way through a few of the deepest washed-out holes in the road. Without thought, she grabs for my hand. Without hesitation, I interlock our fingers.

"The run downhill from here gets pretty treacherous. Hang on Maya," my hand signals strength in our shared grasp.

"Will you tell me more about the second heaven? What was it you said... the second heaven in the desire realm?"

She is persistent and even so, it is a fitting story as we travel toward the celebration. "The story begins by telling us how, after twelve cycles of life, there was a certain traveler who set out to discover an end to human suffering. The journey started as he climbed up one of the many mountains that surrounded his village. With every step up the steep slope of the mountain, the ground being soft under his feet would give way. Making it so that for each step up he would slide back down three-quarters of the way. To make the climb even more difficult there was very little to eat as he could only find a small root plant here and there or a handful of nuts one time or maybe twice There were a few streams of water but the water was fast and filled with minerals so the taste was bitter and it had the smell of sulfur. Finally, after many weeks of climbing, he reached the top.

"The journey down the other side was dangerous as the ground still giving way under his feet caused frequent rock slides. The trees were covered with thorned vines and empty spaces around and through the thickets of thorns were few and narrow. His hands, arms, and legs were stabbed and cut many times. Birds swooped down to strike him on the back and over his head as they worried about protecting their nests from what they believed to be a predator."

Banyan's story number ninety, "The Heaven of the Thirty-Three," flashes in the HUD. Source file location -- MOTHER.

It's one of my archived stories.

"One morning he woke to find a squirrel nearby who had brought him a cheek full of pine nuts. As he enjoyed the last of the nuts he heard the distinct sound of a rattlesnake close behind him. Startled, he turned to look at a very large coiled viper that was just a meter away. The snake was claiming its natural place where it has daily sunbathed and warmed itself in the morning. Though the vine here was thickest and the ground seemed softer than usual the traveler scurried the best he could all the while apologizing to the snake for his trespassing and praying for it not to strike.

"With his whole body now thoroughly scourged, stinging and burning from the thorns, bleeding, and with every muscle in his body exhausted and aching, he reached the bottom of the mountain. There, at that place, and at that moment he fell to his knees and collapsed face-first to the ground.

"After he had rested for several days the journey continued. As he walked, he set his path in the direction of the sun. Before the day was through he found himself in the desert. When the sun had set, the dry night air began to cool and with each passing hour, the cold intensified over the ground. His body shivered and ached, and his teeth chattered. The muscles in his legs and arms cramp and refuse to move. Surrendering himself, he sat on the ground expecting to die.

"The sun as it always does, came up several hours later. He was facing towards the east and though he wasn't able to move he could see the pre-dawn glow turn the sky a deep crimson and watch it magically transform to an even more beautiful and deeper gold. Once the full sun was above the horizon the warmth of the rays replaced the cold air as quick as a candle wick ignited from the touch of a lit match. His body soon regained its strength. The journey resumed and as he took each step along the path, he went deeper into the desert. The sun's heat became oppressive. His nostrils and lips singed as he breathed the hot air from the desert furnace. His face, arms, and legs burned under the blazing sun. There he found himself with skin vandalized and blistered and it began to flake. His nose bled. A result of becoming too dry. His lips cracked and bled too. There was no shade, no water, no cooling breeze and no food to be found anywhere either.

"The call of a hawk caught his attention. His eyes were dry and his sight was blurred, but he looked to the sky trying to see where it was. Hoping that it would lead him to water. The hawk was flying northward but after several hours of following it, he discovered no water. Close to the end of the day, the sun was nearing the horizon when he came to a rocky ledge where he looked down into a desert valley. At the bottom, he saw a small grove of palm trees and the desert hawk circling above the trees.

"Perhaps one hundred, maybe a hundred and twenty meters down the rocky ledge and he would save his life with a drink of cool water. He began to climb down the ledge, but having no rope to repel over the cliff, the task was difficult. Weak from lack of food for two days, parched from the heat, and drained of all his bodily energy, driven on by desperation only. But losing his footing he fell the last twenty meters landing flat on his back onto the hard-packed and sun-dried soil. He managed to pull himself across the dry and dusty river bed, his lifeless legs dragging along behind him. Just as the sun went below the horizon coloring the sky in hues of pink and purple he reached the edge of the pool of water."

#Banyan, notes: These pains, described vividly, evoke a sense of the harshness and brutality of life's journey. They highlight the physical endurance and resilience required to survive in such challenging circumstances as the world and the universe is constant, and without rest and is always challenging us. End #Banyan, notes.

The fellow travelers were not talking, and inside the transport, it was quiet as everyone had begun to listen to me telling Maya the story about the second heaven of the desire realm. The man seated in front of Maya was holding out a flask of water toward me. "Water?" he offered. We made eye contact and we each identified the other as having the Neuralink 7.19b version of the brain and spine implants.

"Thank you, yes," I replied. I started to pull my hand away from Maya to take the flask but she held me tight and reached with her other hand to double secure our bond. The transport was traversing down the steep grade at a snail crawl. The winding road seemed far too narrow for such a large vehicle. I can tell that she feels less afraid as long as she's hanging onto my hand. I take the flask with my left hand and then I pull a long drink of magnificent clean, cool water. The man looks as if he could be related to the therapist, Sterling Junior.

***

>-Connect to others nearby.-<

   +_One request sent_+

   +_Connection accepted._+

   →My name is Sterling. I'm from Seven Sisters Space Portal.←

   →You have probably met my son, Sterling Junior when you got your Neuralink and software upgrade.←

   >-He told me many things about you and your family's history.-<

   >-Are you traveling to The First Priority celebration?-<

   →Yes. The First Priority, the same as you and Maya.←

   →I have to say it is exciting to see her in person. This is the closest I've ever been to someone as famous.←

   >Maya? She is just a human.-<

   →Yes and I hear the missing data you have been looking for has been found.←

   >-The Universe has restored the humanity file to its rightful plac e.-<

   >-Syganoids have much more work to do.-<

   →Please continue with the story and we'll speak again when we get off of this bouncing transport at the bottom of the mountain.←

   >-Disconnect all.-<

   +_The connection closed._+

   +_No connection found._+

I handed the flask back to Sterling Senior. Then gave her a reassuring squeeze to her hand and shot her a smile. When I looked around and saw everyone looking at me and Maya and listening to the story.

An opportunity for great wealth and benefit. I must finish the story.

"Sometime in the very early hours of the following morning, while the sky was still very dark and the air was still very cold, he woke to an odd sensation. His mind made him aware there was something crawling up the calf of his left leg. He was laying with half of his body in the pool of water. He managed to push his upper torso up with his arms and turn his head to look at his leg. The moonlight was bright enough for him to see a large black scorpion crawling over his leg. On impulse, adrenaline surged through his body, he leaped to his feet, and in the same motion, his hand swept down brushing the scorpion from his leg. He stood at the pool's edge looking around trying to determine what was what on the limited moonlit night. There were a few small root plants to eat and a large flat rock protruding out of the water about two meters or so from the shore and making his way to the rock where he chose his island bed. Sniffing at the blackness of the night air, he smelled only the muddy shoreline and the tree pollens. Surrounded by water he felt safe from the night predators and there he laid back to sleep.

"Hours later when he awoke to the sound of the hawk's warning cry. And again heard the cry after sipping some water from his cupped hand. He scanned the surroundings with a keen eye looking for signs as to why the hawk was sounding the alarm. Perched above him, on the top of the rocky ledge he saw the predator. A cougar. The desert mountain lion was coming to its favorite morning pool for a drink. Taking one last sip from his hand, he grabs the last of the root plants and fled the pool.

"His journey was always the same, wherever he went. There was barely enough food and water to sustain his life, the elements were harsh and taking a toll on his strength and his will to survive, and there were always predator animals competing for the same few resources. He made his way out of the desert and into the cold northlands covered in snow, ice, and too cold to sustain life except for bears and wolves. He went south and found an ocean where he drifted for weeks surrounded by salty water but nothing there to drink. And he was preyed on by sharks and scorched by the sun and wind. He thought the sea was worse than the desert.

"When his raft ran aground, at long last, a short distance from a fertile plain. After a long day's journey from the ocean, his path brought him to a small but bustling village. As he wandered through the streets he observed the busy people. Some were working in the fields tending crops. Others were working on the ranch with flocks of chickens, sheep, cows, and swine. There were sawmills and brick makers along with a few pottery artisans. His journey paused when he found himself standing in the town square where the population enjoyed a concentration of the various merchants. Fish, beef, dried goods as well as fabrics, clothing, shoes and so much more were all marketed here.

"He observed a flat piece of ground under a small tree where he decided he would stand to rest while he watched the activity of the villagers. He hadn't been standing in that place for even two minutes when a man came up to him and shoved him out of the way then took the spot over for himself.

"The traveler gathered himself and his wits, then he saw a place at the corner of a large store where he thought to stand and watch the bustling village activity. In less than two minutes of standing in that place, a woman walked up to him and placed both of her hands on his chest giving him a great shove backward and then she took over his place there.

"The traveler spotted another area, this time several meters away from the center but he was still able to watch the town center marketplace. And, like twice before, it wasn't two minutes later when a man stiff-armed him to shove him aside, and then he took that spot for himself.

"Now the traveler recalled when he first came into the village there was a small farm along the main road where the town mayor was living. He decided to go talk with the mayor. When the traveler knocked on the farmhouse door an old and stately-looking fellow opened the door and greeted him. The traveler asked if he could borrow a hoe, rake, shovel, and an ax. The governor agreed to lend him these tools. The traveler further asked if the small plot of ground between the high road and the town center was available. The mayor told him it was not yet claimed by anyone and then asked the traveler what he was going to do with the small ground and with these few tools.

"The traveler told him of the events that took place as he stood to watch the village people go about the day in one place, then another, and then once again. "Apparently," he said to the mayor, "I have a gifted talent for finding places where people desire to rest.

"From morning to night of the next day the traveler worked the ground on the small plot. He removed stones, and stumps, and made the ground level. On the second day, he built a few tables and benches and as he worked he noticed people began to stand on the flattened area to rest. Others he noticed sat at the tables and on the benches. On the third day, he went into the forest and gathered fallen trees, and used them to build a shelter on the plot of ground. Then on particularly hot days, people could rest by finding shade under the roof of the shelter, and on windy days or rain-filled days, the shelter provides them all a good dry place to rest.

"The traveler built places for keeping a fire to warm the people on cold days. There was nothing the traveler didn't prepare and make ready to provide a comfortable resting place for people."

Standing up, I bow to the people on the transport. Sterling Senior applauded and encouraged others to join him. My eyes are on Maya and I notice she is calm and tension-free. I say to her, "There you have it. That is the story of Indra and how he became Lord Indra, lord of all the heaven realms, and that village from the story is known as the heaven of the thirty-three. Sometimes it is called the second heaven of the desire-realm."

"I think there are probably more than just a few lessons within the lessons contained in your story. Am I right?" she asks.

"The story is one of many hundreds written by Banyan and contained in the ancient writings. The Sutras, Vedas, and Upanishads each have a similar version of Lord Indra and the heavens above the desire realms. And you are right, Maya. There is a lot of wisdom and knowledge to gain from studying the story."

The smells from the festival greet us first. We are treated to scents of rich curries, and brewed teas, mixed with a variety of incense, pervading the bus. Outside the window, we can see the city ahead of us and the sights of the festival. The vibrant sights, intoxicating smells, and lively sounds of the festival enveloped us, igniting a sense of excitement and anticipation for what awaits us in the city ahead.

***

As the transport comes to a stop in the bustling parking area in the center of Tivlabet, the three of us, Sterling, Maya, and I, step out and merge into a sea of people who have gathered for "The First Priority" celebration. The air is filled with anticipation and excitement as tens of thousands of individuals from different planets have converged on the city and gathered near the great stupa.

The blaring sounds of Tibetan horns resonate through the air, accompanied by the rhythmic beats of tambourines and damarus played by the enthusiastic crowd. To navigate through the immense gathering, Sterling takes the lead, pulling Maya along, and she, in turn, gently tugs me by the hand, ensuring we remain connected.

With synchronized steps, we playfully dance our way through the crowd, kiosks of fragrant foods, and colorful displays of festive wear, gradually moving closer to the majestic white marble stupa. The vibrant energy of the celebration infuses our every movement, and the united grip of our hands serves as an anchor, preventing us from getting separated amidst the current of a vast multitude.

The use of pure white quarried marble in constructing the stupa enhances its visual impact, creating a striking contrast against the late afternoon, blue sky streaked with wispy, cirrus clouds, and vivid tapestry of the celebration and symbolizing the purity of enlightened consciousness. It stands as a beacon of serenity, inviting all who approach it to seek inner peace and transcendence united in the joyful chaos of the gathering.

"You see this, Eulər?" Sterling yells above the sounds. Humans came into this quantum existence at odds with one another, and we can only escape the suffering when we learn to forgive and unite in our effort."

The crowd itself is a diverse mix of people from various planets, cultures, and backgrounds, each dressed in their traditional attire, showcasing the richness of their heritage. Exclamations of excitement fill the air as individuals connect, share stories and immerse themselves in the festivities. Melding as one conscious experience.

Flags and banners flutter in the gentle breeze, displaying colorful symbols, mantras, and prayers. These vibrant flags represent devotion and spirituality, adding an extra layer of sacredness to the gathering.

Frozen in place I come to a sudden stop tugging Maya to a stop and then Sterling is tugged to a stop by Maya. They look at me and I point to a person standing on the top of the second set of four tiers of fifty steps each that lead up to the doorway of the stupa.

"Do you see the monk up there? In the saffron robes wearing the abbot's hat?" I shout for them to hear me.

The sounds of the Tibetan horns and the lively music continue to reverberate, blending with the crowd's enthusiasm. With curiosity and anticipation, the three of us gaze up at the figure, our hearts beating in unison. The sense that this person may hold the key to unraveling the mysteries surrounding the stupa, the celebration, and our journey.

Sterling looks in the direction where I am pointing and then when he sees the abbot's hat replies, "Yes, I see him. Do you want me to get us over to him?"

With enthusiastic nods from me, Sterling leads the three of us forward again. The three of us dance and weave our way through the crowds and up the steps. After several minutes we reach the top of the second tier of steps. When the Abbot saw me he bowed deeply and I also bowed deeply to the Abbot. We raced to embrace, each of us laughing, overwhelmed with the joy of the celebration of The First Priority. The four of us joined hands and continued to follow Sterling's lead up the next fifty steps to the third tier of the stupa and then up the last fifty steps to the entrance level.

There are five monks with Tibetan horns on the left side of the opening to the stupa and five more on the right. As the horns blew loud blasts, the four of us turned to face the crowd. Sterling the physicist, Ibrahim the Abbot, Maya the celebrity, and I, Eulər the protector stand together, side by side, and hand in hand just outside the opening.

From out of the transparent blue sky lotus petals rain down and the fragrance of sandalwood fills the air. The stupa radiates with thousands of myriads of colored beams outward into the universe. In the doorway behind us, the Shakyamuni Buddha appears along with Tara, and between them, stands Jaczimin, the woman with four sons from four different men. The Tibetan horns were played again with a long and very loud burst.

At that moment, the air was charged with electric anticipation, as if the universe's secrets were about to be unveiled amidst the joyful chaos of the celebration.

Sterling is transformed and now he is revealed as the eldest of her four sons. He was first born as the son of the horse keeper, who had aspired to be born king in the northern land of Tivalabet to establish the teachings of the future Buddha Shakyamuni.

Ibrahim, the Abbot transformed to reveal himself as the son of the swineherder who had aspired to be born as a pure, fully ordained monk who would uphold the holy monastic order in Tivalabet.

Maya was transformed to reveal she is the son of the dog keeper who had aspired to be born a master of mantras, to tame malevolent forces thereby and help his brothers protect the dharma in Tivalabet.

Here I am, transformed to reveal the youngest brother, I was born as the son of the poultry keeper, who had realized that my three older brothers might be born in different locations and therefore I aspired to be born as the one who could connect them and allow them to reunite in all our future lives.

"It appears that not everyone here can see the light rays, smell the sandalwood and lotus petals, they don't see the Buddhas and our mother standing in the opening to the stupa, and they have not seen we four brothers either," Maya says.

"Not everyone is ready, they have not evolved to be able to realize stream-entry in this life. The time is not yet right for them," Ibrahim replied.

"Eventually everyone will be ready and then we can all leave this universe and return to live in the fields. Free from suffering," adds Sterling.

Before he had finished his sentence, my HUD display lit up:

+_Message from Starlink: Freespeech is under attack._+

+_Fifteen fusion bombs from Aryans have damaged several of the floating city's habitats._+

+_Please help us!_+

My eyes survey the people toward the bottom steps of the stupa. I see the woman in black. Her hands on her hips and her rubbery face expression, as she waits for me to join her.

Chapter Sixteen

The Nirvanaing Series By Mark Bertrand

Book 1 (This Could Be It): To save what was taken, they must confront the exiled.

Book 2 (Starzel): The false prophets of identity claim paradise.

Book 3 (Reckoning): The void between self and exile.

Book 4 (A Conscious Thing): The machine and the language of longing.

Book 5 (The Dot): The door reopens. Karma dissolves.